# A GIRL LIKE YOU

Gemma Burgess wrote her first book, *The Dating Detox*, when she and her sister discussed the difficulty of finding a comfort read with cojones. Her second book, *A Girl Like You*, is inspired by her experiences of learning to navigate the bastard-infested waters of the London bar scene after a long time in a relationship. Gemma grew up all over the place and now lives in Notting Hill.

Find out more at www.gemmaburgess.com or follow her on Twitter at @gkateb.

By the same author:

*The Dating Detox*

GEMMA BURGESS

# A Girl Like You

**AVON**

AVON

A division of HarperCollins*Publishers*
77–85 Fulham Palace Road,
London W6 8JB

www.harpercollins.co.uk

A Paperback Original 2011

1

First published in Great Britain by
HarperCollins*Publishers* 2011

A catalogue record for this book is
available from the British Library

ISBN-13: 978-1-84756-190-9

Set in Minion by Palimpsest Book Production Limited,
Falkirk, Stirlingshire

Printed and bound in Great Britain by
Clays Ltd, St Ives plc

**Mixed Sources**
Product group from well-managed
forests and other controlled sources
www.fsc.org  Cert no. SW-COC-001806
© 1996 Forest Stewardship Council

FSC

FSC is a non-profit international organisation established
to promote the responsible management of the world's forests.
Products carrying the FSC label are independently certified
to assure consumers that they come from forests that are managed
to meet the social, economic and ecological needs
of present and future generations.

Find out more about HarperCollins and the environment at
**www.harpercollins.co.uk/green**

For Paul
Because you rock.

*February. (This year.)*

I never thought I'd spend hours crying on the floor of a hotel shower.

The weird thing is that underneath the hysteria, I'm completely aware how dramatic-yet-amusing this is. I'm crying for a soul-shakingly horrible reason, my contact lenses are flipping over in my eyes from the tear-water onslaught and I don't have the strength to get up, turn off the shower and reach for a towel . . . but I can still see that this is a teeny tiny bit funny.

Is it normal to feel so detached from reality after a heartbreak? Is this heartbreak? God, I don't know.

And as usual, my mind is wandering. I can't help but notice how nice the shower gel is, and how I wish I had a dinner plate showerhead at home, because crying under the pathetic trickle in my skinny white bath is *so* depressing.

Home, oh God, home.

Then reality hits me and I start sobbing again.

I wonder how my black eye is coming along, but I can't bear to look in the mirror. I swear my jowls droop when I'm this tired. On top of everything else that life has landed me with (inability to tell right from left, inability to tell lust from love, inability to drink whisky without becoming really drunk), that's just not fair.

1

The sick feeling I've had for days just won't go away. I wonder if it ever will.

I think I'll make the water a little bit hotter and curl up on the floor. There. I'm almost comfortable. The shower is huge, taking up about half the bathroom, which, like the rest of the hotel room, is dark and sexy with a dash of chinoiserie, and flattering lighting that whispers *five star* in a posh accent. Hey, if you're going to have a breakdown, you may as well have it in the Mandarin Oriental in Hong Kong, that's what I always say.

Perhaps I should call my sister. Sophie. She is always good at being comforting. That's the best thing about little sisters: they spend so much time wishing they were elder sisters (when they're waiting to go to big school, waiting to get a bike without training wheels, waiting to get their ears pierced, though wily Sophie got her ears pierced the same day as me, despite the fact that I'd been begging for YEARS and I was 13 and she was only 11) that in the end they're far wiser than the elder ones could ever be. She's in Chicago right now, so that's only . . . Oh, I can't figure out time differences.

I don't even know what time it is here. Late afternoon?

It feels like the sun hasn't properly risen in Hong Kong today. It's grey and humid and thunderstormy. I love it when the weather matches my mood.

I think I'm almost sick of being in the shower. Perhaps I should go and lie on the floor of the hotel room again. I spent a good two hours crying next to my open suitcase earlier. I estimate . . . Wait. Was that the door?

I stare into space, listening intently.

Another knock, very loud and impatient. Not like the soft knock of the hotel staff.

Maybe it's him! Who else could it be? Yes! It must be! It's him!

I scramble up and turn off the shower, shouting 'coming!', wrap the bathrobe around myself and hurry to the door, my hair dripping water all over my face. I knew he'd find out I was here, I knew it was a mistake, I knew—

I'm stunned. It's not the man I was expecting.

'What are you doing here?' I finally croak.

'What are *you* doing here?' he retorts angrily. 'And Christ, what the fuck happened to your face?'

'I got in a fight,' I say sarcastically, as he barges in and slams the door behind him, pushing me through into the bedroom.

'We have to call Sophie and your parents, *now*,' he says.

I sigh. 'Why?'

'Because you've been gone for almost two full days? Because you flew halfway across the world and didn't tell anyone where you were going or what you were doing? Because you turned your fucking phone off?'

'It ran out. Of juice,' I say, very sarcastically, in a way that I know will annoy him. I see his eyes light up with anger and feel a jolt of joy that I'm making someone else feel as bad as I do right now. (Is that evil?)

'Do you have any fucking idea what you've put us through?' he shouts.

'What do you mean "us"?' I reply. I'm so exhausted and miserable that I don't care if I sound like a brat. 'They're my family, my friends! How dare you stalk me like this?'

He stares at me for a second, and then says flatly: 'You stupid bitch.'

'SHUT UP!' I shout. 'Just SHUT the FUCK UP!' I know I'm hysterical, but I'm so tired, and I feel sick, and I can't stop crying. I don't want to be here anymore, and nothing is how it should be, and my life will never work out, because I don't know what I want or how I'd get it if I did, and as I think this I scream so loudly that tiny lights dart in front of my eyes.

Then, to my shock, he slaps me sharply on the cheek. It's not hard, but I'm so stunned that I immediately shut up, mid-wail. He *slapped* me?

I sit down on the bed. Wow, that was dramatic. Especially for me. I've never been a drama queen. More of a drama lady-in-waiting.

He sits down next to me, trying to get his breath back as I stare at him, my mouth still open in surprise. He looks tired, I notice. It must be Friday by now. Is it? What day did I leave London? I can't remember. My throat hurts.

I suddenly can't go on. I can't bear this. I can't bear any of this. So I flop on the bed, curl up in a little ball and start weeping.

Again.

It's so pathetic, I know, but I can't stop myself. How can I possibly have any tears left? Oh, God. I want my mum.

The wrong man puts a big paw out and starts stroking my head, clearing the wet hair off my face and making soothing 'shhh' noises.

'I'm sorry,' I sob. 'Thank you for finding me. You were right. I saw them . . . and my face, my face . . .'

'He's not worth it. I'm sorry I slapped you, I'm so sorry . . .'

He keeps talking, but I can't hear him, because I really can't stop crying now, and I just wish I'd never come here. What on earth was I thinking? I cry and cry until I finally cry myself into exhaustion. The last thing I think, as I go to sleep, is thank God he found me.

# Chapter One

*September. (Last year.)*

This is it. My first ever date.

Not many people have their first date at 27, and I'm not saying I'm proud of it, but it's true, and it's one of the things you should know about me. Another is that I'm nervous. My stomach hurts from nerves. Perhaps I'm coming down with something. God, then I won't be able to snog him. Will I snog him? I don't know. How do you snog someone for the first time? Do people even still say 'snog' at the age of 27?

I haven't had a first kiss since I was 20, for fuck's sake. I've probably forgotten how.

I'm meeting my date at a place called Bam-Bou at 8 pm, and I'm on the tube. In fact, I'm 40 minutes early. Typical.

It's not like I think he's that amazing, or even – ahem – remember him that well. Perhaps my sister was right. I should have picked someone I didn't like at all for the first date. 'Sharpen your tools on someone blunt,' was her exact suggestion.

I wonder if I even have any tools to sharpen.

I'm not a recovering nun, by the way. I've just been in a relationship forever. I mean I *was* in a relationship. I'm not used to using the past tense. I've only just stopped saying 'we' when I talk about things I've done. As in, 'we loved that movie', 'we went there for dinner'. That's what happens when you have one boyfriend from the age of 20 until 27-and-a-half. I left him in July and here I am, just over two months later. Officially single. And officially dating.

Paulie – my date – is the first guy to ask me out. Not the first guy to ask for my number, mind you. One of the things I've learnt in the past two months of singledom is that guys sometimes ask for your number and then don't call, even though you think they will, and you'll work yourself up into a nervous frenzy every night waiting.

I stop for a drink at a bar called The Roxy, to kill time and check my makeup. A double gin and tonic will take the edge off. Possibly two edges.

I met Paulie last weekend and though he didn't take his sunglasses off (well, it's been an unusually sunny September, and Plum and I were standing around outside a pub trying to smoke and flirt, or 'smirt' as it's apparently called) I definitely had the impression he liked me.

He gave me his card at the end of the night and told me to email him. So I did.

And here I am. Losing my dating virginity.

It was surprisingly easy to get asked out, after all the obsessing, I mean light discussing, I've been doing with Sophie, Plum and Henry for these past two months. Everyone had different advice, of course.

'Just laugh a lot,' said my sister Sophie (the only one in an actual relationship). 'It always worked for me.'

'When a guy talks to you, touch his arm and flick your hair,' said Plum (last relationship: depends how you'd define 'relationship'). 'It's subtle body language, and those signals show that you're interested.'

'Why do you keep asking me this shit? Get drunk and jump on him. It would do it for me,' said Henry (last relationship: never).

'I thought you were confident?' said my mother in dismay

(married to my father forever, has hazy understanding of modern dating due to serious period drama box set addiction).

So they weren't much help.

Anyway, I always thought I *was* confident. Ish.

But being single and being confident is a whole different thing to being in a relationship and being confident. It's *easier* in a relationship. Peter, my ex-boyfriend, was an ever-buoyant life-vest of reassurance. I didn't have to make new friends, I just had a handful of old ones and shared his. If I couldn't talk to anyone at a party, I talked to him. If I found a group intimidating, he would talk for me. And so on.

So, the first time I found myself being chatted up by a moderately good-looking guy in a bar, I felt sweatily self-conscious and couldn't wait to get away. (He seemed to feel the same way about me after about 45 seconds.)

Confidence is a stupid word. It's not like I think I'm worthless or anything. Sometimes I just have trouble thinking of something to say. And then, when I say things, I sometimes wonder if they sound a bit shit. I talk to myself a lot, in my head. But everyone does, right?

Perhaps it's not confidence, perhaps there's simply a knack to being chatted up. I think I'm getting better at it. Maybe. I like bars and drinks and what do you know, so do men.

And so here I am. On a date. High five to me.

I wonder how Peter is. We broke up in July, he moved in with his brother Joe, took a sabbatical from work and went on a year-long backpacking trip. He said it was one of the things he felt he missed out on by being in a relationship with me for the whole of his 20s.

I wonder what I missed out on.

I guess I'm about to find out.

Breaking up with him was the hardest thing I've ever had to do. There isn't much in books or music or films that helps you leave someone who is very, very, nice but just not quite right.

He's not mean, you're not miserable, no one cheats. It's just a sad, slow process of ending it.

Peter's such a reasonable guy that he didn't even disagree when I said, 'I don't think we're right for each other, I think deep down you know it too. So I think we should break up.' He just nodded. He would have gone on living with me for years, without questioning if we actually had a good relationship or just a functioning one. All Peter really wanted was an easy life. And – wait, why am I *still* thinking about my ex-fucking-boyfriend? I'm almost on a *date*. Stop it, Abigail.

Gosh, my palms are clammy. Perhaps I'll need Botox shots in them. They do that, you know. I wonder if my armpits are sweaty too. Fuck. I can't tell. I'll just have to keep my arms down all night.

Oh, look, I've finished my drink. May as well have another.

Thank hell I'm finally going on a date. For the six months before we broke up, the flip side to the thought 'I'm not happy, I want to leave Peter,' was the thought 'but then I'll be single, and I'll have to meet new men, and go on dates, and I don't know how.'

For a while, that thought – that *fear* – was enough to keep me from leaving Peter. Fear of never having anyone think I was pretty, fear of never being asked out, fear of never falling in love again, in short: fear of getting Lonely Single Girl Syndrome, of never finding the right person and dying alone. Why take the risk?

Pretty standard stuff, right?

And yet, the last two months of singledom have been infinitely more fun than the last year (or three) of my relationship. After I dealt with the inevitable emotional fallout and guilt from ending my old life (my advice: move out as fast as you can, so your new surroundings match your new state of mind, and get a haircut, for the same reason) I immediately started structuring a new one. Work is the same, obviously, so the focus has been on my previously neglected social butterfly skills. Dinners and drinks and lunches and parties: you name it, I'm doing it. Other nights I rejoice in time alone, reading chicklit in the bath or going to sleep at 8 pm covered in fake tan and a hair mask.

I love it.

I love my new flatshare, too. It's in the delightfully-monikered Primrose Hill. I'm renting a room from Robert, a friend of my sister's fiancé. I haven't seen him much since I moved in a month ago. When we do meet, in the kitchen or the hallway, we make polite small talk and that's about it. Which suits me just fine.

My bedroom is on the top floor of the house. It's small and quiet and best of all, it's mine, all mine. It's not perfect, of course – the ensuite bathroom is poky, and the wardrobe is tiny, but my clothes have adjusted very well to the transition. They're such troopers.

I look down at my black peep-toes. Yes, you, I think. You're a trooper.

What, like you've never talked to your clothes.

OK, it's 7.50 pm. I can walk to Bam-Bou now. I'm sure Paulie will be early. Men are always early for dates, right? I don't know! God. How did I end up being the only 27-year-old I know who's never ever gone out on a date?

Now I'm nervous again.

Could I have a boyfriend called *Paulie*? It sounds like a budgerigar. Right. Here we are. Bam-Bou. He said he'd meet me in the bar on the top floor.

'Hi!' I say, grinning nervously, when I finally reach the sexy, dark little bar. Paulie is sitting on a stool in the corner, wearing a very nice dark grey suit. He's hot, though a bit jowlier than I remembered.

'Ali,' he says, putting down his BlackBerry and leaning over to give me a doublekiss hello. Cold cheeks. Sandalwoody aftershave.

'Abi . . . gail,' I correct him. 'Abigail Wood.' There's nowhere for me to sit. Never mind. I'll just lean. Oh God, I feel sick with nerves.

'Right,' he says, going back to his BlackBerry. 'Pick a drink, I've just got a work thing to reply to . . .'

I nod, and looking around, pick up a drinks menu and start reading it. What shall I pick? I'm puffed! How embarrassing to be panting this much. Why would you have the bar on the fourth floor of a building with no lift?

I choose a martini, and as he orders it, I try to look composed, like I date all the time. Who me? I'm on a date. Who him? He's my date.

'So. How was your day?' I ask, when Paulie returns. Is that a good question? I don't know. My mum would ask it.

'Scintillating,' he replies crisply, leaning into me. Cripes, he is definitely hot. Very dashing eyebrows.

'What do you do?' I am trying to smile and look interested and nice and pretty, all at the same time.

'I work for a branding agency,' he says. 'I'm head of account management.'

'Oh, how interesting!' I say. Wow. I really do sound like my mum. 'Where is your office?'

'Farringdon.'

'How long have you been doing that?' But I can't seem to stop.

'About seven years. I started my own company straight out of university, managing chalet bitches, as that was what I loved,' he pauses, and grins to himself for a second. 'You know. But that got tired after a couple of years, so here I am.'

'Golly,' I say brightly. 'That *does* sound interesting.' Why do I feel like I'm at a job interview?

'It was,' he nods, his smile faltering slightly.

'Where was the chalet company based?' Is this normal?
'Verbier.'

'Do you speak French?' Stop asking questions.

'I can hold my own.'

'Are you from London originally?' But what if there's an awkward pause in conversation?

'I am,' he says. 'Though I left when my parents split up. My mum moved to Devon and I moved with her. I haven't seen my dad in twenty years.'

'Oh, I'm . . . sorry . . .' Shit.

He smiles at me, slightly less enthusiastically than before. Perhaps talking about his mum and dad makes him sad. I'll change the subject. Is it hot in here? My face feels so flushed.

'So, have you eaten here before?' I ask. I wonder if he can see me sweating.

'Yeah, it's great,' he nods. 'The pork belly is historic. In fact, our booking isn't for another 45 minutes, but I bet we could get settled early. Shall we?'

'Yes!' I exclaim, getting up and following him down the stairs. 'I'm so hungry! I had a sandwich from Pret for lunch and I swear they're basically carbs and air, I am always hungry mid-afternoon, so then I had a chocolate bar, which I know is . . .' Oh, my fucking God, I'm babbling absolute shit, and he's not even listening. Shut up. Shut up. Shut up, Abigail.

'Oooh! What shall we order?' I ask, as we sit down at our table. Paulie doesn't say anything. Shit, we can't just sit here in silence. Without even thinking, I start reading the menu out loud. It's not something I've ever done before, but nerves are enough to make a girl a little, you know, antsy.

'Steamed edamame! They're lovely. Saigon-style crepe, hmm, not sure about that . . . Har gau, they're a favourite of mine. Soft-shell crab! I love crab, my sister hates it, she once had food poisoning in Singapore. I'm not—'

'Excuse me, I think we're ready to order some wine,' interrupts Paulie, gesturing towards the waitress at the door.

'Wine! Great,' I say, and take a deep breath. You're being a dickhead, Abigail, I think firmly. Sort it out. But I can't. I'm a

11

rolling snowball of nerves and stupidity, gathering momentum every second. 'I seem to be impervious to alcohol recently, since I left my, uh, in the last few weeks. I mean, I drink, you know, a lot, but I don't get hangovers lately. It's like I'm an alcoholic goddess!' Did you just say that Abigail? You absolute idiot.

'Cheers to that,' says Paulie, and drinks half his glass in one gulp.

I take a deep breath and smile, and drain half my martini in the next sip. Please God. Let this be over soon.

# Chapter Two

Two hours later, I crash through the front door, staggering a little to take my heels off. My flatmate, Robert, is stretched out on the couch, legs up on the coffee table, watching TV.

'Honey, I'm home!' I say.

'Hey,' he replies, glancing at me and back at the TV.

I shuffle into the living room, carrying my shoes, and plop down on the other couch.

'I just had my first date, ever, in my whole entire life,' I say chattily. I close one eye to focus on the TV. It's an old *The Simpsons*, the episode with the monorail. 'They use the M as an anchor to get the doughnut and then there's an escalator to nowhere,' I say helpfully.

'Thanks for the heads-up.' Robert runs his hands through his hair absent-mindedly. It's longish and dark, and sticks up in the most gravity-defying way I've ever seen. I wonder if he uses product and if so, which one. 'Beer?'

I look down and see a small bucket next to the couch, filled with ice and beer. The fridge is exactly nine feet away.

'That is supremely lazy.'

Robert glances over again and grins. 'Well, aren't you chatty tonight?'

'I'm a little drunk,' I confess, sliding down the couch and manoeuvring my foot to pinch a beer bottle between my toes.

Those last two martinis were goooood. We finished the wine, and Paulie switched to beer, and I thought hell, why not?

'Good date?' he asks, not taking his eyes off the TV.

'Yeah,' I say, moving my foot to bring the bottle up to my hand. Good eye-foot coordination. 'He seems really nice. A bit reserved. He's getting up early for a conference call so we called it a night after dinner.'

'Oh, so it was a bad date,' Robert says decisively, throwing me the bottle opener. I catch it perfectly and smile to myself. I cannot play any sports, at all. In fact, team sports make me panic – what if I let people down? (The pressure!) Yet I can always catch anything thrown at me. If only I could market this talent in some way, I'd never have to analyse results again. I could work in a bar, like Tom Cruise in *Cocktail*, and just throw bottles all – wait. I focus on what Robert just said.

'Bad? No!' I say. 'It was fine. I was a little, uh, nervous, but then the conversation was easy. I found out lots about him, he seems very nice.'

'Did you ask him lots of questions?'

'Yes.'

'Did he ask you any questions?'

Pause. 'No . . .'

'Did you laugh a lot?'

Even longer pause. 'We had a few . . . light moments.'

'Bad date,' he says again. 'No kiss, right?'

I admit, that part confused me. When the hell are you meant to kiss? How can you tell if they want to? I tried to look at Paulie meaningfully, but I couldn't catch his eye, and then he opened the cab door and kind of stood behind it, so I just got in and waved goodbye.

God. That *is* a disaster, now that I think about it.

'How did you know that?' I ask.

'Lip gloss,' he replies.

'Well, aren't you Sherlock fucking Holmes?' I say. I feel a bit deflated. 'I think he'll call me, anyway.'

'Right,' says Robert flatly.

'He could be my soulmate,' I say lightly.

'He isn't,' he says. 'I promise.'

'Oh, poo on you,' I say, taking a sip of my beer.

'Nice comeback,' he says.

Luke, my sister's fiancé mentioned that people sometimes find Robert a bit moody. He should know: Robert is one of his best friends. Robert and I haven't spoken much until now. I'm probably out of practice at making new friends, and sometimes I think I wouldn't know small talk if it hit me in the face. But tonight, the booze is helping.

I close one eye and gaze over at Robert. His legs are so long that he can easily reach the coffee table. I try to reach my toes out to it and fail. Robert notices and reaches forward to pull it towards my hopeful toes.

'Thanks.' Maybe I should say what's on my mind. 'It's not my fault that I don't know this dating stuff, you know. I'm a dating virgin. I'd never gone on a proper date before tonight.'

'Mmm,' says Robert, which I take as further encouragement.

'I mean, I went to the movies and things with Peter at the start, obviously. But we'd been friends for so long that it felt natural . . . and we didn't even go on an official first date. I mean, it was university. We were drunk at a party and snogged and voilà, instant boyfriendage. And now it's seven years later and I've forgotten how to be single. What can I do about it?!'

Robert doesn't respond.

'I was just being polite by asking Paulie all those questions. What else could I talk about? He's a total stranger! Better than awkward silence,' I pause, thinking of more reasons. 'And I was trying to be nice, and, um, and interested in his life. It's good manners.'

'I'm sure he appreciated your good manners,' says Robert.

This is not the type of cosy flatmate chat I used to enjoy with Plum and Henry and everyone at university, I must say. Perhaps he's never lived with a girl before. Luke shared a flat with him until he met Sophie and kicked Robert out, which is when he bought this place. It's a funny little place over three stories, with bare floorboards and very masculine furniture. Leather couches and a couple of low wood tables. I described it to Plum as 'butch chic'.

He's obviously not keen on becoming best friends, I muse. He probably only needs a flatmate to help pay the mortgage. He must be old. Luke's 30, but Robert looks older. He seems to permanently need a shave.

'How old are you?' I ask.

'Old enough to know not to talk to a man during *The Simpsons*,' he replies.

We watch *The Simpsons* episode till it ends, and then Robert starts flicking the TV channels. We go past an episode of *Family Guy*.

'Oohh! *Family Guy*. Yes please,' I say. Robert flicks back.

I'm starting to sober up.

'After martinis, beer is like bread, I swear,' I comment during the ads. 'It really soaks up the alcohol.'

Robert doesn't respond.

*Family Guy* starts again. My mind is racing. Was that a bad date? What a lot of effort and excitement and outfit-planning and grooming and anticipation . . . all for one hour and 45 minutes of shit conversation and good food.

Perhaps I haven't missed out on that much after all. Perhaps this dating and being single malarkey is just a lot of fuss about nothing.

But that can't be right. Plum loves being single and meeting men and going on dates and you know, all that shit. It's like the entire focus of her life. And my sister Sophie loved being a single gal about town (as my dad says), that's how she met Luke, and now they're getting married.

And it's the whole point of everything, isn't it? To find someone to love and laugh with. A (whisper it) soulmate. And not settle with someone that you love like a brother and don't ever really laugh with. Like Peter. I left him because I knew there was something wrong, something missing. But there was something missing tonight, too. I – oh, I need to pee.

'I'm just going to the, uh, euphemism,' I say.

'Good to know,' he replies.

Perhaps Robert is wrong I think, as I sit back down on the couch a few minutes later. Paulie will call and we'll go out again and it will be better. Perhaps it will be a date we'll laugh about for the rest of our lives ('I was so nervous!', 'No, I was nervous!'). I mean, he must have liked me enough to ask me out, so wouldn't he like me enough to ask me out again? I don't—

'Don't think about it anymore,' says Robert to the TV. Wait, is he talking to me?

'Huh?'

'You're very easy to read,' he says, without looking at me. 'It was one night. Just learn from it and move on. Singledom is brutal. You need to be brutal too.'

'Learn what? I don't know what I did wrong . . .' I say, quickly adding, 'If I did anything wrong, if you're even right about it being a bad date, which you might not be. I like him . . . I might like him,' I caveat. Do I like Paulie? God, I don't know. I was too busy keeping the conversation going to figure that out. 'The last thing I said was "will you call me?" and he said "yes".'

'Never ask a guy to call you,' says Robert, opening another beer.

'Then I'll call him,' I say crossly.

'I wouldn't recommend it.'

'I'm a feminist. I can call a man,' I'm defensive now. 'Or I'll just text.' Robert shakes his head slowly. Cripes, maybe I should flatshare with girls. I like a bit more compassion in my pep talks, thank you very much. 'Or email. I have his email address. Or I'll casually Facebook him.'

'I'm a feminist too,' he says, rolling his eyes. 'But no. Not after the first date. Be elusive. And there is nothing casual about Facebook.'

'I just don't understand why you think it went so badly,' I say again.

'What gave it away was the questions thing,' he says, more gently. 'Too many personal questions and it becomes an interview.'

'That's just what it felt like!' Maybe he does know what he's talking about. 'This is good. Tell me more. I need baby steps.'

He grins at me. 'Play it cool. You need to be detached from the situation. It's the only way.'

'Wait!' I take out my notebook. I'm never without it: it's the repository of my to-do lists and the only way I can keep track of everything.

'Give me one sec,' I squint, close one eye, pick up my pen and start writing. What was it he just said again? Oh yeah.

**Be cool**

**Be detached**

That seems simple.

'That doesn't mean you should be a mute. Making him laugh is crucial.'

'I need to be funny, too?' I say in dismay. Robert looks amused by this. 'What makes you the expert? Do you have a girlfriend?'

'Not exactly. I'm just very good at being single.'

Ah, a player. On cue, his phone buzzes with a text that I can immediately tell, by the disinterested way he reads it, raises his eyebrows slightly, and then taps out a reply, is a girl.

'Cool, detached . . .' I muse, watching him. 'Do I have to do this forever? Some day I'll fall in love again, I hope, and then I won't have to think about this . . . Right? Like, on my wedding day, do I have to think about acting cool and detached?'

18

His phone buzzes again. Another text. He reads it and raises an eyebrow, before looking up at me and computing my last statement.

'Don't think about falling in love. Don't even say the word. Love has nothing to do with dating. And don't think about your wedding day. Ever,' he says, picking up his wallet and keys from the coffee table. He throws me the remote control and I catch it perfectly. Yes! Two out of two. 'I'm off. Meeting a friend.'

'I figured,' I say. 'Does that mean my how-to-date tutorial is over?'

'Going on a date is just something to do for a few hours.' Robert takes his coat from the hall cupboard. 'It's no big deal, so don't build it up to be something more in your head.'

'But what if I don't feel detached? Or cool?'

Robert pauses as he reaches the door, looks over at me, and grins. 'Fake it.'

# Chapter Three

As I head in to work the next morning, I realise that Robert was right. I'm sure you've already come to the same conclusion: it was a bad date. I'm trying to chalk it up to experience, rather than chalking it up to my so-I-WILL-end-up-alone-and-lonely theory.

My office is just behind Blackfriars. I'm a financial analyst for an investment bank. Basically, I need to know everything about the retail industry in order to help our traders and clients make money.

When I first started working, I *loved* my job. I loved winkling out information that no one else had. I felt like a little truffle pig snuffling for gems. Then the recession hit, and with no gems to snuffle, it became hard to get excited, or even care, about any of it. And then I – rather belatedly, as tends to happen to me quite a lot – realised that my job wasn't about research, it was all about helping rich people get richer. Which doesn't exactly fry my burger. Though perhaps work isn't meant to be enjoyable, you know?

Full disclosure: I only joined this company because its stand was next to the bar at my university careers day.

I am not kidding. I was finishing a difficult and essentially useless degree in medieval French. The university careers day was stressful and weirdly humiliating. Plum and I discovered the bar during happy hour, the two investment guys at the company stand spotted us and, after our second bottle of half-price wine, came over for a chat.

I didn't know what else I'd do with my life, and the salary sounded pretty good, so I applied for the grad scheme, got in, got a couple of qualifications, and now, here I am, an associate analyst. Stuck halfway up a job ladder I never knew existed till I was already on it.

I sit in a quiet corner of a very large, very grey open-plan office, on the 6th floor. My boss, Suzanne, is a managing director and has her own office (glass fronted, so she can keep an eye on us). I work in a small team, specialising in luxury retail, with two other analysts, Alistair and Charlotte. Sitting around us are the other teams: pharmaceutical, automotive, banking, construction blahblahblah.

Today, at 6.40 am, I'm the first one in from my team. The workday starts very early for research analysts. Just one of the many things that I don't like about my job.

I sit down, turn on my laptop and sigh. Oh fluorescent lighting, how I hate you. I swear the one above my head flickers and buzzes an abnormal amount. At least my team doesn't have to present at the 7.15 am sales meeting today. Instead, all I have to do is check Bloomberg and Reuters and see what's happening in the markets. Nothing so far. Yay. If there was, I'd need an opinion. And it's hard to have an opinion when you don't really care.

This is how easy it would be to improve my quality of life: let my work day start after 9 am and let me dress how I want. Today I'm wearing my uniform: a cream top with grey trousers and heels. The top is a bit silky and the trousers high-waisted, so this is haute fashion in my office, which is exceedingly conservative even for the City. Most women here wear utterly boring skirt suits with ill-fitting shirts and sensible, closed-toe low heels; anything too fashionable attracts attention. I think my job is why I don't speak style quite as well as Plum does. You need to

21

be trying out new looks all the time in order to develop a real instinct for what suits you.

I take out my notebook and am looking over yesterday's list (I'm big on lists, as you've probably noticed), crossing off things and rewriting instructions on today's fresh list when my phone rings.

'Plummy plum,' I whisper. 'I'm—'

'I know you're already at work,' she says. Plum works in PR, so her day doesn't start till at least 9 am, and right now I can tell she's still in bed. 'I need 10 seconds. How the fuck was it?'

I sigh. 'Pretty bad. I need more than 10 seconds.'

'I thought perhaps you'd fall in fucking love and end up marrying him!' she says, yawning. Her voice is croaky in the mornings. She smokes too much. And swears too much.

'Dream on,' I reply, and hang up quickly as Alistair approaches. Maybe Robert's right. Love's got nothing to do with dating.

'Everybody's got a dream!' He's very cheerful in the morning. 'What's your dream? What's your dream? Welcome to Hollywoooooooood.'

'It takes a real man to quote *Pretty Woman*,' I say, as he sits down.

'Really? Can I rescue you right back? Remember, you shouldn't neglect your gums.'

Alistair seemed shy and hardworking in his interviews, but quickly revealed himself to be quite the opposite, and we've ended up becoming almost-friends – as much as I ever make friends at work, anyway.

Charlotte, on the other hand, who I can see trudging up the hallway now, is, well, dull. Yes, I feel bitchy for saying that about a colleague who's never done anything bad to me, but honestly, she doesn't inspire affection. I might be a bit quiet sometimes, but she's practically a mute. Her hair, skin and clothes are all varying shades of taupe, and she wears ponchos (ponchos!) over her suits in winter and so inevitably, because she isn't Elle

Macpherson-shaped, looks like a mushroom. I'm not the most stylish person in the world, but I know a 'don't' when I see one.

'Morning, Charlotte,' I say cheerfully, as she sits down at her desk.

'Morning . . .' she says flatly. See? No effort.

A text arrives from my sister, Sophie.

*Date. Details. I need to know everything.*

I sigh. I wish I hadn't talked about my first date so much. Now I have to tell them all how terrible it was. Though one bad date doesn't mean that I'm going to be single forever, right? Or end up with Lonely Single Girl Syndrome, miserable and . . . desperate? (I'm starting to hate that word. The d-word.)

I open a new email to Plum, Henry and Sophie:

*I will only discuss this once, so read carefully. It was a disaster. I had total verbal diarrhoea. Read entire menu out loud. Asked in-depth questions about everyone he knows. Told him all about my break-up with Peter. Made stupid comments constantly. He left as soon as he could. No goodnight kiss. And I was pretty hammered.*

At about 11 am, the replies arrive. My sister, Sophie, is first:

*Oh Abigail. Maybe you should call him to apologise.*

Is she out of her fucking mind? There is no way I am ever calling him again, ever. Why line up to get rejected outright? Far better that he just doesn't call me. Sophie is too sensitive sometimes.

I reply:

*I might be a dating virgin. But I'm not an idiot.*

Plum replies:

*Sounds like you can chalk that one up to fucksperience, sugar-nuts. x*

Ah, thank you, Plum.

Henry replies:

*I can't believe you didn't jump him.*

Another useful response.

I field emails all morning, in between phone calls to traders expressing my opinions on what's happening in the market (very little and very little). Then finally one email, from my ever-perceptive sister Sophie, cuts through all the shit.

*Abigail – do you even want to see him again? If not, stop torturing yourself.*

I think for a few minutes. I don't. I didn't really have a good time. I just feel like, well, since he asked me out, I should really give it my best shot. Try to make it work. Surely if he's a nice person, and I'm a nice person, there's no reason we shouldn't keep going?

This, it occurs to me, is the kind of thinking that kept me in a relationship with Peter for seven years.

God, that's brutal.

Wait. That was something that Robert had said about dating. I should write it down. I take out my notebook and add '**Act brutal**' to the list. Fine. I won't even try to see Paulie again. He is erased from my mind forthwith. How's that for brutal?

'Are you up for lunch later?' says Alistair, shooting across from his desk to mine on his chair.

I frown at him. This is the third time he's asked me out to lunch in the past fortnight. I'm usually too busy, but today is pretty quiet.

'Sure,' I say. 'Charlotte?'

I don't know why I'm asking, she never leaves the office at lunch. As expected, Charlotte declines.

'So, why have you been dying to eat lunch with me?' I ask, once we're seated at the sushi bar around the corner, and I've done my usual wasabi-soy mixing routine.

'Can't a man want to break bread – sorry, raw fish – with his line manager without attracting suspicion?' says Alistair, copying me.

I glance at him and arch an eyebrow.

'I don't want to be an analyst anymore,' he says in return.

I've just put a huge piece of maki roll in my mouth so I chew it slowly, whilst nodding and making eye contact, trying to think of what to say next. Halfway through chewing, my tongue discovers a large gob of wasabi that I didn't stir into the soy sauce properly, and tears immediately spurt from my eyes.

'You don't have to cry about it,' says Alistair.

'Water,' I whisper, grabbing the shiny, utterly non-absorbent napkin in front of me and holding it to my cheeks. Darn, now I'll have streaks through my makeup. 'Well. That is a big decision. What do you want to do instead?' I say eventually. I sound like my mum. Again.

'I want to sit on a trading desk,' he says firmly.

'Sheesh, why?' I exclaim. The trading floor is the Wild West of the office. They're almost always entirely male, and pungent with the sharp smell of testosterone and competition. Alistair is far too silly and funny to be a trader. And he doesn't have the killer instinct.

'Don't you ever get tired of setting up huge kills and never being part of the bloodshed?' he replies. Perhaps he does have that instinct.

'When you put it like that . . . no,' I say.

'You love research, huh?' he says, rolling his eyes. 'Well, I want more . . . more excitement. And more money.'

'You can't just decide to be a trader, you know. You're only one year out of university.'

'People do make the jump, though,' he says insistently.

'Why don't I do some research to help you make sure it's what you want?'

'Anything you can do to help would be great, lovely Abigail. I'm bored.'

We both go back to dipping and mixing and chewing. I am flushed with pleasure that he called me *lovely Abigail*. It's harmless flirting, but hardly anyone has flirted with me, harmlessly or not, in years.

'You know, I get bored sometimes, too,' I admit. 'And I wonder

25

if I'm in the right job. But I think that happens to everyone. I mean, work is work.'

Alistair frowns. 'Work is life . . . Don't you want to spend your life doing something you love? What would you do, if you could do anything at all?'

I gaze at him, speechless.

'I mean, what do you *want*?' he adds. 'What do you want your life to be like?'

I open my mouth to speak, but nothing comes out. My mind is empty. What do I *want*? What kind of a question is that?

'I don't . . . I don't know . . . I don't . . .' I don't seem to have any words in my head at all.

'Until you do, I wouldn't worry about it,' Alistair says, grinning at me.

My sentiments exactly.

When we get back from lunch, I sit down at my desk, and stare at the screen for a second as I try to push out all the disquieting thoughts from my head. But I can't. Alistair is 23, and knows exactly who he is and what he wants. I'm 27 and three quarters, and I haven't got a clue.

# Chapter Four

You know what bites about singledom?

No, not the lack of sex and/or cuddling. Though a little bit of sex would not go astray right now. In fact, for a month after the break-up, sex was practically all I could think about, isn't that weird? Where was I? Oh yeah. Singledom.

I miss not having anyone to chat to about things. No one to nod when I make comments about an inane TV show, or share a new song with, or to make porridge for on a chilly morning. I'm so used to having someone around that sometimes I come out of the shower and say, 'Can you remind me to get more razors?' before I remember there's no one there. Companionship, in other words.

I'm finding that social butterflying is the best way to fill the companionship void, so I try to make sure I'm almost never alone. At least once a weekend, I meet one or all of the girls to go 'shopping', a catch-all phrase that covers fashion, coffee, gossip, errands, people-watching, and sharing cupcakes or other baked goods as, of course, calories shared don't count (like calories consumed standing up, drunk or on an airplane).

Today is an important day: my best friend, Plum and my sister Sophie, are helping me refresh my singledom wardrobe and teaching me to speak style.

I'm trying on a trench coat in Whistles, and Plum is telling us a story about her colleague.

'And then Georgina is like, since the little fucknuckle hasn't rung her, she's going to organise a party just so she can invite him. I have to say, I admire her balls.'

'Yeah,' I say, exchanging a glance with Sophie. All of Plum's non-fashion conversation so far has, as usual of late, centred on men. Men she knows, men she likes, men other women know and like.

Plum walks over. 'Push the sleeves up,' she instructs me, undoing the belt and tying it in a half-bow-knot instead. 'Pop the collar. Never wear a trench the old-fashioned way. This isn't Waterloo fucking Bridge.'

I nod obediently, exchanging a grin with Sophie. Plum has a bossy-but-charming manner that you could put down to her Yorkshire roots, five years working with posh girls in PR or growing up with four younger brothers. We met at university when she borrowed my French notes, and became best friends when she began dating one of Peter's friends. That didn't last, but our friendship did. She was the centre of a much wider group while I was in a relationship with Peter and didn't really get to know many people . . . I wonder if that's why I get so socially nervous sometimes. Hmm.

Plum has always been sunnier and more easygoing than me, though the recent months – or is it years? – of man troubles are getting her down. She's also very pretty, with a smile so perfect, it's almost American. I've had braces twice and my teeth still retain a certain kookiness.

'Anyway,' she continues airily, backcombing her light brown hair with her fingers and pouting in the mirror. 'I told her that was silly. I mean, maybe he lost his phone. Or maybe he saved her number incorrectly. A hundred things could prevent him from calling her. That's what I always tell myself when I'm in that situation.'

I nod, unsure what to say. When I was in a relationship I didn't really see this side to her. The man-hunter side.

'Perhaps I'll just go back to Yorkshire,' she says glumly. 'I'm running out of men in London. My mother would be thrilled.'

'Don't be a dick,' says Sophie gently. She's the only person I know who can call someone a dick and still sound nice.

Sophie is two years younger than me. As children we were both very shy and spent a lot of time reading and drawing in intense, creative silence. But then, at 12, she developed this calm confidence while I remained quiet and prone to inner panic. For a few years I was jealous of her – she went to more parties and no matter what she did, was unable to keep platonic male friends where I was depressingly capable of it – but that soon faded. And now I just adore her. (Which is fortunate, as her engagement coinciding with my break-up could otherwise have been difficult.) We look very similar: straight, dark brown hair, slim but utterly un-athletic, with blueish eyes. Her teeth are better than mine too.

'Easy for you to say, you're the one who's getting fucking married at the age of 25,' says Plum.

Sophie doesn't say anything to this. She told me once that she feels embarrassed about jumping the marriage queue ahead of us both. That is typical Sophie. She's kinder than anyone I know.

Plum is now trying on the trench I just had on, and is gazing at her reflection in the mirror in that detached, assessing way that all girls have when they're shopping, like they're examining fruit in a market. 'I look like Inspector fucking Clouseau,' she says. (Plum has to be extremely 'on' for her job in PR, which I think is one of the reasons she swears like a sailor with Tourette's when she's with us. Another is that she's just really good at swearing.)

I pick up a dark-blue mini-dress. 'Good? With a belt?'

'I'm over belts,' says Plum. 'Actually, I'm over dresses. They're so un-versatile. It's all about separates now. But that would be OK with some drop earrings and some chic little flats.'

'I don't own drop earrings or chic flats,' I say sadly. 'How can

I have been shopping my whole fucking life and still have nothing to wear?'

I take out my notebook and write 'Flats, earrings' in a page I keep specifically for sartorial learnings.

'How's this?' says Sophie, coming out of the changing room. 'It's not revealing, it's informative.' Her dress is cut to well below boob-crease.

'When the fuck are we going wedding dress shopping, by the way?' says Plum, perking up considerably.

'We?' repeats Sophie dubiously.

'You need me, I'm your other big sister,' says Plum firmly, putting her arm around Sophie and shepherding her back to the changing room. 'I'm not leaving the Wood sisters alone with that decision.'

'Fine. After work next week,' calls Sophie through the changing room curtain. 'I know a vintage wedding dress company. We did a shoot there once.'

Sophie is an agent for photographers that you've almost heard of and soon will. She discovered she loved photography temping in a gallery in San Francisco, then rang 20 London agents every week till one of them gave her a job to shut her up. Another person who knows what she wants and makes it happen. Argh. Did I miss a Figure-Out-Your–Life-Day at school or something?

'Right, stick a fork in me, I'm done,' says Sophie, handing the rejected dress back to the saleswoman with an apologetic smile. 'It's lovely, I'll probably come back later, thank you so much for your help!'

She once told me that she feels bad when she doesn't buy something. It's why she owns eight identical V-neck black jumpers.

'Let's go to Zara for non-basic basics,' says Plum decisively. 'That's what Abigail's missing.'

'How are you so good at this stuff?' I ask as we head outside.

Plum shrugs. 'My brain automatically co-ordinates outfits. Like that magic fashion computer in *Clueless*. I can even do it with things I haven't bought yet.'

With Plum's help, Zara is a success. I find a sexy nude pencil dress, a slightly-longer-than-any-of-my-others-and-therefore-apparently-completely-different black skirt, and some totally inappropriate green high heels that I just want. Plum tells me how I should wear all these things, and I take out my notebook and write everything down till she starts laughing at me.

'How are you getting along with Robert, by the way?' says Sophie.

'Fine,' I say. 'He's not around much. He gave me some good "surviving singledom" tips the other night.'

'He'd be good at that,' says Sophie. 'He's a total ladykiller. One of London's premier playboys.'

'Description, please,' says Plum.

'Dark hair, dark green eyes, high cheekbones, chiselled jaw line, lips arrogantly curled into a perma-snarl,' says Sophie, as though she's reading the back of a Mills and Boon novel. 'Gorgeous, brooding and manly.'

'Frowny,' I add. 'Grumpy. Needs a shave. Hair's a bit messy. He's very tidy around the house, though. Thank God.'

'Good body?' says Plum.

'Yes,' says Sophie. 'You really don't find him hot, Abigail?'

'I haven't seen his body. It's not like I'm going to run into him coming out of the shower, we have separate bathrooms.'

'Shame,' says Plum wistfully.

'Anyway, when we met I was still in break-up recovery mode,' I say. 'I only ever saw him as a potential flatmate.'

'Domesticity breeds contempt,' says Plum. 'He sounds like just my kind of bedmate. Roll him in honey and bring him to me.'

'He's not the relationship type,' I say, shaking my head.

'Totally,' agrees Sophie. 'He's sort of unobtainable. Great guy, but . . .'

'Marvellous, another fucknuckle, that's just what I need. Hey, did you hear what happened to Henry?' asks Plum. 'He woke up this morning with a bite of unchewed kebab still in his mouth.'

Henry is my other best friend. He's a real *boy*: uncomplicated, very good-natured and permanently hungry. He shared a house with Plum and me at university. We went through a phase of calling him Miranda, but he said if he was anyone, he was Charlotte, so we stopped. He's not gay, by the way, and he has lots of guy friends (all mined by Plum a long time ago). But we've known him for so long, he's one of us.

We head towards Marylebone and sit at a table outside the first coffee shop we see, just as Plum's phone rings.

She pops her Bluetooth earpiece in her ear (she was convinced that her mobile was giving her blackheads), and trills, 'Henrietta! No, the BabyCare Show is the 25th this year, darling! Mmm. Righto. Byee!' She hangs up and rolls her eyes. 'You'd think we were saving the world, not launching a new fucking nappy range.'

Sophie frowns. 'Plummy. Language.'

'Well, she always panics on weekends and calls me from her boyfriend Sebastian's fucking Range Rover as they're off shooting yachts, or whatever it is they do,' says Plum crossly. 'I'm fed up with posh girls, I really am.'

Sophie and I look at each other and start to giggle. I wonder if people I work with do things like that. Then I remember work, and sigh deeply.

'What's wrong, kittenpants?' asks Plum.

'Do you love work?'

'I love my work *friends*, even the posh ones,' says Plum. 'But the pay is shit, I'm permanently broke and because the office is all women we all go on the blob at the same time, which is a fucking nightmare.'

'I do love my job,' says Sophie. Plum throws a sugar cube

at her. 'Sorry, but I do! . . . It's stressful but I look forward to Mondays.'

'Fuck me,' says Plum in dismay. 'You look *forward* to Mondays? Honestly . . .' she turns to me. 'Why do you ask, sweetie?'

I sigh deeply. 'Work is basically somewhere I go for free internet access. I don't like it, I never laugh . . . But I don't know how to do anything else.' Oh God, I'm getting emotional. Tears, down boy.

'Remember it pays well,' says Sophie. I nod. I get paid more than Plum and Sophie put together, which I feel guilty about so I try to surreptitiously pick up the cheque whenever I can. For the record, I'm not the flash-your-cash bankery type: the idea of spending thousands on a handbag is obscene (practical and annoying, but hey! that's me). I've also saved quite a lot over the years without really trying. (I know how practical and annoying that is too.)

'I don't think that . . . I don't think that I care about the money that much,' I say.

'So you're in the wrong job,' says Sophie calmly. 'It's not the end of the world. You can change.'

'How can I have spent the last six years in the wrong fucking job?' I exclaim. 'Then again, I spent the last seven years with the wrong man. I clearly have a talent for ignoring things.'

'Isn't it time you bought a house?' says Plum. 'You should get a mortgage while you still have a good job. Then you can quit and do what you want.'

I wince. The buying-a-house conversation comes up with my parents every year. I always fudge it. The idea of committing to something so huge makes me feel sick. I can't imagine it, I don't want to imagine it. So I ignore it.

'Maybe you shouldn't worry about it just now,' suggests Sophie quickly. She can read me so well.

'And remember, you are recovering from breaking up with the man you spent a quarter of your life with,' says Plum, slipping straight into supportive-friend mode. 'I mean, I need fucking months to get over relationships that didn't even last as long as a season of *The City*.'

'But . . . I am fine about Peter,' I say uneasily. I really do feel fine. Perhaps I'm in denial. 'Never mind. It's too late to change careers now.'

'It's never too late. What would you do, if you could do anything?' says Sophie.

Pause.

I'm staring at her, unable to respond. She stares back for 10, 20, 30 seconds . . . I'm speechless, mouth opening and closing like a goldfish. My inability to answer that simple question makes me want to be sick even more. What's *wrong* with me?

Plum exchanges a glance with Sophie.

'I don't know!' I say eventually. 'I don't want to talk about this anymore. I'm going home to get changed. I need to put my singledom skills to the test again.'

The best thing about a busy social life? It helps you avoid reality.

# Chapter Five

Whenever you break up with someone, you don't just break up with one person. You break up with their family, their friends and their dog. It's sad, inevitable and kind of annoying. But it's just the way it is. Which is why this weekend has been a bit . . . urgh.

For a start, Peter's mother rang yesterday morning, talking about how much she misses me and how love is something that you have to work at. Bloody nightmare. Then last night Plum, Henry and I went to a party which turned out to be a minefield of Peter's friends who either asked me about Peter, ignored me or gave me death stares. At 10 pm, my cheeks aching from fake smiling, I made eye contact with Plum and raked a finger across my throat to indicate that I wouldn't mind leaving. We grabbed Henry, who had been rejected by every girl in the bar anyway, and took a cab to a late-night bar in Victoria.

We had a long chat about singledom on the way.

'I need to hang out with guys more,' said Henry. 'I think you chicks are the reason I never get any action.'

'You don't think it's because you tend to wake up with bites of unchewed kebab in your mouth?' I said.

'One time!' shouted Henry. He paused. 'I could murder a kebab now, actually.'

'I am so over that crowd,' I said, applying lip gloss. 'They all think I'm an evil bitch for dumping Peter.'

'Me too,' said Plum, taking the lip gloss from me. 'But only because I've slept with all the decent men.'

'You didn't sleep with me!' exclaimed Henry, slapping Plum away as she tried to put lip gloss on him too.

'I snogged you at my 21st, sweetie,' she replied. 'And it wasn't great kissing, so I didn't bother to defile you.'

'Maybe you're a bad kisser,' he said. 'Because I'm awesome.'

There was a pause, probably as we all wondered if we were, in fact, bad kissers.

'I'm starting to think I'm bad in bed because men keep dumping me after I sleep with them,' said Plum glumly.

'I heard that you were bad in bed, actually,' said Henry. Plum punched him, quite hard, in the shoulder. 'Ow.'

'I have only kissed or slept with one person since my teens,' I said. 'So both of you can just shut up.'

Poor Henry, I reflect. My mother would be so happy if I fell in love with and/or married him. So would Plum's. But we've known him too long. I don't even think of him as having a willy. I sort of imagine he has a mound down there, like a Ken doll.

Today, I'm dragging Plum to meet my sister and her fiancé at a pub called The Cow in Notting Hill.

'I fucking hate Sundays,' says Plum, lighting a cigarette as we walk towards the pub. She's in a mood. 'Every Sunday I go to bed alone and wake up on Monday alone and think, oh, another week, a whole week till the weekend when I might, *maybe*, get to meet someone new, someone who isn't a total cockgobbler . . .'

'Plum!' I exclaim. 'That is melodramatic. And untrue.' Her hung-over negativity scares me. Is that attitude inevitable? Will I end up like that? I did meet someone last night, between you and me, but I don't want to bring it up now and make Plum feel worse.

'Churchill had a black dog. I have singledom,' she says, exhaling theatrically. 'I will die alone.'

'Plummy—'

'It's enough to make me completely desperate—'

'Don't! Don't say that word,' I exclaim. I don't want to catch her Sunday blues. 'I don't like it.'

Plum looks at me strangely. 'Alright. Jeez. Oh, there they are. Sitting outside. Yay.'

Luke is half-Dutch, and inherited white-blonde hair from his Dutch mother so it's easy to spot him in a crowd, like a little ray of light. He and Sophie met a year ago and got engaged two months ago. Just before I left Peter. I'd tell you that their perfect, blissful love had no impact on my Peter decision, but well, I'd be lying. It was a major catalyst. Sophie wanted to marry Luke, I didn't want to marry Peter, the contrast was too huge to ignore.

'About time!' says Sophie, standing up to hug and kiss us hello. I note, as usual, how she seems to glow with happiness whenever Luke is around. That's what love should be like. Maybe I'm just not capable of it. Argh. *Love.*

Time for a drink.

'So tell me about last night,' I say a few minutes later, Corona in hand.

'Another fucking 30th. A dinner party,' says Sophie. Luke is 30, so their social life seems to be 'another fucking 30th' every weekend. 'Started with wine and nibbles, ended with straight men doing synchronised dance routines to Backstreet Boys songs.'

'I rocked out like AJ McLean,' adds Luke. His phone buzzes. 'That's the hotline . . . ah. Dave can't make it. He's unable to get out of bed, apparently.'

'Anything exciting happen last night?' asks Sophie. 'I mean men. You know I mean men.'

I grin, and shrug coolly. I want to get the subject off men so Plum doesn't get even more depressed. I'm also trying out the don't-think-about-him-don't-talk-about-him attitude I've been working on since Robert's post-Paulie peptalk.

'*Bonjour tigre,*' says Plum under her breath. I look up.

It's Robert, striding towards us, up Westbourne Park Road, talking on his phone.

'That's my flatmate,' I say. 'Robert.'

'Fucking hell,' she says quietly, glancing at Sophie and Luke to see if they're listening, but fortunately they're cooing at each other like pigeons. 'He *is* gorgeous.'

Robert is clearly trying to end the phone conversation. He's wearing a kind of cool, albeit wrinkled, khaki shirt. Combined with the furrowed brow and stubble, I have to admit he looks pretty good. He'll need Botox soon if he doesn't stop frowning, though.

'Right . . . Is that all? . . . Well, thanks for calling . . . I don't know yet. It's six days away . . . I will. Yes.' He finally hangs up, shakes his head and runs his hands through his hair, and turns to us.

'Luke, you look fantastic. Hello Sophie, Abigail,' he says, leaning over to give me a kiss hello. His stubble is longer than usual, and he smells slightly of whisky.

'Long night, huh, sailor?' I say, wrinkling my nose.

'You have no idea,' he says. His voice is very husky. 'God, even my eyebrows hurt.'

'You bad man, why are you in the same clothes that you were in last night?' asks Sophie. Robert winks at her. Plum is practically panting.

'Robert, meet Plum. Plum, Robert,' I say.

'Hello, Plum,' says Robert, sitting down at the table next to me. 'What a delightful name. It's one of my favourite stone fruits.' Hung-over Robert is infinitely more relaxed than After Work Robert, I notice. I wonder if his job is stressful.

'So you were out last night? Were you dancing too? Hung-over today? I hate hangovers, don't you? I had one earlier but it's gone now!' babbles Plum, as she frantically flicks her hair. I glance at her in shock. Is that her idea of subtle body language? And is Robert really that gorgeous?

'No questions, please. I need a drink,' he says. Luke hands him the beer he has waiting for him. 'Thanks. Christ, it's sunny. I'll pay you a thousand pounds for your sunglasses, Abigail.' His eyes are dark green, I notice, with irritatingly thick eyelashes. Why do men always get them? Is it the gene pool's idea of a joke?

I hand over my sunglasses, which are sort of Fifties and cat-eyeish, and to my surprise he happily puts them on and beams at us all.

'Do I look like Audrey?'

'Audrey is boring,' I say. 'Katharine Hepburn was so much cooler.'

Robert gasps in mock horror. 'How could you say that? I heart Audrey!'

'How come I've never met you before?' says Plum. She's cool again. At least on the outside.

'I was seeing a girl in Italy,' he says, turning to her with a grin. The cat-eye glasses give everyone killer cheekbones. Including Robert. 'Lots of weekends away.'

'And another girl in Edinburgh,' adds Luke. 'And one in Bethnal Green, and one in Highgate . . .' Robert shoots him a shut-up look and Luke responds with a wide – albeit slightly watery – grin.

'Well, I'm free again now, so all's well that ends well,' Robert says.

Funny, how men call it being free and women call it being alone, isn't it?

Soon Plum is talking about the lack of men in London. She's either already pissed, or wants Robert to know she's really, definitely, totally single.

'I go out four motherfucking nights a week. I am in bars and parties and I'm not obese or revoltingly ugly. And yet I cannot meet a decent man. It's just fucknuckle after fucknuckle, time after time . . .'

39

'Seriously, can you please not swear for just one minute?' says Sophie.

'No I cannot! There are no fucking men in London.'

'That's just not true,' says Robert.

'Are you saying I am meeting men without my knowledge?' Plum reaches out and pokes Robert in the arm.

'No,' says Robert matter-of-factly. 'I'm saying you're closed to opportunity. Take right now: you've got your back to the crowd. You can only see us. I've seen every woman who's walked in . . . and out . . . and in again. 'Scuse me,' he adds, getting up.

We all turn wordlessly and watch him walk up the steps to inside The Cow, where I can see a pretty, model-esque blonde wearing a bowler hat and pretending not to see him.

'He's not *that* attractive,' says Plum decisively. She's evidently decided, in the face of his utter non-flirtation with her, to stop throwing herself at him. 'And he's a smartarse.'

'That must be why you've stared at him nonstop since he sat down,' says Sophie. Plum flicks a piece of ice at her.

From my seat, I can see Robert quite clearly. He's standing at the bar, still wearing my cat-eye sunglasses, and is grinning down at the bowler-hat girl. Then he takes them off and leans in, as though he didn't hear what she said the first time.

Robert doesn't have the sleazy, shark-like twinkle of other lothario types. He just seems calm and certain about – well, everything. It's obviously charming to other women. I'm clearly immune to it.

I tune back into the conversation for a few seconds. 'Italy, I think, and then driving to Provence—' Sophie is saying. Luke gazes lovingly at her when she talks, it's so cute. They met when he walked past a pub in Soho, saw her through the window, went in and drank alone at the bar till he had the courage to go and talk to her. And that was it.

I hope it's that easy for everyone, i.e. me.

Robert soon returns, putting his phone back in his pocket. He must have just got her number, I think to myself. Smooth.

'Have you recovered from your disastrous date, Abigail?' he asks. He maintains very steady eye contact, I've noticed. I bet that's part of the whole calm thing.

'Yes, thank you. So, are you taking bowler hat to dinner?'

'Who? Her? No. She's not dinner material.'

'What is she then? Tell me you don't booty call. It's so five years ago.'

'I'm not that kind of boy,' he says, sipping his drink thoughtfully. 'They booty call me, if anything . . . No, she's a fancy-a-few-drinks-if-you're-out-at-about-10 pm text.'

'A short-term investment,' I suggest. 'You're a bit of a bastard, aren't you? I suppose your singledom rules will make me a bastard, too.'

'They're just survival skills, Abigail,' he replies easily. 'Don't overthink them. So. What did you get up to last night? Give your number out to all and sundry?'

'Yeah, I got stickers printed up,' I reply. His know-it-all attitude is kind of annoying. 'Aren't you tired of talking about my dating life?'

'I find it interesting,' he says. 'Like a parallel universe of naivety and optimism.'

I glare at him for a moment, and then start to laugh. 'Fine. His name is Josh,' I whisper, so Plum can't hear. 'He works in HR, and I met him at the bar, and we snogged on the dance floor. My first snog since Peter and I broke up!' I pause. 'I wish I could remember it better.'

'Wow,' says Robert. 'I haven't snogged on a dance floor in years. Did you feel his excitement thrusting against you?'

'Ew,' I say. 'Seriously, ew.'

Robert laughs. He has one of those laughs that makes everyone else feel like they might be missing out on something funny.

'*Que*?' says Sophie.

'I, um, met a guy last night. Robert reduced it straight to sex, immediately,' I say petulantly. 'Deviant.'

'Who's the guy?!' says Sophie excitedly.

'No one, no one, I haven't heard from him yet, he probably won't even call,' I say, glancing at Plum, who is carefully lighting a cigarette. She left soon after we got to the bar last night: no one was chatting her up so she couldn't see the point in staying.

'Doesn't it seem a shame to spend all night chatting to just one person?' asks Robert.

'No,' I say, though now that I think about it, there was a tall guy at the bar who I thought kept looking at me. I wish I'd talked to him a bit, too.

'I knew it,' he says smugly.

It's kind of annoying how he can read my mind. 'You want me to' – I pause and look for the right word – '*multitask* my flirting?'

Robert nods. 'Meet, greet, move on. Unless you just want, you know, a one-night-stand.'

'Men don't think like that,' says Plum, who looks a bit upset. I know she's thinking about a guy she met a few months ago. She talked to him all night, thought a thunderbolt went off, went home with him and shagged till 5 pm on Sunday. She hasn't heard from him since.

'Enough about this,' I say hurriedly.

'But I thought you were the fuckmerchant!' she blurts at Robert.

He shakes his head. 'Casual relationships. Very different thing.'

'You make it sound so noble,' I say.

Robert ignores me. 'I bet, if you two did exactly what I say, you could meet a guy within the next hour.'

'How?' interrupts Plum. 'Write my number on the back of the boys' toilet door?'

'Go over to The Westbourne,' that's another pub just about 30 feet up, always surrounded by enthusiastic outside drinkers on days like this. 'Walk in the side entrance and order two pints of beer and a vodka and tonic at the bar. Carry them out the main door—'

'But how can I carry three drinks?' asks Plum. 'I'll drop them.'

'Exactly. Pause when you get outside, like you can't see your friends. It's packed, so that's not surprising. Act like you're having trouble holding all the glasses. Someone will offer to help you. Talk, laugh, flirt. Job done.'

'Will that really work?' I ask, as Plum heads off.

'No reason it shouldn't. The first step to being chatted up is being visible,' says Robert. 'She's a pretty girl and she swears exceptionally well . . . Of course, she's also transparently high-maintenance, and that's her Achilles' heel.'

'What's mine? Achilles' heel, I mean?'

'Lack of confidence,' says Robert instantly. Ouch.

'I have confidence,' I protest feebly. (This, of course, isn't the correct response when someone accuses you of lacking confidence. The correct response is a derisive 'blow me'.) 'Dating is just out of my comfort zone.'

'Well, you also often look preoccupied, like you're arguing with yourself. It gives you a fuck-off aura.'

'Suck my aura,' I say sulkily.

Robert smirks.

'It's not my fault,' I say, after a pause. 'You need experience to be confident at anything. Driving. Putting on make up. Flipping pancakes. I have no experience at being single. How could I possibly be confident at it?'

'We're working on that,' he says. 'You're next.'

I sigh. I really don't want to set myself up for another terrible Paulie-date.

'Relax,' he says. 'You'll be fine. It won't be like Paulie. Experience, remember?'

His mind-reading trick is getting really annoying.

43

'There she is!' exclaims Sophie a few minutes later. I look over. Plum is sauntering over the road towards us, an enormous grin on her face. She holds her fist in front of her chest and flips up her index and little finger in the heavy metal, devil sign.

'Victory is mine, beetchez. First, a man at the bar gave me his card,' she says, sitting down. 'And I met two guys outside. One went to make a call, and the other asked for my number and asked if I would like to meet for a drink on Wednesday!'

Sophie and I reach over to give her surreptitious high-fives.

'Ditch the card,' says Robert. 'It's lazy. If he was really keen, he would have asked for your number.' Plum obediently tears the business card in two and drops it in the ashtray.

Paulie gave me his card. No wonder the date sucked.

Plum sits back, smiling peacefully to herself. Funny how happiness is tied in to feeling wanted, isn't it? Or not feeling unwanted, anyway.

'Abigail, your turn,' Plum grins at me.

Oh God no. I couldn't bear to have everyone watch me fail.

'No point,' I say quickly. 'The guys at The Westbourne have seen Plum do exactly the same three-drinks-lost thing. If I did it, it'd look weird.'

'Forget The Westbourne. Try the bar here. Go in, order five drinks,' says Robert. 'Stand next to someone decent. When the drinks arrive, look perplexed. He'll offer to help.'

'I don't want to,' I say in a faux-whingey voice that I hope hides how nervous the idea makes me feel.

'Go on, darling,' says Sophie. 'I need a drink, anyway.'

'There's nothing to be nervous about, Abigail,' says Robert.

Sighing, I walk into The Cow, stepping over a couple of sprawling dogs and the long legs of a model on the way in.

I size up the bar. There are three guys standing together, all wearing knee-length khaki combats that remind me of Peter, so I dismiss them instantly. A curly-haired woman is next to them gossiping with the bartender. I decide to stand next to two guys studying a wine list down the other end of the bar. God, nerves suck.

'Montepulciano,' one is reading. He's cute, wearing skinny jeans and a slightly too-tight T-shirt. 'Or Valpolicella.'

'You can't choose a wine just because you like saying the name,' says the other, who's wearing just a waistcoat and shorts. He's carrying it off, surprisingly.

'I think I'll call my first child Montepulciano,' replies Skinny Jeans pensively. 'Monty, for short, obviously.'

I grin to myself at this, and duck my head to hide that I'm eavesdropping.

'See? The lady in red thinks it's a good idea,' says Skinny Jeans. I glance down. I'm wearing a loose red mini dress and Converses. He means me! I don't know what to say, so – cool! detached! – rather than gabble, I look over and smile mutely. Skinny Jeans is cute in a skinny, media-boy kind of way.

'She thinks you're a drunk,' replies Waistcoat.

OK, now I need to speak.

'Actually, I'm thinking that I always wanted to name my first child Mascarpone, but I may have to rethink that now,' I manage to say.

'You choose, then,' says Skinny Jeans. He hands me the wine list and I scan it slowly, trying to think of something to say.

'Quite the wine buff,' comments Waistcoat. I look at him and raise an eyebrow. To disagree would look falsely modest, to agree would be idiotic.

'The Brunelli is nice, if you want Italian,' I say calmly. 'Personally, I like Malbec.' Actually, it's the only wine I remember drinking recently.

'Malbec it is,' replies Skinny Jeans. 'Care to join us?'

'Alas, I cannot,' I say quickly. 'I've got to get a round . . .' I turn to the bar and see the bartender looking at me expectantly, and quickly order. I ignore the guys while I wait. Nerves, my nemesis (nemeses? Nemesii?) have overcome me, and I don't know what to say. I hand over my money, take the change, feeling painfully self-conscious the whole time . . .

'Need a hand with those drinks?' asks Skinny Jeans.

'Uh, yes, please. Thanks,' I say.

'Alfie, order the Malbec,' Skinny Jeans says over his shoulder as he nods to me to lead the way.

'Thanks . . .' I say again, as we're walking outside.

We reach the table, and Sophie and Plum beam at Skinny Jeans. Could they be any more obvious?

'Next time you need a drink, you should come and find me first,' says Skinny Jeans to me, after he sets down the drinks. 'It makes sense. Logistically.'

'Yes, sir,' I say. He walks back inside and I sit down nonchalantly.

Everyone makes an 'oooooo' sound.

'Shut up,' I say. I can't help smiling. Confidence, engage! Experience, add one point!

'Did he get your number?' asks Plum.

'No,' I say. Everyone except Robert murmurs 'oh' disappointedly. Confidence, dash yourself against the nearest rock! Experience, minus two! See? I do suck at being single! 'This is weird, guys. Stop it.'

'Play a long game,' says Robert. 'He'll be after you next time you're inside.'

'OK,' I say glumly.

'Why are you being so fucking helpful, Rob?' says Luke suddenly. 'This is completely unlike you.'

Everyone looks at Robert. He stares into space for a second and then frowns, 'You're right. I have no idea. Back later,' and stalks off towards The Westbourne.

'Have you spoken to the folks this weekend, Abs?' asks Sophie. Our parents have retired to a little village in the south of France, which is just as idyllic as it sounds, and twice as boring. When they moved there six months ago, our mother rang us both once a day, sometimes twice. Then, thankfully, Sophie got engaged, and Mum threw herself into Mother Of The Bride work with fervour. She started a MOTB blog and even tweets about it, much to Sophie's horror.

'Yep, she's organising an expat MOTB tweet-up,' I say.

'A what?' say Luke and Plum in unison.

'A meeting of Twitterers. Tweeters. Whatever,' I say.

'It's her new career. She'll be dying for you to get married next,' says Sophie.

'She'll be waiting a while, at this rate . . . Oh my God, I'm the elder sister spinster,' I realise. 'How depressing.'

'It's not your fault Sophie is a child bride,' says Plum.

'And it's not my fault that Luke is ancient and wants to settle down,' replies Sophie.

'I'm not that old,' protests Luke half-heartedly. 'But it is past my bedtime. Can we go home please? I need to tuck my hangover into bed.'

Plum and I decide to go home too. It's nearly dark now, and getting that chilly September Sunday feeling.

'Should I wait for Robert?' I wonder aloud. We all look over. He's pouring a bottle of wine for two uber-cool girls in jumpsuits, who are laughing at something he has just said. Wowsers, how does he do it?

'You'll be waiting a long time,' says Luke.

Before we leave, I walk back into The Cow to go to the bathroom in the basement. On my way back up the stairs, Skinny Jeans is coming down. We do a polite little side-step-side-step dance, and I smirk and head past him without saying anything.

'What . . . that's it? No conversation? After all we've been through?' he says, and we pause on the same step.

'Oh, did I hurt your feelings? I am sorry,' I say. 'What would you like to discuss?'

He chuckles and looks me right in the eye. 'Your phone number.'

47

High five! Robert really *is* good at this. Looks like someone isn't failing at being single after all. (That someone is ME. In case you're wondering.)

'I'm Mark, by the way,' he says.

'Abigail,' I nod. You don't look like a Mark, I think. I'm going to call you Skinny Jeans.

At home, I potter around for a while, remembering to drink water and eat crumpets to soak up the booze. I try to read in bed, but almost immediately fall into a slumber with Jilly Cooper's *Polo* open on my chest. When I wake up it is midnight, and I can hear voices downstairs. I wake up long enough to focus on them. It's Robert and a girl. Good for him, I think to myself, then turn off my light and fall back to sleep.

# Chapter Six

I'm finally embarking on my second-ever date. YES! I know. I'm happy for me, too. I'm not quite as nervous as I was last week. You can tell I'm not as nervous tonight, right? I had a mini confidence crash earlier, but I closed my eyes and took deep breaths till it passed. I just have to fake it, that's what Robert said. Fake it till you feel it.

It's Josh from HR, the guy I met when I was out with Henry and Plum on Saturday night. We're meeting at the Albannach bar, just off Trafalgar Square, for a couple of drinks. Robert recommended I make it drinks, not dinner, as it saves time if you decide you don't like them. If you like them, you can do dinner on date two. I shared that piece of genius with Plum.

'But that makes the date so much shorter, so they have less time to get to know you and decide they like you!' she exclaimed in dismay.

I thought for a second, and replied, 'Shouldn't you be deciding if *you* like *them*, not the other way around?'

Silence.

Perhaps I'm wrong. As previously established, I don't have much 'experience' or 'confidence' in dating. (Harrumph.) Plum is seeing the guy she met at The Westbourne tomorrow night, by the way. And no, I haven't heard from Skinny Jeans guy yet.

I'm early, so I sit in Trafalgar Square for a little while and text people.

To Sophie: *Yes to shopping on Saturday. How was the wedding place?*

To Henry: *Remember to chew.*

To Plum: *Any news from Westbourne Guy? Thank you for clothes help.*

Plum helped me work out what to wear tonight over a series of long, highly specific emails today. The result – a pretty, pale pink mini-dress with brown platform sandals – feels both comfortable and confidence-boosting. 'Pretty with a punch, in the form of the unexpectedly chunky sandals,' said Plum. I think that might be my special flavour. Pretty With A Punch. Hell yeah, I speak style.

I wait for a few minutes, but no one texts right back. I'll take out my powder and check my make-up. Yes, good: smokey eye, nude lip gloss, check teeth, yes, good, fine. Right. Time to go . . .

Boom! In a split-second, my stomach goes from mild nerves to hyperactive butterflies – no, that's far too pretty for how it actually feels. My stomach is moths. Flappy, molty-winged moths. Deep breaths, Abigail. You can do this. It's just a date. You won't mess it up this time.

Oh God, I think I'm sweating again.

Text! From . . . oh, Robert.

From Robert: *You left your keys here.*

I check my bag to make sure. Yep. No keys. Shit.

To Robert: *Oops. Are you at home all night?*

From Robert: *At The Engineer for a few drinks. Call in on your way home.*

How does he know I won't be on this date till past midnight, I think. Josh From HR could be my soulmate, for all he knows.

Ooh, another text.

From Robert: *Unless Josh From HR is your soulmate, of course.*

Bastard.

To Robert: *OK. Thanks. I'll call you later . . . ps any advice for me, o dating sage?*

From Robert: *Act like you don't care.*

His tips are getting annoying. Isn't that kind of the same as 'act detached', anyway? I check my watch. It's 8 pm! I'm going to be a few minutes late. What a novelty. Time to go.

The Albannach is a dark, masculine bar, with deer antlers on the wall giving it a slightly creepy look, and it's full of business types having a post-work drink. I hope Josh sees me before I see him. I was tipsy when I met him last weekend, and yes of course I remember what he looks like but, well, I don't want to have to gaze into the face of every man between 25 and 40 to make sure . . .

'Abigail,' says a voice behind me, and I turn around with a smile. It's Josh. Slim build, slightly oversized pink shirt that gapes around the collar, pukish-taupe tie, little wire-rimmed glasses.

'Josh!' I say, and we kiss hello. No aftershave. Cheeks very warm.

'I got us seats over here,' he says. Following him, I look down and see that his trousers are about three inches too short. 'Want to look at the drinks menu?' he says, handing it over. He's drinking a pint of beer.

'Sure thing,' I reply easily.

My nerves disappeared the moment I saw him. I can't believe I snogged him . . . He's not quite how I remembered, ahem. I'm not sure he's much more than 25 and he looks even younger. I study the cocktail menu for a few seconds, and automatically start reading the names aloud thoughtfully à la Bam-Bou.

'Pea—'

I stop.

'I'll have a Pear Sour, I think,' I say. He smiles back and I realise that he has no intention of going to the bar for me. Of course! HR. Equal opportunity. 'Back in a sec,' I say, and walk up to the bar. What an awkward start.

I get back to find him absent-mindedly squeezing something on the back of his neck.

'I'm back,' I say, slightly pointlessly.

'Did you have any trouble getting here?' he says quickly, taking a large sip of his beer and spilling a little on his tie.

'Um, no,' I say. 'Did you?'

'I did,' he says earnestly. 'I thought Trafalgar Square was near Leicester Square and, well, you can imagine!'

It is near Leicester Square, I think, but don't say anything. It's not nice to make someone feel stupid. Even if they might be stupid. (Is he stupid?) Instead I smile. 'Central London is designed to confuse. Perhaps next time you should bring a compass and some sandwiches in case you get lost.'

Josh From HR continues, completely missing the compass/ sandwiches thing. 'I know! I hate it! I never come here if I can help it. I never leave Wandsworth if I can help it, actually, except to go to work.'

'Wandsworth is delightful,' I agree, as it seems like something to say, though actually I have never been there. And why live in London if you hate the place? Move somewhere else. It'll bring rent prices down for the rest of us. Gosh, I've got a feeling he's a dweeb. I didn't think I was *that* tipsy on Saturday. Perhaps I shouldn't make dates after more than three drinks.

'Isn't it?!' he exclaims, smiling and revealing a large piece of food lodged between his teeth.

Oh God, he *is* a dweeb.

For the next ten minutes, the conversation continues like this. Question, answer, comment. I realise I'm acting like Robert told me to – I'm cool, detached, offering a funny/teasing comment here and there (that he never picks up on), and generally acting friendly. It's easy to act like I don't care with Josh, because – yup – I really *don't* care. At all.

Despite not caring, I discover that he works in Croydon for Nestlé, studied geography at university, grew up in East Anglia, loves his mum's Sunday roast more than any restaurant meal and has every episode of *Little Britain* memorised. He, in turn, discovers that I studied Medieval French, work in a bank but find it boring, love reading, live in Primrose Hill and have never, ever, watched a single episode of *Little Britain*.

I finish my drink quite quickly, and though he's finished his, he doesn't offer to go to the bar. So I do instead.

As I stand waiting at the bar, it finally hits me: I don't want to be here. And that sounds obvious, but really, it goes against every stick-it-out, wait-and-see, have-you-thought-this-through? instinct I've ever had. It's a revefuckinglation.

I order our drinks, and get out my phone to text Robert. He's the only person who seems to be able to provide textual healing tonight.

To Robert: *Please help. Give me an excuse to get out of here.*

Robert replies: *He could be your soulmate.*

I narrow my eyes at the phone. Nice one, smartarse. I reply: *Seriously. Should I fake a burst appendix?*

From Robert: *I'll call you in ten minutes. Have your phone out.*

I head back with our drinks and sit down with a bright smile. 'Saturday was fun, huh?'

'I know! We got the overland to Victoria and then the train to South Kensington, and got off there by mistake instead of High Street Kensington, and—'

Hurry up, Robert, I think. Please hurry up. I'm trying to engage Josh on the marvellous subject of Wandsworth ('When the shopping centre was opened, it was the largest indoor shopping centre in Europe! That was 1971, of course . . . but it has all the shops I need now: Burtons, JD Sports, Primark . . .' 'Oh, I adore Primark!' I say, grateful to finally have something to say about Wandsworth), when my phone rings.

'It's my flatmate, I'm so sorry, I must get this,' I gabble. 'Hello?'

'Abigail, I've locked myself out of the flat,' says Robert.

'You've locked yourself out of the flat?' I repeat, very loudly and clearly.

'Yes, I have. And I need you to come and let me in.'

'You need me to come and let you in?'

'Yes. Fast. I'll be in the pub.'

'I'll be there as soon as I can!' I say, and turn apologetically to Josh. 'I'm so sorry, I have to go . . .'

'I had a great time,' Josh says. 'I'd love to see you again,' he stands up awkwardly and moves towards me. Cripes, he's not going to try and kiss me at 8.20 pm in a Central London bar, is he? I make myself all elbows putting on my jacket, and turn away whilst picking up my bag.

'That'd be great,' I lie, and smile at him. 'Don't worry about walking me to the tube. I'll be fine. No, no. Bye!'

Walk fast, woman, and don't look back.

Why bother to make dates when they're going to be that boring? Was I that boring when I was with Paulie? No, perish the thought.

Seriously, though: is dating always this difficult and/or dull? Why is everyone always talking about dating if it's this turgid? Life with Peter was a non-stop rave in comparison.

Do you think I'm being terribly mean? Look, I can't help it. Josh is a dweeb. He wasn't funny or interesting. I just don't fancy him. I did fancy Paulie, a bit. Having said that, Paulie got my name wrong and didn't make much effort even before my nervous meltdown. Hmm.

If you were me, would you get the tube home? Me neither.

I get in a black cab and start giggling to myself in the back. Not one but two bad dates! At least that one wasn't stressful. How silly the whole dating thing is! I mean, really. Oh well, experience equals confidence, right? I just – oh, more texts.

From Henry: *If you were a real friend you'd blend all my food from now on.*

From Sophie: *Wedding dress hell. I'm getting married in jeans. How's the date?*

From Plum: *Seeing the guy from The Westbourne tomorrow!! ARGH!*

By the time I get to The Engineer, I'm in a really good mood. I walk in and see Rob in a corner talking to a very pretty girl with long dark hair. Interesting body language: she's leaning forward in her chair, and he's leaning right back. Something not fun is happening.

'Hi!' I say brightly, when I reach their table. The girl – the tanned, glamorous type that you see on holiday, the kind with no body fat and improbably full lips – turns towards me, and I see that she's been crying. Her long fingers are curled around tatty little tissues. She seems unable to speak.

'This is Antonia,' says Robert shortly. I look at him, and back at her. His face is completely closed, giving nothing away.

'I'm Abigail, Robert's flatmate,' I say. She blinks and looks away. 'I'll get a . . . bottle,' I add, and turn towards the bar. Yikes. This is going to be awkward. Third-wheel-tastic. Should I just leave? I pretend to look around the bar and see Antonia storming out. Problem solved.

By the time I get back with the wine, Robert has sprawled himself over the two seats. He has a habit of taking up all the space at a table, or a sofa, or anywhere, I've noticed. Anyone else feels like they're encroaching on his territory just by being in the same room. I push his feet off the chair with my knee, sit down with a dramatic flourish, and pour us each a glass of red. I feel slightly euphoric to have got away from Josh From HR so easily.

'You need to shave,' I say.

'So, did you break his heart?' replies Robert, ignoring my shaving comment. I notice again how green and steady his eyes are. He really nails the whole self-assured eye contact thing.

'I don't think so. We had nothing to say to each other.' I sigh. 'My second date in my whole life was a dweeb. And the first was a fucknuckle.'

'You now think Bam-Bou Paulie was a fucknuckle?' says Robert in surprise, his eyes lighting up in amusement.

'I'm always more discerning in retrospect.'

'Aren't we all, Abigail darling?'

'I'm not your darling. You clearly just broke your darling's heart.'

'Oh, no grief, please . . . she flew here from Milan. I didn't ask her to. Fucking nightmare.'

'I expect you led her on,' I say.

'I did not,' he says defensively, running his hands through his hair. 'I never do, I always say "this is just casual" and then before you know it, it's where-is-this-going, what-am-I, and what-do-you-take-me-for . . .'

'How awful it must be when the easy sex starts asking hard questions.'

'Quite. I admit, it got a little too serious with Antonia . . . I mean, that's been going on for months. My bad.'

I snort with laughter.

'But the rest of the time, I'm totally honest that I am not looking for, uh, anything, and I end it within a month. I mean, that doesn't make me a bad guy, does it?'

'You're such a cliché.'

'How amusing, because you're not at all. Newly single girl, late 20s, trying to bag a boyfriend . . .'

'Shut up. And I'm not trying to "bag a boyfriend". I'm just trying to survive singledom and make up for lost time.'

'I've given you a few tips. You'll be fine.'

'Tonight was easy,' I admit. 'I had no problem walking out. I felt totally in control.'

'Of course, Christ, you should always feel in control,' says Robert in surprise.

I take out my notebook and write **Stay in control** on the list. Robert watches me with a bemused look on his face. As I look up our eyes meet, and I raise an eyebrow at him.

'Nice dress by the way. It suits you.'

'But what if I meet someone I like?' I don't want to talk about my dress, I want to talk about my dating.

'Then you see them as much as you want. Whatever blows your hair back. The point is, you're calling the shots.'

I hear my phone beep from my bag. 'Ooh! Text,' I say excitedly, reaching for my bag. 'It's the guy I met at The Cow on Sunday! Skinny Jeans guy!'

'What's he say?' he asks, trying to read my tiny phone screen. 'I haven't seen a Nokia like that since Britney was a virgin.'

'I like this phone, why change?' I say, and clear my throat. 'Ahem! He says . . . *Princess Malbec Of The Cow. I need a recommendation for a wine bar. You seem like the boozy type who'd know somewhere good. Any ideas?*' I make an excited-grin face at Robert. 'What should I reply?'

'Well, what do you want to say?'

'Well, I'm going to ask where he lives, and then what area he wants to go to. That will help me narrow it down, right? And then I'm going to tell him I'm most certainly not the boozy type, thank you very much . . .'

'No, no, no. Don't jump, don't be serious, don't respond to every point, it's too anxious. And don't ask so many questions. You're in control, remember?'

'OK,' I say, and take a long drink of wine. I like the way that Robert doesn't make me feel too stupid for not knowing this stuff. 'Like . . . umm . . . *Are you asking me out? Before I recommend anything, I want to know which area, and when . . .*'

'No, no, that's still jumping.'

I bury my face in my hands and squeal. 'This is hard! I can't play this game . . .'

'You keep saying that, but you seem to be learning quite fast,' says Robert drily.

I peer at him through my fingers. 'What would you say, then . . .?'

'I'd wait for a bit, then say something like: *I'm flattered to be your drinker of choice. Mention my name at Negozio Classica on Portobello Road and they'll look after you.*'

57

'That's so arrogant! And I've never even heard of that place. And shouldn't I say what time?'

'Arrogance is good. Keeps him on his toes. Let him take care of the details. Don't be obvious. It's needy.'

'But . . .'

'Send it.'

I obediently tap it in, reading aloud as I go, and press 'send' before I can think about it. Goodbye little text. God speed.

'Tell me more about Antonia.'

Robert sighs and rubs his eyes. 'I met her in Croatia last summer. She's beautiful. And crazy . . . We had a hedonistic week drinking and sleeping and swimming all day, staying on her dad's boat . . .'

'Seriously. What happened?'

'That's exactly what happened,' he says in surprise.

Wow. That's unlike any holiday I've ever had. Peter and I went on a boat trip off the coast of Majorca once, but Peter was seasick and I got a headache and we were only out for six hours, anyway. Then he went to bed and I lay by the hotel pool and watched other people having a good holiday. God! Enough about Peter.

I pause, as a dark-haired girl in a tiny black dress and huge black boots walks past us to the bar. She's trying to give Robert some intense eye contact as she passes, but – unusually – he's oblivious.

'Do women always just present themselves to you on a scent-spritzed platter?'

'Sorry?'

'Nothing. So, you fell in lust with her, then what?'

He shrugs. 'We've been stealing weekends together here and there, but it was never going to last, was it? She lives in Milan, for God's sake . . .' He shakes his head. 'I'm surprised she's surprised, if you know what I mean.'

'I don't think women think like that.'

'Well, guys do.'

'Do you want to know what I think?'

58

'If it's anything other than that I should end it, no.'

'You don't have to be such a bastard about it. I think you need to make her feel better. Did you tell her you're sorry?'

'Never apologise, never explain.'

I'm about to retort when my phone beeps.

'Ooh!' I read the text aloud. *'For my safety, you should probably escort me. Negozio Classica, tomorrow, 8 pm?* What should I say?'

Robert reads it. 'Short notice. Do you want to see him?'

'Yes . . .' I say, thinking about Skinny Jeans' blue eyes and engagingly bold manner. 'I think so. Yes.'

'Leave it for twenty minutes. Then text him back "sounds good, see you there".'

'Shouldn't I say something funny?'

'Leave him wanting more. And don't use an exclamation mark or a smiley face.'

'Like I would!' I exclaim. We sit in silence for a few moments. I might have used an exclamation mark, actually. 'I wonder if I'll ever date someone I actually like,' I say. 'Instead of just saying "yes" to any random man I meet.'

'Course you will. But you have to slay a lot of dragons to get to the princess, that's what my mother always says.'

'What a peach.'

'She is,' he agrees.

'I have to use the euphemism.'

'You know, "loo" isn't a dirty word. You can even say "bathroom" or "toilet".'

By the time we finish the wine, I've sent the second pre-agreed text to Skinny Jeans, and receive a reply as we're contemplating getting a second bottle.

'Ooo! Another text!' I say excitedly. Robert grins. It says . . . *"I'll see you there. You lucky girl."* What should I reply? Something about him being the lucky one?'

'No,' says Robert. 'Don't reply. Remember, always leave them wanting more.'

'Yes, master. Any other advice?'

'Make this one work hard. He's slick.'

'What if I need help? Like once I'm on the date?'

'Text me,' he says, grinning. He seems to find my dating panic highly amusing.

'Thanks,' I grin at him. Maybe having a male flatmate will work out after all. His phone beeps again. 'OK. I have to go, I'm afraid. Lady Caroline. Here are my keys. I'll be home at 6.30 am, will you be there?'

'Yep. I'll make us breakfast,' I say. Yay! I hate eating breakfast alone. I get up and put my coat on.

'Don't all your tips kind of defeat the point of dating?' I wonder aloud as we walk towards the door. 'You know, to get to know each other and see if you like each other?'

'Don't be silly,' he replies. 'The point is to have fun.'

All the way home, this thought plays over and over in my head. Dating is supposed to be *fun*?

# Chapter Seven

'Appetite for Western brands is undiminished, and contrary to early-recession reports, China's millionaires were largely unscathed by the global downturn. The overall economy and the diversification of wealth will continue to grow—'

I clear my throat. I loathe presenting. Whenever I stand up in front of all these men (and yep, apart from me, today they are all men) I think 'firing squad'.

I actually find the subject – luxury in China – fascinating. Through this project, and others like it, I've learnt all about the political and economic history of China, particularly the cultural changes of the last 20 years, and what companies are succeeding (or failing) and why. But it's just another report to them. They'll go and buy and sell shares and make recommendations based on it, and make or lose money. And then I'll come back in a few weeks and do it again about something else. It is never-ending.

I start talking about the new generation of millionaires in China, the people that the luxury brands need to be aiming for. Out of the corner of my eye, I see one of the traders, a young American jock-type, send a text. The other takes out his phone, looks at it, glances quickly at me and grins. I start stammering 'Um, ah, ummm . . .' for a few seconds before I find my place in my notes again. Stay in control, Abigail. In. Control.

Finally, it's question time. One of the senior traders asks about

LVMH, and I talk for a few minutes about numbers and expect-ations. 'Louis Vuitton, the company's fashion and high-end leather goods brand,' (out of the corner of my eye, I see the same trader make a tiny whip-cracking motion to his friend, and they both stifle grins), 'is leading the growth. This year alone they're opening new stores in Beijing, Shanghai, Guangdong, Chengdu, Wenzhou and Beihai. Exactly where the millionaires are.'

Flushing with relief to have it over and done with, I look up the table to the whip-cracking guy. I've seen him before. He catches my eye and grins. I ignore him.

As we're walking out of the room, I feel a tug on my hair and turn around. It's the trader.

'I just wanted to follow up on the leather and saddlery divi-sion of Louis Vuitton,' he says, grinning. 'So, demand for bridles and whips are up?' I hear the traders behind him explode with stifled laughter.

All of a sudden, I don't feel intimidated. Just irritated.

'Yes,' I say. 'But if you're looking for something kinky, try Ann Summers. It's more your league.'

What a fucknuckle. At least I got through my presentation with only one mistake, I reflect, as I get in the lift. Today seemed easier than usual . . . a knock-on effect of the fake-it-till-you-feel-it I'm-so-confident attitude, I guess. Thanks, Robert.

When I get back to my desk, Alistair is comforting Charlotte. She's – what? – crying.

'Are you OK?' I ask, slightly redundantly.

She looks up, her face swollen and pink, hiccuping with sobs. Gosh. She's never shown any emotion, in all the time I've known her.

'Abigail, thank God you're back,' says Alistair, relieved.

'Let's get a coffee,' I say. There is nothing worse than being upset in our office. People can smell the scandal, and walk past super-slowly to get a good look.

Charlotte nods and gets up to put on her poncho.

'I need to talk to you today, too,' says Alistair, as we go.

'Yep, no problem,' I say. 'Everything OK?'

'Yes, m'lady,' he says, grinning and spinning in his chair. 'Very much so.'

We walk to a tiny Italian coffee shop that I'm pretty sure has been here since the 1950s. One guy to make coffee, one guy to make sandwiches, and a linoleum counter at the window to sit and watch people go past. It makes me happy, somehow, to be here where they've been serving coffee for 60 years, rather than at a big Pret-A-Costabucks chain. And the coffee is amazing.

I order for us, and sit down. Charlotte hasn't spoken a word. She has been crying so hard, and so silently, that she's having trouble breathing.

'Do you want to tell me what happened?' I say.

Charlotte starts to hiccup out the words: 'Last night—'

'Deep breaths,' I say. 'Just relax. Everything will be fine.' Wow, cliché after cliché from me.

'My boyfriend Phil broke up with me last night,' she finally says.

'Shit,' I say, and without thinking about it, reach forward and give her a hug. I don't think I've spontaneously hugged anyone except my family or very closest friends, possibly ever. It's nice.

Charlotte starts to cry again and a large gob of spittle swings out of her mouth and splats on my trousers. Ew.

Over the next half an hour, between semi-hysterical tears from her and gentle questions punctuated with reminders to breathe from me, it emerges that after nine years together – from the age of 17 to 26 – she's been with the same guy. And he's just broken up with her, saying 'I love you, but not enough'.

'I don't know what . . . to do, I don't know what to do,' she says, when she's calmed down and cried out. 'All through school and university and work, we were together, our parents play bridge, we were saving to buy a house, we share a car, we had a 10-year-plan that was going to end next year with us getting eng – eng – eng . . .'

'Engaged?' I suggest.

'We have a budgie,' she says, crying even harder. 'My mother is so upset, I told her last night and she hung up on me, she's already bought her outfit for the wedding—'

'Shh,' I say, stroking her shoulder in an – I hope – comforting way. This is so different to my break-up. I cried, but I knew it was the right thing to do. I think Peter did too. In fact, the only person who got really hysterical was his brother Joe. He came over as I was moving out of the house and called me a 'stupid bitch'. God, that was a horrible day, I feel sick about it even now. Oh dear, must think about Charlotte.

'Breaking up is awful,' I say unoriginally.

'I've never broken up! I've only ever had Phil!' she says.

'Do you have a friend you can stay with? Brother? Sister? Parents?' I know nothing about her, I realise. I've simply never asked.

'My parents – no, no way. But my brother lives in Stoke Newington,' she says. 'N16,' she adds helpfully.

After she's called her brother, cried some more, established that she can stay in his spare room, and had another coffee, it's past 9 am.

'I feel much better,' she says. 'Thank you so much, Abigail.'

'You know, I broke up with someone in July,' I say. 'After seven years together. It's awful, it really is horrible. But you'll get through it. You will.'

'Really?' she says, turning her pale, reddened eyes on me.

'Yes,' I say, wondering if now would be an appropriate time to suggest a lash tint. Probably not. 'Honestly, Charlotte, from now on, every day will get a little bit better and easier . . . You just have to hug yourself tightly and ride through the next few weeks.'

'But I've never been single!' she exclaims tearfully. 'I have no idea how to date! None! I'm going to be one of those single women in bars! Desperate!'

'No, you're not,' I say, ignoring the fact that she's thinking exactly what I thought for years, and that Plum and I are now said single women in bars. But we are not desperate, I think firmly. Not. The d-word. 'Being single is fun,' I say. 'You can do whatever you want, whenever you want, go to sleep early or stay up all night . . .'

Charlotte doesn't look impressed.

'You can go out and flirt,' I say, as enthusiastically as I can. 'Go on dates. I've got a date tonight, actually.' With a man named Skinny Jeans. I mean Mark. 'Kiss other men and, you know, all of that,' I say. This too isn't impressing her. Guess I won't actually mention sex, then. 'It's so much fun, Charlotte. Honestly. You won't know yourself in a few weeks.'

She looks at me blankly and wipes a last solitary tear from the corner of her eye.

'Think about all the things that made him irritating,' I say, trying another tack. 'Like, lazy around the house? Bad dresser?' I realise that Charlotte wouldn't recognise a bad dresser if he stamped on her foot wearing Crocs and hurried on. 'Messy drunk? Moody? Bad cook?'

'Oh, he never cooks,' she says. 'I do. Every night. And he won't try new foods so it's always chicken and chips. I did an amazing sushi course and he never lets me make it at home because he hates the sight of fish. And seaweed. And rice.'

Wow, I think to myself. What a fucknuckle. 'Well, there you go,' I say. 'Now you can make and eat sushi to your heart's content.'

Charlotte gazes into the distance and smiles. 'And he never cleans up after himself. He just expects me to do it for him. And he's gained quite a lot of weight recently.' Charlotte's on a roll now. 'And he thinks no one is as good as his mum. And he makes me pull his finger when he farts.'

What the devil were you doing with him for nine years, I think to myself. But I refrain from saying it. I am not one to talk about the comfort of habit.

'Well, you never have to deal with that stuff again,' I say cheerfully. 'Now, Charlotte, if you want to, please take today and tomorrow off.' I have no authority to offer that to her. Oh well. 'And whenever you mention his name, pretend to spit over your shoulder. It's very cathartic.'

'Thank you,' she says gratefully, looking slightly mystified at the spitting comment.

As we leave the coffee shop, and Charlotte heads off for the tube, I lean over and give her a proper hug.

'You'll be fine,' I say. 'Feel free to call me if you need anything.'

'Thank you, Abigail,' she says. 'I never thought I'd feel so cheerful about being dumped!'

I walk back in the office, swinging my security tag around in little circles, smiling to myself. How did I become the motivational speaker for single girls? It's so nice to be able to comfort someone and feel like you've made their day a bit better, I've never really done it before. And you know, I think I've misjudged Charlotte all this time. She's not blah at all.

When I get back to my desk, Alistair is waiting for me.

'I need to talk to you,' he hisses. 'Can we have a coffee?'

God, I've had four coffees already and it's only 9. 30 am.

'Of course,' I say, my heart sinking at the thought of more caffeine. 'Give me ten minutes to check emails.'

There are over 50 emails in my inbox, and I can see I've got a few phone messages to answer too. Ah well. Fuck it. Alistair wants to talk. That's more important, surely.

'I have been offered a job,' says Alistair, the moment we're seated. 'With UBS. On a trading desk. As a desk assistant.'

'You'll be a glorified coffee maker,' I say, aghast. 'I mean,' I continue, quickly composing myself, 'Are you sure? That's an entry level job.'

'It's what I want!' he says. 'Look, I'm impatient. I want what I want now. I can't afford to waste any more time here.'

'You know, you're only 23. There's no rush—'

'Yes, there is. I'm sorry, Abigail. I know you've been doing research for me, but I wanted a job.'

'We only spoke like, two weeks ago . . .'

He shrugs. 'I had already been talking to people. I was just asking for your help to be polite, really. And because I wanted to have lunch with you.'

'Gosh, thanks,' I say sarcastically, then realise he's looking at me anxiously, wanting my approval. 'Of course, I totally understand. And congratulations,' I add. 'It's great, I'm really happy for you.'

'I'm sorry I'm leaving your team, you know I love working with you. I feel like . . . like I could get stuck here.'

I nod, thinking: I am stuck here.

'I don't have a passion for it, like you clearly do,' he says apologetically, reading my face.

'I wouldn't say I have a passion for it,' I say, tearing my napkin into little shreds. 'But I do . . . I do know it inside out.'

'That's why you're the best.'

We both take a careful sip of our drinks, and I try to ignore the thought that I am stuck in a job I don't love.

Now I'm going to have to tell my boss Suzanne. Holy shit.

I dread dealing with Suzanne. She is very short, very blonde and very frightening. She joined six months ago from another bank, replacing my unusually easygoing last boss. (He was either pushed out or jumped, depending on who you believe.)

Suzanne works at least 14 hours a day, and is constantly barking into a headset that's permanently attached to one ear whilst simultaneously reading reports, checking numbers, pushing sales and sending snappy/terse emails. She spends all her spare time walking around Bluewater and Westfield, taking day trips to Edinburgh or Paris, surveying the stores and the shoppers and the atmosphere. It all goes into forming a detailed picture of the retail market in her head. She's like a megacomputer for retail analysis.

'Why is he leaving?' she snaps.

'He's bored.'

Oops. That came out without me thinking about it. There's a pause and she stares straight at me.

'*Bored*?'

'Research just didn't, um, stimulate him . . .' I say helplessly. 'He wants to be on the floor, making things happen.'

There's a beat whilst she looks at me. She is nailing the eye contact thing. It would be inspirational if it wasn't so fucking scary. She wears too much black eyeliner.

'I'm not seeing enough drive in you, Abigail,' she says, finally. 'You have the knowledge and the experience, but you don't care. Your reports are always bang-on, but you're totally reactive and you never over deliver, you just . . . deliver.'

I nod, trying to look as composed as I can. Since when was this a critique of me?

'I've been monitoring you since I arrived. You only make two or three calls a day. I expect you to make 15. You're too passive. I expect you to know the luxury retail market; to eat, breathe, and fucking sleep it.'

I nod. I don't even know how to respond to a speech like this. Is everyone else really doing this? Is Charlotte doing this? I haven't noticed, but then again, I've been a bit distracted over the past six months.

She sighs. 'I've been trying to get hold of you all morning. Where were you?'

'Um, Charlotte was upset—'

'You're not here to help Charlotte. You're here to figure out how to make money.'

I bite my lip. She's right.

'I need someone who can create volume, stimulate sales. I don't need someone who just sits back and reads. You're too passive.'

I flinch.

She isn't done yet. 'I expect more. Step. It. Up.'

I am nodding so hard that my neck is starting to hurt. The 'you're too passive' remark particularly stings.

I clear my throat. 'Yes, thank you, I know, I know.'

Suzanne narrows her eyes. 'It's up to you. The question you need to ask yourself is, *what do I want?*'

I stop nodding and stare at her for a second. It's that fucking question again. She raises an overplucked eyebrow and looks at me.

'What do you want, Abigail?'

I open my mouth to speak and shut it again. I have no answer, none at all. What's wrong with me? For a second I fight the urge to cry. What the fuck *do* I want?

'That's all,' she dismisses me. I walk out, shaking my head to clear my thoughts. What a day. And it's not even lunchtime yet.

The last thing I'm in the mood for is my date with that Skinny Jeans guy tonight. But I'm damned if I'm going to miss out on a chance to get the dating experience I need. I'm meant to be meeting him at 8 pm. I think I should have a couple of drinks at home first to get me in the mood.

# Chapter Eight

Friday morning, 8 am.

My phone wakes me up, which is lucky, since I'm (a) meant to be at work by 7 am every day (b) not in my own house (c) naked.

I'm on the edge of a double bed with strange pale blue sheets, and as I turn my head to figure out how the hell I came to be here, I spy a naked man sleeping next to me. It's Skinny Jeans guy.

I gasp in shock, fall onto the floor and scramble around the bedroom frantically looking for my phone. My heart is beating violently, my head pounding at the same pace, oh God, oh God – ah, it's in my bag. Under my bra.

I look at the caller ID. It's Plum.

'Fuck!' I whisper, instead of hello.

'So, how was it?!' she says excitedly.

'Wrong tense,' I mumble, as I crawl frantically around the bedroom on my hands and knees looking for the rest of my clothes. Knickers! On the bookshelf. Sweet.

'Don't tell me you're at his house?' Plum starts to laugh hysterically.

'I don't remember, I don't remember anything,' I mumble.

'What the fuck happened?'

I grab my jeans from their hiding place half under the bed, whispering furiously. 'We were on our date, in a bar, and I called

Robert for advice, and he suggested I have a shot for liquid confidence, and I did, but then I think I had too many . . .' I writhe on the floor to pull on my jeans without standing up, accidentally drop the phone and pick it up quickly.

'So! Do you like him?' asks Plum chattily.

'No, yes, I don't know, I have to get out of here, I have to call in sick . . .' I decide against putting my bra on and stuff it in my bag. My top is, oddly, folded on the floor. Why would I do that, I wonder? Then again, it is one of my favourite tops. I just bought it on the weekend with Plum and she suggested I wear it on my date. It's the most perfect, dove-grey asymmetric top from Cos and I can't tell you how much I wish I'd bought it in black, I might go – oh, shit. Back to the nightmare.

'OK. Sorry. Get home and call me. I'll call in sick for you,' she says.

'God, I love you,' I whisper.

We hang up, and I open the bedroom door silently and crawl out on my hands and knees, my handbag strap firmly in my mouth. Skinny Jeans hasn't even stirred. I wonder why he isn't at work. What does he do again? I try to remember. Ah, yes – he works for a film production company. His day doesn't start till 10 am.

I find myself in a living room, and spy the detritus of last night: an overflowing ashtray, empty wine bottles and – oh please God no – a bottle of whisky. My jacket is on the couch, along with my shoes. I put them on, fumbling over the stupid finicky fucking shoe straps on these YSL-via-Zara beauties, and stand up for the first time today. I nearly faint from the sudden rush of blood/oxygen/booze to my head. I feel simultaneously hot and cold, nauseous and fuzzy, and I'm trying not to think about the fact that maybe, yes, I might, possibly, yes, I probably, definitely had sex with Skinny Jeans last night.

The used condom on the floor next to the bed kind of gives it away. Three cheers for safe sex.

I close the front door as quietly as I can and, squinting help-lessly as the grey morning burns my eyes, look around for some kind of sign that will let me know where I am. Think woman, think . . .

I hurry to the end of the street to look at the street sign. It says W10, what's that? North Kensington? Ladbroke Grove? I don't know! It's so fucking quiet! There's no traffic noise, nothing . . . I walk as fast as I can to the end of the road and look up and down the next road. Which way should I go? The street at the bottom looks busier, so I speedwalk towards it, silently vowing to never leave the house without sunglasses and Panadol again. And a personal chauffeur and car.

I reach the end of the road and pivot around and around on one leg like a drink-defiled netball player, desperately looking for a street sign. Chamberlayne Road, that sounds familiar, doesn't it? Kensal Rise? I think so.

Where the fuck is a black cab? Please God, please send me a black cab. One finally turns up, and I bleat 'Primrose Hill' as I get in, collapse on the back seat, and take a deep, shaky sigh.

What the fuck happened last night?

The first hour or so was fine. We met at Negozio Classica, made chatty, flinty, witty repartee that was one part fun and one part hard work, and one part petrifying nerve-wracking hell, and shared two bottles of wine. I was in a bad mood about my disastrous day at work, so I definitely drank faster than I usually would have. (Too passive, my arse, I remember thinking, as I flirtily ordered a second bottle of wine from the waiter.)

Then we went on to a restaurant called Taqueria where I was overjoyed to discover they had margaritas and other potent liba-tions of the Tex-Mex persuasion. Robert's right, I thought happily, as the waiter whisked away my picked-over tacos and delivered my fourth tequila-based cocktail, dating *is* fun.

Skinny Jeans was slick, flirty and very confident. I laughed at everything he said, laughed even harder at everything I said, and after a few drinks, found it easy to play the cool/detached card as instructed. Right up till he started playing with my hands after dinner. Curling his fingers around my fingers, tracing my palm with his thumb, smiling at me, looking into my eyes . . . It was completely unnerving. I ran to the toilet in a panic and rang Robert.

'What do I do, what do I do?' I gabbled.

'What's going on?' asked Robert.

'Umm, he's looking me in the eye a lot, and playing with my hands, and it's like, I don't know, a seduction thing. I'm finding it very hard to be cool and detached when it makes me want to run away . . .'

'You can leave anytime you want.'

'No, I want to stay,' I said bravely. 'I'm going to have a proper date if it kills me.'

'If you don't like the seduction routine, just take your hands away. You're in total control.' I made a hurrumph sound. 'Maybe you should have a shot of something. Liquid confidence.'

Good fucking idea, Robert, I think now. The cab is nearly home, and going past our local shops. Do I need anything? Because I sure as shit am not leaving the house once I get there. I might never leave it again. I have bottles of water in the fridge (hydration is urgently needed), and lots of those dissolvable sparkling vitamin tablets and please God let me have painkillers. I don't have any crumpets but fuck it, I can do without.

All I need to do is survive the rest of the day, one minute at a time.

I finally get into my tiny en suite bathroom, nearly dying of exhaustion from the effort of climbing the stairs, and gasp in shock for the second time today: last night's carefully applied make-up is now Courtney Love On A Bender, and my smooth ponytail is an Amy Winehouse-y rat's nest: knot upon knot upon knot. I look like that anti-binge drinking ad. God! It's so not me. Social drinker, enthusiastic drinker, animated drinker, yes – but not binge drinker . . . I can't bear to deal with it right now. I'll just wash the rest of me and worry about the hair later.

Then I start gagging in the shower, and, spilling water everywhere, have to hang on to the toilet seat to vomit up the poisonous sour taste of half-digested wine and whisky.

Hello, rock bottom. Fancy seeing you here.

Finally, I'm in bed with the curtains closed and my room nice and cold and dark. My heart is still hammering and I'm panting light, shallow breaths.

I hate alcohol.

What else happened last night? After Taqueria, we went to a pub around the corner, which I can't remember very well, and we did tequila shots at the bar, and then we went to a downstairs bar with a DJ, and I have a feeling more shots were involved. I remember rubbing the belly of a fat man at the bar 'for luck'. And I gave a girl in the toilets a make-over, and showed her the importance of blending. I think I was dancing to Marvin Gaye, yes I was and oh God, I think I did splits on the dance floor.

WhyLordowhy.

We definitely snogged in the last bar, and then we were in a cab snogging more, and I think I was on his lap but I can't remember, and oh God, I am a slutbag, we were back at his, and we drank more (more?!) and that's about it. Blackout before the R-rated bit starts.

I'll try to drink the first bottle of water.

Fucking hell, that is exhausting.

I need a hug. I make a little whimpering mew sound to myself, then stop. Even that is exhausting.

My phone rings. It's Plum again. It takes me a long time to pick it up, press the right button and hold it to my head.

'Fuck,' I say again.

'Are you OK? Are you home?'

'Yes,' I say. 'Did you call work?'

74

'You have a throat infection that will keep you in bed all weekend,' she says crisply.

'Oh, that's lovely,' I whisper. 'Oh God, Plum, I'm dying, I'm fucking dying . . .'

Plum is openly laughing now. Why is someone else's hangover and drunken remorse always amusing?

'I just threw up,' I whisper.

'If I were there I'd hold your hair back,' she says. 'I'd even braid it for you.'

I moan slightly. 'It's fucking Robert's fault. I hate him. He told me to have shots for confidence.'

'How many shots did he tell you to have?'

I pause. 'One.'

'How many did you have?'

About sixteen.

'Shut up, Plum,' I instruct. 'I am hanging up now.'

I decide to lie as still as I can to get the poundpoundpounding in my head to go away. I'm sweating and shaking lightly. My scalp hurts. I try to ignore the waves of drunken remorse that are washing over me, the flickering images of last night that are moving around my head in a nightmarish kaleidoscope . . . Don't think about it now, Abigail, just don't think about it.

Somehow, by holding my head at just the right angle, the bottle of water clasped to my chest, I fall asleep.

# Chapter Nine

I wake up just past 5 pm to see Robert in my doorway.

'What the hell happened to you?'

I feel like I've just been hit in the mouth with a bucket of sand. I sit up unsteadily, try and fail to croak hello, and after several attempts, hold a bottle of water to my lips and drink till I have to collapse back on the pillow. God, water tastes good. So good.

'Nice hair,' he says. 'Very sexy.'

'Well, Robert,' I say finally, ignoring the hair comment. 'Some idiot told me shots would relax me.'

'I said have a shot, not a bottle,' replies Robert, leaning against the doorframe and folding his arms. He's trying not to grin. And failing. 'How was your walk of shame?'

'It wasn't a walk of shame,' I moan. 'It was a dash of total fucking mortification. I am full of remorse. I showed my fifi to a strange man. And I don't even remember it.'

'Your fifi doesn't care. Have a shower and get dressed, Abby. We're going out.' I've noticed him calling me Abby recently, which no one has done since I was little.

'I can't possibly face the world. I am a harlot and a lush. I should be branded.'

'We can brand you later. We're going out,' Robert says firmly.

'I can't possibly leave the house after my behaviour in the past 24 hours. I'm putting myself under house arrest.'

'Get dressed,' he yells, walking down the stairs.

Leaving Skinny Jeans' house this morning has turned into a fuzzy half-memory. Just like most of last night. I wonder what time we got to bed, I mean sleep.

Flashback: lying on a pillow, kissing Skinny Jeans and looking over at his bedside clock as it hit 5.03 am.

'Fuuuuuuuuuuuuuuuck!' I shout.

'Get up!' shouts Robert up the stairs.

I reach into my drawer and pull out my dissolvable vitamin Cs and Solpadeine stash, pop them into the remaining water and swirl them around till they're all dissolved. Sipping it, I lean over and switch on my iPod player. Quite randomly, it's 'Get Over It' by OK Go. How appropriate.

Ah, the joy of a hot shower. I lather up with as much soap as I can and scrub my head with my poshest shampoo, and spend a careful ten minutes on my bed hair with a wide-tooth comb and half a bottle of conditioner.

'Where are we going?' I yell down the stairs at him. 'What should I wear?'

'Something sharp,' he replies. Something sharp?

I open my wardrobe doors. Come on, Abigail. It's time to start speaking clothes. Not what Plum tells you to wear, not what Peter used to like you to wear . . . but what you want to wear.

I feel like looking invincible and effortless tonight, because I feel just the opposite on the inside. So I take out my new Topshop jeans that make me feel extremely tall and thin, and pair them with a super-lightweight white vest. I add a blazer and a long, skinny red scarfy thing, and put on a pair of boots that add a good four inches to my height.

Invincible. But effortless. Yes.

Halfway through blow-drying my hair, Robert knocks on my door.

'Room service.' He walks in with a Bloody Mary and two crumpets smothered liberally with peanut butter. 'I thought you might want to line your stomach.'

'How did you know I love crumpets?' I say, delightedly. 'I thought I'd run out.'

'You've always got a crumpet attached to your face on weekends, it doesn't take a genius to figure it out . . .' he says. 'I picked them up on the way home. And everyone loves Bloody Marys.'

'Thank you . . . but I don't think I should drink again. Ever.'

'A Bloody Mary isn't drinking, it's like nature's Solpadeine.'

I look at him expressionlessly and sip the Bloody Mary.

'Wowsers, that's good . . . You've shaved,' I comment.

'You told me to,' he replies. 'Did you just say "wowsers"? Like Inspector Gadget?'

The next half hour is a mix of chewing, slurping, make-upping and smiling. I almost feel better. The Bloody Mary is extremely spicy. The peanut butter is chewy and just a tiny bit salty. And my make-up is – God bless it – working wonders. I need a little extra highlighter and concealer tonight, but apart from that I look surprisingly alright. I've had about 10 hours sleep, I guess.

I suddenly feel inexplicably cheerful.

I wonder what Robert has planned for us tonight. I hope it's fun.

I check my phone for the first time since this morning. Seven missed calls and four texts. I love feeling popular. The texts are from Sophie, Josh From HR and ohfucktwofromSkinnyJeansguy. I listen to a message from Mum, asking me about my bridesmaid dress preference. No one else left a message. Everyone I know is too impatient to bother leaving a voicemail.

Sophie: *So I hear you've been a very bad girl. Details.*

Josh From HR: *Hi!!! What are you up to this weekend? Fancy a catch-up? Maybe dinner in SW17? xxx*

Skinny Jeans: *Devastated. I am devastated that you would leave me like this. x*

Skinny Jeans: *Well, you can ignore me, but I had a great night. Let me know if you fancy it again some time.*

'Fuuuuuuuck,' I say to myself, and flop facedown on my bed and moan. I feel sick again.

If I was going to have the first one-night-stand of my life, wouldn't it be good if I could actually remember it?

And yes, by the way, it was definitely a one-night-stand. I'm too mortified given my drunkenness, and I don't want to see him again, anyway. He's kind of cute, but his anecdotes centred largely on getting stoned. I kept thinking, *Stick it out, Abigail, this is experience, this is experience . . .*

I'm going to be brutal, as per Robert's instructions. Josh From HR is just ew, and Skinny Jeans . . . I can't face it. So I won't. For some reason, the decision to ignore them both makes me feel stronger and in control.

I flip through the rest of my texts from last night. They're all from Robert, all in reply to apparent text questions from me. From the end of the night, backwards:

*1.32 am I am sleeping Abigail.*

*12.37 am Don't worry about it. Lots of people get caught snogging in bar toilets.*

*12.20 am Have a glass of water. I don't speak drunk.*

*11.57 pm Maybe he doesn't know what comatose means.*

*11.41 pm Everyone's seen Pretty In Pink. He's lying. PS I can't believe you'd choose Stef.*

*11.37 pm Try this, then. Ducky versus Blaine – who should Andie have picked?*

*11.16 pm How about this: You look like the kind of guy who sings in a choir. Am I right?*

*10.24 pm Dater's block, huh. Very funny. Try complimenting him on something he's wearing in a slightly sarcastic way.*

*9.43 pm Relax. Are you even having fun? Did you have a shot? Remember, you can always leave.*

We were kicked out of a bar for snogging in the toilets?

I never want to see Skinny Jeans again. It will be easy because I am never going to get off my bedroom floor. I will die here. Of mortification.

I moan at the ceiling pathetically for a few seconds.

Ooh, text.

It's Henry.

*Abigay. What are you doing tonight and can I join?*

I invite him along, and resume my position.

It's at this second that I remember that I have not had a bikini wax since quite a long time before Peter and I broke up. My moan turns into a loud squeal of anguish.

'What now?' Robert is in my doorway again.

'Nothing,' I say sulkily. 'My friend Henry is coming along, by the way.'

'Tell Uncle Robbie what's wrong,' he says, coming into the room and crouching down next to me.

I sigh, and meet his amused eyes. 'I just realised that I have not had a bikini wax in a long time. It's pretty bad. I should have had a sign on my knickers saying Abandon Hope All Ye Who Enter Here.'

'Only the penitent man shall pass, huh?' Robert starts laughing. 'Hey. I hear the full bush is coming back into fashion anyway.'

'"The full bush"? Says who, the pubic topiary style mavens?' I pause. 'I'm sorry I bothered you so much. With the texts, I mean.'

'There was nothing good on TV. It was a nice distraction.'

'You were at home?' Robert is never home on a Thursday.

'Of course not. I was with bowler-hat girl. She has a TV in her bedroom.'

'That's nice.' I peer at him through my fingers. 'I'm a woman of easy virtue,' I add mournfully.

'Oh, come on. What is this, 1955? No one is judging you except yourself.'

'Sleeping with a virtual stranger and being too drunk to even remember it is a pretty bad fucking mistake, Robert. It's just not something I *do*. Ever . . .'

'Just shake it off. Remorse is a pointless emotion. Be bullet-proof. That's key to surviving single life . . . What did he say this morning?'

'Nothing,' I say, taking out my notebook and adding **Bulletproof** to the list. That's a good one. 'I crept out before he could wake up and act like men in films do, all awkward and uninterested . . . what's that line in *When Harry Met Sally*? Pretend he had to, you know, clean his andirons.'

'What's an andiron?'

'I don't know.' I sigh deeply, and look at the ceiling. 'I don't want to stay here tonight with nothing but my remorse for company, that's for sure. OK, let's go.'

'Well, at least you pre-empted the number one rule, princess,' says Robert as we leave the house a few minutes later.

I almost can't bear to ask. 'What's that?'

He holds the front door open for me. 'Always leave them before they leave you.'

Oddly, that does make me feel better. I pause on the doorstep to add it to my notebook list.

**Always leave them before they leave you.**

# Chapter Ten

It's raining. Not real, hard rain, but that autumn perma-drizzle that ruins your hair and make-up. Robert and I stand under an umbrella on the corner of our street, waiting for a black cab to take us to a pub in Belgravia called The Pantechnicon Rooms.

'You look alright, by the way. Considering.'

'Gosh, thanks,' I say, slightly sarcastically, to hide the fact that actually, I can feel myself blushing. Compliments have been quite light on the ground since I left Peter.

'Sorry, Abby. You look stunning. Gob-smackingly stunning. Now, let's get you a drink.'

'I don't think I can drink,' I'm trying to angle my words to the side in case, despite cleaning my teeth and scrubbing my tongue three times, my breath still smells like booze and/or vomit. This umbrella seems abnormally small.

'Alright, alright. You're in charge, OK?'

I'm so achey. I think it's the remorse, not the hangover. Can you believe I was kicked out of a bar for snogging in the toilets? And I did splits on the dance floor. Oh the self-loathing . . .

Once we're in the cab, I look out of the window at rainy, grey Friday-night London, and sigh deeply.

'Do you want me to tell you a story to make you feel better?' says Robert. Mind-reading again.

'Yes please,' I say in a small voice.

'When I was 22, I secretly started seeing one of my mates'

older sisters. She was 27 and clearly slumming it with me . . . Anyway, I was still at Cambridge, doing a postgrad, which by the way was an utter waste of time, in case you're thinking about doing one.'

'I'm not. But thanks.'

He continues. 'So, I came down one weekend and she took me to a London party,' he says, enunciating 'London party' with all the excitement he clearly felt at the time.

'How glam.'

'I was very nervous, drank half a bottle of Jäger, got naked, threw up on her housemate, passed out on the dining room table wearing nothing but a pair of washing-up gloves, woke up three hours later to find the party still going and asked her to marry me.'

'What did she say?' I gasp through my laughter.

'She said no,' he says, looking out the cab window for a second, before turning back to me. 'Unsurprisingly. So, still drunk, I put some clothes on and stormed out to a train station, slept on the platform, got on the first train at dawn the next day, passed out again and ended up in Scotland.'

'Wowsers,' I say, trying not to laugh.

'You think a walk of shame is bad. Try a six-hour train ride of shame back to Cambridge, wearing nothing but boxers, a rugby jersey and washing up gloves as shoes.' He pauses, and starts laughing despite himself.

Our cab pulls up outside The Pantechnicon Rooms.

'Making a fool of yourself at least once is a rite of passage,' he says, as we walk in and get enveloped by the serene, happy buzz. 'Onwards and upwards.'

'Onwards and upwards,' I agree, looking around. Robert was right to force me out of the house. This morning's dash of total fucking mortification in Kensal Rise suddenly seems a long time ago.

I sit down and look around happily. You get the feeling that nothing bad could ever happen in this pub. It's clean and warm and just so. I want to move in and live under the stairs like Harry Potter.

'So, is bowler-hat girl your main squeeze right now?' I say, turning to Robert, once he has a pint and I have a nice calming lemonade.

'Interesting terminology. Nope, she's going travelling next week.'

'You sound devastated. Do you actually like women, Robert?'

'I love them!' he says, an injured expression on his face. 'Don't give me the you-must-be-a-misogynist crap. I love talking to women, I love their company. I simply prefer their company on a very, very casual basis.'

'Lucky them. Why don't you invite bowler hat to join us?'

'Maybe later. What about you? Seeing Skinny Jeans again?'

'Oh, fuck me, no. No way,' I sigh. 'I suppose I had to get it over and done with. First person since, you know. Peter.' I pause to pretend to spit over my shoulder.

'That's the spirit.'

I frown into space for a second. Peter. Paulie. Josh From HR. Skinny Jeans. God. What a mess I'm making of this whole singledom thing. Robert's still looking at me and grinning.

'Can we change the subject from my love life?' I ask.

'Tell me about your job. You never talk about it . . .'

'Neither do you!' I exclaim.

He smiles, but doesn't say anything.

I sigh. 'My work life is, to misquote The Breakfast Club, unsatisfying. I don't enjoy it and I'm not very good at it, either,' I add, thinking about my meeting with Suzanne yesterday. Fuck, and I didn't turn up today. She'll love that. 'I know I have to do something about it,' I say. 'I just don't know where to start.'

'What's wrong with it?'

'It's just . . . I don't like it anymore,' I say. 'I don't find it interesting. I used to love taking a wide-angle lens to the world and then zooming in on specifics, does that make sense?' Robert nods. 'But the rest of it, the calls, the sales . . . I just don't care about. My boss told me I had to start delivering and stop being so passive,' I sigh. 'Whatever the fuck that means. But I can't. I am not very good at making, uh, decisions.'

'That's not true . . . You decided to leave Peter.'

'Yeah, about five years after I should have,' I reply, shaking my head. God, he's good at making me talk. I can't think of the last time I chatted like this, even with one of the girls. 'Oh well. At least the money is good, why take a risk?' I sigh, and try to sound cheerful. 'And if it ain't broke, right?'

'Isn't that the kind of thinking that kept you with Peter for so long?'

'Ouch,' I say, wincing.

'Sorry. My big sister rang from Dublin earlier. She always asks me pointed questions like that. It's catching.'

'I didn't know you had a big sister.' The idea of Robert being a baby brother is strangely delightful.

'I have two. Both older, both boss me around constantly. Alice is married with children in Dublin. I see her every couple of months. Rosie is in London, but south of the river. So I see her even less. Is Sophie your only sister?'

'I most certainly am!' Sophie, Luke and Henry have arrived. I feel almost surprised to see them. I was enjoying talking to Robert so much that I forgot why we were here.

We stand up for the inevitable hug-and-kiss hello dance. Robert hasn't met Henry before, and I can see them sizing each other up the way men do. Henry still looks about 21: his rugby brawn is somehow boyish. In comparison, Robert looks like his dad.

I briefly recount the highlights of last night. Everyone tells morning-after stories to make me feel better.

'My worst walk of shame was Battersea Bridge to Clapham North,' says Luke. 'I'd just moved here and knew Battersea was

85

next to Clapham so figured it couldn't take more than ten minutes . . . I took a detour in Clapham Junction and it took an hour and a fucking half to get home.'

'I had a window-jump of shame because the girl didn't want her flatmates to know she'd pulled me,' says Henry.

'I've never had a walk of shame,' says Sophie. 'Because I have always been an angel.'

I raise an eyebrow at her doubtfully. That is *so* not true.

'Except for the time at university that I went to a ball and wore my then-boyfriend's tuxedo shirt and boxers back to halls the next day, still drunk, smoking a cigar *then* ran into Mum and Dad, who I'd forgotten were visiting,' she says thoughtfully. 'There was that time, I guess.'

'And to think that you two look sweet and innocent,' comments Robert.

'We are sweet and innocent!' exclaim Sophie and I at exactly the same time, with exactly the same intonation. We do that sometimes. I think it's a sister thing.

'They're not,' says Henry. 'Sophie especially.'

Sophie punches him lightly and he grins at her. I think Henry had a crush on Sophie a few years ago, but never acted on it.

'What are we eating, kids?' says Luke.

'Steak and chips,' says Henry. 'With extra chips.'

'Abigail wants low-maintenance food,' I say, scanning the menu. 'Ooh! Risotto.'

'Are you talking about yourself in the third person?' says Robert.

'Abigail likes it,' I nod. 'She thinks it's funny.'

Luke laughs at this, nearly choking on his drink. 'I would never have thought a girl like you would say things like that . . .'

'Things like what?' I say, frowning at him.

'Just . . . your little comments. You used to seem kind of, um, subdued,' he says, exchanging a quick glance with Sophie. 'In a good way. Sweet, you know.'

86

'Why are you exchanging looks?'

'I'm telling him to shut up,' says Sophie calmly. 'He just means that you were a bit quieter before.'

'Do you think I was quieter before?' I ask Henry. He shrugs. Mr Observant.

I stare into space for a second, trying to remember. Have you noticed it's impossible to look back and remember how you used to act? You can remember how you felt, that's all. I remember letting Peter talk for us, as it made my life easier. And I remember feeling a bit, I don't know, out of place sometimes. I don't feel like that anymore. Despite today's remorse-packed hangover. I just feel like myself.

The waiter comes over to take our order. Sophie, as always, agrees to everything he suggests, so we end up with every side dish on the menu.

'Why did you order honeyed carrots?' says Luke.

'I feel bad saying no!!' she exclaims. 'He put so much effort into telling us the specials . . .'

'I'll eat them,' says Henry.

'I will too, of course,' says Luke quickly. Nothing like competition to make a man loving.

Robert changes the subject. 'So, Abigail tells me you play for Richmond, Henry?'

Henry goes into a long diatribe about his team's strengths and weaknesses. I've heard it before, and start gazing around the room. A few after-work drinkers, a romantic couple, another romantic couple, three guys at the bar . . . and one of them is looking right at me.

*Zip.* (That's the record in my head.)

Guy. At bar. Looking *right at me*. And he's good-looking. Short dark hair, slight stubble, wide smile that's now grinning with just a hint of cheekiness . . . What the devil? Men never stare at me like that. I must have something on my face.

I turn back to our table, and quickly but casually, check my face and hair for problems. I seem clean enough . . . I glance back at him. He's now talking to his friends, but a moment after I look over, we meet eyes again.

'There's a guy at the bar looking at me,' I whisper across the table to Robert. 'What do I do?'

'Feign nonchalance,' he replies straight away. 'We'll work out a game plan.'

'Feign nonchalance?' I reply. 'What big words! I guess we can tell who went to Cambridge . . .' Robert smirks. I lean back in my chair and pretend to yawn and stretch as nonchalantly as I can. I'm only doing it to make Robert laugh, and it works.

'We are thinking about having a weekend in France in November,' says Sophie, interrupting us. 'Mum and Dad are visiting Aunty Peg and Aunty Pat for the weekend.'

'Smashing, go for it,' I nod. I haven't spent a lot of time at the house in France; Peter and I didn't do weekends away. I stopped booking longer holidays with him about six months ago. That's a sign, by the way. You know you're about to leave someone when you don't want to plan holidays with them.

'Actually, we were thinking it would be a get-to-know-you weekend for the wedding party,' says Luke. 'All the bridesmaids and all the groomsmen.' He glances at Henry. 'Um . . .'

'Don't worry,' says Henry. 'I've got rugby anyway.' He smears butter on his third bread roll and tips salt on it. I reach over and take the salt away from him.

'And Robert,' says Luke. 'I've been waiting to ask you if you'd be my best man.'

Robert looks up in shock. 'Mate! I'd be honoured!' They stand up and hug as Sophie beams on adoringly and I – I admit it – take the opportunity to steal another look at the guy at the bar. Bar guy smiles openly at me. I smile back. Cripes, I *am* more confident than I used to be. This experience thing works.

'I thought you'd ask Dave!' says Robert, sitting down again. He's beaming from ear to ear. 'I was hoping for a groomsmanship and trying to be cool about it . . . This is fantastic, Lukey!'

'Lukey?' say Sophie and I in unison.

'Dave is a groomsman, so is JimmyJames,' says Luke. 'But you're the one who's been with me through all the shit times . . . and you know Sophie better, too.'

'I voted for you!' said Sophie happily.

Our food arrives at this point, and Robert, Henry and Luke happily tuck into their identical dinners: steak for main, medium rare, with a side of chips. Men are so predictable.

Robert is smiling into the distance and sighing happily. 'Best man! Tell the other bridesmaids to watch out.'

'Oh, we will,' I say. Sophie's bridesmaids, apart from *moi*, are Vix, Sophie's best friend who lives in Edinburgh, and Luke's younger sister Bella, who I haven't met yet as she lives in Bath and has somehow missed every post-engagement family get-together. Sophie has confided in me that she finds Bella 'a bit tricky'. This is Sophie-speak for 'a difficult and unpredictable bitch'.

'Please don't plunder and pillage the wedding party, Robert,' says Sophie. 'Really. I will go bridezilla on your arse.'

'I might plunder the wedding party,' pipes up Henry hopefully.

Sophie pats his arm condescendingly. 'Sure you will.'

'I promise to behave,' says Robert. 'I've known little Bella forever, anyway, so that would be disgusting.' Then his face drops. 'Shit. Does being best man require a speech?'

Luke and Sophie smile at him.

'Is that a yes? That's a yes, isn't it . . . Oh, God.' Robert pushes his chair away from the table and pretends to hyperventilate. I think he's pretending, anyway. He puts his head between his knees, as Luke pats him on the back soothingly. 'Public speaking.

And talking about love. Both my fears. Together in one place. In black tie.'

'You have like, six months to prepare . . .' says Sophie hopefully.

'I think I'm going to throw up,' says Robert. I've never seen him lose his cool before. Or be so silly. Whichever it is. I stifle a laugh. 'Shut up, Abigail,' he calls from between his knees. 'You'll be helping me write the speech in return for all the dating help I've been giving you.'

'Lucky me,' I say.

I steal a glance at the guy at the bar, and he makes a 'what the fuck?!' face at our table. It does look funny: four people eating calmly, one person having a panic attack. I shrug a 'Search me' face at him and turn back to the table. Cool and detached! And I'm drinking lemonade. I don't need alcohol to be confident. Oh no.

The waitress comes over and puts a glass of champagne in front of me.

'From the gentleman at the bar,' she says.

Is this a set-up? I look suspiciously at the others, but they've all turned to stare at the bar, where the guy who's been looking over all night is now deep in conversation with the guy next to him.

'There's a note!' I exclaim. It's a little folded sheet of paper. I pick it up and open it. On it is a list of questions with check boxes marked 'yes' or 'no' next to them.

**Q1. Are you single?**

**Q2. May I buy you a drink later?**

**Q3. My name is Adam. (Dammit! That's not a question.)**

I snicker to myself. Funny and hot! I look up at the others. 'Does anyone have a pen?'

'Not the old "do you like me" note trick! God! I've been using that for years,' groans Robert.

'What a surprise,' I say.

'Does it work?' says Henry.

'It's ballsy,' comments Luke. 'Chatting you up without talking face to face.'

'We've been exchanging looks all night,' I say pertly.

'Do you want to meet him?' asks Sophie.

I nod as timidly as a girl who woke up in someone else's bed this morning can. (Don't look at me like that! This is all so new and *fun*. Imagine, you just go out to dinner, and by the end of it, you could meet someone new! Someone who might be your soulmate! Singledom! Best thing in the world, seriously.) (Look, please forgive the 'soulmate' comment. I know I'm not supposed to think like that. But in a tiny corner of my mind, the thought is there.) So I tick 'yes' and 'yes' and write 'Abigail' on the note. I add 'Thank you for the drink'.

'Add "meet me at Motcombs in ten minutes",' suggests Robert. 'It's the bar a few doors down.'

'I thought I was supposed to let him make that decision,' I say.

'No, in this instance, a little bull-by-the-horns is good.'

'OK,' I say. I wait for the waitress to come by, then give it back to her.

I take a calming breath. Henry is still eating, Sophie and Luke are nibbling and kissing each other, as they tend to do whenever they think they're unwatched, and Robert is texting someone with a little half-smile on his face. He glances up at me, and presses 'send'.

'You alright? This is good. This is just what you need to get over last night. You know you can text me if you have any problems,' he says.

'Yes sir,' I nod, taking a careful sip of my champagne and trying not to look around at the bar. I glance up and see Luke and Sophie staring at us. 'What?' I say.

'What is going on here?' asks Luke slowly, his eyes going from Robert to me. 'I thought Robert was giving you advice. Not virtually dating for you.'

91

'He's not!' I protest, at the same time as Robert says 'I'm not!'

'He's more of a . . . singledom coach,' I say. 'Teaching me how to be like him.'

'Right,' says Sophie, looking from me to Robert suspiciously. Then she grins. 'You know, I never even liked dating. It was like . . . I don't know, performing, or something. Stressful.'

'That's because you didn't have me to help you,' says Robert.

'Thank fuck for that,' says Luke.

'Could you be a singledom coach for guys?' says Henry self-consciously. He clears his throat. 'I'm shit at, uh, that whole thing.'

'No, you're not,' chorus Sophie and I loyally.

'I've been reading this book about being a pick-up artist,' says Henry shyly. 'It's about playing the game. I'm sure you know it,' he adds to Robert. 'It gives you loads of techniques . . .'

'Like what?' say Sophie and I in unison. I'm shocked: I had no idea Henry felt he needed pulling help so badly.

'Like, you should wear something to make you stand out. It's called "peacocking". Like my red belt, see? Or, there's this thing called a "neg". So I might say, "I love your hair, but you should wear it up more". It's a negative compliment – so it confuses the girl and makes her want to impress you.'

'That is ridiculous,' I say, at the same time that Luke says 'I get it . . .'

Henry sighs. 'It's not working for me so far.'

'"Confuses" the girl?' Sophie repeats. 'What, like we're farm animals that need herding?'

'Like drawing a circle in the ground and putting a chicken in it,' I suggest. I'm trying not to look at the Tick Boxer guy to see if he's reading my note.

Henry ignores us and looks at Robert for validation. 'I bet you do that, right, Rob?'

'Uh, no, I'm sure it's a great book, but no,' says Robert.

'What do you do?' Henry persists. 'What's your secret?'

'No secret. I just ask questions, and listen to the answers,' says Robert. 'Conversation is pretty much all it takes.'

'Well, I can't do that,' says Henry. 'I can't get past the asking-for-a-number stage. I need the girl to make the first move.'

'Good luck with that,' I comment drily. I cannot imagine ever making the first move.

'Make eye contact and if she's looking at you, go and talk to her,' says Robert. 'If she's looking, she's interested.'

'Are you saying that girls need to be visibly available for dating, and guys need to be proactively ready?' I say, trying to fit this into my working knowledge of Robert's surviving singledom techniques. 'That's sort of primal, isn't it?'

'Uh, yeah, sure,' Robert grins at me and shakes his head. 'Don't analyse everything so much.' He turns to Henry. 'You'll be fine. Try it the next time you're out.'

'I'm not that guy,' says Henry. I wonder if most men feel like Henry does. I can't imagine it.

'We'll go to a bar after this,' says Robert reassuringly.

'You can be my wingman!' says Henry excitedly.

'Right. I need a make-up pit stop,' I say, standing up and still not looking towards Tick Boxer at the bar. 'Sophie?'

'Roger that,' she nods, and we get up to go to the bathroom together.

As we're in the bathroom side-by-side, silently make-upping, Sophie turns to me. 'Look, I've just got to ask. Do you fancy Robert?'

'No!' I say, surprised. 'Not at all!'

'Really?' says Sophie.

'He's not my type. Far too . . . tall. And he's a player, did you not hear the advice he was giving Henry? He's only friend material.'

'But you get along so well . . .' says Sophie.

'No,' I say firmly. 'He doesn't fancy me, I don't fancy him. We're just friends.'

'Robert doesn't have female friends,' she says. 'Luke told me. And everyone fancies him. Even me. A little.'

'Well, not me,' I say, zipping up my bag and taking one last look in the mirror. Dismissing the conversation, I head for the door. Come on, Adam The Tick Boxer guy. Let's see what you've got.

# Chapter Eleven

'No milk, no eggs, no bacon, nothing,' says Robert, leaning into the fridge. 'Fuck this. We're going out.'

It's Saturday morning, a week after the The Pantechnicon Rooms evening, and I've just returned from spending the night at Harry The Tick Boxer's house. Robert's just returned from a night with – actually, I don't know. (I've stopped asking their names.) I'm mildly stubble-rashed, a little tired, and, after a shower and new clothes, feeling rather pleased with myself.

'Look at you, practically skipping around the house,' says Robert, grinning.

'Thank you so much for your advice,' I say happily. 'I think it's made all the difference with Adam The Tick Boxer. I've been cool. Detached. Funny. Ended dates first. And he likes me and I like him! It really worked!'

'Good,' he says. 'Let's eat.'

We walk down to The Engineer and enjoy a lovely, almost completely silent breakfast (eggs Benedict for him, pancakes with bacon and maple syrup for me), reading newspapers someone else has left behind. Neither of us is feeling chatty, which suits me fine. I'd rather be alone with my thoughts. Which are mostly about Adam The Tick Boxer.

As mentioned, he's lovely. And smart and genuine and funny. He works for an IT company. He rock-climbs. He has a movie poster of The Fifth Element on his bedroom wall. He lives with his brother in a flat in Ealing, which, let me tell you, was a bitch to get home from this morning. And he likes me. Me!

I've seen him three times since we met in The Pantechnicon Rooms last Friday. Three! In a week! And this morning I even felt comfortable enough to invite him to Henry's brother's goodbye party tonight. He has other plans, but he is going to meet me quickly beforehand. Isn't that nice?

'I feel like shopping,' I say absently. The pancakes are all gone now, even the syrup-soaked crumbs. 'The girls are all busy though, and I can't shop alone with a slight hangover. I'm just a bit . . . meh.'

Robert's amused eyes meet mine, and he pretends to sniff the air. 'Is that . . . apathy I smell?'

'Yes!' I exclaim, pretending to smell my wrists. 'It smells like British trains.'

'I'll go shopping with you,' he says.

'Wowsers, that's verbal Rohypnol,' I say. 'Seriously. It's the best pickup line I've ever heard.'

'Right then, funny girl, let's go,' he says, standing up.

We head to Westbourne Grove and windowshop, spending an inordinate amount of time in Reiss – it seems to be Robert's sartorial homeland – then eat some absolutely delectable Ottolenghi cupcakes that we nickname 'Heaven for babies'.

'Because what's better than heaven? Heaven for babies,' nods Robert sagely.

I pause. 'So, this is like – a dead baby cake?'

Robert immediately spits the bit of cake in his mouth onto the ground.

Then we walk to Portobello market. It's October, so it's not prime tourist time, and we don't have to fight the crowds.

'I can honestly say I will die without ever a) buying or b) wearing cowboy boots,' I say thoughtfully as we pass a boot shop.

'Gosh, you're so interesting. Do go on,' says Robert.

I convince him to buy a second-hand tweed blazer with patches on the elbows.

'I look like a prat,' he murmurs under his breath, as he tries to see himself in the cracked mirror hanging on the back of the stall.

'It's ace,' I say firmly, with all the confidence of someone who discovered how to speak style about eight days ago. 'It works. Buy it.'

We start walking back up Portobello Road towards Notting Hill Gate. Robert's fielding text messages, as usual. I've only had one from Plum saying '*I'm taking a vote. Dress vs sexy jeans?*' I replied '*Dress. Obv.*' I do speak style! Even Plum trusts me.

I smile to myself. I just remembered something about Adam: when we had that drink last Friday, he leaned in and said, 'I don't normally do that sort of thing . . . I just felt like I had to talk to you. I couldn't approach your table or just send over my number. That would be weird.'

'Yeah, *that* would be weird,' I agreed. 'Whereas, the check-a-box note is totally normal. Predictable, even.'

See? Me! Acting cool! And I like him. Have I mentioned that?

The best thing about dating Adam The Tick Boxer is that it distracts me from work. The past week has been pretty ghastly: I've diligently obeyed the face time rule (part of the culture in my office – i.e., when your boss is in, you're at your desk, sending emails and visibly being a hard worker. Obviously it's bullshit as half the floor goes to the gym at 6.30 pm and comes back at 8 pm to write a few emails, eat dinner on the company and then get a taxi home on the company account, but never mind). I suggested three more reports (the luxury booze market! The luxury car market! The effect of sales on luxury stocks!) and generally, have been a good little associate. I really am trying.

Charlotte and I have met up for coffee almost every day. She's actually very funny, underneath the timid exterior. She spent the weekend moving out of the flat she shared with Phil and in with her brother, and seems impossibly cheerful about the whole thing.

She said yesterday that every time she starts feeling sad, she just remembers all the things that she doesn't like about him, and feels sure that breaking up was the best possible thing that could have happened to her. Isn't that incredible?

Still, every day this week I've been looking forward to the second I can leave work. I'm ignoring the fact that I shouldn't think this way about my job, particularly not when I have a reasonably serious one that ought to take up more of my attention. I guess if I was ambitious, it would. But – and this is a newsflash, since I've worked 12-hours a day, every day, since the day I started – I'm starting to think that I'm not ambitious – at least, not for anything that's on offer for me here. Which I suppose means I'll be an associate forever.

What a fucking awful thought.

'Distract me,' I say. 'I'm thinking about work.'

'On a weekend?' gasps Robert in mock-horror.

'Any funny stories for me?' I say.

'Nope,' he says. 'Bowler-hat girl has gone travelling. Lady Caroline continues to use me when she's bored. Miss Felicity is seeing someone else but calls me now and again. Nothing very funny there.'

'It's bizarre, more than funny,' I agree. 'Let's talk about your best man speech for Luke and Sophie's wedding. Any ideas? Thoughts? Themes?'

'No,' says Robert, his face creasing with stress. 'I'm considering curling up in the foetal position and whimpering.'

I pause. 'That could work.'

At about 3 pm, we head home, as Robert has the all-important job of sitting on the balcony in the sunshine, reading the papers. This is one of Robert's rituals. He hates the idea of missing something interesting, so he buys every broadsheet and reads them cover to cover. It's like a news binge. I sit next to him, alternating between skimming the business section and staring into space, daydreaming.

'How excessive,' I comment, looking at the floor. We're practically drowning in newspapers. 'At least you recycle.'

'Mmm,' says Robert, folding the paper over expertly. I find it so hard to fold broadsheet newspapers backwards like that, I think. Sometimes it's enough to put me off reading an article I know I'd probably enjoy.

You know, I'm still mortified about my drunken behaviour on the Skinny Jeans guy date the week before last. I've swept it under a carpet in my mind – yes, the same place you'll find work, and the place that up until a few months ago, you could find Peter. Ahem.

Am I meant to not reply to Josh From HR's texts, do you think? Hell, maybe I am. Maybe he liked me the way I like Adam The Tick Boxer. Maybe every single person in London is hoping for a text from someone else, and we're all connected in a chain of waiting. I wonder who's at the top of the chain?

Robert's phone beeps. He picks it up, reads the text, makes a derisive little snorting sound and puts it back on the table without replying.

That answers that question, then.

I sit back and study Robert thoughtfully. All 6'4" of him is leaning right back, legs stretched over the side of the balcony, taking up every bit of available space around him. As usual, he's frowning, giving him a serious look that I think is actually just a squint. He probably needs glasses. Adam The Tick Boxer wears glasses for work, they're adorable, and –

'Stop it,' Robert says to the back of the Sports section. 'Read something else, or drink your coffee, or something. But don't stare at me and don't think about Adam The Tick Boxer.'

'But he's so gorgeous. He goes to the gym every day, did I tell you that?'

'You did. I bet he looks at himself in the mirror as he's working out, too.'

I narrow my gaze. 'Do you do any exercise? Your body won't stay so fit forever if you don't.'

'Do you?'

'Yeah, I'm going to start playing croquet.'

Robert laughs, as I wanted him to, and folds down the newspaper to smirk at me. 'You don't seem like the croquet type, Abby, darling.'

'I think I need a party nap,' I say.

'Me too,' Robert says, cricking his neck.

But I can't be bothered to get up just yet. I think I'll just sit here and daydream about Adam The Tick Boxer some more.

'What should I wear tonight?' I ask Robert.

'Are you going to ask me that every night?' he says. 'Because it's been coming up a lot.'

'It's rhetorical,' I say. 'I'm saying it aloud to prompt myself to think about it. I'm going to Henry's brother's goodbye party. I'm meeting Adam The Tick Boxer first, so I want to look sexy, and tall, and—'

'What happened to the nice shy Abby I met all those months ago?' he says to himself. 'She was great. Practically a mute. This Abby never shuts up.'

I give him the finger as I leave the balcony.

'That's very childish, Abby,' he calls after me. 'I expect more of you.'

I don't really need his sartorial advice, of course. I speak style pretty well these days. I'm going to wear my nude pencil dress and my grass-green, very high heels, and my hair parted on the side and tied in a low, chignon thing . . . Pretty With A Punch.

I lie on my bed for a while and try to nap, but my mind keeps drifting to Adam The Tick Boxer. I think I'll take him as my date to Sophie's wedding next year! Do you think it's too early to ask him? I wonder what his plans are for New Year's Eve. It's my birthday on January 1. Maybe we could go away for the night . . .

I take a long shower, and enjoy a surprisingly successful blow-drying-and-straightening session. Then I get dressed. Some natural-ish makeup, with brown smoky eyes, and voilà! All done.

I stalk out of my room, picking up my white wrappy coat on the way and stomp down the stairs (you have to stomp or stride in heels this high; at least until your second drink, when you can strut or slink). I catch Robert coming out of his room with wet hair pulling a T-shirt down over jeans. He makes a whistling sound at me.

'Sexy outfit.'

'Sexual harassment in the home environment,' I say sniffily.

'Sorry. You look like shit. Go have some fun.'

'I intend to,' I grin. Adam The Tick Boxer, here I come.

# Chapter Twelve

8 pm Saturday night. South Kensington tube station. And my night hasn't started well.

'Abigail!' exclaims Plum. 'Finally!'

'Cocksmoker!' I reply.

'Do I have something in my teeth?'

'Adam The Cocksmoking Tick Boxer just dumped me,' I whisper furiously, taking her arm. 'Let's walk. I need to smoke.'

'No,' she gasps.

'I really do, I need to smoke.'

'I mean – he dumped you? And you don't smoke.'

'I do tonight,' Plum hands me her lit cigarette so I can inexpertly drag on it. 'I was meant to meet him at the Grand Union in Camden, for a drink, you know, as I was coming down here and he has a thing somewhere else, and then he didn't show, so I rang him, and he didn't answer, and I texted him, and he replied "I'm back with my ex-girlfriend. I'm sorry."'

'Oh, that's fucked,' says Plum sympathetically. 'I hate it when that happens. What a fucknuckle.'

'Does that happen a lot?! I just can't believe it. I don't understand what I did wrong,' I say, exhaling quickly. Why isn't Plum more shocked by this? I feel like having a tantrum. Keep your cool, Abigail . . . ah, fuck it, I can't. 'This is not fair! I have never felt this confused and helplessly single before!'

'Wait till it happens eighteen times in a row,' says Plum. 'Westbourne guy,' she pauses, and spits over her shoulder, 'didn't call. I texted him, and he didn't reply.'

'Oh God, I'm sorry,' I say. Poor Plum. I wish I could erase all the shit things that have happened to her so she could start again. How would I feel if I'd met someone I liked and had it inexplicably go bad time after time after time, for years and years? I can't imagine.

Plum shrugs, and puts on her best I'm-in-a-great-mood smile. 'Don't worry about it. Here. Vodka?'

Plum always has a small water bottle of vodka in her bag on nights out. It's a necessary strategy she explained once, to combat London bar prices. I have a quick swig and, coughing, take out my phone to check (just in case) if Adam The Tick Boxer has texted again (he hasn't). And the only thing that stops me from bursting into tears is the determination that I am not going to be the kind of girl who gets stood up on a Saturday night and cries about it.

Instead I will just rant for a while.

'I don't get it,' I splutter, puffing violently on my fag. 'I just don't get it. Who does that? Who pursues someone and goes out of their way to spend time with them and then discards them?'

Plum and I lock eyes. 'Robert,' we say simultaneously.

'I'm going to call him,' I say. 'He'll know what we should do.'

'How may I assist you,' he says, instead of hello.

'Adam The Cocksmoking Tick Boxer' – I pause and spit, as Plum looks at me supportively – 'fucking dumped me, and you need to fucking tell me why.'

'Whoa, psychogail,' he says, laughing. 'What?'

'Adam. The Cocksmoking. Tick Boxer. Dumped. Me.' I take another dramatic drag. 'I don't understand, I thought it was going well—'

'Abby, you weren't going out with him. You've only known him a week,' says Robert bluntly.

'Well, I felt like I was going out with him,' I falter. 'Not dumped, then. Rejected. Is that better?'

'I thought you said you were cool and detached.'

'I *acted* cool and detached,' I say. 'Mostly.' Though I did suggest the last two dates, now that I think about it. And I suggested staying at his house last night. And I did text him first every day since Tuesday. Shit, that's not cool or detached. 'Ah, fuck it.'

Plum hands me the vodka-water-bottle again, and I take another swig.

Robert's grinning, I can tell. 'OK. Well, don't worry about that. He's clearly stupid, blind and probably gay. So shrug it off. Being tough is absolutely key to surviving single life, Abby. You can't compete in blood sports if you faint at the first shot.'

'Tough,' I say tentatively. 'I am tough. I am a bastard, just like you.'

'Uh, sure, whatever . . . Now. Delete his number.'

'Seriously? But what if I need to—'

'Abby, darling, for your own good, delete his number,' instructs Robert.

The sound of Robert calling me darling makes me feel even more like crying. I don't know why.

'I'm sorry I'm interrupting your date,' I say, with a choking sound.

'I'm not on a date,' he says. 'I'm with your sister and Luke, actually. We're heading out to another fucking 30th in a bit. Sure you'll be alright?'

'Yep,' I say, snuffling into the phone as we walk. Plum looks over sympathetically and squeezes my arm. 'I'm with Plum. I'm good.'

'Good,' he says. I can hear that he's smiling. 'Remember, this is experience.'

'Experience,' I repeat, proudly. 'Experience equals confidence. Tough.'

'Exactly. You're in control. You're tough. You're bulletproof. Now go out there and batter up: make this party your bitch.'

I hang up, delete Adam The Cocksmoking Tick Boxer's number, square my shoulders, and look Plum in the eye.

'Batter up!'

'What does that mean?' whispers Plum.

'It means: bring on the next man! We are bulletproof! Say it with me.'

'Batter up! We are bulletproof,' she snarls. 'Fuck, yeah.'

We bump fists in a semi-and-therefore-not-really-ironic way, I stub out my cigarette, and we resume marching towards the Hollywood Arms and the party.

With every step, I imagine myself shaking off the rejection and becoming stronger and tougher. Everything is perfect. I will not end up bitter or miserable or angry or desperate. I will make this party my bitch, in fact, I will make being single my bitch. Experience. Confidence. Bulletproof. Yes.

'Abigay!' shouts Henry from the other end of room when we finally get to the Hollywood Arms, a glossily posh pub with a private upstairs room for parties. 'Pruneface! Finally!'

'I wish he wouldn't call me Abigay. It's really inappropriate,' I mutter to Plum.

'You want to complain about Abigay when he calls me Pruneface?'

'Your real name *is* Prunella,' I remind her.

'Shut it, Abigay,' she retorts with a dazzling smile.

'My girls!' he shouts, enveloping us in a boozy hug. He's three weets to the shind, as per usual on a match day.

'Beetchez! Are you two ready for a big night?' he bellows. 'I

105

had a nice little Saturday: house hunting all morning and got the shit beaten out of me at rugby. So I'm going to raise the roof.' He does a little 'raise the roof' motion with his hands, causing a few of the boys around him to join in.

The party is well underway. I vaguely recognise some of Henry's rugby friends. I wish I'd mingled more in the past. I wonder if everyone in relationships becomes socially lazy, or if it was just me.

Come on, social butterfly, unfurl your wings.

'How was house hunting? Where are you looking?' says Plum.

'A *ballache*. The underbelly of Chiswick,' he answers.

'No!' I gasp. 'Seriously. Don't. We would never see you again. Hammersmith is the Hadrian's wall of West London.'

'You talk nice,' grins one of Henry's drunker rugby friends, Gaz, as Henry orders drinks. Gaz came to a Christmas party that Peter and I had in our second year in London, and threw up in the kitchen at 10 pm. I arch an eyebrow instead of replying.

'I've snogged at least three men in this room and screwed two others,' says Plum in a low voice. 'Ah well. Live and learn.'

Henry hands us our drinks.

'What's that you're drinking?' asks Gaz. He is seriously invading my personal space.

'Uh, vodka and cranberry,' I say.

'Cranberry juice,' he says, nodding. 'That's good for your vagina.'

Plum splutters into her drink, unable to control her laughter. I flash Gaz a please-fuck-off grimace-smile. I am in control. One more drink and I'll start butterflying.

'I've invited a friend along later,' he says, swaying slightly. 'She's fit. And gagging for it. Once women hit 30, there's only one thing they want.'

Plum's smile freezes and I narrow my eyes at him. Fucknuckle. 'Really?'

'Marriage. Babies. Ring on the ol' finger . . . She's desperate for it.'

Gaz is saved from my heel in his jugular by the arrival of Henry's brother Rich.

'Late to your own party!' shouts Henry, tucking Plum under his arm like a teddy bear. She pushes him off with pretend irritation and tries to fix her hair.

'Punctuality is an overrated virtue,' Rich says, accepting a beer from one of the guys. He looks a bit like Henry, only without the puppyness. More of a grown-up dog. And rather attractive, I've always thought. 'Good evening, Plum, Abigail. Looking lovely, as ever.'

'We thought we'd make an effort,' I say. 'Since you're heading off to deepest darkest China, after all.'

'Hong Kong isn't exactly deepest darkest China,' he says. 'But I appreciate the thought. How's single life?'

I think for a second. 'Surprising.'

Rich grins. 'I've been looking forward to you coming back on the market for years. Never thought Peter was in your league. What a shame I'm leaving.'

'Tragedy.' Hell yeah, I am a flirting machine tonight. The phone chat with Robert was a life-saver. Bulletproof. I am bulletproof.

Rich's attention is taken by one of his ex-work colleagues trying to give him a very unwelcome Jägerbomb, and I look over and see Plum's now standing at the bar, being ignored by the bartender. She suddenly looks a little bit lost and, to be honest, not bulletproof at all.

I walk over to her. 'You OK?'

She shrugs. 'I just got an encouraging text from Thomasina saying: if he wasn't quite right, he wasn't Mr Right.' She sighs, her I'm-in-a-great-mood mask dropping again. 'Can you believe that shit? I love my work friends, but seriously. I am so glad I have you. Especially now . . .'

107

'Now that I'm single and going through the same thing?' I say, laughing.

'Well, now that we're in this together. My mother has even stopped telling me to come home to Yorkshire so she can find me a nice local man. She thinks you're a good influence . . . I just don't feel as alone as I used to.'

I'm shocked. I didn't know Plum ever felt alone.

'I think we should date more than one guy at once,' I say flippantly. 'Spread the risk. Mix the good guys with the bad guys. Like an investment bank.'

'Isn't it that kind of thinking that started the global financial meltdown?' asks Plum.

I shrug. 'Yeah, you know, churn and burn them . . .' I pause, and look at her. 'That's exactly what we should do!'

'You're turning into a bastard commitment-phobe, now?'

'It seems better than the alternative.'

'Alright, girls,' says Henry. 'I'm going to introduce myself to some chicks.'

'Don't call us chicks,' say Plum and I in unison.

'Ladies, then,' he says.

A few hours later, I'm having a brilliant time. Farewell parties can be risky: the mix of school, work and university friends results in either a seriously segregated party, or a free-for-all social orgy where everyone talks to everyone else. This is the latter.

Henry's in the corner with a girl Plum and I helped him meet, and Plum's over the other side of the room talking to a couple of guys I don't know. And I'm talking to Rich again. He's been discussing the ideal time to send out group emails. His invitation to the farewell party – 2 pm last Thursday – was apparently very carefully thought out.

'Friday is the best day for group banter,' he nods. 'I'm at my funniest on Fridays. Wednesdays you'd have to email me something pretty damn good to get me to respond. And on

Mondays and Tuesdays, I don't want to hear from anyone unless I skipped out on a bar bill or trashed your gaff on the weekend.'

'Maybe you should write up these guidelines and send them to all your friends,' I suggest.

'I know,' he sighs. 'But they'd label me, you know. "Pushy". "Bossy".' He holds his hands up in an exaggerated 'quote mark' mime.

'"Anti-social". "Surly". "High Maintenance",' I continue glibly, then look at his pretend-hurt face with mock surprise. 'Too far? Did I go too far?'

'Fuck it, Abigail, why are you single now, when I'm leaving?' says Rich, leaning back and looking at me.

'You'll get over it,' I say tartly. *Bonjour* confidence. Churn *et* burn.

'Dreadful timing. Dreadful.'

'By the way,' I say. 'Who's Plum talking to?' This flirting is good, but Plum's admission about feeling alone has made me feel protective of her.

'Dan and Pete. I work with them.'

I look over and see Plum laughing and shaking her head at something one of them is saying. She looks her happy, pretty self. High five, Plum, I think. Bulletproof.

A second later, my sister Sophie and Luke walk in to the party, followed by Robert. Sophie and Luke look worried, and Robert is squinting and tripping over something at the door.

Sophie searches the room and we meet eyes. Something is wrong. Weren't they supposed to be at someone's 30th tonight?

'Excuse me, Rich,' I say, and hurry over to Sophie. Before I can get there, I'm almost knocked over by a bear hug from Robert.

'Abbbyyy,' Robert croons into my ear, and leans back to beam at me. I realise that he's absolutely hammered. He's actually cross-eyed. I look at Sophie and Luke in alarm.

'What the fuck?'

'He said he had to talk to you about being bulletproof,' says Luke, sighing. 'We were just up at The Anglesea Arms, so we thought the walk might sober him up.'

'It's been an eventful night,' adds Sophie quietly. 'We'll tell you more later.'

I turn to Robert. He's staring into space. 'Are you OK?'

He focuses on me. 'Oh Abby . . . I want you to know . . . I am so full of shit. You should not listen to me. I know nothing.' He can barely talk, he's slurring so badly.

'Do you want a glass of water?'

'I'd like a pint of WINE!' he shouts excitedly. People around us start looking over. It's only 10.30 pm. 'What are you looking at, googly?' Robert points at a guy with glasses. 'Do you google in your googlies? HA!' He turns back to us and puts up his hand for a high five.

'Shut. Up!' I hiss at him through clenched teeth. I turn to Sophie and Luke. 'Let's get him downstairs.'

'I'm going to talk to Rich,' nods Sophie. 'We can't turn up to his party with a gibbering drunk he doesn't know and not even say hi.'

'You're a hi,' says Robert, and starts laughing helplessly.

'OK,' I say. 'I'll get him out of here.'

I turn to Robert. 'Robert. Robert.' He turns to me and closes one eye to focus. The other is bloodshot. 'Let's go downstairs.'

'Abby-gail,' he singsongs, obediently following me out the door. I turn as we leave and see Plum looking over. She's just talking to the tall guy now, who looks completely besotted by her. I give her a questioning thumbs up and she nods.

'I'm not ash drunk ash I'm pretending,' whispers Robert, extremely loudly, stumbling down the stairs to the main bar.

'Really,' I say, scanning the room for a spare table. Spying one, I grab Robert, sit him down, and then get a pint of water for him and a glass of wine for me. When I get back, he's slumped in his chair, blinking groggily.

'What happened, Robert?' I say.

'You never call me Rob,' he replies, making a valiant attempt to sit up straight. 'Everyone elsh does. Why?'

'I don't think of you as a Rob,' I say. 'You're a Robert.'

'I am. I am Robert.' He sighs. 'Was at another fucking 30th. For Dave. Another fucking groomsman.'

'Dave, Luke's groomsman, yes,' I nod. 'I've never met him.

'And his sister is the . . . the one I told you about.'

'Which one?' I say, confused. Robert never talks about his ladyfriends in any kind of detail.

'The one. The one from the party. With the train and no shoes.'

'Dave's sister is the girl you proposed to?' I ask. 'Like, 10 years ago?'

'Yes. Her. Stupid. Stupid Robert.'

'Did something happen?'

He sighs, and swings his head to the side and gazes at me. 'You're so pretty.'

'Robert!' I snap. I'm intrigued. 'Tell me what happened.'

'She was there. Louisa.' He rolls out the name slowly. Looooeeeeeeessaaaaa.

'Oh, shit,' I say. 'But, surely . . .'

'Surely it was years ago. Surely you're over it, Robert. Don't call me Shirley. HA!' Robert laughs and slaps his knee.

'How's it going?' says a voice, and I look up. It's Luke.

I stand up and, with my back to Robert, ask quietly: 'What happened with Louisa?'

'He told you about her?' says Luke in surprise. 'God, she's an evil bitch. We saw her, she's with her husband, everyone was very civil, then Rob drank straight whisky for two hours.'

'That's such a bad idea,' I shudder at the thought.

Luke nods. 'So was Louisa.'

'He told me about proposing to her,' I say as quietly as I can, so Robert won't hear.

'Which time?' replies Luke with a wry smile.

'It happened more than once?'

Luke nods.

'What are we whishpering about?' says Robert, who has hopped up out of his chair and is propping his chin over my shoulder unsteadily.

'Whisky,' I say. 'You are one messy drunk.'

'I'm not,' he says indignantly, and belches pungently. 'Oops. Damn wine.'

I look down and see that he's just drunk my entire glass of white wine.

'Nice move, hotshot. That was mine. The water is yours.'

Robert sighs, hiccups and assumes a hangdog expression. 'I'm sawry . . .'

Luke and I exchange glances as Sophie comes up.

'How's it going down here?'

'Disastrous,' I say.

'Soph-AY!' exclaims Robert delightedly. He pushes past Luke and I to hug her, but loses his balance and tackles her to the floor, knocking over a table and chair on the way. The noise is almighty. Everyone in the pub immediately falls silent and looks over.

'Ow,' says Sophie, blushing scarlet as she gets up, trying to look extremely sober and disapproving so everyone knows she's not the drunk idiot in this situation.

Robert is lying groggily on the floor, looking mildly confused. He is clearly the drunk idiot in this situation.

'We have to get him out of here,' I say to Luke and Sophie, looking over at the bartenders who are talking amongst themselves. 'We are two seconds away from being kicked out.'

'Agreed,' says Luke, and leans over to hoist Robert up.

The three of us drag/support him out of the bar and into the cool night air. God, he's heavy. I immediately light a stressed cigarette.

'Oh! Yes. Cigarette for Robert,' says Robert, pushing us off him and trying to walk alone.

'No,' I say. God, drunk people are annoying. 'We're taking you home and putting you to bed.'

'Naughty!' exclaims Robert, and promptly falls over again.

By the time we find a black cab willing to take us home, it's past 11 pm. I text Plum on the way, saying an emergency came up and I had to leave. We carry a nearly-asleep Robert to bed ('On his side!' I say. 'He might choke on his own vomit.' 'He's not Jim Morrison,' replies Sophie. 'I thought it was the lead singer from AC/DC?' I say. 'It was Jimi Hendrix, but is this important right now?' says Luke) and then we retire to the living room.

'What a car crash,' I comment, opening a bottle of wine and getting out three glasses. I haven't heard from Plum yet, but I think I should probably go back to the party.

'You should have seen him when it happened,' says Luke. 'Poor bastard. She annihilated him.'

'I can't imagine it,' say Sophie and I in unison.

'Tell me the whole story,' I say.

'Ah, look, Robert will tell you himself one day,' says Luke uneasily.

'God! I hate the way you won't gossip,' says Sophie despairingly.

'Sorry, darling,' says Luke, grinning at her. She smiles hopefully back, and he relents. 'The short version is: Rob and Dave and I were friends at school. Our dads all went to university together, and we all used to go on holiday in the same village in France and have BBQs together every night, that sort of thing. And Rob always had a thing for Louisa, who is Dave's big sister . . . With me so far?'

Sophie and I nod.

'Then they finally got together when we were about 22. It was pretty serious, he proposed when he was hammered, then came down the following weekend and proposed properly. With a ring and everything. She said no and broke up with him,' – Sophie and I gasp – 'and he ploughed his study and came down to work in the City instead – I think just to be closer to her . . . and then she continued to string him along. For years, she turned to him whenever she broke up with someone. He moved to Boston to study, to get away from her, but still, he'd fly back whenever she asked.'

'Bitch,' say Sophie and I in unison.

'I know,' says Luke. Like most men, Luke's very good at gossiping, despite pretending to hate it. 'And when he was 26, they began seeing each other properly again, and after six months, he proposed. Again.'

'No!' hiss Sophie and I in unison again.

'Yep. And she said no. Turned out she'd been cheating on him the whole time. With the guy who is now her husband. It wasn't a car crash. Rob was roadkill.'

'NO!' we shout.

'Poor darling Rob . . .' says Sophie sadly. 'No wonder he's so allergic to commitment now.'

'Wowsers,' I say. 'That's so awful.'

'Oh, God, pity is the last thing he wants,' says Luke, groaning. 'I should never have said anything. He's a very private guy.'

'I'll never say a thing,' I say.

'Me either,' says Sophie. 'Cross my heart.'

She makes a very serious cross-my-heart sign, and then a zipping-her-mouth-and-throwing-away-the-key gesture.

My phone beeps. It's a text from Plum.

*Where are you??? We're going to Chloe . . . I need you! Get the fuck back here x*

'Can I be bothered to go all the way back down to South Ken?' I ask.

'No way,' says Sophie.

A second text. From Henry.

*Abigay. Please come back. I need you to help me be bulletproof too.*

They're in league. I sigh and look up at the guys. 'My public needs me. I must venture forth once more. It's only 20 minutes. Will you come?'

'I'll call a cab,' says Luke. 'We'll drop you on the way home.'

# Chapter Thirteen

By the time I get back to Chloe, a basement bar and club in South Kensington, it's nearly midnight. Sophie and Luke drop me on the corner, and trying not to feel self-conscious, I stride towards the 30-people-long queue.

'Um,' I say, to get the list bitch's attention. (I'm not being rude. It's what they call them.) She turns to me and blinks heavily-mascara-ed eyes. She's blonde, older than she wants to be, with major attitude.

'I'm on the list,' I say tentatively. 'Abigail? Wood? My friends are inside?'

'I don't have your name, join the queue,' she turns away abruptly.

I'm contemplating begging or bribing, and wondering how you do either of those things, when—

'Imma!' shouts a male voice. 'She's with me!'

I look around to see where the voice is coming from, but can't see anyone.

The list bitch, her face blank, points me down the stairs leading to the basement courtyard.

As I walk down the stairs, I try to ignore the tiny thrill from (a) going to a club I've never been to before (b) going to a club at all because Peter and I never ever did and (c) skipping the queue.

A few intrepid smokers are down in the courtyard, risking the rain.

'I hope I get a thank you for that,' says the same voice, and I look up into the eyes of a rather handsome blonde guy smoking a cigarette.

'Thank you,' I say. 'That was you?'

'Indeed,' he nods. He talks like Roger Moore, sort of posh and knowing. 'Cigarette?' Why not. 'Imma isn't the friendliest, but that's her job.'

'I bet she's a real bleeding heart the rest of the time,' I nod, trying to smoke coolly and ignore the headrush.

'Oh, she is,' he says. 'Nurses a sick grandmother. Adopts kittens. The works.'

'I should get her number. We could hang out.'

He grins. 'I'm Toby, by the way.'

'Abigail.'

We smile at each other. I'm enjoying this, somehow I feel far less nervous than usual. All I have to do is maintain steady eye contact and not babble.

The rain intensifies, and Toby pulls an umbrella out of his blazer pocket.

'You were a Boy Scout, weren't you,' I say, arching an eyebrow.

'Well, I tried to be a Brownie, but they wouldn't let me. Bastards,' he says sadly. I can't help but smirk. (Darn, flirting is easy tonight!) 'So, Miss Abigail. What brings you here?' he asks.

'My friends are inside,' I reply. 'We were at a party earlier but I had to tend to someone who was unexpectedly taken drunk. I mean, ill.'

Toby grins. 'I hate it when my friends do that. Let them sleep on the street, I say. Teaches them a lesson.'

I nod. I don't know what else to say, so I think I'll end the conversation. How's that for detached? 'Well, I'd better go and find everyone,' I say, stubbing out my cigarette. 'Thanks again for the door help. And the cigarette.'

'My pleasure,' he says.

I walk away, not looking back. I am bulletproof. Hell yeah.

117

Once I'm inside, it doesn't take long to find everyone.

'AbiGAY!'

Ah. Henry and Plum are standing near the bar in a big group of people that I recognise from the Hollywood Arms earlier.

'What the fuck happened to you?' says Plum. 'We thought you'd been kidnapped.'

'Sorry,' I say apologetically. 'Robert needed to be taken home.'

'Are you sexing your flatmate?' asks Henry loudly.

'No,' I say. 'And that's not a verb, Henry.'

'I thought verbs were doing words,' he replies. 'And sex is a DOING word.' He turns to high-five one of his rugby friends.

'What have I missed, then?' I say, rolling my eyes as I turn back to Plum. At about midnight, Henry always goes from puppy to smutty. I glance quickly around the bar, lock eyes with Rich, and nod in greeting. He looks like he expects me to go over and say hi, but I'm quite happy here for now. If he wants to talk to me, I suddenly realise, he'll come over. Then my attention is taken by Plum telling me all about Dan, the cute guy she was talking to at the party earlier.

'He's from Yorkshire! Can you believe it? And he asked for my number, so I gave it to him,' finishes Plum proudly, and then pauses. 'Not like that.'

'Good for you,' I say. 'Bulletproof!'

'I know!' says Plum. 'We haven't spoken in over an hour, though. Maybe I should go and find him and talk to him some more,' she adds worriedly. 'What if he finds someone he likes more than me?'

She never used to be like this. Where did this insecurity come from? Years of disappointing singledom, comes the answer right back. 'Don't stalk him. Do a lap of the club, and if you see him, grin or raise an eyebrow, but don't stop. Go straight to the bar. I bet Dan follows you and starts talking to you.'

'Who made you the queen of pulling?' says Plum.

I do sound extremely sure of myself. And I feel it, too. How strange. I shrug. 'What have you got to lose?'

'Absolutely nothing,' says Plum cheerfully. 'Back in five.'

Hmm.

I think I've just learned how to be single.

I look around the bar, make eye contact with Rich, raise an eyebrow, and then turn back to my drink. I bet you five pounds he comes over within 10 seconds.

'I hope you came back to the party just to see me,' says a voice five seconds later. I look up at Rich, stifling a victorious grin. Ha! 'But I wouldn't be so egotistical as to assume so.'

'Humble, yes, that's how I'd describe you,' I nod. 'So are you learning Cantonese for Hong Kong?'

'Come on, everyone knows other languages don't actually exist,' he says conspiratorially. 'We go travelling and hear them speaking Italian and Japanese and so on, but the minute we turn our backs they're all talking in good old English. It's all pretend!'

I smile at him. He's very cute.

'I like your hair,' I say thoughtfully. 'You look like Henry will when he's a big boy.'

Rich smiles at me and leans forward, and for a second I think he's going to kiss me, when out of the corner of my eye I see Plum returning from her lap around the club, and quickly turn my head to watch her. To the outside observer, she's another leggy, nonchalant girl wandering to the bar. But I can tell that she's melting inside, thinking Dan hasn't followed her. Fuck it, I think, sighing. I want to fix things for her.

'Plum!' shouts a voice, and Plum and I both turn and see Dan striding over towards her. 'There you are. Can I buy you a drink?'

Yes! I want to punch the air. I am the singledom coach! I am the love sage! Move over, Robert!

'Love Is A Battlefield' comes on, and I look up at Rich and grin. 'If you'll excuse me . . . I need to watch your brother dance to this song,' I say.

Henry likes Pat Benetar. No, Henry *loves* Pat Benetar. And he has a handful of dance moves (the Shopping Trolley, the

Sprinkler, the Reverse Park, the Tennis Serve, the Ear Cleaner and the Cake Mix) that I love. He and I also have a special dance move called The Fisherman, where he pretends to have a fishing rod and I pretend to be a fish and have to get hooked from across the dance floor; and the Skipping Rope, where another person and I mime holding two skipping ropes as he pretends to skip over them faster and faster. He is always the skipper, and *never* lets me skip.

I'm having such a good time. A drunk guy approaches in that flirty/sleazy way that guys do when they think they're Al Pacino in *Scent Of A Woman*, so I hit Henry in the arm and he starts twirling me. The pretend boyfriend: every single girl's must-have. The two of us acting like dickheads isn't going to help Henry's case with the opposite sex either, but he seems to be having a good time.

Eventually the DJ starts playing Europop, so leaving Henry doing the Running Man, I head to the bar to look for Plum.

'So, as I was saying earlier, we should go out,' says Rich, sidling up next to me immediately. 'Don't make me ask again.'

'You're leaving for Hong Kong!' I say, stalling for time. Do I really want to go out with Henry's brother? And I don't think I should make a date on the same night that Adam The Tick Boxer rejected me and almost made me cry, do you? Though between me and you, I don't feel upset about him anymore . . .

'Not for a few more days,' Rich says.

I pause. 'OK, I'd love to.' Batter up.

'Great,' he says. 'Give me your number.'

As I give him my number, I look up and see posh Toby from the courtyard. He's looking over at us – me, sipping my drink; Rich tapping my number into his phone – and grins knowingly. I narrow my eyes and scowl at him. He pretends to be hurt.

Flirting without words. Wow, I can't wait to tell Robert about this.

Henry comes up. 'Where the bloody hell are all the girls?'

'Everywhere, Henry,' I reply. 'Everywhere. Remember what Robert said? Right, I'm going to the bar, boys.'

When I get back with our drinks, Henry is still talking about not being able to meet girls.

'Abigay's flatmate Robert – total legend, by the way – gave me a few tips. But I just don't know if I can be that guy.'

'You can be that guy,' says Rich solemnly. 'I believe in you.'

'You're a very handsome man,' I say, feeling like Henry's mother. 'Just channel confidence.'

'There are two girls over there,' says Rich. 'Go on—'

'What if they tell me to fuck off? I—' Henry pauses.

'If they do, then just assume they're talking about something traumatic,' I say. 'Girls sometimes have private conversations. It's not personal.'

'OK,' he says. He takes a deep breath, squares his shoulders, and walks over. I look over at Rich again and we both start laughing.

'Ah, the pull,' he says, grinning. 'You seem awfully knowledgeable for someone so newly single, by the way.'

'Shit! Plum!' I say. 'I have to do a recon. Back in a mo.'

She's not on the dance floor, the other seating area, or the smoking courtyard, so I make a bathroom pit stop. As I wash my hands and make awkward chitchat to the bored woman they don't pay to stand in the tiny bathroom and hand out free paper towels, Plum bursts in happily.

'I've been looking for you!' She pretends to faint against the wall. 'He is so fucking dreamy.'

The toilet attendant woman tsks, and taps a door, indicating Plum should go in and stop wasting her time. She looks over at her perfectly arranged perfumes and hairsprays, and sighs with boredom.

'Sorry,' we chorus. She nods without making eye contact. Why is it people who work for nightclubs act like your existence annoys them?

121

'Wait for me, sugarnuts, I'm bursting,' says Plum.

I look over the array of seriously minging perfumes on offer. Who wears Paris Hilton's Heiress? And why offer Chupa Chups? What are we, five years old?

A heavily fake-tanned girl with serious hair extensions and spray-on jeans comes out of a stall, washes her hands, glosses her lips, tips the attendant and takes a Chupa Chup. She unwraps it and carefully places it between her glossed lips, then twirls it with careful practice.

Ah. I understand now. Sucking a Chupa Chup equals pouty, fellatio-y lips. Some girls must be pre-programmed to ooze that kind of sexiness. I don't think I'm one of them.

'Right. Tell me everything,' I say, as soon as Plum comes back out.

She beams delightedly. 'We're going out on Thursday.'

'Smashing!' I say. Please, let this work out, I think to myself.

She smiles to herself. 'Now, listen. I have to leave now, Abigail, because otherwise I'll probably get drunk and make a fool of myself and go home with him.'

I'm done with tonight, too. I only came back to support Plum. Getting asked out by Rich, rather than the high point of the night as it would have been a few weeks ago, is just a nice bonus. The high point of my night, in fact, was probably Henry's mimed skipping.

We head inside to say goodbye to Henry and Rich.

'Abigail,' says a voice behind me. I turn around. It's Toby. 'I realise you're highly in demand tonight,' he starts. I grin. 'But I'm going to a restaurant launch party on Wednesday, and seeing as you make friends with the door people so easily, I thought you might like to come with me.'

I don't reply. Is it bad to make two dates in one night?

'She doesn't eat carbs on Wednesdays,' says Plum coquettishly.

'I promise to personally check every mouthful she eats,' he says. 'I can even pre-masticate, if you like. Like a Mummy bird.'

'Well, everyone loves a man who's into mastication,' I say, I can't think of a reason to say no, other than that it feels a bit naughty when I just gave Rich my number. But we had that little frisson outside. And he's so good-looking . . . Before I can decide yes or no, Toby takes out his phone, and I give him my number. Batter up indeed.

'We're heading off now, so have a good night . . .' I say.

'You, too,' he says, leaning forward to kiss me goodbye on both cheeks. 'May I arrange a car for you?'

'No, uh, I'm good,' I say, grinning awkwardly as we walk away. 'Thanks, though.'

'He's gorgeous,' hisses Plum, as we walk away. 'Funny, charming, tall . . .'

I wrinkle my nose. 'He's a bit smooth.' Plum looks at me in shock, and I start laughing. 'Come on, let's get out of here.'

# Chapter Fourteen

The next day, at the end of a lazy morning on the balcony reading *Cold Comfort Farm*, drinking coffee and eating crumpets with peanut butter, I decide enough is enough. I need company and he needs food.

'Knock knock!' I say at Robert's door, and immediately curse myself for sounding like both of my parents. 'Robert?' I say, pushing open the door. 'You OK?'

I hear a grunt, and tiptoe in. 'Robert? There's a girl outside who says she's pregnant. She says it's yours?'

'What?' he croaks, shocked out of his hangover coma. He sits up, still wearing his clothes from last night. Through the gloom I can make out puffy eyes, stubbly cheeks and wild man hair. Then he realises it's just me, and flops back down with another grunt. 'What time is it?' he whispers hoarsely.

'It's high time you got up. I brought you water, a Bloody Mary – good for hangovers I hear – and peanut butter crumpets,' I say, holding up the tray.

'This isn't a hangover,' he croaks. 'It's the plague.'

'Poor baby,' I say, sitting on the edge of the bed and handing him the water first. He takes a feeble sip and hands it back to me.

'I wonder what time I got home last night,' he muses. 'And how.'

'What's the last thing you remember?'

'The Anglesea Arms . . . it's a pub in Chelsea. Drinking whisky. Why? Did I see you?'

'Let's talk about that later. For now, just recover. Can I open a window? This room smells like a boys' school.'

'How do you know what a boys' school smells like?' asks Robert through a mouthful of peanut butter.

'My boarding school only accepted girls in the last two years. It stank like unwashed hair and pubic teenage lust.' I draw the curtains open a few inches, and then push up the windows.

'My eyes!' screams Robert. The more I get to know him, the sillier he is. He tucks the duvet high under his armpits like the wolf in Red Riding Hood, and continues to eat and slurp. 'And I don't have dirty hair, by the way. I wash it every day. And condition it.'

'Figures. You scream like a girl, too. I'm bored. Will you play with me today?'

'Ah, if I had a pound,' says Robert.

'I had so much fun last night,' I continue. 'And two men asked for my number. The party was officially my bitch.'

'Come and sit here and tell me absolutely everything,' says Robert. 'And if I close my eyes, don't be alarmed. I'm just resting them.'

I perch on the edge and start chatting about last night, carefully skipping over the and-Robert-turned-up-shitfaced-and-we-had-to-take-him-home bits, because I don't want him to be reminded about Louisa and get upset again. Fifteen minutes later I'm sprawled across the entire bottom third of the bed, checking my hair for split ends.

'You're taking over my bed. You are like a Labrador,' says Robert.

'Labradors have split ends?' I say.

'Glad the upset over Adam didn't last, anyway,' he says, finishing the last of the Bloody Mary with a satisfied sigh.

'Adam who?' I say.

Robert grins, but I'm actually not joking. It takes me a moment to realise he's talking about Adam The Tick Boxer. Of course! I was upset about him. Oops.

'If you loved me, you'd get all the papers and maybe a car magazine as a little treat, and some croissants and a latte,' he says. 'I'm sick and need looking after.'

'Alright. But only because you're teaching me how to be a bastard.'

'What? Oh, right. No problem. God, I feel like I was beaten up last night.'

We spend the next few hours watching a *Curb Your Enthusiasm* mini-marathon. I consume yet more coffee and simultaneously read glossy magazines, clipping out pages that will help me further refine my sartorial instincts. (I like to multitask while I watch TV.)

Robert, showered and still feeling rotten, is curled up in his duvet. He's trying to read the paper but holding it up is proving difficult, and he keeps putting it down with a deep sigh. I'm surprised he's not holding onto a teddy and sucking his thumb, the big baby.

'You know, you can't sulk your way out of a hangover,' I say.

He looks at me and grunts.

I love being single, I muse, as I reach for US *Vogue*. I can do whatever I want. Even if that means nothing. Anyway, there's no one else around today. I've texted Plum, who is starry-eyed about Dan, and has floated off to visit her sister in Richmond, safe in the knowledge that questions about her love life won't bother her today. Henry ended up in a house party till 6 am and isn't taking calls. My sister and Luke have gone to see his parents in Bath.

'Are you making a collage?' asks Robert. I am carefully cutting out the latest Miu Miu ad.

'I stick pictures I like on the inside of my wardrobe to

help me decide what to wear,' I say brightly. 'It's my new idea. Good, huh?'

'How much time do you spend thinking about what to wear?' says Robert. 'Honestly. How many minutes a day. Ballpark.'

'I can't count that high,' I say. 'It's one of life's most surprisingly smashing pleasures, though . . .'

'Smashing,' says Robert, without looking up from the paper. 'Why is it you say quaint little things like "cripes" and "smashing"? It's like hanging out with Julian from the *Famous Five*.'

I ignore him. I *love* Julian from the *Famous Five*.

His phone beeps and he looks at it quickly and deletes the text. He's been swatting off texts all day.

'Ah, the trials of a man in demand,' I say. 'Ladyfriends after a little action, are they?'

'I think any action would kill me today.'

'Poor Lady Caroline.'

'No, darling, Lady Caroline only texts me when she's drunk and bored. That was Janey. She only texts me when she's tired of shopping.'

'She sounds awesome.'

'She is for me,' he says, flashing me a grin.

Toby and Rich both text and ask how I'm enjoying my Sunday. I'm happy they texted, but I'd be happy if they hadn't too. I'm not faking this either. I *am* cool and detached.

'You're not replying?' says Robert in surprise, as I look at Rich's second text and put the phone down with a little snort of laughter.

'Maybe later. Keeps them on their toes.'

'Attagirl. Adam who, indeed.'

I stick my tongue out at him, pick up the paper and realise with a shock that yesterday was Peter's birthday. How could I have forgotten that? How can you share your life with one person for so many years, cook and plan holidays and talk to his mother

127

on the phone, and then move on and be a complete person with a completely different life, all by yourself, within months? Does it mean I never loved him? Or just that I was ready to change? Or is it just the power of the human id? (Or is it ego? I can never remember.)

'I've got cabin fever,' I comment at 4 pm.

'Mmm,' replies Robert.

I stare at the ceiling for a while.

'Abigail wants to go for walkies,' I say. 'She wants to go to Regent's Park.'

'Robert doesn't feel very well and shouldn't do anything strenuous,' says Robert.

'Get up. We're going out.'

Regent's Park on a Sunday afternoon in October is delightful. Especially today. It's blustery and grey, but not too cold. Robert and I stroll in unison, hands in our coat pockets, only talking occasionally. I instinctively knew these clothes would make me happy today: tight jeans, new biker-y boots, a red hoodie and a navy peacoat. Pretty With A Punch. I never used to like what I was wearing. Now I do.

I love people-watching. Guys playing football, dogs running around, kids screaming, mums and dads with strollers looking tired. Everyone here to escape Sunday blues for a few hours.

Without discussing it, we both slow our pace and my brain stops racing. I suddenly feel very peaceful and relaxed.

Two yummy mummies steering those four-wheel-drive type prams stare at Robert as they walk towards us. It's kind of fun having a platonic male friend that every woman in London seems to find ridiculously attractive.

I wonder whether I'll ever be a mother. I wonder if I'll ever fall in love and get married. It seems so utterly impossible right now. Then again, I used to find it impossible to imagine not living with Peter. That's one of the nicest things about life, I think to myself. You never know what's going to happen next.

Both lost in our own thoughts, Robert and I stroll all the way down to the Marylebone entrance, when his phone rings.

'Mum!' he says, and then listens for a minute. 'Well, which button did you press? . . . OK. Is the Sky Box on? . . . Well, is the light blue or red? The light in the middle?' I start to laugh. 'I don't think it's the Sky, then, Mum . . . Try the other remote. Press the upper right hand corner . .' He pauses, and glances at his phone screen. 'Mum, that's the home phone. You just called me. You did, you're on call waiting. Hang up with the home phone and—' He pauses and looks at me in shock. 'She just hung up on me.'

I'm in a giggling fit. 'What a lovely son you are.'

'Of course I'm lovely, I'm the only boy and the baby, to boot . . . ah,' he says, as his phone rings again. 'Mother! Always a pleasure. Yes, I think I meant the other phone too. Right, so that wasn't the TV remote, that was the home phone, so find the TV remote, it's the one that says Sony . . . Sony. SONY. Yes . . . And press the green button. It's in the top corner, Mum. Turn the remote the other way . . . there you go. Only press it once, it takes a few seconds . . . and now press "guide" on the Sky remote and you'll get the menu you want. The Sky one, Mum . . . Yes. Yay! Well done, you.' He pauses and grins widely. He looks very boyish when he's happy, I suddenly think. He's got lovely white teeth, with pointy incisors that give him a wolfish air. His features are all lit up and his thick floppy hair is going in a million directions, as always. He catches my eye and grins. 'I'm walking with Abby, so I shouldn't chat . . . she's the girl I live with, remember?' He pauses and rolls his eyes. 'No, Mother, you can't. I have to go. I'll call you during the week. Love you too.' He hangs up and lets out a bark of a laugh. 'God! I have at least one of those calls a week.'

'Robert loves his mummy,' I say in a happy voice, as we turn right and start walking up the other side of Regent's Park.

'I do, I love my mummy. I have never caused her any

trouble . . . though when I was nine, I made her cry. I accidentally-on-purpose smashed my birthday cake on the floor right before my birthday party because I was angry that it was football-shaped, not cricket-bat shaped like I wanted.' He pauses. 'She'd worked all day on it and burst into tears . . . Then I felt too guilty to enjoy my party. I still feel bad about it.'

'What a brat you were. I never did anything bad,' I say proudly, then remember, 'except steal a viola bow.'

'A what?'

'A viola bow,' I enunciate carefully. 'I was seven, and I snapped it when I was running around the house, and I knew I'd be in deep shit. So the next day, I stole someone else's bow before orchestra practice. Isn't that awful?' I sigh at the memory. 'I'm a thief. I felt sick for months about it.'

'I'm shocked,' says Robert.

'I know,' I say sorrowfully. 'It was a dreadful thing to do.'

'No, I'm shocked that a seven-year-old would ever play the viola,' he says, looking mystified. 'Come along, let's walk faster. I want something to eat.'

'How about Carluccio's for coffee and pannetone?' I suggest.

I put my arm through his as we stride along together. He's much taller than me, with infinitely longer legs, so I do a skippy little pony-trot every few steps to keep up. The second time I do it, Robert notices and slows down. Enveloped in our happy silence, we walk in the direction of St John's Wood. Suzanne lives in St John's Wood, I think. Urgh. Work again.

'Work? That was a work sigh,' says Robert. Mind-reading again.

'I don't want to go to school tomorrow. I'm starting to hate it . . . Suzanne has been watching every move I make. It makes me so self-conscious.'

'Find a job you love, and you'll never work a day in your life,' suggests Robert.

'Thanks for the hot tip,' I say sarcastically. 'You should be a careers counsellor.'

'One of my dad's edicts. He has better ones. Like "Never waste an erection" and "It's not about how big or small it is, it's how angry it is".'

'You should put that on a T-shirt. Or better, a tattoo.'

He turns to look at me as we stop at Prince Albert Road. 'Why don't you just quit? You'd figure out what you want pretty fast once you stopped earning a salary.'

'No,' I say immediately. 'Not an option. I just want, um, life to be easy. And I want to not feel sick whenever I see my boss.'

'Then start doing what she wants.'

'Smashing. "Step it up". "Be proactive". Make more calls. Meet more clients. Introduce more sales. All that shit.'

We walk in silence for a few seconds.

'Try not to worry about it,' says Robert. 'Any of it. Work, dating, none of it matters. Just . . . detach.'

'I want to be like a female version of you,' I say. 'Without quite so much meaningless sex.' Not that I'd mind a bit of sex, I think to myself. But not like the Skinny Jeans one-night-stand. He'd have to be gorgeous and we'd need some kind of, what's the word? . . . Oh yes. A spark.

'Good. Most things in life are only as difficult as you allow them to be.'

'What the devil do you do, anyway? Why are you always giving me advice? Are you a careers consultant or something? A life coach?'

Robert shakes his head.

'Are you a lawyer? You have that bossy lawyer thing going on.'

'Nope,' he says.

'Are you a spy?' I say. 'That makes sense. You won't tell me what you do, you're a control freak, you went to Cambridge . . .' I shiver as we walk past the church and the October wind hits us.

'Yes. I am a spy,' he says, putting his arm around me. It's like

131

being tucked under the arm of a very large, warm bear. For a second, I press my head against his chest as we walk, then I realise it's an almost girlfriend-like sign of affection, so I pull away and go back to linking arms.

Just as we reach Carluccio's, Robert's phone rings again.

'Lukey!' Robert says with a grin. Oh, goody, I think, I want to talk to Sophie. There's a pause. 'Pretty tender. Your future sister-in-law has been looking after me.' Pause. Robert's face drops. 'You did?' Pause. 'I did?' Pause. 'No. She didn't.' Robert looks at me, his face now a blank. 'Yeah. Fuck, thanks. Sorry about that . . .' Pause. 'Well, yeah. Talk later.'

'Why didn't you tell me that you had to carry me home last night?' he asks. His voice is perfectly neutral, and his green eyes have gone very opaque. I look into them uneasily. What is he so upset about?

'I didn't want to worry you. You were in a miserable state over Louisa . . .'

Robert throws a hand up as if to stop me, like he can't even bear to hear her name. 'You should have fucking told me, Abigail. Christ!'

'But I thought it would upset you! Let's eat cake and talk about it.'

'I don't want fucking cake.' Shit, he's furious. He won't even look at me.

'I was going to tell you later. I didn't want to make your hangover even worse,' I say. 'I had no idea it would upset you this much. You're totally overreacting. I was trying to be a good friend.'

'No,' he says furiously. 'I'm going home. Just leave me alone. You're my fucking *flatmate*, Abigail.'

Is it me, or is the unspoken end to that sentence 'and not my friend'? I can't believe that he'd throw a tantrum like a huge fucking baby, and I'm about to say something to that effect when he starts walking away. I stand in the street for a few seconds, watching Robert hail a cab, get in and slam the door, feeling like I've been slapped. You stupid prick, I think. The 'you're my fucking flatmate' call was designed to hurt me, and it does.

I take a moment to centre myself. I didn't do anything wrong. He blew it completely out of proportion. He'll realise that.

But I can't go home now. I don't want to see him. That's why Plum never socialises with her flatmates. So home is still private and a place to escape to.

I sigh, and take my phone out of my bag to call Henry, the only person who might be free. He takes a long time to answer.

'You have won dinner with Abigail Wood, one of London's hottest bachelorettes!' I exclaim. 'You lucky boy. The Windsor Castle, Notting Hill, in one hour.'

'Abigay!' says Henry. 'I can't. I'm busy.'

'With whom? Someone with chesticles?' I say coquettishly.

'Well, actually, yeah,' he says. 'Sorry.'

'Oh, OK,' I say contritely. Robert's advice is obviously working. 'Well, um, have fun.'

The day is now devoid of all cosiness. It's grey and empty and Sundayish. I don't want to go home, but I have nowhere else to go. Lonely Single Girl Syndrome has never seemed such a likelihood.

I start walking, because standing still is making me cold. Wanker, I think with every step. Silly, silly wanker. I know he only reacted that way because he's a control freak, but he tried to hurt my feelings and it worked.

I walk back down through Regent's Park, which is far less delightful now that I'm alone. Everyone else is walking with friends and partners and babies. Even a dog would be good company right now, I think fretfully. I am just not enjoying myself. The happy peace I felt earlier is gone.

Fuck it, I suddenly think. It's my home too. I pay rent.

Robert can just deal with me being there. Stupid man, losing his temper because he's embarrassed about the way he acted over Louisa. I know that's all it is, but he'd better fucking apologise.

When I get back, Robert is in his usual position on the couch, legs on coffee table, reading the papers. I decide not to say hello (screw him!) and stride up to my room. I sit on the bed and sigh. It was such a perfect day up till we started fighting. Now I have cold, hard Sunday blues.

Then there's a knock on my door.

'Yes?' I say, as though it could be anyone else but Robert.

'Can I come in?'

'Yes,' I say, turning to face him. He's a picture of hungover, stubbled contrition.

'I'm sorry,' he says. 'I was a dick. I'm sorry.'

'A total dick.'

'A total dick,' he repeats. 'Will you forgive me?'

'Say that I'm your friend as well as your flatmate,' I say petulantly.

'You are a brilliant friend *and* flatmate,' he says, coming in and sitting next to me on the bed. 'I'm sorry that I was so drunk last night and you had to see me like that. I was embarrassed when Luke told me, that's all.'

'There's more to it than that,' I say.

He sighs. 'I was angry that I let myself get like that. And I took it out on you.'

'Yeah, you lashed,' I say thoughtfully. 'You were lashy.'

'I promise not to lash out again,' he says ruefully.

'I promise to tell you next time you turn up shitfaced to a party that you're not invited to,' I say. 'I didn't know it would upset you so much.'

'Thanks for looking after me,' he says. 'Last night and today. I've had a really good weekend apart from that.'

'Anytime,' I say. 'And I've had a really good weekend too. Even though whatsisname dumped me.'

We pause.

'Do you want a hug, or something?' I say. 'Because that's probably asking too much.'

'Let's go to the pub. Steak, chips and red wine. Yes?'

# Chapter Fifteen

Six weeks is a long time when you're single.

It's been just six weeks since Adam the Tick Boxer, the little fucknuckle, dumped me, but I could walk into any busy bar in London right this second, certain that I'm likely to meet a guy. Certain that if I make eye contact he'll probably come and talk to me, probably ask for my number and probably text within 48 hours. Plus – and this is key – certain that if he doesn't, I'll have a good time anyway.

Sound arrogant? I think of it more as a victorious circle of self-assurance, where if you're breezily confident that you'll be asked out, then you'll be asked out because you're so breezily confident.

It's so easy to be this bulletproof. All you have to do is fake it and – boom! You're there.

I'm in control. I don't respond immediately to texts, don't analyse everything, and most importantly, I don't worry about any of it.

In other words, I'm dating like a man.

I went out with Rich, Henry's brother, twice before he left for Hong Kong. He's nice, but almost *too* nice. Know what I mean? And I went out with Toby twice before I decided he was probably too much of a high-flying social bunny for me (he spent most of our dates talking to other people).

Anyway, neither of them made my heart beat wildly with excitement. So why bother seeing them again?

'Because you want to get to know them better?' suggested Plum when I said this.

'But that's just it. I don't,' I replied.

Once you get the hang of dating, it's kind of hard to stop. What did I do with my Wednesday and Thursday nights before I dated? I don't remember. (Fridays and Saturdays are still for friends. Obviously.)

One of my dates, Mark, wore a T-shirt saying 'I'm not a gynaecologist but I'll take a look' which rendered me helpless with laughter at such an error of judgement.

Another date, Patrick, was ridiculously good-looking. I met him at a terrible nightclub called Embargo's, and it wasn't till he said he was hoping to go to Sandhurst next year that I said, 'How *old* are you?' and he said 'Well, how old are *you*?' I said, 'Twenty-seven,' at the same moment he said, 'Eighteen.' We both stared at each other for a few seconds and called it a night 10 minutes later.

I snogged a guy called Tom at one of Henry's rugby parties, and we went out once, but he ruined it for himself by texting me eight hopeful 'Are you still out' texts at 3 am the following weekend. ('That just means he likes you! That's a good sign!' exclaimed Plum when I told her. 'No,' I said. 'One drunk phone text means he likes me. Seven drunk texts means he's an idiot.')

I also went out with an American called Chad (honestly, that was his name, though he didn't laugh when I asked if I could call him Dimpled Chad) a couple of times, but he was rude to the waitress.

And lastly, I went out with a charming guy called James twice, who read the *Daily Mail*. Enough said.

So I ditched them, and haven't thought about them since. Delete, ignore, continue.

Plum and Sophie think I'm strange. Henry thinks I'm awesome, having taken similar advice from Robert.

'It's you and me, Abigay! We rock singledom!' said Henry.

'You are acting like a man,' said Sophie. 'A bastard man.'

'A bastardette,' corrected Plum. 'A fucknuckle bastardette.'

'Plum. Language,' said Sophie.

'Sorry.'

I shrugged. 'I'm just acting the way men act. Why pretend to like them when I don't?'

'Because you'll hurt their feelings?' said Plum.

I thought about this for exactly one second. 'I don't care. I'm having fun.'

It's true. Who wouldn't like to get dressed up and sit in a bar with someone who is at least slightly attractive, and who has never heard your best lines and stories before? If it's a bad date, it's a great story. If it's a good date, then – hell. It's a good date!

Yes, I am still nervous, but I just keep smiling – cool! confident! – and it's always fine. More than fine. Smashing.

Tonight is a new experience in the dating spectrum: a blind date.

It's the brother of a guy Sophie works with. All I know about him is that his name is Jon, he's 29, does something in media, and is apparently 'really quite good-looking'.

Sophie's colleague was whingeing that Jon kept meeting absolute cows and 'he just needs someone nice'. She texted and I thought, why not?

It's Thursday night, and we're meeting in Soho. You'd think, since this is media-land, that Jon would know all the best places to go, but in the few texts that we've exchanged, he's been startlingly ambivalent about venues.

'He's easygoing,' protested Sophie, when I rang her to point this out.

'You say easygoing, I say wishy-washy,' I replied. 'I want someone to take charge so I don't have to decide everything.'

'God, you're turning into a ball-breaker,' she said.

I was thrilled. 'Thank you!'

Ball-breaker is *such* a nice change from always being called nice, dependable, sweet, subdued . . .

We eventually agreed to meet at 9 pm at 22 Below, a cocktail bar in Soho.

I put on my fail-safe date outfit: extremely high black heels, black tights and a short black dress. I add a white jacket, tied with a big, black Obi belt. (Pretty with a monochromatic punch.) Hair down, in case I need to hide behind it. There. I feel slim and tall and confident. And when it comes to dating, that's half the battle already won.

I head downstairs at 8 pm to get myself some crumpets with peanut butter (strong drinks on no dinner is not a good idea for me), and turn on the TV to 'You Belong With Me' by Taylor Swift. I love teen girl-pop. I was quietly obsessed with Avril Lavigne's 'Sk8ter Boi' and 'Girlfriend' for years. (Immature, I know, but Plum loved Justin Bieber so I feel OK about it. Fucknuckle.) I stretch my feet out to the coffee table, admire my heels, and sing along loudly. I know every word.

'That's a fucking naff song,' says a voice behind me. It's Robert.

'Don't care,' I reply.

'Seriously. You're too old to like teen pop.'

'LOVE. LOVE teen pop,' I correct him. 'Right, I'm off. I've got a date.'

I stand up and head to the kitchen to put my plate in the dishwasher. Robert's unpacking a little take-away box from Marine Ices. I know it is spaghetti napoletana without even looking at it, as it's his standard dinner on weeknights.

'You're going to get sick if you don't eat some vegetables soon,' I tell him.

'Thanks, Mum,' he replies. 'Don't think I don't know what you just ate. You are the laziest cook ever.'

'I had vegetable soup and a chicken salad at lunch,' I protest, leaning over to flick his ear with my index finger as I leave the kitchen. 'Anyway I cooked for Peter for years. I'm officially exempt from cooking until, well, until I feel like it again. What are you up to tonight?'

'Not sure yet,' he shrugs. 'I could do with some sleep. Lady Caroline was exhausting last night.'

'So I heard,' I call, as I head out the front door.

It's much easier to make dates for a bit later in the evening, as you can call it quits after an hour at 10 pm and no one's feelings are hurt, I reflect, as my cab pulls in to Great Marlborough Street. Jon told me he'd be outside 22 Below, and made some slightly lame joke about wearing a carnation.

I text Sophie quickly.

*He'd better not have a ponytail or you're dead.*

I pay for the cab and get out, and see a tall, skinny guy. He's in a slightly crumpled suit and satchel, with a nervous expression on his face. Cute, with hair in a sticky-looking quiff.

For a second, nerves overtake me, as they always do, and my heart puckers in apprehension. I'm about to make conversation with a virtual stranger? Easy, Abigail, breathe. It's just a couple of hours. Cool and detached. Elusive and alluring. Bastardette.

Jon walks forward and smiles. 'Uh . . . Abigail?'

'Jon!' I reply, and we both half-giggle at the awkwardness of the whole blind-date situation. He has a very nice smile.

'Thank God it was you, you're the third girl I've asked and the other two thought I was nuts. Shall we get a drink and get this thing started?' he says.

'Sounds like a plan,' I nod. Nice voice, soft Welsh accent.

We walk down to the basement bar, which is small, sexy and very, very red.

'Cool bar,' says Jon.

'It's like being in a blood clot,' I agree.

Jon barks with surprised laughter and, showing a decisiveness missing in his texts, grabs a menu. 'You choose. I'll order.'

I choose quickly. 'Uh, a Russian Rocket, please.' Our eyes meet and he nods, a little grin on his face. He fancies me, I think suddenly. I can tell, I don't know how – the glint in his eye? – but I can. That makes things easier.

'Cocktail aficionado?' he says.

'You can't go wrong with anything with vodka and lemon,' I reply.

'Do you want to—' he gestures towards the bar. Go with him? Why would I want to do that?

'I'm good here,' I smile calmly.

Once seated, I check my phone, more as a look-busy mechanism than anything else. There's a text from Robert.

*Remember, he could be your soulmate!*

Ha. I laugh out loud, and quickly reply.

*Mummy is busy. Be a good boy and hush.*

Jon comes back with our drinks, and we start by talking about the only thing we have in common, i.e. my sister working with his brother. This segues easily into his job, which is in media sales (yep, I have no idea what that is either), and then my job, which I dismiss quickly with, 'If you ever have trouble sleeping, call me and I'll tell you all about my day'. We talk about *Battlestar Galactica*, which both of us loved (Peter insisted on watching it, and I discovered I loved sci-fi); and pork belly, which we agree should always be ordered if it's on the menu, if only to encourage the restaurant to keep offering it; and Playstation and Nintendo Wii, which I have never played (and have no desire to) and which he adores. It's a pretty easy, seamless date, in other words.

'So, is this something you do often? Set-ups?' asks Jon at one point.

'Yes, it's a hobby,' I say airily. 'More of a lifestyle than a hobby, actually.'

Jon laughs. He finds me a lot funnier than I find myself.

'Right, I'm going to the bar,' I say eventually, when our glasses have been empty for several minutes.

'No, no,' he replies quickly. 'It's mine.'

Here are my thoughts: Jon's fine. He's good-looking, and polite, and quite funny, and well, there's nothing *wrong* with him. But I'm pretty sure I can't be bothered to see him again. He's failed a

141

few tests: he hasn't made me laugh much, I feel like I'm carrying the conversation too much, and he didn't suggest the second drink. There's just something a bit passive about him, something that doesn't quite click . . . The big test, of course, is coming. Later.

He returns with the drinks, and I ask him where he's from, and we get into a long conversation about Bristol, where he went to university.

'When I was little, I thought Blame It On The Boogie went "I spent the night in Bristol, at every kind of disco",' I say.

Jon grins. 'There are two kinds of nightclubs in Bristol. The ones that are awful, and the ones that are closed.'

I laugh at this. Perhaps he is funny after all.

'So, what's a nice girl like you doing on a blind date?' he says. 'You must have guys falling – over, um—' his confidence stalls halfway through the sentence.

'I thought it might be fun, I guess,' I say. 'I'm not looking for a relationship. I just broke up with someone. So this is all new to me . . .'

'And is it fun?' he says hopefully.

I can't answer honestly (I'd say 'meh'). So I smile instead. 'It is.'

I get us the next drink, and as we finish, I notice that it's 10.45 pm. I think I'll call it a night. I don't want to ignore my self-imposed midnight date curfew.

'I have to get up at 6 am,' I say apologetically. 'I must take my leave.'

'Oh, that's a shame,' says Jon, looking slightly crestfallen. 'I've had a, er—'

'Best night of your life?' I suggest, standing up to put my jacket on. He stands up to help me, a second too late. 'I thought so. You lucky man.'

He grins again. My cocky-little-madam act works a charm on dates, I think to myself. Men have no idea what to do with it.

'Will you escort me to a cab?' I ask. 'I may need your protection on the dark streets of Soho.'

This is, obviously, a lie, but he says 'Of course!' and escorts me upstairs. I stand back for a second, so Jon can hail an oncoming black cab for me, the way Toby and Robert and other take-charge types always do, but he doesn't move. So I hail it myself. The cab pulls up just as Jon reaches out and takes my hand. I pretend not to notice, and lean in the front window to ask the driver if Primrose Hill is OK. (For some reason we do this in London, as though the driver might say 'Hmm, I don't fancy that direction' and we'd say 'Oh, of course, so sorry to bother you, silly me'.)

The driver nods, and I turn to Jon. His hand is very warm and ever so slightly sticky. I hope that's from cocktail dribble, rather than from not washing it the last time he went to the bathroom.

He clearly wants to kiss me, but his nerve is failing. I smile up at him expectantly. Seconds pass. Nope, nothing. Come on, man, I think to myself. Grow a pair.

'I think you should kiss me now,' I say finally.

Jon grins, his face lighting up with relief, and leans forward. It's a pretty nice kiss, as kisses go. It lasts somewhere between 10 and 12 seconds. He has soft lips and he smells of one of those watery aftershaves.

But there's no spark. No frisson in my body, no racing heart, no excited feeling. And that's the ultimate test.

I lean back and smile at him.

'I'll text you,' he says.

'Look forward to it,' I reply.

I get in and close the door, and take out my phone and call Sophie.

'Negatory,' I say, instead of hello.

'Already? You've decided *already*?'

'He's too passive,' I say. 'And he loves Nintendo Wii more than anything in the world.'

There's silence on the other end of the phone, and then Sophie starts laughing. 'You really have turned into a bastardette,' she says.

'I know!' I say happily.

'I'm not sure it's a good thing.'

'Don't hate the player,' I say, quoting something Robert said the other day. 'Hate the game.'

'Do you think he wants to see you again?'

'Probably,' I say. 'But I told him I wasn't looking for a relationship.'

'Oh God, are you crazy? That's like catnip to men,' Sophie says, laughing.

'Not my problem.'

'Instead of looking for reasons *not* to see him again, why not look for reasons you *should*?'

'Why waste my time?'

'The Nintendo Wii stuff doesn't matter,' she says. 'What matters is that spark. You need to take a risk sometimes . . .'

'But I *am* looking for the spark!' I protest. 'That's why I always kiss them. And there was no chemistry. I could have been shaking his hand, it was so unexciting.'

'That's not what the spark is,' says Sophie. 'The spark is the feeling that you'd rather be talking to him than any other person in the world.' She pauses. 'The kiss is important too. But you could have that kiss chemistry with someone who is totally wrong for you. Remember Brian? Worst boyfriend ever, but his kisses were . . . God, they were awesome.'

'Well, there was no spark or chemistry of any kind,' I say. 'Good to have the blind date experience out of the way though. Cheers for that.'

'You're going to run out of men soon,' she says.

'I bet you a tenner I kiss someone with whom I have a real spark by the end of the year.'

'Deal.'

We hang up. I've just received a text from Robert.

*I'm in the pub. Last orders. Chop chop.*

I grin, and lean forward to redirect the driver.

# Chapter Sixteen

Tonight I'm going to wipe my date slate clean and find some fresh men to play with.

I'm going speed dating.

'Why don't you come?' I say to Robert over breakfast. 'Speed dating! Don't you want to try it? It's run by a workfriend of Plum's. Lots of posh PR girls . . .'

'I did try it,' says Robert. 'More coffee . . . Years ago. When everyone else was trying it. It sucks arse.'

'Well, bully for you,' I say, taking my mug. 'I can't imagine why you're still single, with that attitude.'

'Not single, baby,' he says, smiling lasciviously and stirring honey into his porridge. 'Multiple.'

'You are beastly,' I say sniffily.

'Why are you talking like the lost Mitford sister?' asks Robert.

'I'm rereading *The Pursuit of Love*,' I say, thrilled that he noticed. 'It's utter bliss.'

'Are these chopped almonds on my porridge?'

'Yes,' I say. 'Full of happy fat and very good for you.'

'My digestive tract has been delighted ever since I stopped having a ham and cheese croissant for breakfast,' admits Robert.

'What a shock,' I say, hopping down from my chair. 'Right. Ready to go? I'm just going to clean my teeth again.'

'Cleaning your teeth both before and after breakfast is a little weird, you know,' he shouts after me as I head up the stairs.

'So is having four ladyfriends on the go at once,' I shout back. 'But no one is judging you. Except God.'

Last night's blind date with Jon is long forgotten. It's a crisp November morning, the sun is just coming up as we get on the moped, and London is so new and fresh that I feel like singing. For all that everyone always goes on about summer, and heat, and parks, and ice-cream, London can be a real armpit in August. Dawn in autumn, on the other hand, feels clean, and when the sky is clear and the sun is promising to do its very best to shine, the whole city sparkles.

My I-love-London attitude is helped by the fact that I always get a lift to work with Robert on his moped, rather than taking the tube. (In winter, the London underground becomes a warm, pungent hug of humanity-infused air.) I love the moped, and I've even purchased my very own helmet. It's black. I am thinking about adding little glow-in-the-dark stars. Unless that's childish. In which case I won't. I'm 28 in January, after all.

'You're going to need proper protective weather gear soon,' says Robert, as I zip up my warmest coat.

'You're protective weather gear,' I say with a dazzling smile.

Robert grins to himself and gets on. I prop myself on the back, and off we go. It's chilly, but such a smashing way to get around London. The hours I used to spend waiting for buses and trains! What a waste of time.

I do miss tube flirtations though. (Accidental eye contact, grin to yourself, repeat.) But the moped is an improvement in every other way. I feel very safe sitting behind Robert. And very warm. His body temperature is, I swear, about five degrees warmer than mine at any given time. He's so broad and tall, and I hang on to him like a baby koala all the way to work. With Robert, I'm always sure he knows what he's doing.

We're at Blackfriars in minutes, and Robert nods goodbye and heads towards Liverpool Street. I still don't know what Robert does for a living, you know. He will not discuss it.

146

Today, I have to announce the quarterly figures to the trading floor. This is usually my least favourite part of the job (it's seriously intimidating), but new cool-and-bulletproof me is faking that I LOVE it. And to tell you the truth, whether as a result or by coincidence, I am almost looking forward to it today. So I stride down the corridor, past Suzanne's office, with a spring in my step and sit at my desk for a few minutes.

Then I take the lift up to the trading floor. I read out the above-average results, and say that we expect the stock to go up. I have a little tummy-wobble of nerves just before I start speaking, but apart from that I'm fine. I even finish with a big, beaming smile. Wow. Fake it till you feel it, indeed.

As I walk back to the lifts, a guy bounds ahead of me. He presses the button and turns around, and I see it's the same guy who asked me about whips and bridles all those weeks ago. The jackass. The lift opens and he holds it open for me, grinning broadly. I get in, and still grinning, he steps in next to me.

'Hey,' he says casually. 'Going down? . . . I mean, uh, which floor?'

'Sixth,' I say. 'Thanks.'

'So, I had the craziest night last night,' he says. 'Cuckoo Club till 4 am.'

'Wow,' I say.

'Yep,' he says. 'Uh, great report, by the way. A couple of my clients will be pleased to hear about this. Perhaps we could, uh, meet up—'

'There's a full report on the way,' I say. 'You can read about it.'

Silence.

The lift gets to my floor and I get off without looking at him.

As we walk to our desks I see a very tall, broad-shouldered man coming out of Suzanne's meeting room. He reminds me of Robert from this distance.

'Abigail,' barks Suzanne. I walk over with a ready smile. I quite like standing up next to her, as I'm about nine inches

147

taller than her and she doesn't scare me quite as much. 'This is Andre.'

I turn to smile at him, and he fixes me with a charming grin. 'Nice to meet you.' French. Long eyelashes. Charm oozing from every pore.

'Andre is going to be in the London office a lot over the next few months. He's currently in the Paris office and is heading to China in February.'

'Smashing,' I say, meeting Andre's warm, chocolatey gaze without flinching.

Suzanne continues to talk about the project he's here for, and I concentrate on not breaking eye contact with Andre first. The longer I hold his gaze, the more he's trying not to smile. I wonder if it's unprofessional of me to date you, when you're living here, I think idly to myself. To hell with it, I want to. And I bet you do, too.

'Andre!' barks Suzanne, and Andre is forced to break the stare first, as she introduces him to one of the other managing directors on our floor.

'Shall we luncheon today?' suggests Charlotte as I sit back at my desk. 'And who the devil is that?'

'Yes we shall,' I reply. 'And *that* is Andre.'

It's now been over six weeks since Charlotte broke up with whatever-his-name-was, and she's undergone a dramatic trans-formation. Drab Charlotte is gone. She's highlighted her hair a buttery shade of blonde that makes her skin look luminous rather than washed out, started wearing make-up and heels, and stopped wearing ponchos. As a result she seems to stride and stand out, rather than sit and slouch. See? Singledom. Best thing ever.

It's like having a brand-new workmate. In fact, at Alistair's leaving party a few weeks ago, he told us he'd been asked three times who the new girl was, a fact that made Charlotte and I cackle with glee. Best way to turn a friend into a close friend,

I've discovered, is to have a crisis. Or discover a shared love of *Grease 2*. (We did that, too.)

And the best thing? She smiles and laughs all the time. That's what I didn't understand about her before: she wasn't boring. She was just bored.

'Perhaps I'm in denial,' she said blithely last week, when we went for an after work drink together and accidentally ended up in a dodgy late-night bar near Temple, swapping our newly-single stories. 'But life really seems better without him. I'd rather be single than in an unfulfilling relationship.'

'I'll drink to that,' I said, raising my glass to hers.

'Have you spoken to Alistair?' she asks.

'No,' I say quickly. 'I'm sure it's crazy over there.'

Charlotte doesn't know that at Alistair's leaving party, at a typical City wine bar under the nose of our entire floor of colleagues, he made a play for me. An enormous, fumblingly drunken play, that consisted of flirty smiles and meaningful eye contact (7 pm to 8 pm), questions shouted at me over whoever else I was talking to (8 pm to 9 pm), and attempts to hold my hand and grope my waist when I was waiting for drinks at the bar (9.05 pm to 9.15 pm). Then I stormed furiously to the bathrooms to calm down rather than shout at him in front of everyone.

And he followed me. Right into the bathroom.

'What is this, fucking *Top Gun*?' I snapped. 'Get out.'

'Oh Abigail, I like you, so much, I want – I want to – you, with . . .' he said, suddenly looking very young and vulnerable.

'No,' I said firmly. 'You don't.'

'You don't even know what I'm about to ask!' he said, then looked around and started laughing. 'Tampon machine!'

'It doesn't matter,' I said. 'The answer is no.' I walked out, leaving him shouting my name in the bathroom and haven't seen him since. He emailed me a couple of days later, saying sorry and asking me out for a drink, but I haven't replied. I think it's the best way.

Sophie and Plum think that was too brutal, considering he was a friend – I believe Plum's term was 'fucking harsh' – and I'm sure Charlotte would not approve of my behaviour either. But it made sense to cut him off before he went any further, right? Am I fucking harsh? Or am I just taking cool and detached to the next, logical level?

Perhaps most girls are just too nice. Perhaps we get dumped because we date guys who just aren't right in the first place. For example, if I'd been properly brutal about Adam The Tick Boxer, I would have dumped him because he said he played Doom for 10 to 12 hours every weekend, which is – let's face it – weird. Instead I ignored that, went out with him, got a bit emotionally attached and then, well, you know. Boom.

'I've decided I'm ready,' Charlotte says over lunch. 'To start dating. A new boyfriend might be nice.'

'Yay,' I say, holding up my bottle of water to clink with hers. 'Though wanting to date and wanting a boyfriend are completely different things. In my mind, anyway.'

'Then . . . why are you dating?' says Charlotte reasonably.

'It's fun,' I shrug. 'And I'm making up for lost time . . . But I'm not getting carried away with some asshat like Adam The Tick Boxer again.'

Charlotte nods sympathetically.

'That was a mini-disaster. I really fucked up,' I add.

'You did not fuck it up! You liked him,' she exclaims. 'There's nothing wrong with that. Don't be cynical. You need to keep a positive mental attitude.'

'This is a positive mental attitude,' I say. 'I can have fun and date without actually getting emotionally involved.'

'OK,' says Charlotte doubtfully. 'If you say so.'

'One day I might find someone . . . perfect,' I pause, thinking about my fruitless search for a spark, and the someday-I'll-fall-in-love-and-find-a-soulmate thought that Robert told me to ignore. 'Until then, I'm having fun and staying in control.'

Charlotte laughs. 'I don't think I can be as . . . strong as you.'

'I don't think I'm that strong,' I say, surprised. No one's ever called me strong. 'I just try to ignore my brain when it tells me I'm a bit shit. Robert told me to fake being bulletproof until I felt it, and that worked . . . Hey, what are you doing tonight?'

Charlotte shrugs. 'Nothing. All my friends are in relationships, so Friday is usually quiet . . .'

'Friday! Quiet!' I am appalled. 'Come to this speed dating thing with me.'

'Are you sure?' says Charlotte.

I nod my head firmly. 'Definitely. Without question. Plum just forwarded an email saying they were still short of girls – there's too many men! So you really should come.'

Charlotte bites her lip. 'Well . . . alright.'

# Chapter Seventeen

The speed dating tonight is being held at a Bloomsbury pub called The Perseverance, which is a singularly appropriate name for a speed dating venue.

The attendees include Plum, me, Henry and now Charlotte. We're meeting at The Lamb, a Victorian pub with the original, frosted-glass 'snob screens' so you can order a drink without people in different parts of the bar seeing your face.

I hope everyone's on good form tonight. Plum had four seemingly perfect dates with Dan, but he went to Atlanta for a work conference three weeks ago and she hasn't heard from him since. She seems to have borne the disappointment surprisingly stoically so far, i.e. she's not talking about it.

'*Bonsoir*,' I say breezily as we finally locate Plum on a table at the back. Henry's at the bar, getting drinks. I introduce Plum to Charlotte, and Henry returns with a bottle of champagne and four glasses. He's wearing his glasses, something he never does on Saturdays and Sundays when I usually see him, and a suit.

'Looking sharp, Henry! Champagne! What's the occasion?' I exclaim, kissing him hello.

'I got a promotion today,' he says. Henry works for an IT company, and from what I can understand, he is in 'logistics'. Which seems to mean Sorting Shit Out.

'Yay!' We all chorus our congratulations and ask for details that we don't understand. Henry pours the champagne and we toast to his promotion.

'By the way, Henry, this is Charlotte,' I say. I can tell by the slightly shy way Henry smiles at her that he thinks she's cute.

'Right then. I need tips from experienced speed daters,' I say. 'Plum, that's you.'

'My tip is to drink a lot beforehand,' says Plum. She's quite tense tonight. 'Because it will be fucking excruciating.'

'That's not very helpful,' I say, seeing Charlotte's face fall.

'I am going to ask "would you rather" questions,' says Henry. 'Like, would you rather smell like a goat for a year or shave your entire body, including eyebrows? Would you rather be a fairy or a mermaid? Would you rather eat steak or chicken if you had to eat one of them, at every meal, forever?'

'Shave, fairy, steak,' I say automatically.

'No! Goat, mermaid, steak!' shout Henry and Charlotte in unison, and then glance at each other with delight.

'I'm a mermaid, can I sing underwater like Ariel?' asks Plum.

Henry doesn't reply, because he's grinning at Charlotte now. 'No one ever says goat!'

'I would hate to draw on my eyebrows every day,' Charlotte explains matter-of-factly. 'And if I'm a mermaid, well, I'll be swimming most of the time anyway, so if I smell goaty, it won't matter.'

'Exactly!' says Henry.

'I may have to borrow the "would you rather" icebreaker, Henry,' I say. 'Good technique.'

'What techniques does your esteemed bastard mentor recommend?' says Plum.

'Robert? I forgot to ask him,' I say glibly. 'I must have graduated from his School O'Lurve.'

'Clearly,' says Plum, leaning back in her chair and pulling up one ankle to rest on her other knee.

'Why are you wearing flats?' I'm shocked. Plum's wearing

153

ballet shoes with very pre-loved jeans, a tank top and a blazer. She doesn't look bad, exactly, just as though she's made absolutely no effort at all. Very unlike her.

'Because I don't want to be crippled by walking on fucking tippytoes all night?' she replies.

'You always say wearing flat shoes on a Friday night is a sign of depression,' I say.

Plum raises an eyebrow and doesn't reply for a few seconds. 'You look good, by the way.'

She says it without much enthusiasm but I flush with delight. I'm wearing a very crisp white shirt over tight jeans, with my white wrappy coat on top, and my favourite green heels. I did think that I was channelling Pretty With A Punch, but it's nice to have it confirmed.

'I can't believe you roped me into this,' sighs Henry. 'The rugby boys can never find out, OK? Never.'

'Shall we make up pseudonyms tonight?' suggests Charlotte. 'It might help nerves. I'll be Cherry. Cherry Buns.'

'I'll be your brother,' says Henry, grinning. 'Honey Buns.'

'I'll be Chastity Rocks,' I say.

'Chastity! As if,' says Plum, grinning at me as if it's a hilarious thing to say. That's a bit harsh. I've only done the wild thing with Skinny Jeans since I became single, and she knows that, and anyway, who is she to judge? 'I'll be Debbie,' she says, adding, 'I've always wanted to be called Debbie. Debbie Dateless. Or, ooh, I know – Debbie Desperate.'

She grins gleefully at me. She knows how much I hate that word. *Desperate.*

'Do you have any lip gloss?' says Charlotte, cleverly knowing that the best way to diffuse tension with girls is to discuss something shallow.

'I have MAC Big Baby,' I say, taking out my make-up bag.

'I have MAC Nymphette, Pink Poodle, and Prrr,' says Plum, taking them out of her bag and fanning them out in her hands.

'I could write a thesis on the anti-feminism and female infantilisation of MAC lip gloss names,' I say thoughtfully. 'But they're really good lip glosses.'

'I love MAC,' agrees Charlotte. 'I also have one by Chanel, called Glossimer—'

'That's a fucking amazing lip gloss!' exclaims Plum. Charlotte looks delighted to have had the approval of someone who clearly considers herself a style maven. 'I also use this one from Rimmel, called—'

'Vinyl?' suggests Charlotte excitedly. 'I love that stuff! My friend Janey lives in Tokyo, and has trouble getting hold of it, so I have to bulk buy them for her . . .'

'I really need to hang out with guys more,' says Henry flatly. 'Seriously. You're killing me.'

'Does anyone have a tampon?' says Plum by way of response.

'Where's your flatmate?' Henry asks me. 'Why isn't he here? He'd clean up at a night like this . . .'

'Robert hates speed dating. You have a boycrush on him, don't you?' I say. Henry talks about Robert with a sort of reverence. We all went out recently for drinks, and they ended the night with a pair of Swedish twins, eating falafels in Maroush. Robert went home with one of them. Henry didn't go home with the other. But it was still one of the best nights of his life.

'No,' says Henry defensively. 'I just wish he was here to balance things out.'

'Henry's got a bromance,' says Plum.

My phone beeps. It's a text.

*Great time last night. Would absolutely love to do it again. What about Sunday lunch? Jon.*

'Oh, it's blind date guy,' I say. '*Sayonara*, big guy.' Delete, ignore, continue.

'Fucking hell,' says Plum under her breath.

'Right, let's go,' says Henry, getting up. Charlotte quickly follows him and they start chatting on the way out the door.

155

As Plum and I walk out of the pub, I sigh happily. After two glasses of champagne, I feel ready for whatever this speed dating night has in store for me. I may be the last single girl in London to try it, but by God, I'm going to give it my best shot.

'Try not to hog all the fucking men tonight, alright, Abigail?' says Plum, as we reach the street.

I instantly realise what her problem is: she thinks I'm taking male attention away from her.

It crosses my mind to say that describing herself as Debbie Desperate and/or Dateless isn't the most attractive thing in the world, and maybe that attitude is why she's not getting as much dating action as she'd like, but I'm a firm believer in not kicking someone when they're down. Even if she's being – frankly – a bit of a cow. So I just ignore her and keep walking.

Charlotte and Henry are striding ahead, chatting away flirtily.

'Looks like Charlotte and Henry are getting along,' I say happily.

'Why'd you have to bring the extra competition?' says Plum crossly.

That's it. Fuck firm beliefs.

I stop walking and turn to her. 'Plum, what the hell is wrong with you tonight?'

'Nothing,' she says defensively.

'Then why are you acting like this?' I say. 'You don't need to take out your bad mood on me. You're ruining the night.'

Plum starts scrabbling in her bag, and I notice the tears streaming down her face.

'I'm sorry,' I say immediately. Fucking hell, I didn't expect her to explode with misery. 'Plum, please, don't cry, it's fine . . .'

'It is *not* fucking fine,' she says, through sobs. 'I can't face tonight, I c-c-c-can't take the rejection. Dan was the last straw, I really thought it was different, I really, *really* fucking liked him and he's disappeared like the rest of them. I have nothing left. I am toxic with singledom.'

'Oh, Plum,' I say, putting my arm around her. The others are still walking ahead of us to The Perseverance, oblivious to what's going on. 'Can't you just . . . detach from it all? Just have fun? Just fake it?'

'No I fucking can't,' she snaps furiously, pushing my arm away. 'Stop giving me Robert's advice. Everything is so easy for you. You break up and boom, you're on dates all the time. You don't even want them to text, and they still do. It's *so* unfair.'

'I am *not* on dates "all the time",' I exclaim. 'And it's not like any of them are any good . . . Fucking hell, Plum, being single is a novelty for me, of course I'm going to enjoy it.'

Plum makes a sarcastic snorty-huff sound.

'None of them are amazing or even that interesting. I can't even *imagine* ever falling in love again, I'm just trying to enjoy myself . . . And just so you know, everything is *not* easy for me,' I add. That particularly upset me. She knows how hard I fight to keep my nerves under control.

'It looks easy,' she says glumly, holding a tissue gently under each eye to dry her tears without ruining her makeup.

'Well, that's your perception,' I reply. 'Try to think of it from my perspective. I'm just trying to, I don't know, do my best. You'll find a good guy. Both of us will. One day.'

'I know,' she says chokingly. 'I'm sorry . . . It's just . . . it's so hard.'

I sigh. There's nothing I can say to change how she feels about that. Too many shit things have happened for her to be happy right now. It's almost scary: when someone as cool and confident as Plum can't handle singledom, what hope is there for me? No, I'll be fine. I have Robert to help me. Plum just needs a Robert, but I don't think she wants to hear that right now.

'Shall we have a *Good Will Hunting* moment, where I tell you over and over again that it's not your fault?'

Plum smiles, sighs, and shakes her head. 'No. You know, I thought Dan was a good guy. Maybe there are no good guys left.'

'Come along tonight and have some fun,' I say. I take her bag, take out her cigarettes, put one in her mouth and light it for her. 'Let's see what's out there.'

'Let me save you the bother,' she says, exhaling smoke dramatically. 'Nothing, and no one, is out there. I don't even know why I suggested fucking speed dating. I give up. Do you hear me, universe?' She shouts. 'I give up!'

At that moment, her phone rings.

She locates it in the side pocket of her bag, and looks at the screen.

'No fucking way . . .' she says quietly, and presses the answer button. '. . . Hello?'

There's a pause, and I see her eyes scanning space as she listens. 'Yes, oh, oh, hi,' she says, and quickly covers the phone while she wipes her nose and clears her throat. 'I'm marvellous, thanks, Dan. How are you?'

Dan! Her good guy! From the nightclub! Who hasn't called in weeks!

'It did? . . . You did?' she pauses, and smiles. 'Really? What a nightmare.' Seeing Plum grinning is one of the nicest things I've seen in days. Like cold feet in a hot bath, my worry slowly eases. She mouths that she'll catch up, and I nod and skip to where Henry and Charlotte have stopped to wait for us.

'Sorry,' I say.

'Everything alright, Abigay?' asks Henry.

'Smashing,' I nod. 'She'll just be a second.'

Plum runs up to us, buzzing with happiness. 'Dan's suitcase was lost on the way to Atlanta! And his phone was inside it as he'd changed jackets at the last minute! And he was emailing Rich, trying to get in touch with me! But Rich wasn't responding cos he's got a new job in Hong fucking Kong! And then he tried to find me on Facebook but my privacy levels were too high! So Dan finally got back to London yesterday and just got his suitcase back today and the first thing he did was call me! He said he was sitting on the floor of his flat because he had to charge it at the same time because the battery was dead! I'm seeing him tomorrow!'

We all start cheering and high-fiving, even Charlotte, who seems pretty confused by the whole story but just rolls with it. By the time we reach The Perseverance, I am feeling uber-confident and ready to go. I am going to make this speed dating night my bitch. We walk in, and I look towards the bar.

And then I see Josh From HR.

And Skinny Jeans guy.

And Peter's brother, Joe.

Shit.

# Chapter Eighteen

'Fuckety fuck, fuck, fuck it,' I say. I'm saying it to no one, because the minute I clocked the three of them, I ran straight for the bathrooms. Now I'm locked in a cubicle, having what I suppose is a very mild version of a panic attack: I'm looking at my shoes and saying 'fuck' a lot.

What do I do now? I have to leave, right? I cannot brazen my way out of this, no matter how detached and cool I pretend to be. I'll text Plum and ask her to come in here, perhaps we can fashion a burkha of some kind out of her scarf, and I can escape without them seeing me—

'Abigail?' says a voice. It's Plum. 'Why did you just do a pirouette and leap for the ladies?'

I open the toilet door and walk out just as Charlotte bursts into the bathroom.

'What's going on?' she says. 'You left me with Henry!' she stops short. 'Not that I mind . . .'

'I have to leave,' I say, fighting the urge to laugh hysterically. 'The dweeb is here and the guy that I, you know, was a drunken slutty nightmare with, and Peter's brother, Joe, who hates me and called me a selfish bitch. What are the odds? I can't possibly stay and sit face-to-face with them for three minutes each!'

'You can't leave!' they say in unison.

'I need you here,' says Plum. 'And if you leave, you'll fuck up the guys-to-girls ratio.'

'I only came because of you!' says Charlotte nervously.

Fuck. It's true, I really can't leave Charlotte since I invited her. Plum was practically hysterical on the street just now, I mean, she seems stable since Dan rang but God knows what might happen if something went wrong. And it really would be difficult to hold a speed dating night with too many guys.

'Oh God, I'm having a hot flush from nerves, this may have brought on The Change,' I say, leaning over the sink and running my wrists under the cold water.

'I find it unlikely that you're going through menopause at 27,' retorts Plum.

'When were you a drunken slutty nightmare, by the way?' says Charlotte. Ah yes, I pretended I was sick. Oh well, we're friends now. I give her a quick rundown on the Skinny Jeans date, and she laughs so hard I think she might be ill.

Then we're all silent for a second. 'There's what, seven million people in London? What are the odds?'

'I thought it was eight million,' says Charlotte.

'Whatever,' I say. 'I need some thinking time. What time is it starting? We're just butterflying now, right?'

'We're supposed to go to the private room upstairs by 9 pm,' says Plum, glancing at her phone. 'You have half an hour.'

'I'll tell Henry what's going on,' says Charlotte, dashing back out. 'He'll be worried.'

'I'll get us some drinks,' says Plum. 'Then we can figure out what to do.'

And I'm alone again. I feel sick, like I've been caught doing something I shouldn't . . . I never responded to any of the texts from Josh From HR or Skinny Jeans. Perhaps this is my comeuppance for being so arrogant. Karma is a bitch. Should I say I lost my phone? Or that I just never got their texts? Perhaps I could pretend to have amnesia. Like Guy Pearce in *Memento*.

Fuck it, I'm calling Robert.

'Why are my spidey senses telling me that you need advice?' he says, instead of hello.

'Total fucking meltdown. Can you talk?'

'I learned to talk when I was a year old, but I was advanced for my age. What's up?'

'I'm at speed dating, you know, and Skinny Jeans the one night stand guy is here, and Josh From HR, remember that bad date at the Albannach? And Peter's brother Joe who hates me, and called me a stupid bitch, and I'm going to have to talk to them all for three minutes each, and I can't leave or the girls will kill me.'

There's a pause.

'You'd better not be laughing!' I say.

'Sorry,' he says. I can tell by his voice that he's smiling. 'Why is it echoing?'

'I'm hiding in the, uh, euphemism.'

'Right . . . So, who cares? Three minutes. You can do anything for three minutes.'

'No! I need help!' I am overreacting, but I can't help it. 'Joe was so horrible to me the last time I saw him, and I couldn't even say anything back, I just clammed up and ran away and cried. And last time I saw Skinny Jeans guy, he was passed out in bed and I was crawling around his room looking for my knickers. I will die of mortification when I have to face him.'

'If you die, text me.'

'I don't think that the state of deadness – or the speed dating environment, for that matter – is conducive to texting.'

'Drinks!' says Plum, bursting back in with two very large vodkas. 'Is that Robert? Hi, Robert!'

'Is that Plum?' he says. 'Christ, she's cheerful.'

'I'm putting you on speaker,' I say, and press loudspeaker. 'Robert is my scriptwriter.'

'Right then. To the Josh guy, you say that you lost your phone,' he says, his voice sounding all tinny over the loudspeaker.

'Roger that,' I nod. 'But he might ask me out again.'

'Then say that you're, God, I don't know . . . working through a few issues with a recent break-up,' he says.

'So she's allegedly working through break-up issues by going to a speed dating night?' says Plum dubiously.

There's a pause. Plum and I stare hopefully at my mobile.

Robert clears his throat. 'Let's move on. Skinny Jeans. Just act like you're mildly amused to see him again.'

'That's no help!' I exclaim. 'I need a script, Robert. What if he asks me why I left before he woke up? Or why I ignored his texts? I'm too embarrassed to tell him that I was too embarrassed.'

'What?' Robert starts laughing again. 'Why do you care what he thinks?'

'And what if Joe picks a fight again? I'm not good with people being mean! What if – I mean, what if—'

'I can't script non-specific "what if" situations, Abigail,' says Robert. 'You can handle this. Come on. Be a man. Pull yourself together.'

'I've got an idea!' exclaims Plum. 'My earpiece. The Bluetooth thing on my phone. We can arrange your hair to hide it, and Robert can call my phone and listen in and suggest things to say.'

I gaze at Plum for a second. It's the perfect solution.

'Yes! Awesome idea!' I say. Plum starts high-fiving me and jumping gleefully around the bathroom. I turn back to the phone. 'Robert! Will you do it?'

'Um . . . OK,' says Robert slowly. 'Can you really hide it, though? And I need to be able to hear what he's saying, too.'

Plum brandishes a hairclip. 'Side part, so all your hair is over your ear. Voilà.'

'Got it,' I say. 'In that case I need another double vodka, please. My shout. Take my card. You know my pincode. Robert, I will call you back in a few minutes.'

'Roger that,' says Plum, and runs out of the bathroom. I get my make-up out of my bag and start reapplying. I need more warpaint for this battle.

Twenty minutes later, my hair is now in a (rather becoming, actually) bouffy side-swooped ponytail, entirely covering my right ear. Plum's phone earpiece is tucked safely behind said side-swoop, and Robert is sitting on the couch at home with a bottle of wine, his voice beaming into my ear via the magic of Bluetooth. Or wireless. Or whatever it is.

'*Can you hear me? Testing, testing.*'

'Affirmative,' I say into the bathroom mirror.

'You can't see a thing,' says Plum admiringly. 'God, I am brilliant.'

She's bursting with sunny positivity. What a difference a date makes. I also notice that she's backcombed her hair and done a sex-kitten-swish with her eye make-up.

'Miaow,' I say.

'I know,' she beams. 'I'm seeing Dan tomorrow. But the admiring male gaze is good for the soul.'

'Amen to that, sister,' I say, and we clink glasses. 'Robert, can you hear us talking?'

'*Loud and clear,*' says Robert. '*And heavy on the oestrogen.*'

'OK,' I say. My nerves have solidified into a tiny fist in the pit of my stomach. I can handle anything tonight throws at me . . . with Robert's help.

'Robert, thank you so much for doing this,' I say. 'I mean really. I owe you.'

'*Add it to my tab,*' says the little Robert voice in my ear.

'OK, team,' I say, as a bell rings outside. 'Let's go.'

We walk outside and upstairs to a private room, where Charlotte, Henry and the rest of the speed-daters have already congregated. Forty of London's young singles, all in the one room. I can practically smell the hormones.

Keeping my head down, I take a seat at a table for two with a bottle of wine and two glasses. How thoughtful to provide a conversational lubricant, I think, pouring myself an extremely large glass, drinking half of it and then refilling it. There's also a pencil and a sheet of paper with 20 numbered lines on. I'm supposed to make notes? Fuck that.

A girl at the front is calling out instructions to people, but I'm having trouble paying attention. I look around and see Charlotte and Plum at their own little tables, and give them little thumbs up and nods. The rest of the speed daters are all in different stages of nervousness and excitement. I can't see any particularly good-looking guys, by the way. Which is good: the next hour is about surviving, not flirting.

'You OK, Abby, darling?' says Robert.

'Smashing!' I exclaim brightly, scaring a guy walking past who thinks I'm talking to him. 'Sorry, sorry!' If I'm not careful, I'm going to look absolutely cuckoo. Thinking this, I say 'cuckoo!' aloud, and I hear Robert laughing.

'Hi, I'm Christopher,' says a shaven-headed man in a suit, shaking my hand. 'I think I'm your first victim.'

'Tell him you'll take it easy on him, but you like to draw first blood,' says Robert. I crack up and Christopher looks at me oddly.

'If you find that amusing, we're going to have a great time.' he says.

I raise an eyebrow at him. Two can play the arrogance card, my friend.

Then a bell rings again, and the speed date has officially started.

'So, what brings you here tonight, Christopher?' I say.

'I'm a journalist. I'm reviewing this for *Time Out*,' he says.

'*He's lying*,' says Robert in my ear. '*He's trying to look cool.*'

'Really,' I say. 'Do you work with Kristina O'Shaunnessy?'

'Yeah, I think she's on another floor,' he says smoothly. He is lying. I totally made that name up.

'Do you live, um, in London?' I say.

'*Oh God, I'm so bored already*,' says Robert.

165

'Shut up,' I say. Christopher looks at me oddly. 'I mean . . . don't shut up! Talk! Talk!'

Robert starts laughing in my ear and I'm having trouble holding it together. The rest of the speed date is a complete catastrophe, as all I can hear in one ear is Robert laughing, and Christopher, clearly thinking I'm mad, in the other.

Then the bell rings again. Christopher can't wait to get away.

'Listen, dammit, I need you to be serious,' I whisper fiercely. 'I'll be sectioned if it continues like this.'

'*Sorry,*' Robert says. '*OK, OK, I will be serious now.*'

Then the bell rings again, and I look up, and it's Josh From HR.

'Abigail,' he says awkwardly, sitting down.

'Josh!' I say loudly.

'*Who?*'

'From HR,' I add quickly.

'*Got it.*'

'How've you been? What have you been up to?' I gabble. Ah, job interview mode. We meet again.

'Great,' he says, and pauses. 'Look, I don't want to make this awkward . . .' he trails off, clearly trying to think of how to ask me why I ignored him. I clear my throat, hoping Robert will take that as a cue to talk. He does.

'*I've been meaning to text you,*' says Robert.

'I've been meaning to text you,' I say.

'*I just think I'm not ready. Uh, to date. I was in a very serious relationship and meeting someone straight away wasn't part of the plan.*'

'I just think I'm not ready to date. I was in a very serious relationship and meeting someone straight away wasn't part of the plan.'

'I totally get it,' says Josh. 'And actually, I wanted to ask you about the girl I just met. I think she's a friend of yours. Plum? . . . She's amazing! Tell me everything about her!'

Robert starts laughing again.

'Plum!' I say brightly, trying to ignore Robert. 'Of course. She's one of my best friends. What do you want to know?'

'Where does she live? I want to meet someone who's also south of the river,' he says.

The rest of the three minutes is filled by telling Josh all about Plum. Hopefully she won't get annoyed.

By the time Josh leaves, I'm sweating lightly.

'Thanks for nothing,' I hiss into my earpiece.

'*And you thought it was going to be all about you. Serves you right for being arrogant.*'

'I thought arrogance was good.'

'*Only if it's funny.*'

The next dates are easier: perfectly nice guys, none of them particularly interesting, funny or good-looking. I'm not feeling with it enough to apply myself to the task of conversing, so each speed date drifts pointlessly through predictable questions and answers. All of them probably think I'm strange, as I keep grinning when Robert makes little comments about them into my ear.

'I'm an entrepreneur,' says one.

'*Pimp,*' says Robert.

'I love travelling,' says another.

'*Sex tourist.*'

'Have you been to Canada?' says the smoothest of the bunch.

'*Serial killer.*'

And then Skinny Jeans sits down.

'Abigail,' he says. 'I thought it was you.'

'Hi!' I say loudly. 'Mark!'

'*Who?*' says Robert. Fuck, he doesn't know his real name. Why do I give everyone stupid nicknames?

'I almost don't recognise you out of your SKINNY JEANS,' I enunciate carefully. He's wearing grey flannel trousers and a pink T-Shirt with leather Converses. He speaks clothes exceptionally confidently for a straight man. I wonder if he'd take me shopping.

167

'*Oh, right. Got it.*'

'That's odd,' says Skinny Jeans. 'Since I was wearing nothing at all when you left my room without saying goodbye . . . let's see, seven weeks ago?'

'Um, yes. Well, you know . . .' I trail off. Come on, Robert, I think desperately.

'*I'm sorry, were you planning on making me breakfast in bed?*' says Robert. Yes! Make a joke!

'I'm sorry, were you planning on making me breakfast in bed?' I say.

Skinny Jeans grins.

'*Scrambled eggs? Toast? On a little tray?*'

'Scrambled eggs? Toast? On a little tray with a rose on it?' I say.

'*Don't fuck with my script*,' says Robert, which makes me grin slightly more broadly.

'Find yourself hilarious, huh?' says Skinny Jeans.

'I'm a great audience,' I reply, without thinking.

'*Cute line*,' says Robert.

'Well, whatever . . .' says Skinny Jeans. 'I had a good time anyway. I was just . . . surprised not to hear from you.'

'*I'm sure you got over it*,' says Robert.

'I'm sure you got over it,' I say, in a slightly teasing tone.

'I don't know why I expected a girl like you to want to see me again, anyway,' says Skinny Jeans, half to himself.

'What does that mean? A girl like me?'

'Cocky. Funny. Hot,' he says.

I start laughing. 'I was *so* nervous on our date . . .'

He raises an eyebrow. 'You *were*?'

'*Don't talk about feelings . . . talk about booze*,' instructs Robert.

'Have some more wine,' I say. I fill up his glass as slowly as I can, and then mine. How long can three minutes possibly last?

'Do you remember rubbing the fat guy's tummy for luck? Holy shit, that was hilarious.'

'Uh, yeah,' I say. I do remember it, kind of.

'And singing all the words to *Smokey Joe's Cafe* in that kebab shop on Portobello Road? And getting everyone in the shop to join in?'

'Erm, yeah, that was smashing.' Nope, don't remember that at all.

'*You are one classy lady.*'

'It was one of the best nights I've had in a long time,' says Skinny Jeans.

'Yeah . . .' I say doubtfully. 'What are you doing here, anyway? You don't strike me as the speed dating type.'

'I lost a bet with Alfie,' he says. 'You met him at The Cow that day . . .?' Waistcoat Guy, I think, nodding. 'I said to him that if you didn't text me back then I'd try speed dating, because I'm officially the worst single man in London.'

'You're not!' I say. 'I mean, it wasn't a bad date. I was just . . .'

'*Don't say you were drunk! It's the biggest post-sex insult ever.*'

'. . . drunk, I mean drinking, a bit more than I ought, and I was, uh, cringing at the thought that I'd been a nightmare date.'

'No. You were great,' says Mark/Skinny Jeans.

'*Actually, the biggest post-sex insult is "we did?"*' says Robert. '*But that's another story.*'

I laugh out loud and quickly turn it into a girlish giggle and try to focus on Skinny Jeans. 'Well, anyway. It's nice to see you now.'

'You too,' he says. 'Any chance of a second date?'

'*This is a second date,*' says Robert.

'This is a second date,' I say. Good time-buying, I think.

'Then . . . a third?' he says.

'*Sounds like fun. Have your people call my people.*'

'Sounds like fun,' I repeat. 'Have your people call my people.'

'I get it,' says Skinny Jeans, laughing to himself as the bell rings again. 'You are one tough customer.'

I'm so not, I think, but I grin at him and take a long slug of my wine. Thank God that's over.

'Thank you,' I whisper into my earpiece.

'*Pleasure*,' Robert replies.

Next I have to sit opposite Henry. He interrogates me about Charlotte and Robert starts giving Henry advice through me. After that, the rest of the dates are pretty easy. Robert is mostly quiet – in fact, for a moment I think he's dropped off to sleep until he sneezes very loudly and I squawk in surprise, scaring the guy opposite me half to death.

'*Anyone worth a date?*' says Robert as I finish date 18 – or is it 19? – pour myself another glass of wine and sit back with a happy sigh. This is easy!

'No,' I mutter. 'I need to get out of here, soon. Let's get drunk.'

'Abigail,' says a deep voice, and I look up to see Joe, Peter's brother, walking towards me. Fuck.

'Joe . . . hi,' I say, all thoughts of Robert forgotten.

'I'm just coming over to tell you that I'm not going to sit opposite you for three minutes, so you're saved,' he says.

'Fine,' I say.

'*What an asshat*,' says Robert in my ear.

Joe nods and gives me a look of utter disdain.

'I didn't do anything wrong, you know,' I say involuntarily.

'*What?*' says Robert.

'What?' says Joe.

'I didn't do anything wrong. With Peter. I broke up with him, but I didn't hurt him and he's fine, he's totally fine, right?' I stammer hopefully.

'I'm not telling you how my brother has been since you walked out on him, without so much as a backward glance,' he says, every word dripping with contempt. 'But I want you to know something. He had an affair. Two years ago. With a girl he worked with. He ended it because he couldn't bear the thought of hurting a girl like you, even though he loved her. And she's with him in Thailand now.'

'*Fuck off*,' says Robert.

'Fuck off,' I repeat, and immediately clap my hand over my

mouth. I didn't mean to repeat that, it just came straight out because I was too shocked to process what I was saying. I stand up, my eyes filling with tears. Peter had an affair. And Joe hates me enough to tell me.

'I, uh, I, uh, I'm going d-d-downstairs,' I stammer, picking up my bag and wine and hurrying past Joe.

'See ya,' he says.

I stumble down the stairs, trying to stop the tears that are welling up in my eyes.

'*Abby? Are you OK? Abby? Say something . . . Do you want me to come down there and punch that guy?*'

'I'm fine, I'm fine,' I say, stalking through the bar to the front door, ripping out the earpiece as I go. 'I'm hanging up. I'm having a fag.'

'*But you don't smoke—*' says Robert, as I pull the earpiece out. Peter had an affair. At the same time that I was trying to ignore the fact that I felt like something wasn't right, like the relationship was missing something, but thinking that I should do my best and keep trying and above all not hurt him because I was responsible for his happiness, he was banging someone else on the side. How stupid I must be. When I broke up with him he looked at me with his sweet, sad face and said 'I'll always love you, no matter what. Even if we're not together.' God, he must have thought I was so gullible. Just think! All that worry and uncertainty, the guilt about leaving a man who I thought was so fundamentally good and decent . . . who cheated on me. And Joe thinks I should feel bad because he didn't want to hurt me? Why not just leave me?

What a fucking liar.

Maybe Plum was right. There are no good men. Only different degrees of bad ones.

I only smoke when I'm stressed and I am really, definitely stressed now. With trembling hands I put the coins into the cigarette machine, beg a lighter off the bartender, tear open the pack and am outside lighting up within 60 seconds.

Just as I exhale, and take a huge slug of wine, my own phone rings. It's Robert again.

'Abby, are you OK?' says Robert, when I finally answer.

'Yes,' I say, my voice high and quivery.

'Are you crying?'

'No,' I lie, as another tear escapes out the corner of my eye. 'I'm just, I don't know, in shock. Joe has a nasty vindictive streak . . . And he never liked me. Peter took me on a family skiing holiday the first year we were together and Joe hated it . . .' I take a shaky drag. 'Can you believe Peter had an affair?'

'No,' says Robert. 'He's clearly an asshat, too. And Joe probably fancied you.'

'Yeah,' I say, laughing and blotting tears with a tissue. 'I wonder who she is?'

I suddenly remember a girl in his team at work, a sporty type I always thought was odd; she stared at me a lot but never started any conversations. I mentioned to Peter, after his work Christmas drinks one year, that I thought she was weird. He jumped to her defence, saying that she was just very shy. 'I know who it is,' I say now. 'I mean, I know who she is. I'm sure it's her.'

'I wouldn't waste any time thinking about it,' says Robert.

'I wonder how long it went on for,' I say. 'And how it started. And it ended. And how often he lied to me . . .'

'Abby, darling, you'll never get the answers you want,' says Robert. 'It will just torture you. You left him. You ended it, you walked away and you were loyal while you were with him.'

'Yes,' I say uncertainly.

'So forget about it. Otherwise it will drive you crazy. Trust me,' says Robert. I suddenly think about him and Louisa, and how the man she'd cheated on him with is now her husband.

'What an asshat,' I say.

'Yes,' says Robert. 'He is.'

There's a pause. Actually, I meant Louisa, I want to say, but don't.

'Thanks for calling back,' I say.

'Anytime.'

'And helping me survive tonight. I feel like you're my therapist sometimes.'

'That's what friends are for.'

'Actually, that's what *best* friends are for. You just got a promotion.'

'Lucky me. And you didn't even need me. Not really. You could have handled all of that on your own.'

'Yeah, but our way was fun.'

There is silence for a few minutes. I take another sip of wine and hear Robert taking another sip of his. It's oddly comforting.

'I told you speed dating sucked,' he says finally, and I start laughing despite myself. Fuck Peter. I am bulletproof.

'Are you OK? What the hell happened with Joe? Let's get out of here!' exclaims Plum, bursting out of the pub and onto the pavement. 'Can I have my phone back? Like, six guys want to ask me out! I'm saying no, of course. My heart belongs to Dan.'

'Plum's here,' I tell Robert.

'Good. I'm late to meet your sister and Luke for a house-warming party. Why don't you come and join us?' he says.

'Maybe later, I have to talk to my homeboys,' I hang up and turn to Plum, who is having trouble lighting a cigarette through the ecstatic smile on her face. See what I meant about the victorious circle of self-assurance?

'Hey chicks,' says Henry, following her out with Charlotte by his side. 'Would you stop running off and leaving us alone? You're giving us a complex. That was shit, by the way. I don't know why I let you talk me into it.'

'Let's get out of here,' I say. 'Anyone want to go for a few drinks? My shout.'

# Chapter Nineteen

Speed dating left us all with post-traumatic euphoria. We found a new bar around the corner, took over a table and started to tell dating stories. Plum and I pressed olives in our cheeks and did our Stockard Channing imitations, Henry told a story about a friend of his who had a weekend in Ibiza that started with a small glass of white wine on the flight over and ended in being airlifted out by helicopter.

'I've never been to Ibiza,' said Charlotte shyly. She's completely out of her shell; Henry's puppyish openness seems to reassure her.

'Neither have I,' said Henry. 'We'll go together. What's your favourite place to go on holiday?'

They've been flirting a lot. Henry is following Robert's just-make-conversation tip, and Charlotte is twinkling back. Plum is in brilliant form, and I've laughed so much that my face is aching. Even the inevitable discussion about Peter doesn't upset me.

'Now's the time to tell you, I never liked the guy,' says Henry.

'But . . . I thought that you got along!' I say. 'You always came over for dinner, and we watched rugby together . . .'

'We did get along,' he says. 'But we were friendly. Not friends.'

'You're way out of his league,' agrees Plum. 'You smile so much more now.'

I put a small black olive over my incisor and grin at them all. There's no point in talking about Peter. Or his brother. Who cares about the affair? I am bulletproof. Nothing affects me.

Another text arrives from Jon, the blind date guy.

*Hey! Just checking you got my text earlier. I had an awesome night. Would really love to do it again. Jon*

Delete, ignore, continue. To hell with karma.

And now we're at the housewarming. It's in a top floor flat in Notting Hill, and you can hear the party from the street before you even get in.

'Raise the roof, raise the roof,' sings Henry as we walk up the stairs, and does a little dance. Plum, Charlotte and I fall against the wall giggling.

As we walk in, the first person I see is Robert, propped in a doorframe with his arms folded, talking to a blonde girl wearing, frankly, way too many sequins.

'Survive, did you?' he calls to me, turning away from her.

'Just,' I say, and turn around to help the others with the wine that we picked up from the off-licence. Charlotte and Henry have already charged into the overcrowded kitchen, and Plum is talking to the guy who opened the front door for us. I turn back to Robert, and see the girl he was talking to gazing at the back of his head balefully, before stalking quickly down the corridor.

'Your sequinned blonde is leaving,' I say in a low voice, walking over to him.

'She'll be back,' he says. 'Come on, let's find your sister. She's pretty hammered.'

'Thank you for tonight,' I say. 'Especially the Peter thing.'

He grins. 'Enough with the thank yous. I've had experience in dealing with similar revelations.'

As we walk into the living room I'm hit by a tsunami of happy, party noise. There's about sixty or seventy people in here drinking, whooping, dancing, smoking, laughing or shouting over each other. The music is turned up full blast and half the crowd is wearing wigs and sunglasses for no apparent reason.

It's not one of those parties where everyone looks to see who you are and then dismisses you. It's a party where you walk in and immediately feel like laughing for the delightful indulgent silliness of it all. I also immediately identify five girls wearing outfits I want to copy.

'I was going to introduce you to everyone,' says Robert. 'But I think we're one drink too late for that.'

We smile at each other for a second, but I'm quickly distracted by a guy charging into the wall next to me in an attempt to walk up it, à la Donald O'Connor's 'Make 'Em Laugh' routine from *Singing in the Rain*. It fails miserably, and he crashes noisily to the floor.

'Are you alright?' I ask, leaning over him gingerly.

'Did anyone see?' he squeaks through his armpit, which is somehow over his face.

'Um . . .' I'm not sure what to say.

'That's JimmyJames,' Robert tells me. 'He'll do anything for attention . . .'

'I will NOT do anything for attention,' says JimmyJames from the floor. 'I draw the line at nuns and dogs.'

He grabs Robert's proffered hand and pulls himself up with a bounce. Jimmy, I can now see, was built for power, not for speed. Or climbing up walls. He's about my height and barrel-shaped, with scruffy brown hair.

Before I can reply, or ask why he's called JimmyJames for that matter, I'm distracted by a shout behind me. 'Sistaaaah!'

I turn around. It's Sophie, uncharacteristically dancing on a coffee table to 'Bust A Move' by Young MC. She screams my name in joy and reaches her arms out to me, and promptly falls off the table. For a split second, I imagine her plummeting headfirst onto the floor and breaking her nose, too drunk to even put her hands out to stop herself, but a moment later Robert has caught her and places her safely on her feet. She doesn't even seem to notice, and collapses happily into me. 'I missed you so much!'

'Thank you, oh my God, that was close,' I say. Robert smiles and turns back to JimmyJames.

'Tell me everything about speed dating!' says Sophie. She doesn't usually get drunk like this. Someone has been giving her shots.

'Tomorrow,' I say, shaking my head.

Sophie grabs my hand and makes me do the (rather pathetic) bendy arms breakdancing move we perfected as children. Laughing, I turn to look at Robert, but he's staring at a very pretty girl, with big slanty eyes like a Siamese cat.

'Robbie, can I have a quiet word?' the girl murmurs in a husky voice. God, I wish my voice was deeper. I swear I sound about seven on my voicemail.

'Olivia! Of course. I'd love to,' he says. 'Let's go to the kitchen. Abby, do you want a drink?'

'Lukey is over there, come and say hi,' Sophie says, grabbing me by the hand.

'Yes, and I'll have anything,' I call over my shoulder as Sophie leads me away. 'I'm clearly too sober for this party,' I add to myself.

'Sobriety kills,' says the guy standing in front of me. We make eye contact. Holy sensory overload of gorgeousness. I turn to Sophie to break eye contact with him.

'Abigail, this is Dave,' says Sophie.

'Hello,' I say, and – stunned into rudeness – turn quickly to Luke before Dave can say anything back. 'Hi, Luke.'

'Hello, nearly sister-in-law,' says Luke, kissing me on the cheek, before dipping Sophie into a huge movie star snog. I have no choice but to turn back to Dave. Oh God. The handsomeness.

'Can I interest you in a shot?' says Dave. He has a bottle of tequila strapped to his chest in one of those water bottle holders normally used by runners, with six shot glasses on either side like bullets. In an iPod holster on his left arm is a small salt shaker, and he's holding a plate of sliced lemons in his right hand. He's clearly responsible for my sister's present state.

'You couldn't rig up a contraption to hold the lemons with?' I say. Hold it together, Abigail. His eyes meet mine and my face tingles painfully. I'm blushing.

177

'I was hoping to strap this plate to a dwarf's head,' he says. 'But my go-to dwarf is on holiday.'

'Bummer,' I reply, my eyes flicking up to meet his and then quickly away. Funny too. Shit. Come on, Abigail. Pull yourself together.

He's just so *handsome*. Short dark blonde hair and extremely blue eyes that I can't look into for more than a half-second. Very tanned, like he's just been skiing or sailing or something. A huge smile that almost takes over his face. Tallish and fit, perhaps a little on the thin side, but as long as his jeans aren't smaller than mine I don't care. In summary, hot as hell. And probably out of my league.

'Places!' shouts Dave. Sophie and Luke stop kissing and stand to attention as he hands us all shot glasses from his holster, and fills them up with tequila.

'I'm not sure that I like tequila shots,' I say, thinking of that night with Skinny Jeans. Ew. Block it out.

'No one *likes* tequila shots, Abigail, my darling,' says Dave, raising an eyebrow. 'Obviously.'

Lick hand. Sprinkle salt. Do the shot. Suck the lemon. As I shake my head at the disgusting taste, I look up and meet Dave's eyes again. God. It's like being punched in the stomach with – well, sorry, but it's true – desire. I have never felt like this in my life. I bet we'd have that spark, if we kissed . . .

There is nothing cool or detached about me right now. In fact, I'm quite sure he can read my mind and it's saying, in very large print: *I would like to be naked and in bed with you.*

I turn to Sophie.

'You should call that guy! Jon!' she exclaims. 'I heard he really likes you. Did he text you?'

'Uh, yeah,' I say distractedly. 'But I'm not into it.'

'Can you make up a lie rather than ignore him? Like, that you're getting back with your ex? At least he won't have to wonder . . .'

'Nah,' I say. 'Can't be bothered. I told him I wasn't looking for a relationship.'

'You're being mean. Apparently he's really lovely . . . Oo! I ran a marathon today!' she says proudly.

'I thought it was a charity 5k in Hyde Park at lunchtime?' I say. God bless drunk attention spans.

'Whatever. The point is, I ran a long, long way,' she says. 'Then I went home to recover, then I met Luke for dinner at Bumpkin, and then Dave announced himself as the captain of fun,' she says, hiccupping slightly. 'It's been a bit crazy ever since.'

'No, no,' Dave interrupts. He has a very self-assured way of speaking. 'Captain Fun. Not the captain of fun. It's a legitimate name. Abigail, you can see the difference, can't you?'

'Absolutely,' I nod, again stupidly. I wonder if he heard that thing about Jon. At least he'll know I'm single, right? (Does that sound desperate? Oh God.)

I charge towards Robert, who has just come in with two beers and no Olivia, hissing 'follow me!' as I reach him. The moment we're in the corridor, I collapse dramatically against the wall.

'Dave. You're like, best friends with him, right? How have I never met him before? Is he single?'

'Yes, why?' says Robert. Then he clicks. 'Really? Him?'

'Yes, yes, he's the first guy I've met since breaking up with Peter that I find just – argh, divine,' I babble. 'Tell me about him, does he have any deal-breaking faults? Is he nice to waitresses? Do you think he'd like me? Would he ask me out? I think I might take him as my lover.'

'Your lover? OK, just relax, Abby,' says Robert. 'Dave is one of my oldest friends, I can help.'

'You can?' I say. 'Yes. Please. If he's your best friend, he must be normal! Isn't this exciting? Finally, I know what I want! I want him!'

'Just one thing,' he says, pausing to think for a second. 'Dave—'

A shout from down the other end of the corridor draws my

attention, and I see Henry and Charlotte holding hands and heading out the front door.

'Look!' I say, grabbing Robert's arm. 'Henry and Charlotte!'

Robert nods. 'I saw them doing a mating dance in the kitchen.'

'So, what do I do about Dave?'

Robert thinks for a second. 'Just ignore him. That's the best thing you can do.'

'Really?' I say doubtfully.

'Yes, definitely,' he says.

Plum comes bounding up. 'This party is awesome! I *beg* your pardon,' she says before I can reply, turning around to face the guy behind her. 'Did you just place your hand on my bottom?'

'No . . .' he says. He's cute, in a beardy way. 'Maybe. Can I get you a drink to apologise?'

'I suppose,' she says, and skips after him into the kitchen, turning to flash us a manic grin.

'Come on,' says Robert. 'I'll introduce you to everyone.'

The people at this party come not only from all over the country, but all over the world. A Greek girl called Aphrodite is teaching a Liverpudlian called Dylan how to say 'I'm pregnant with your child', an American who is, rather fabulously, called Vlad, is standing on a chair having a Cypress Hill song competition with JimmyJames, and a Canadian guy called Matt asks for my number but then repeatedly calls me Jessica.

'Where do they all come from?' I say.

He looks around and shrugs. 'That's London for you. I guess JimmyJames and Dave are very good at making friends.'

I love it. As much as I enjoy the warmth of having friends I've known since I was 18, these people don't know me as Peter's quiet girlfriend, or the girl they always saw in the library, or Plum's subdued friend, or Sophie's less fun, elder sister. I have a blank slate. As a result I'm a bit louder and more confident than I've ever been before. I talk more and laugh louder. It's brilliant.

Throughout all of it, I'm acutely aware of exactly where Dave is on the other side of the room, what he's doing and who he's talking to. I'm discreetly tracking him. He's so good-looking and funny, and exudes confidence and charm. If he was to come and talk to me, could I be cool and detached? Would I clam up or babble? I have no idea. But I'm following Robert's instructions and ignoring him.

Then I head into the kitchen for a refill.

'You're Robert's flatmate,' says the girl in too many sequins that I saw talking to Robert earlier.

'Yes,' I say, though it wasn't really a question. 'I'm Abigail.'

'I'm Emma,' she says. 'I expect Robert's told you about me.'

'Oh, yes, Emma! Of course.'

Her eyes fill with tears. 'He hasn't ever mentioned me, has he? Bastard.'

'Um, I'm sorry,' I falter. 'What . . . are . . . did he do?' I can't think of what else to say, though it's pretty obvious what she's upset about.

'What he does to everyone,' she says, flailing her arms wildly and spilling a little bit of gin on the floor. 'Slept with me three times and then told me it was better we kept it casual.'

I grimace. That sounds like Robert alright. Though according to him, it's always mutual, and the girl doesn't expect anything else. Like hell.

'He makes you feel special, like he's going to look after you, you know?' she says. She's slipping into full rant mode. 'And he always says how he's not looking for a relationship but he's so kind and sweet and hot and seems like perfect boyfriend material. But it's all a front, it's a game to him, he's just a big fucking slut.'

'He's not,' I say defensively, though actually, if Robert wasn't such a good friend of mine, I'd probably think he was a big fucking slut, too. 'He's a great guy to have as a friend,' I say. 'He's just not looking for a relationship.'

181

'He told me that, too, but it's like part of the attraction!' she says hysterically. 'He's unobtainable. You must be the only female friend he's ever had that he hasn't slept with. And I bet he will,' she spits bitterly. 'I bet he sleeps with you. And then you'll know.'

'Well, thanks for the heads up,' I say. This conversation isn't going anywhere. 'Lovely talking to you.'

I turn around and leave the kitchen and run straight into Robert. 'I wouldn't go in there,' I say. 'Emma's waiting for you.'

'Fuck, thanks,' says Robert, doing a 180 and walking back quickly towards the living room.

'You know, you should stop having sex with girls and then dumping them. It's just not nice,' I say.

'The sex is very nice, actually,' he says.

'That's not what I mean. That girl is miserable and it's your fault.'

'I never lied to her. I never pretended it was going to be anything more than it was,' he replies easily. 'I always say "I am not looking for a relationship, this is just casual". It's perfectly clear.'

'You may think that, but they don't,' I say, frowning at him. 'I guarantee it. Girls get involved . . .'

'You slept with Skinny Jeans and didn't get involved,' says Robert, raising his eyebrows at me.

I grimace at the memory. 'That was a mistake. And an aberration. I had to leave when he was still asleep so as to avoid the morning-after awkwardness . . . Anyway, I'm talking about your so-called casual relationships, not one-night-stands,' I pause, thinking. 'Maybe you shouldn't be so kind to them.'

'I admit, Emma wasn't my best idea ever,' he admits. 'Too sweet. I've since moved on to tougher girls who will love it when I avoid morning-after awkwardness.'

'Like Olivia?' I say. The Siamese-cat-eyed girl from earlier is now sitting on some guy's lap on the sofa a few feet away, but staring at Robert.

'Olivia, if you must know, uses me whenever she's between boyfriends,' he says in a low voice, running his hands through his gravity-defying hair so it's almost completely upright. He grins wolfishly, showing his very white, straight teeth. 'See? Victim. *Moi.*'

'My heart bleeds,' I say, looking up at him with a frown on my face. 'You should tell Emma you're sorry, or something.'

'Never apologise, never—'

'Explain,' I interrupt, finishing the sentence for him. 'You told me that one already . . . Shit. Hang on. Where is Dave?'

I suddenly realise that my Dave-o-meter has lost track of where he is. I scan the room and can't see him, then scurry to the corridor and poke my head around the corner. Dave! Leaving! With sequinned Emma! He doesn't even turn around to say goodbye. He just puts his hand on her back and shepherds her out. Argh!

'He's leaving! With Emma!' I hiss at Robert.

Robert mutters something about a death wish, but I can't catch it.

'Sorry?' I say. 'Dave has a death wish? Emma didn't strike me as a genuine bunny boiler . . .'

'No . . .' he sighs. 'Don't worry about Dave. Trust me, that won't be anything serious.'

'Really?' I say. 'Why did you tell me to ignore him, you doofus?'

'You'll see him soon. We're all going to your folks' house in France in two weeks, remember? Bridal party get-together.'

'Yes!' I say, punching the air in delight. 'OK, between now and then, I want you to tell me everything there is to know about him. I need a game plan.'

'Yes, ma'am,' he says, swigging his beer.

Luke comes up, half-carrying Sophie. 'She's toast. We're heading.'

'It's because I ran a marathon!' exclaims Sophie, slurring slightly. 'Alcohol hits the system fast when you run fast. That's a biological fact.'

'I'll come with you,' says Plum, bounding up. 'I've got a hot date with Dan tomorrow. I need my beauty sleep.'

'I'm ready to go too,' I say. 'Robert? Or do you have things to see, people to do?'

'Ha,' he replies. 'Well, Felicity has requested my presence. But I'll see you home safely first, of course.'

'You're such a gent,' I say.

We find two black cabs within minutes of standing on Westbourne Grove. Sophie, Plum and Luke take the first one, and Robert and I jump in the second.

'That was fun,' I say, turning to him.

'It was,' he agrees, looking over at me.

We smile at each other in the silent darkness for a few seconds.

'You look nice tonight,' he says. 'I like your shoes.'

'Thanks. I like yours too.' I lean my head back and close my eyes. 'Thank you for everything tonight,' I murmur. 'You're the best.'

'That's what they tell me.'

'You're my Cyrano de Bergerac,' I mumble.

'Does that make you Roxane?'

'No . . . Christian. The guy he helped was Christian de Neuvillette.'

I'm so tired. Such a long night. Between counselling Plum, the speed dating car crash, the shock of Peter's affair, and finally the stomach-thumping discovery of Dave, I am absolutely exhausted. Thank God it's only Friday. I'm going to have the laziest Saturday morning ever. I might even cook. No, who am I kidding? I won't cook. I'll pick us up something at Melrose and Morgan. Or, ooh yes. I'll have crumpets with peanut butter. I wish we had one of those foursome toasters. Sometimes two crumpets just isn't enough . . .

'Abby, darling, wake up, we're home,' whispers a voice, and I open my eyes. I'm lying down in the cab, my head on Robert's thigh, his big hand on my arm. I am unbelievably warm and sleepy and comfortable. My hair falls over my face and Robert smooths it back.

'But I'm so cosy,' I murmur.

'Come on,' he says, and takes me by the hand. I slowly get out of the cab. There's a big jacket around my shoulders. It must be Robert's. He pays the driver through the front window and takes me by the hand. I am so sleepy, I can't open my eyes. My brain feels like it's made of warm honey.

I follow Robert up the stairs and wait for him to open the front door, and then he takes my hand again and leads me inside and up the stairs towards my room.

'What big hands you have, grandmamma,' I say, half to myself.

'Shh,' says Robert.

'Shh,' I repeat.

We stop on the landing outside my bedroom door and I lean over to take my heels off. It's difficult with my eyes nearly closed. Robert crouches down and helps me, and I fall against him slightly.

Then we're in my room, and I can't even be bothered to take off my make-up or get undressed. So I let go of Robert's hand, shuffle across the room and flop down on top of my bed. I sense him leaning over me and for a frightening second, think he's going to kiss me, but then he just pulls half of the duvet over me and tucks it over my clothes.

'Night night,' I whisper, letting my brain relax completely into warm sleepiness.

'Night night,' whispers Robert, closing the door. I hear his footsteps going down the corridor, and then his phone ringing.

'Ah, Miss Felicity,' I hear him saying. 'Now what is a girl like you doing awake at a time like this?'

And then I'm asleep.

# Chapter Twenty

You won't believe what happened at the airport this morning. We got to Gatwick at an ungodly o'clock, for the 7.05 am flight to Montpellier. It was just the four of us – Luke and Sophie, Robert and me. Luke and Sophie were zombies after a late night with too much wine. But Robert and I watched 30 Rock, ate takeaway Thai and went to sleep early, so the 4.45 am wake-up call wasn't difficult at all. (We were ever-so-slightly smug about it.)

So there we were, in early-morning airport hell, slumped against each other with bad coffees and unopened papers, when a shrill voice screamed 'Robbie!'

We all turned at once. The voice belonged to Antonia, the impossibly beautiful Italian girl I saw Robert breaking up with that night at The Engineer.

'Antonia!' he said in surprise.

He walked over to her and kissed her on both cheeks. She was wearing – and I'm sorry, but this is worth relating, because no one should look this good at 6 am – white jeans that made her legs look endless, a white skinny knit top and a white furry gilet, with huge white-rimmed sunglasses pushing her long shiny hair back. Add tanned skin and a little Louis Vuitton bag in the crook of one arm, and the overall look was unquestionably Eurotrash, but on someone so beautiful, it worked. Sophie and I exchanged glances and scowled: we looked like scruffs.

'Who the fuck is that?' said Luke.

'Robert's ex,' I said.

'Fucking hell,' he said.

'Do you want a smack?' said Sophie, and he started to laugh and grabbed her hand to kiss it.

Robert and Antonia were too far away for us to hear anything, but after a minute or two of smiley-chats, the conversation clearly became more intense. Antonia seemed to be giving a little speech. She took her sunglasses off her head and put them on her face, then alternated between crossing her arms and using them to gesticulate wildly.

No one was even pretending to doze. We were too mesmerised by Robert and Antonia.

'Such a glamorous couple,' I murmured.

'I thought you didn't fancy him?' said Sophie.

Then Robert started talking, and Antonia listened intently. Over the course of a minute, she took off her sunglasses, smoothed out her hair and even smiled. Then – surprise of surprises – they hugged.

And a minute later, after another hug and a kiss on the cheek, Robert turned and walked back to us.

'Are we ready?' he said, as though nothing happened.

'What the fuck was that?' said Luke.

'That,' he said, picking up his overnight bag, 'was Antonia.'

'I meant, what happened?' said Luke.

'Nothing,' he replied, walking off towards the gate. 'Our flight is boarding. Come on.'

The rest of the journey has passed without incident. We all fell asleep on the plane and woke up in sunny Montpellier, and if there is a better way to re-start a Saturday in November than speeding through the French countryside towards Autignac in a hire car that goes at – max – 60 km an hour, then I don't know it.

I'm dying to know what Robert and Antonia were talking about. Is that nosy of me?

It's only 10 am, and the whole weekend is stretching out in front of us in all its French deliciousness. Work troubles? What work troubles?

Dave (Dave!) lands at midday, so my excitement is just about under control right now. Is it immature to have a crush like this? Fuck it, I've got one.

I haven't seen him since the speed dating/housewarming night two weeks ago, but his group emails – short, sarcastic, amusing – have made my crush even more, uh, crushing. I've Facebook stalked him, Googled him, and most of all, interrogated Robert about him. And he really does seem perfect. Sporty, does some charity stuff, works in finance, loves music festivals, took his mother to a holiday safari in Kenya for her 60th. You know: perfect.

Luke's sister Bella, and her boyfriend Ollie, JimmyJames and Sophie's best friend Vix are also on the later flight.

'We're here!' crows Sophie, as we turn off the motorway and along a little road surrounded by vineyards. Autignac is a very small village in the Languedoc region. My parents retired here three years ago, but they're away this weekend.

Their house is lovely: quite narrow, with peeling green shuttered windows and a big courtyard where they eat every day and night, unless it's raining. My parents spent an age renovating the rather poky interior. It now has a big eat-in kitchen and a sofa-strewn living area, which opens up onto the large courtyard with a long wooden dining table. Stairs in the front hall lead up to two more floors with various bedrooms and a study. It's still odd seeing all the family furniture from our old house in Surrey here; familiar and strange all at once.

There's a note on the kitchen table.

*Hello, my little darlings. Milk in the fridge! Ham, olives, cheese, crisps etc help yourself. Call us if any problems. LOL Maman et Papa.*

'I must tell Mum that LOL doesn't stand for lots of love,' I say thoughtfully.

'I'm going to bed for a few hours,' says Luke. 'Sophie, I need you to help me sleep.'

Sophie raises an eyebrow at him, and follows him out of the kitchen with a little grin on her face.

I turn to Robert. 'Ew.'

'I know,' he says.

'Nearly time for Daaaaaaave,' I singsong, bounding into the kitchen joyfully.

'Why are you leaping like that?

'It's my nimble-footed mountain goat leap!' I call back. 'I was watching a David Attenborough documentary the other night, and these little goats were leaping and I thought, that looks like fun.'

'And it does,' he agrees. He attempts a manly leap and crashes into the wall.

'You are not a nimble-footed mountain goat,' I say sadly. 'You are more like a bear . . . big and grumpy. Now that we're alone, will you tell me about Antonia?'

'Nope,' he grins at me.

'Fine,' I say, exasperated. Why is he so private? What's the point of having a male best friend if he won't tell you gory ex-girlfriend details, or what he does for a living, for that matter? 'Well, will you at least help me unleash my fiendish plan to make Dave my lov-ah?'

'I don't think you need my help, Abby,' he says shortly. God, he's moody. He was fine earlier. We shared coffees and papers before we slept on the plane. He did his gentlemanly folding-over-the-paper-for-me thing, as he always does these days. I shouldn't have brought up Antonia.

'You're right. I am going to make this weekend, and Dave, my bitch.' Robert doesn't even react. 'Gee whiz, tiger, you're on great form today. Want to see your room?'

'"*Gee whiz*"?' he repeats incredulously.

As we start walking up the stairs, we pass family photographs of Sophie and me as children. Robert pauses and stares at each one.

'Childhood was difficult for you, wasn't it,' he says. 'Ages, say, two through 14.'

'Charming,' I say, looking at photos of myself. 'I was a late bloomer.'

'You bloomed?' he says in mock surprise, and I hit him on the arm. 'Look at this one!' He stops at my seventh birthday party. 'You look like Grayson Perry. You know, the cross-dresser . . .'

'I know who Grayson Perry is, thank you,' I say, and lean over. 'I remember that dress. It was my party dress. So much easier when you only had one.'

Robert keeps walking. 'Uh-oh! Nude shot. On the beach. Wearing nothing but . . . Elton John sunglasses?'

'I was two. My parents thought that was hilarious,' I say. 'The bastards.'

'Look at the tummy on you,' he says, grinning. 'And your legs! Seriously. Like John Candy.'

'Right, that's enough family history,' I say, pushing him to the top of the stairs. 'This is my bedroom. You're across the hall.'

Robert doesn't even bother to look at his room, and just walks straight into mine. It's pretty bare, with not much more than a double bed, a chest of drawers, and a bookshelf stacked with all my favourite childhood books. My parents have been meaning to hang pictures for the past three years, but I think my dad is saving it as a daddy-daughter activity for when I'm back at Christmas. The shutters are open on the large windows, showing the pale blue sky outside.

'Hmm,' says Robert, walking over to the bookshelf. '*Milly Molly Mandy*. All the Famous Fives, in order, of course. All the Roald Dahls, including *Kiss Kiss*? That's a bit racy. Oh, smashing! I love Malory Towers.'

190

He lies down on the bed and starts reading *In The Fifth At Malory Towers* in a posh 1950s-English-schoolgirl voice.

I try to look disapproving but fail (it was my favourite! After *Anne of Green Gables*, anyway) – and keep giggling. After a few minutes he stops reading, and we lie side by side on my bed with our eyes closed.

I feel deliciously relaxed, and after about 20 minutes of hearing nothing but the occasional twitter of birds and the deep, even breathing of Robert next to me, I'm about to drop off to sleep when—

'Did you hear that?' whispers Robert, sitting bolt upright and looking at me in alarm.

I shake my head, and, staring at each other, we both listen to the silence in the house. Then I hear it. From the bedroom above our head is the distinct sound of Luke and Sophie either playing vigorous tennis or—

'RUN!' I hiss at Robert, who's already halfway out the door.

'Let us never speak of that again,' says Robert approximately 15 seconds later, when we're safely out of the house.

'Deal,' I say. I link my arm through his and we walk up through the village. 'Let's have a cafe crème,' I say. 'Ooh! And a brioche.'

'Ooh,' echoes Robert.

The first walk through Autignac is always slightly surreal. After the noise of London, the silence of a tiny French town is almost scary. The streets are slightly wonky, the houses a little higgledy-piggledy, and the effect – though charming – is like being in a fairytale.

We can't hear anything except the birds, and very occasionally the sound of French radio or TV comes floating down from open shutters. And we don't see anyone on the walk to the *boulangerie*, except two old ladies in black who are gossiping on a corner. Both have walking sticks and scrappy little dogs, and stop talking as we approach to take a good hard stare.

'*Bonjour!*' I say cheerfully. Don't you think French sounds like a pretend language when you just drop into it like that? I do.

'*Bonjour*,' they both mutter suspiciously.

I shoot a look at Robert as we pass them. 'Such friendly locals.'

'I wouldn't like us either, if I was them,' he says. 'This is a beautiful town. How did your folks find it?'

'A lot of holidays in France,' I say. 'They're dedicated researchers.'

'So that's where you get it,' he says.

I grimace. I don't want to think about work. It's been stressful recently: a lot of projects and meetings with people asking questions to which I'm meant to know the answers. Plus, Andre's been sitting with us and is very chatty. He's always asking me about projects and clients as well as non-work things, like travel and my social life. I'm not sure if he's flirting: he's professional, but the intense eye contact is verging on ridiculous.

Charlotte and I have escaped for a couple of lunches. She works harder than anyone I know. She told me that a horrible teacher in Birmingham once said she shouldn't even try to do A-levels, so she always thinks of her when she's tired of working. She also said she never felt pretty because she'd been chubby as a teenager, and her ex was the only guy who'd ever asked her out so that was probably why she stayed with him for so long.

I wonder why I lived with Peter for so long. I don't think it was a confidence problem. I'm just *un peu* lazy and *très* indecisive.

Ooh, pastries.

With warm brioches in hand, and a pocketful of Carambars for Robert ('I just love them so much,' he says), we walk across the little sun-drenched square and sit at a table outside the Bar du Sports.

'Man of few words,' comments Robert, when the owner and bartender Frank accepts our request for two coffees with a curt nod.

'When he speaks, it's worth it,' I say. 'I wish I could be like that.'

'I wish you could be like that, too,' says Robert. I throw a bit of brioche at him, and he catches and eats it. I narrow my eyes at him and pretend to frown, and he smiles smugly at me.

'Dave is here in . . . one hour!' I say, making a manic-happy face. 'He's so pretty, Robert. He's like that guy from *The Fast and the Furious*.'

'Vin Diesel?' says Robert, taking out his phone.

'No, the other one . . . You know, you're not being very helpful. Are you in love with Dave, or something?' I say.

Robert puts his phone back in his pocket, and looks me straight in the eye. 'Look, Abby, about Dave . . . he had a fling with Luke's sister,' he says. 'When we were younger.'

'So?' I say. 'And how much younger?'

'Uh, five or six years ago . . . So, I'm just saying . . . it could be awkward. If you were to, you know, hook up with him tonight. In front of her.'

'Hook up with him? What are you, a cheerleader?' I say. 'And it was six years ago! Why would she care? She's got a serious boyfriend now. Ollie, isn't it? He's coming along this weekend.'

'I know, but . . . Look, I feel awkward, and Dave and Luke and I have an unspoken agreement not to . . . get involved in each other's, uh . . .'

'Love lives? Sex lives? Fuck ups?' I suggest, realising we're not just talking about Bella and Dave. I always wondered how Dave handled it when his sister Louisa dumped Robert and broke his heart. Apparently he ignored it.

'Exactly,' he says, unwrapping a Carambar and taking a big chewy bite. 'I feel weird even saying this stuff to you. Just be careful. OK?'

'Yes, Daddy,' I say. 'And he's definitely not seeing that girl in sequins that he left the party with?'

'Emma? Definitely not,' he says, through a mouthful of Carambar. 'I met her for coffee yesterday, actually. She works near me and I wanted to explain to her why I didn't want, uh, a relationship.'

'I've never seen a man eat five Carambars at once. You're so butch,' I say. 'Hang on. I thought your policy was "never apologise, never explain"'

'It was,' he says, chewing. 'But I started thinking about what you said. About making her feel better. And I started feeling, I don't know, guilty . . .'

'Wow. You're evolving,' I say. 'We should take a photo to commemorate this, or engrave a plaque, or something.'

He shakes his head. 'I knew I shouldn't have told you. Anyway, she's fine. She said she tends to cry after a few drinks and that she wasn't helplessly in love with me, contrary to what you assumed.'

'Oh, well. That's nice,' I say.

'She did, however, say Dave—'

I put my hand up to stop him. 'It was a one-off, right? Apart from that, I don't want to know. Anyway, it's no wonder he didn't pay any attention to me at that party when I avoided him all night, thanks to you.' I decide to change the subject. 'I'm looking forward to seeing Vix.'

'That's Sophie's best friend, right?' says Robert.

'Yep,' I say. 'She's hilarious. I've known her since she was eight. She and Sophie were best friends through the three key phases of girlhood: ballet, friendship bands, and Pacey from *Dawson's Creek*.'

Robert puts his sunglasses on and smirks at this. I knew he wasn't really in a bad mood.

Over the last two weeks, in addition to my internet stalking-I-mean-research, I've grilled Robert on Dave's interests (skiing, surfing, sailing), favourite drink (red wine), film ('Are you serious? I don't fucking know, Abby'), where he lives (Camden), where he works (an American bank) and his taste in women ('drunk, usually'). I wrote everything down in my notebook, but backwards and in French so no one would know. (I should have worked on the Enigma project, honestly.) He really does seem perfect.

I take a moment to check my notebook singledom list, as I have many times over the past three months.

**Be cool**
**Be detached**
**Act brutal**
**Stay in control**
**Bulletproof**
**Always leave them before they leave you**

I wonder if I'll find him as knicker-droppingly gorgeous as I did last time. The memory of meeting his eyes across the empty tequila shot glasses makes me squirm with excitement (and a tiny bit of revulsion – tequila, ew).

I'll be far more in control this time, of course. I shall be myself (in a calm-cool-collected kind of way), and he shall find me irresistible, and we'll flirt and kiss and then I will take him as my lov-ah. Right?

God, it feels nice to relax. I've had a hectic week. I was at a client dinner on Thursday that didn't finish till almost midnight, then was in the office for 6.15 am for a trader announcement on Friday. Suzanne almost smiled at me towards the end of the client dinner. That's got to be a good sign, right?

'Why are you thinking about work on a weekend?' says Robert, coming back outside with two more coffees.

'Fucking well stop that,' I say. 'Your telepathy freaks me out.'

He grins. 'Want to talk about it?'

'No,' I say, chewing my lip. 'I mean, it's fine. I'm working as hard as I can. I'm doing everything just like I'm supposed to.'

'Do you mind if I ask why?'

I gaze at him for a second. What does he mean, why?

'It's a job. That's what you do. You do your best. I can't just quit and navel-gaze till I find something better.' I sound a little harsher

195

than I mean to, but his needling questions are clearly intended to make me question my place in the world. 'Work is just work.'

My phone beeps. It's a text from Plum.

*Dan invented a new swearword. Fuckwart. Isn't he talented?*

I show Robert and we both start laughing. 'God, she makes me laugh,' I say. 'And she's so fucking happy. I love it.' Dan is utterly enchanted by Plum, who seems to have become an uber-version of herself in the past two weeks: happier and more calmly confident.

'How's the H-Bomb?'

This is the nickname that Henry made up for himself last weekend, and insisted that everyone – especially Robert – call him that.

'Yep, he's a smitten kitten with Charlotte,' I say. 'I think your advice helped; he really was the worst single man in England . . .' I pause for a second. 'Hang on. Are you telling me that I'm the only single one left?'

Robert leans back in his chair, sunglasses on, hands folded behind his head. 'You tell me.'

'I cannot fucking believe this,' I say in shock. 'For seven years, Henry and Plum and even my sister have been almost constantly single whilst I was in a relationshit. Now I'm finally able to have some fun and they all fuck off and desert me.'

'Relationshit? Nice.'

A frantically beeping horn makes us turn to see a Hertz rental car squealing to a halt in the centre of the square. The driver beeps a few more times for good measure and jumps out.

It's Dave.

My entire body does a back flip inside my skin, and my breezy plan to take him as my lov-ah collapses. This is like, the worst nerves in the world. Times a thousand. How the hell am I meant to handle this? I'm all hot. And sweating slightly. Are my sunglasses on? Yes. Good. Fine. Breathe. Smile serenely. Chin up. Stomach in.

'*Bonjour, mes amis,*' says Dave, coming over to kiss me – oh hot flush! – hello, and then leaning in to give Robert a loud smacking kiss on both cheeks too. 'Robair,' he says, pronouncing it as though he was French. 'Don't be shy, *mon petit fleur.*' Robert pushes him away and starts laughing. Dave, with a satisfied smile on his face – oh perfect teeth, beautiful smile – stands up and looks back to the car.

I'm dazed by my body's pathetically hormonal reaction to Dave, and fight the urge to give myself a good slap. Then I take an extra moment to check him out behind my sunglasses. Not super-tall but very fit and good God, he really is gorgeous. I wonder if he has those little muscle-lines above his hip bones. I've never seen them in real life. (I am so deprived.)

'Come on, team, we haven't got all day . . .' he calls.

Vix and JimmyJames, and the two people who I surmise must be Bella and Ollie are slowly getting out of the car.

'I tell you, if it wasn't for my cheerful disposition, riding in the car with this lot would have killed me,' says Dave, putting a piece of chewing gum in his mouth. 'Fucking hell! I've met brick walls with more banter.'

Vix and JimmyJames are both wearing dark glasses and clearly suffering from very bad hangovers. Bella, despite her unhappy pout, is extremely pretty, with very long hair, the same flaxen blonde as Luke. Ollie has sandy hair and an open, freckled face, and looks like he'd probably be great fun, if it wasn't for the fact that he looks ready to punch someone.

Hmm.

Vix and JimmyJames are speechless with relief to be out of the car, and Bella and Ollie take their tight little smiles and sit at opposite ends of the table. I'm unable to speak because the penny has just dropped that I fancy Dave about a thousand times more than I thought I did, and Robert has gone inside to order coffees for everyone.

Only Dave seems unperturbed, sitting back and swinging his feet up on the table.

'Pretty town. Ugly locals. Typical France. Is there a bar scene here?'

'This is it,' I say finally, after several seconds, when it's quite clear that no one else is going to speak. 'Um, shall I walk down and wake the happy couple?'

'No, no, you stay here, angel. I'll take care of it,' says Dave, standing up and taking out his phone from his jeans pocket. He puts aviators on at the same time, and gazes across the square waiting for Luke to answer. Oh. The chiselled jaw line.

'Luke. What's your poison?' Dave pauses. 'Well, we're in the bar now, what's the point in coming all the way back there? . . . OK, see you in five.' He hangs up. 'He's coming.'

'With Sophie?' says Bella. Dave nods. 'Then why not say "they"? Women count, Dave. We even have the vote now.'

'I know! It's so exciting. Well done, you,' says Dave, smiling his blindingly perfect smile as he walks away from the table to make a phone call. I giggle, and Bella coolly lights a cigarette and starts texting someone. My giggle trickles off into a gurgle, and finally stops. I am an idiot.

I turn to Vix and JimmyJames, the hangover twins, and finally find my tongue. 'Look at you reprobates. Honestly.'

'I seem to have developed an allergy to alcohol. Whenever I drink it, I black out.' JimmyJames coughs for several seconds, pauses, swallows, and looks up at me. His shirt is done up wrong, I notice, which doesn't sit well at all on his short, stocky physique. 'Right. Snack time. How do you say croissant in French?' He wanders across the courtyard, looking like an unmade bed. The French housewives won't know what to make of him, I think.

'I had a fight with a bottle of gin last night,' says Vix croakily. 'I lost.'

'Hair of *le chien* will sort everyone out,' says Dave, returning to the table. He sits down next to me and gestures for Frank's attention. '*Garçon!*'

I raise an eyebrow at him. 'Robert's getting coffees inside.

And I don't think they say *garçon* anymore.' Yes! I spoke to Dave. High five to me.

'Of course they do. "*Je joue à la guitar.*" "*Où est l'auberge de jeunesse*" and "*Garçon, il y'a une mouche dans mon potage.*" I passed GCSEs with these three sentences . . . *Monsieur! Trois biéres, s'il vous plait, un carafe du vin rouge. Merci.*'

He didn't even ask who wanted beer. Just assumed he knew best. The arrogant take-charge attitude makes me wonder what he'd be like in bed.

Oh God. Blushing.

Robert returns with the coffees. Vix falls on hers with little cries of glee.

'You shouldn't have bothered, Robbiekins, I've got it covered,' says Dave. 'So, Abigail,' he adds, turning to me. 'What do you have planned for me, then? I'm assuming you're in charge of administering fun.'

I hope Robert can't really mind-read me, as I just thought exactly how I would like to administer fun for Dave. I open my mouth, and close it again. My tongue is in knots.

FuckingsaysomethingAbigailgoddammit.

'Actually, Luke and Sophie are in charge. I'm just here for the ride,' I finally say.

'That's practically my catchphrase,' he says, eyes back to his BlackBerry.

I giggle slightly (OK, very) inanely, but no one else is laughing, in fact, the entire table is silent again. I look over at Robert for help, but he's wearing sunglasses so I can't catch his eye.

'How's work, Bella?' says Robert, after a just-too-long-to-be-comfortable silence.

'Marvellous.' Bella, it turns out, is a paralegal for a leading divorce lawyer in Bath. 'I help nail bastards to the wall all day,' she adds, by way of explanation to Vix and me.

'How wonderful that your job is also your hobby,' says Dave sweetly.

There's another long silence.

'Does anyone want any peanuts?' I say eventually.

'Yes, please, angelface,' says Dave.

Does anyone want any peanuts? I repeat endlessly to myself as I stand at the bar. Why not just say 'I carried a watermelon', Abigail, you fucking doofus?

Peanuts in hand, I walk back outside, just as JimmyJames returns with bags of croissants, Sophie and Luke arrive, and Frank brings out everyone's beer and wine. The sudden injection of the happy couple, caffeine, alcohol, carbs and sugar, gives everyone a second (or in most cases, first) wind, and the table is happy and animated for the first time.

'Right,' says Luke, clapping his hands after a few minutes. 'Welcome to Autignac. Thank you for coming all this way. Let the bridal games begin!'

'Fuck me, is this a swingers' party?' says Dave in alarm. 'I haven't prepared. I need to freshen my manscaping.'

'Manscaping?' says JimmyJames.

'Trim the undergrowth. Tidy the hedgerows so my bloom may grow, unfettered.'

JimmyJames stares at him blankly. Dave makes an exasperated face and points to his crotch. With serious effort, I control my giggles.

'What? Are you kidding?' says JimmyJames, astonished. 'Rob. Do you do this?' asks JimmyJames. Robert nods. 'Bullshit! Luke? Ollie?'

'It's under control,' nods Luke. Sophie grins at him and they snigger at a private joke.

'I like to keep the playground clear of weeds,' nods Ollie. It's the first thing he's said today, and we all laugh a little more than he deserves, to make him feel welcome.

JimmyJames is stunned. 'When did this happen? Was there a memo? Why didn't anyone tell me?'

'All men should trim,' says Vix. 'I don't want to floss and blow at the same time.'

I open my mouth to speak, but can't find the words, so I close it again.

'Right,' says Dave. 'Enough about your pube-fro. Let's talk about my lunch. I want ice-cold lettuce, local cured ham, fresh-baked bread, creamy brie and lashings of wine.'

'I think you mean lashings of ginger beer,' says Luke.

'I definitely mean lashings of wine,' says Dave.

I giggle inanely again. Oh God, I hope I calm down soon.

# Chapter Twenty One

A weekend with people who don't all know each other is always a gamble. All you need is one no-speakies couple, one tired/insecure/premenstrual girl who wants to take it out on everyone else, one hammered guy and well, the whole thing becomes a disaster time bomb.

As I'm discovering.

I don't know what Bella's problem is, and I'm not sure that I care. She's being what my mother would call 'a right little madam'. Snapping at her boyfriend Ollie, snapping at Dave, snapping at Luke, offering negative comments whenever she can – in fact, the only person she's nice to is Robert, whom, slightly irritatingly, she seems to adore. It's adding a distinct edge to the day.

Not that we're not having a good time. We are. We're the noisiest and least popular people in Autignac, and our loud, tipsy voices continually echo around the quiet village square. Sophie hates tension, so she's dealing with the Bella situation by getting drunk with Vix and JimmyJames.

'I went on a weekend away with just Robbie once,' says Dave thoughtfully. 'And it was, second to none, the best three days of silence I've ever had.'

'Perhaps there was nothing worth saying,' says Robert.

'Well, you say nothing very well indeed,' replies Dave.

Robert ignores him. Sitting in between them has been like

watching a tennis match for much of the afternoon. There's been a lot of biting put-downs.

Dave starts talking with JimmyJames about the time they stole Luke's phone and changed all the contact names to 'The Mexican'.

At one point during the story, Dave stretches out his arms to rest behind my chair and Sophie's on the other side. His arm is just touching my back and a bit of my hair, but I feel like sparks are flying off me. It's the kind of move Robert makes all the time, but with Robert I tend to lean back on his arm like it's a pillow (sometimes I even pretend to plump it up to make it more comfortable). I can't be that unselfconscious now: I fancy him too much.

As well as being incredibly, head-turningly good-looking, Dave is quick and witty and deeply, deeply confident. A killer combination. Every time his laughing blue eyes meet mine, my stomach flickers with nerves. It's the kind of attraction that makes you crease up with longing. The kind that I've never, ever felt before. I'm sure it must be obvious to everyone around me.

So where is everything I've learned from Robert's boot camp for single girls, you ask? I have no idea. I seem to have regressed to my early teenage years, when shyness made me silent and prone to nervous giggling around every boy in the entire world, whilst eternally longing/fearing that they might kiss me.

'Why are you called JimmyJames, by the way?' asks Vix.

'Because on his first day of university, when he met the three of us, we said, what's your name, and he said "Jimmy – uh, James"', replies Dave on his behalf.

'Thanks, pretty boy. It was my one chance to not be called Jimmy anymore,' says JimmyJames sadly. 'And I fucked it up.'

'It's kind of weird how you three went to the same school and the same university,' says Sophie.

I find my voice. 'You're in love with each other,' I croak, and immediately blush as everyone looks at me. Argh. My nerves are getting on my nerves.

'She's right,' says Bella. 'It's sick. I mean, it's just fucking weird.'

I didn't mean it in a derogatory way, I want to say, but Bella has twisted the conversation into a nasty corner. Everyone moves on.

'I'll always be the new boy in the group, and I've known them for 12 years,' says JimmyJames.

'Hardly a boy anymore,' says Dave. 'And Robbiekins and I fell out of love a long time ago, though he secretly still adores me and I enjoy patronising him.' He turns to Robert and sweetly adds : '"Patronising" means when people are talking down to you, dearie.'

Robert's face doesn't change.

Dave's phone rings. 'It's my mother,' he says, and presses 'answer'. 'Mummy dearest! How may I be of service?' He pauses, and, clearly playing to his audience, rolls his eyes. 'Why are you calling me about this again? I thought that – well I'm just – but I don't – fine. I'll put him on.' He throws his phone to Robert. 'Explain the Sky box to her. I can't do it again.'

Covering the phone speaker with his hand to drown out everyone's shouts of laughter, Robert walks away from the table.

Dave sighs. 'I can't handle my mother when she's being like that. I always tell her to call him. She loves him more than me, anyway.'

'She does,' agrees Luke. 'She loves me more than you, too.'

'So, the wedding,' says Sophie. 'Can we talk about that? Since it's what we're here to do? Sorry, Ollie, I know this is boring for you.'

'Not at all,' he says, smiling tightly. He and Bella have been talking via eye-contact for the past few minutes, I've noticed. Funny how fighting couples do that.

'What am I wearing?' says Dave. 'I look exceptionally nice in a morning suit.'

'None of that shit,' says Luke dismissively. 'Just a well-cut dark grey suit.'

204

'What?' says Dave, outraged, as Robert sits back down at the table. 'Robert, have you heard about this? Plain suits? Is this a wedding or another day at the office?'

'Your mother sends her love . . . to Luke,' says Robert, throwing the mobile phone at Dave.

'Think *Oceans 11*, OK, Dave?' says Sophie placatingly. 'Sheesh! You are a diva. And girls, how do you feel about pale silvery-grey dresses, I've bookmarked a few different styles so you can choose one that suits you.'

'Sounds like a fairytale,' says Bella acerbically.

Sophie's face falls. She's spent hours looking for dresses, and was so worried about what Vix and Bella would say that she was almost ill. In the end, I spent an entire Sunday with her going over her shortlist, and we agreed that if we all wore identical dresses we'd look like cushions on a sofa. Plus, Vix is short with enormous boobs, so she'd be the overstuffed cushion.

Now, Bella doesn't know all this. But it shouldn't matter. God, I hate rudeness. I turn and stare at Bella pointedly. No one fucks with my sister.

'I can't wait,' says Vix pointedly, glancing at Bella and then back at us with a big smile. 'I look fantastic in pale grey.'

'Bella doesn't like anything that's not about her,' says Dave. 'Just ignore her. I do.'

'Oh, fuck off,' snaps Bella.

Sophie smiles glassily, but her eyes look sad. And I'm furious. I narrow my eyes at Bella. Just shut up.

'The night before the wedding, we're having a rehearsal dinner,' says Luke.

'Can I give a speech at that? I want to give at least one speech, somewhere,' says JimmyJames cheerfully, tossing a peanut into the air to catch in his mouth. He misses it completely, as he has every other time he's tried all afternoon.

'What's the date again?' asks Dave.

'Are you serious? March 7,' says Luke, throwing a cork at his head. 'I will tattoo it to your chest if I need to.'

'Chill out, groomzilla,' says Dave, calmly. 'Now, listen. I want four buttons on the cuff. And just half an inch of sleeve showing.'

Vix and Sophie start talking about necklines and dress lengths, and JimmyJames, Luke and Dave about three-vs-four buttons. Bella and Ollie are staring at each other furiously again.

I glance at Robert, who's turned very pale. I immediately know why: he's just remembered that he has to make the best man speech. I've witnessed him remember it every couple of days ever since that night in The Pantechnicon Rooms. The warning signs are always the same. His colour drains, he stares into space, his brow furrows even further than usual, and he starts to bite the cuticle on his left thumb.

I put a reassuring hand on his shoulder.

'It'll be fine,' I whisper. 'We'll write it together, remember?'

Robert takes a deep breath and nods. 'OK.'

'I've got notes. There's a formula for how you do it. I found it on the internet.'

Robert glances over at me and grins. 'Thanks, Abby, darling. Such a geek, always making notes.'

'Shut up. You need me.'

'What's all this?' shouts Dave. 'You two are very close, aren't you? Let's make it a double wedding!'

'No!' I exclaim, a bit too quickly.

'Finally,' says Dave, clapping his hands and staring at me with his ridiculously blue eyes. 'Someone impervious to Rob's endless charms.'

'The competitive streak between you two is weird,' says Sophie.

'You're just saying that because you went for the albino,' says Dave.

'I think he's far more handsome than either you or Rob, actually,' she retorts, flushed with angry loyalty.

'I agree,' I say, trying to help, then realise I sound like I fancy my future brother-in-law. Ah well, may as well roll with it. 'I mean . . . yeah. Luke is totally hot.'

'It's true, I am extraordinarily good-looking,' nods Luke, swigging his beer. 'Shame no one knew it when I was growing up with these two. They used to have snogging competitions at our school socials. It was disgusting.'

'It's not a competition when one of you is a born winner,' says Dave.

'It's certainly not a competition when one of the contestants was 5'4" until he was 18,' says Robert. 'You were far prettier than most of those girls, I admit.'

'Until I was 15,' says Dave loudly, to drown out everyone's laughter. 'I was 15 when I had my growth spurt, actually. I can't help that my voice didn't break when I was six, like some people.'

'Nature picks the real men early,' says Robert, grinning. Finally, he's snapped out of his mood. When he's quiet, it's very noticeable.

'Why don't you real men go to the bar, then?' suggests Sophie. 'We've run out of drinks.'

The guys get up and run towards the door of the bar, pulling each other and fighting to get inside first. Robert wins, followed by Dave. Luke walks in with JimmyJames hanging onto his back like a koala. Ollie follows them sedately, and would appear to be the only sober one if it wasn't for the fact that he misses the step and stumbles inside.

'Frank's gonna love them,' says Sophie drily.

'Are they always like that?' asks Vix. 'So, um, competitive?'

'Yes,' say Sophie and Bella in unison, and both start laughing. I think it's the first time Bella's laughed today, though I'm still peeved with her for the fairytale comment. Then there's an awkward pause.

'Ollie seems lovely,' says Vix. Untruthfully.

'You think? He's fucking furious at me. We've never fought for 24 hours straight,' she says, and pauses. 'It's actually kind of fun.'

There's a pause, but no one is game to ask her what they're fighting about. Bella lights a cigarette and sighs, and for a second, I think she might cry.

Then she looks up and assumes her normal sexy-bemused mask. I wonder if she's just unhappy.

'I heart Robert, by the way,' says Vix. 'He's gorgeous. I bags being his partner in the ceremony.'

'I don't care who I'm partnered with, as long as it's not fucking Dave,' says Bella.

Sophie smiles nervously. 'I'm sure you two can get on for one, um, night?'

'I wouldn't bet on it,' says Bella.

The inevitable awkward pause that follows is relieved only by the guys spilling out of the bar, shouting at each other.

Dave and Robert are stuck in the doorway, shoulder to shoulder, as neither will let the other out first. Robert eventually wins, as he's the taller and broader one. Dave looks thunderous, and immediately heads across the square to make a phone call. Robert sits down next to me.

'Abbyyyy . . .' he croons, propping his legs over mine as though they were a footstool.

'Oh, no. When you're singing at me, I know we're in trouble,' I say, swinging my knees away so his feet crash to the floor.

'A bit like when you're sleeping on me,' he retorts.

'One time!' I say. 'I fell asleep in a cab once! And you won't let me forget it.'

'Actually, you did it that night we went out in Shoreditch about a month ago, too, remember? And you snogged that hipster guy with a beard,' says Robert.

'Beardy!' I'm delighted at the memory. 'He was far too cool for me, though. I mean, I was a Brownie. I just don't think ex-Brownies can ever be hipsters. We're a bit uncool forever.'

'Do you still have your Brownie uniform? I love playing dress-up,' says Dave, who has finished his phone call and is back at the table. I didn't realise, or I'd never be able to talk so unself-consciously. My face is hot again, and I don't know what to say, so I just frown up at him.

As I look away, I meet Bella's eye, she stares at me without expression for a second, and then looks away. God, she's unpleasant. So unlike Luke. He's sitting on Sophie's lap now, nuzzling her head lovingly. JimmyJames starts singing 'That's amore'. Robert and Dave join in, very loudly.

'I think we should take this party home,' says Sophie, as yet another local woman pauses and frowns at us.

'I *knew* it was a swingers' party,' says Dave.

'Christ, can you keep it in your pants for one night?' snaps Bella.

'Easy, kids,' says Robert. 'Everyone be nice.'

Sophie and I exchange a worried glance as we leave the square. This is not going as we planned.

# Chapter Twenty Two

By 10 pm, the atmosphere has improved. A bit.

We're sitting around the courtyard table, with a smorgasbord of bread, cheese and pâté, and about 16 bottles of wine. It's getting cold, but we've drunk enough not to care.

And I'm feeling less self-conscious. With the help of wine, Sophie and Vix.

'And the moral of the story is that snowflakes are not an adequate form of rehydration,' says Vix, finishing a story about a house party in Scotland.

'But the condensation from a cold beer bottle is OK, right?' says JimmyJames.

'Definitely,' agrees Vix, leaning over to bump her fist against his.

'We should make up a secret handshake!' says JimmyJames.

'Let's not, and say we did,' says Vix.

'Robbie! Robbie. *Robbie*. Robert!' says Dave. Robert, who is trying to talk to Bella and Ollie, ignores him. 'Fine, ignore me. JimmyJames and Luke, what do you think about the Vegas plan?'

'Vegas, baby,' grins Luke.

'Vegas!' shouts JimmyJames.

Why is it that you mention Las Vegas to any man aged between 20 and 40 and he starts shouting 'Vegas' like a fratboy on spring break?

'Aw, it's so cute that you think you're allowed to go to Vegas for your stag,' says Sophie tenderly.

'Vegas,' whispers Dave hopefully.

I laugh, and he grins at me.

'I'm having a low-key hen, with a fireman stripper, blow-up penises and L-plates,' says Sophie. She's joking, obviously. That's her worst nightmare. She's banned us from organising any kind of hen night.

'Fucking hell, this wedding is just cliché after cliché,' snaps Bella.

The table falls silent. Ollie gets up and walks inside without saying anything.

There's a pause. Sophie stares into space. She's pretending she's not here. But I'm furious, and I can't hold it in any longer. How dare Bella take her mood out on my poor sister?

'What the fuck is your problem?' I say. She looks at me unblinkingly, then slowly gets up and follows him inside. I shake my head to myself. What a cow.

'Love on the rocks!' shouts Dave. He turns to me conspiratorially. 'It's a Neil Diamond song. Love on the rocks, ain't no surprise . . . pour me a drink and I'll tell you some lies . . .'

'Shut up, Dave,' says Luke. He looks upset.

'To be honest, I'm not surprised it's not working. Bella lives in Bath, for fuck's sake,' says Dave amiably. 'You know, I realised recently I don't trust anyone who lives outside of London. In fact I don't trust anyone who lives outside Zone 2.'

'Then you're a prat,' says Vix. Dave grins at her.

The sound of angry shouting drifts from the kitchen. We all fall silent and listen, but I can't make out any words other than 'I'm sick of you—' and 'I've had enough of this bullshit, you never—' and 'I didn't even want to—' and then the kitchen door slams.

Sophie puts her face in her hands and starts crying. Shit. She really hates confrontation.

I quickly get up and walk over to her. 'Honey, just ignore her. She's a complete fucking bitch.'

'Do you mind? She's my sister!' says Luke.

'Well, get her a muzzle,' I snap.

'I don't want her to come to the wedding,' says Sophie, through her tears. 'She'll ruin it. I'm de-bridesmaiding her. I'd rather have Plum, anyway.'

'Don't talk shit!' says Luke. 'You do that and this wedding will implode.'

'Fine!' snaps Sophie through tears, and runs into the house.

Luke looks into space for a second. 'Fuck!' he mutters, and follows her.

There's a very tense silence at the table again. JimmyJames and Vix start giggling slightly hysterically.

'I love these group bonding weekends,' says JimmyJames.

'I think Bella and I could definitely be best friends,' agrees Vix.

'Bella likes drama, that's all,' says Dave. 'Everyone just calm down.'

I'm biting my thumbnail worriedly. Robert looks up at me and our eyes meet. Please fix this, I think desperately. Thank God for mind reading: he nods, and turns to Vix.

'So, Victoria, tell me more about this guy,' says Robert quickly, pouring her another glass of wine. JimmyJames immediately starts to tease her, and the night – or what is left of it, anyway – picks up slightly.

Then Dave leans right back in his chair, his legs stretched out under the table, and our feet touch. I meet his eyes and, feeling cockier than I have all day, I don't look away. He narrows his gaze and I can feel my heart beating in my throat for several seconds. Oh God, this is unbearable . . .

I look away.

Robert is now analysing a text from the date Vix had a few weeks ago.

'That doesn't mean he regrets the night,' he says. 'It means he regrets the hangover.'

'Should I text him back, then?' she says. 'I mean, I took it as rejection, it's been like, two weeks. What's the statute of limitations on that stuff?'

'You are breaking my heart, Victoria,' says JimmyJames loudly.

She turns to him and presses her finger to her lips. 'Shh. Let's play a game called Shut The Fuck Up.'

'Sounds fun! What are the rules?' he says.

'I'll give you some love life advice, Victoria,' says Dave. 'Don't ask what he's doing, or what he's thinking, or when you'll see him next. Christ, I hate text-terrogations.'

'Ignore him,' says Robert to Vix.

'I need some new friends,' says JimmyJames. 'You lot fight more than my parents.'

'Do you think I should go and check on Sophie?' I say worriedly.

'No,' says Robert. 'Luke will sort it out.'

I can't bear the squirmy feeling in my stomach any more. Combined with the wine and cheese, and the worry about Sophie, Dave's presence is genuinely making me ill. Perhaps I should go to bed. He keeps looking at me with those laughing eyes, like he knows how much I'm attracted to him and thinks it's just a big joke.

Then, as if he's reading my mind, Dave meets my eye again. I hold his gaze for as long as I can, and feel my face start to boil. I will not look away first, I will not look away first . . .

'I think we should buy more wine, don't you, Abigail?' he says quietly.

'Ye-yeah,' I stutter, and then swallow. 'The place shuts in 20 minutes, though.'

Dave stands up. 'Abigail and I are going to get more booze. You three hold the fort.'

I stand up and, without making eye contact with anyone, leave the courtyard.

We walk through the house and out the front door silently. I feel even more conscious of Dave's presence than ever. I didn't think that was possible.

213

We start walking slowly up the quiet, dark street towards the centre of town.

'Don't worry about Bella,' says Dave after a minute or so. 'She doesn't mean that stuff. She'll make it up to your sister.'

'I hope so,' I say honestly. 'Sophie would never upset someone on purpose. Bella is totally out of line.'

'Bella will feel bad tomorrow, trust me.'

'Good,' I say firmly.

I glance at him. He's going to kiss me, I realise with a jolt of certainty. The only question is when.

The village shop sells everything from pâté and wine, to figurines of ice-skating teddy bears. Dave holds open the door for me and we head towards the wine section together. We don't speak, but oh God, the pressure is ridiculous. I'm hyper-conscious of his every move.

At the cash register, I put my hand out to pay. Dave grabs it and moves it away, giving the shopkeeper money with his other hand. He keeps hold of my hand as we leave the shop.

Finally, as we reach a quiet, dark patch of street about halfway between the shop and the house, he stops walking. The cold November night is completely still.

I turn to face him, trying to look cool and detached, rather than anxious and lustful.

I wonder if you can die from sexual tension.

'Cocky little thing, aren't you?' he says, very quietly.

I raise an eyebrow. 'I'm actually quite tall.'

'So there's nothing going on between you and Robert?' he says.

I don't trust myself to speak, so I just shake my head.

Then Dave leans forward and kisses me.

And it's a very simple kiss. No tongues, no pressure. Simply his slightly cool lips pressed against mine. But – and I am not exaggerating here, I swear – an electric jolt goes right through my body, all the way to my toes and back. I want to gasp, but my lips are busy.

This is it. This is that spark I've been looking for.

After what feels like an hour, but is probably only about a minute, he leans back and raises his eyebrows at me. Even in the dark, he's so fucking good-looking, I think for the eleven-thousandth time today. 'Well, that was unexpected, wasn't it?' he says.

I grin at him, and he grins back. Oh, perfect sexy smile.

We put the wine bottles down and start kissing properly. Fucking hell, I keep thinking, fucking, fucking hell, this is amazing . . . My body is a tangled mess of electrical wires. He's not too tall, so even in flats I can kiss him perfectly.

With one hand on my neck and one around my back, Dave walks me back a couple of steps till my back is up against the side of someone's house, his whole body pressed against mine. Good thing downtown Autignac is basically asleep at 11 pm on a Saturday night I reflect, then I get lost in the kissing again.

'I couldn't take the way you were looking at me any longer,' he says at one point.

'Me?' I gasp back a few seconds later. 'You were the one staring at me all day.'

'Let's leave the wine in the kitchen, and take this upstairs,' he says.

'Won't they miss us?' I say.

'Of course they will,' he says. 'But I couldn't give a shit. Let's go.'

# Chapter Twenty Three

'Hello.'

I open my eyes. It's a second before I remember where I am.

I am in my bed in my parents' house in Autignac. Very naked. With Dave next to me. Also very naked.

'Hello,' I whisper.

We're lying side by side, facing each other, in my little bedroom. The house is totally quiet: no one else is up yet. My chin feels hot and chafed – damn thee, stubble rash – and my breath is, I suspect, kittenesque. But I can't bear to move. I'll just breathe through my nose.

'I was magnificent last night, wasn't I?' he whispers.

I start to laugh. Hell of a way to break the morning-after ice.

'Come here,' he murmurs, and pulls me towards him for a kiss.

'Gently,' I say. 'My lips are swollen from all the snogging.'

'I'll kiss them better,' he whispers, moving me underneath him and placing his hands on either side of my face.

And now, I must briefly draw a veil over your eyes, or perhaps cut to a scene of a rocket launching, a flower coming into bloom in fast-forward, or train pistons shunting back and forth. We all know how great sex is (unless you haven't had sex yet, in which case: don't rush, the first time sucks, and remember to play it safe). So just imagine it with a smooth-skinned, flat-stomached, very enthusiastic man who you fancy so much that you want to grab and paw and bite every inch of him. That's what this is.

My God, sex is amazing. To think that I used to actively try to avoid it when I was living with – no, no. Don't think his name. Just think about Dave. Concentrate on the now. (How zen I am.)

'Ahh, *la belle* France,' says Dave, an hour later, as we lie on the seriously rumpled sheets.

'My poor childhood books, seeing this sort of activity. They've led such sheltered lives,' I say. 'What time is it?'

'I don't know,' says Dave.

I grab his watch from the bedside table. 'It's 10 am. I'll go to the bakery,' I say. 'I wonder if everyone is awake. I hope Sophie and Luke made up. I've never seen them fight . . .'

'Of course they made up, don't be ridiculous.'

'Do you think everyone drinks coffee? Maybe I should get some orange juice, too . . .'

'Who cares what they drink? Come here, angel. I'm not done with you yet.'

'No,' I say, wriggling out of his grasp.

'Abigail. I said come here,' he says.

'I'm not steak. You can't just order me,' I say. It's a quote from *Working Girl*. I wonder if he got it. I shuffle off to the tiny en suite off my room and try to ignore the inevitable 'he's-looking-at-my-naked-arse' thought.

Remain in control of this situation, Abigail, I think, turning on the shower.

'Do you have any soap to drop?' says Dave, stepping into the shower with me, and the next second he's kissing me against the shower wall and well, again I must draw a veil over your eyes.

When I finally get downstairs, leaving Dave upstairs 'to make some calls', only Sophie and Luke are awake. They're draped over each other on the sofa, watching French cartoons on TV.

217

'Morning,' I singsong. Looks like they've made up.

They both look over and smile. 'Morning, sweetie,' says Sophie.

'Sorry about all the drama, Abigail,' says Luke. He leans over to kiss Sophie's head. 'I was a brute. Your sister has forgiven me.'

'I'm sorry too,' says Bella, coming into the kitchen. 'It's all my fault.' She walks straight over to Sophie and Luke. 'I really am sorry, Sophie. I was so rude and I didn't mean any of it. I was premenstrual and drunk and Ollie and I were fighting . . .' Bella seems genuinely contrite. 'Please forgive me?'

'Of course!' says Sophie, brightening. She is clinically unable to hold a grudge. 'Are you and Ollie OK?'

'Ha, sort of,' grins Bella ruefully. 'He ordered a taxi at 7 am and took the early flight home.'

'Ah,' says Sophie. Bella shrugs. I can't read her face – is she upset or relieved? She's so self-controlled.

'Well, I'm going to get bread and croissants for breakfast,' I say. 'It's lovely and sunny. We can eat in the courtyard. Back in 20 minutes.'

I'm so giddy with happiness, I have to fight the urge to skip up to the bakery. Just 24 hours ago, I hadn't kissed Dave yet. Now I have. Our first kiss was right there, against that wall. And it was amazing. It was sparktastic. I can't wait to do it again. I feel all hot and tingly at the thought.

But what if that was just one night for him? I feel a strange flutter of panic: I want him, and I desperately want him to want me . . .

Hang on. Did I just use the d-word? *Desperate.*

Fuck.

Stay in control, Abigail. Remember Robert's tips. I can be cool and detached. And anyway, it can't be just one night for him. Not the way he was looking at me, and the, frankly, utterly incredible sex . . .

'*Bonjour!*' I exclaim, walking into the *boulangerie* with a huge smile. Ten croissants, ten *pain au chocolats*, three baguettes and some brioches should do it. I also pick up some orange juice and some flowers for my mum.

When I get back to the house, Bella is lounging on the other couch, and Dave is lying on top of Luke and a shrieking Sophie.

'Hold me,' begs Dave. 'You two have each other. All I want is a little cuddle. Maybe you could stroke my hair.'

'I'm not going to cuddle you,' says Sophie, giggling. 'Get off. You're squashing me.'

Standing up, Dave looks over and winks at me and I wink back. Suddenly I see Bella staring at Dave, and her gaze slowly moves to me. I look away, but not before I see the look of shock on her face.

She's not over him, I realise. The idea makes my stomach flip.

'I'm going to call Ollie,' Bella says, bounding up and heading towards the stairs.

No, she's fine, I tell myself as I walk into the kitchen. She's calling her boyfriend. I'm imagining things.

Dave sits down on the other couch.

'So, Luke, are you playing nice again? You know how much I hate fighting.'

'Then stop fucking stirring everyone,' replies Luke.

Sophie comes into the kitchen and sidles up to me, whispering: 'Am I imagining things, or did you and Dave . . .?'

I meet her eye and grin. Sophie chortles with glee, and then, as Dave and Luke both look over, pretends to have a coughing fit. I deliberately hadn't mentioned my uber-crush to Sophie, as I knew she'd tell Luke. (Not that I'd blame her, that's how relationships work.)

'Something funny to share with the rest of the class?' calls Dave.

'Scuse me, something in my throat,' she says, taking the orange juice and glasses out to the courtyard.

219

'Morning, all,' says Robert, coming into the living room, followed closely by Vix. I look at them delightedly. They scored! I thought JimmyJames fancied Vix. Typical Robert. Oh well.

'Coffee for you, sire?' I say to Robert cheerfully, as Luke and Vix help Sophie carry the rest of the breakfast things outside.

'Yes, please,' he says. He's not as grinny as I'd expect, having just scored with one of the bridesmaids. I would have thought that'd be the kind of thing that'd make him happy.

'Victoria,' I say, waggling my eyebrows at Vix, as we walk outside.

'Calories don't count in France, right?' says Vix, picking up a *pain au chocolat*.

'Not when you've burned them all off during the night,' says Bella, coming back out into the courtyard. I glance up immediately, but she's not looking at me. Guess Ollie didn't answer her call.

'I bloody love everything French,' continues Vix airily, ignoring her. 'French pastries, French wine, French cheese—'

'French fries, French kissing—' inserts Sophie.

'*Écoute*, Robert,' Vix calls into the kitchen. 'We need more milk! How do I say milk in French?'

'*Lait*,' Sophie and I say in unison.

'*Plus de lait!*' she shouts. Robert returns with the milk, and Vix winks ostentatiously at him, mouth full of *pain au chocolat*. 'Thanks for the *lait*.'

I smirk to myself. They'd make a good couple, wouldn't they?

'Please move to London,' says Sophie mournfully to Vix. 'I'm tired of only seeing you on one drunken weekend every three months. And I'm too old to make a new best friend.'

'I might,' replies Vix. 'I'm running out of men in Edinburgh, fast.'

'Sleep well, princess?' I whisper, as I pour Robert some coffee. He looks tired, I suddenly notice.

'Pretty good,' he whispers back, putting his sunglasses on. 'Well done, by the way. Looks like you made this weekend your bitch. Attagirl.'

'High fives to me,' I agree, smiling to myself.

Everyone's eating with hungover enthusiasm. Dave is down the other end of the table, talking to Luke and Sophie about the wedding. It is just not fair the way men can wake up and look gorgeous even when they've been drinking. I needed ten minutes of careful make-up just to look human.

Suddenly, there's a moan from the side of the courtyard, and a figure wrapped in the waterproof barbeque cover rolls across the courtyard, unravelling as it goes. It's JimmyJames.

He has leaves in his hair and his face is marked where he used the barbeque cover rope as a pillow. He looks like Edward in an amateur production of *King Lear*.

'You locked me out,' he says indignantly. 'I could have frozen to death. To *death*. Oh, goody. Breakfast.'

JimmyJames came outside for a cigarette when everyone moved inside at midnight, and the courtyard door locked behind him. Everyone assumed he'd gone to bed.

'I scaled the outside of the house using the barbeque cover rope to help me,' JimmyJames tells us, tearing into a *pain au raisin*. 'I knocked on all the shutters, till I fell off and lacerated my arm – see? Look,' he rolls up his sleeve to show off a very mildly grazed elbow.

The girls all make sympathetic noises. I splutter into my coffee with laughter, catch Dave looking at me in mock-alarm and blush. Darn it, I thought I had this self-conscious thing under control.

'I shouted for a bit, till your neighbour yelled at me.' Sophie and I exchange a grimace. 'And after about an hour, I decided my priority was survival.'

Luke laughs so hard at this he starts to gag and has to leave the table and lean over, hands on knees, gulping deep breaths till he feels better.

JimmyJames carries on.

'Temperatures can get down to six or seven degrees celsius in France at this time of year. And, as we all know, it's imperative to keep your head warm. So I fashioned a sockturban, thusly, wrapped myself in the waterproof cover, using leaves and the rope as a pillow.' He smiles proudly at us all.

'Very, uh, impressive,' says Robert.

'So, what have I missed?' JimmyJames says. 'I'm glad to see Lady Bella is smiling again.'

Bella grins and blows JimmyJames a kiss.

'Oliver has, sadly, left us,' says Dave solemnly. 'Rest in peace, Oliver.'

Sophie, Vix and I all immediately glance at Bella, anticipating fireworks, but she just grins and lights a cigarette.

'What an exciting weekend it's been,' says JimmyJames, reaching for another croissant. I catch Dave's eye and can't help but grin helplessly. Blushes be damned. 'Right. Who was bad with whom? And why do you look like the cat that's got the cream, Abigail?'

The last activity of the weekend is a *boules* tournament in a nearby town. Personally, I think we could do without it, but Luke is set on us all bonding as a wedding party.

*Boules*, in case you've never seen it, is a French version of bowls, and the specific game they play in our area is known as *pétanque*. The Béziers *boules* tournament is taking place on the long gravel pedestrian area in the centre of town, and there's a carnival atmosphere. It's a much bigger town than Autignac, and all the cafes and restaurants lining the street have installed outside seats and heaters so people can witness the game while they eat.

Dave and JimmyJames immediately decide to have a glass of wine 'for sustenance'.

222

'I need it,' says JimmyJames earnestly. 'I think my platelets are down.'

'I just really like wine,' says Dave. He leans over to me. 'Can I get you some wine, hot stuff?'

I grin, shaking my head. Out of the corner of my eye I can feel Bella staring at me, but when I turn, she looks away.

The tournament has three different levels: the professionals, who take it so seriously that they're barely speaking to each other; the middle league, who seem to be mostly couples and friends pretending not to take it seriously; and the bottom league, which is a shambles of fights and laughter. Just our style.

'I think I should probably concentrate on staying alive, given my last 24 hours,' says JimmyJames in a slightly martyred voice. 'I'll just have a nice sit down here and drink wine,' he pauses. 'I'd feel a lot better if Victoria would stay with me.'

'Get used to disappointment,' she replies.

'I speak disappointment fluently,' says JimmyJames. 'Please?'

'Fine,' she says. 'If you get me a chair and table, I will sit.'

'Fine. We'll register the six of us, then,' says Luke. 'We can play triples. Robert, Dave and I against Sophie, Bella and Abigail.'

'Aces,' says Bella, lighting her eighth cigarette of the day.

'I notice you still smoke like a Russian peasant,' comments Dave.

She blows a smoke ring at him and he grins. She's extremely cool. So much cooler than I am. I bet she never needed a singledom coach.

'What are the rules?' says Bella. 'How does it work?'

'Toss a coin, draw a circle, throw the ball, person nearest the jack wins,' says Robert shortly. He's kept his sunglasses on since breakfast. A sign of remorse, or else just his usual hangover grumpiness. Poor Vix. It's a shame she didn't kiss JimmyJames.

'This is so heavy!' exclaims Sophie, picking up one of the *boules*. 'Right. I'm ready.'

223

'I'm going to beat you lot like a Christmas puppy,' says Dave with an evil grin.

'I'm going to beat you like a foster child,' says Bella, squaring off against him.

'I'm going to beat you like a Mormon wife,' retorts Dave.

'Ha! You're such an idiot,' she replies.

'You can't resist me, Bells,' says Dave, reaching out to pull her hair as she walks away.

My hackles are raised. What the devil is this? Last night it looked like they couldn't stand each other. Now they're flirting.

'OK,' says Robert, interrupting them. 'Let's toss the coin and find out who's doing the circle.'

*Boules* is a gentle, slow game, or at least it is the way we play it. There's just the occasional cry of 'oops!' and 'sorry!' from the girls, and 'fuck!' and 'you distracted me, you penis' from the boys.

After we've played a few rounds, the teams are neck to neck. Bella – having clearly decided to behave – is being very chatty and playful, and she and Sophie and I have forged a surprisingly strong camaraderie. I'm glad that they're getting on, but I wish my sister wasn't quite such a pushover. I want to be a little cold to Bella, to show that even if Sophie has forgiven her, I haven't, but it's hard in the face of her charm offensive.

Luke's his usual jovial self, and Robert's granite face is barely moving, while Dave is keeping up a hilarious and irritating running commentary. However – and this is not just because I shagged him all night, I swear – he's so charismatic that even when being deliberately annoying, he's irresistible.

'Right. Bella, Bella. Beautiful girl, ugly underhand bowl. It lands next to Robert's last throw, which I understand he aimed for Paris . . . And here's Robert again, he takes his shot, now he's leaving the grounds, I'd say he's probably going for a pee, are you going for a pee, Robert? And he's ignoring me. Right. So

224

and now we have Luke, who lives up to his nickname "The Fluke" and oh, lands just inches away from the jack, sadly a good inch and a half behind my last throw which is by far the best of the round so far.'

'Wanker,' says Luke to Dave. The rest of us are in fits of giggles.

'Penny in the swear jar for you. Right! Next up is Abigail, approaching with the delicate baby foal wobble she's perfected over the last few rounds, and oh dear, she lifted a foot. Disqualified.'

'What?' I gasp. 'I didn't!'

'You did,' says Dave patronisingly. 'Left foot came up and off the ground.'

'It did fucking not!' I exclaim, annoyed now.

'Vote!' says Dave.

'Safe,' says Sophie loyally.

'Out,' says Bella. Typical.

'Safe,' says Luke.

'Out,' says JimmyJames. 'I didn't see it, but fuck it, let's create another drama.'

'Safe,' says Vix, raising her glass of wine to me.

'Looks like we have an impasse,' says Dave.

'It was safe,' says Robert, striding back into the ring.

'You were having a slash, you didn't see it,' snaps Dave.

'I was getting a bottle of water. My eyes were on the game the whole time.'

'She was fucking out,' insists Dave.

'She was in,' says Robert.

'I was in,' I echo. 'And the vote reflects it. So bite me.'

Dave gazes at me delightedly. Suddenly I realise that he wants a sparring partner. He likes the attention and frisson that arguing gives him, no matter who it's with – Robert, Bella, or me. That's why he's always stirring.

Well, I can do that.

'Chalk it the fuck up, Dave,' I say. 'Robert. Your ball.'

Robert hits my ball out of the circle. Dave whoops in delight. 'The flatmates! Drawn together, yet always apart.'

Robert and I both narrow our eyes at Dave.

'Try to shut up, David my boy, or we'll put you on the naughty step,' I say. He grins, kicking some gravel onto my shoes as he passes me. Yep. Definitely likes a sparring partner.

Dave bowls, hitting Robert's ball away from the jack.

'We'd get two points if you'd aim near the jack,' says Luke irritably.

'I want to deny Robert the pleasure of scoring,' says Dave, batting his eyes innocently.

'*Plus ça change*,' says Luke.

I glance at Robert, who is really overdoing it on the grumpiness front today. I wonder if he can read me. I hope not as I keep replaying some of the more R-rated activities from last night over and over in my head . . .

After an hour of playing, the entire game falls apart. We keep arguing, and though Dave announces himself victor, Bella and Sophie and I agree that we won. Vix and JimmyJames start cheerleading, and everyone joins in. It's one of the few genuinely successful, light moments of the weekend, and Sophie looks thrilled. Bridal party bonding at last.

Dave also spars with me for the rest of the *boules* game, the more I push him away and play it tough, the more he loves it. It's exhilarating.

But he hasn't asked for my number.

Of course I'll see him at the wedding next year, he's a groomsman. And I could probably organise a night out with him, with Robert and Luke's help . . . but I want him to just ask me out. I really do.

If he doesn't, then I just had another one-night-stand. Oh, God, what the fuck was I thinking?

'Time to go,' says Luke, looking at his watch. 'Everyone in the cars.'

I hate flying, I reflect, as we make our way to the airport. It was alright yesterday morning, as I was kind of on early-morning autopilot, plus Robert, who knows I hate flying, distracted me by talking the whole time. I don't think he'll be as chatty today. He's so grumpy that he hasn't even taken his sunglasses off, and when I offer to get him a Coca-Cola and a baguette to help with his hangover, he just grunts 'I'm fine'. So moody.

We get to the airport, check in, and go through the security.

'I should pee,' I say to no one in particular. The group has gone very silent, as hungover groups tend to.

'Thanks for sharing,' says Vix. 'Have fun.'

I always go to the bathroom before I get on a flight, even if I don't actually *have* to go, as otherwise I'll have to go in the air and I'm scared of the sound of the toilet flush in planes. (Yes, it's a completely rational fear.)

I wash my hands, and take a dismayed look at myself in the skewed mirror above the airport sink. No wonder Dave doesn't fancy me. My lack of sleep, stubble rash and mild hangover have combined to make my face eat my make-up. I slap on some more and head back out to the boarding lounge, sighing deeply.

'Hello, angel,' says a voice. It's Dave, leaning against the wall, waiting for . . . me? The others are all sitting down on the other side of the lounge.

'Well, hello,' I say.

'You and me. Tonight. My house. I'm not quite done with you yet.'

I start laughing despite myself. 'Oh . . . Dave. What an invitation.'

Dave leans forward and looks me in the eye, and despite my laughter at his terrible line, I feel my chest contract with the familiar nervous, squirmy heat. 'It's not an invitation. It's a fact. I stole your number from Sophie's phone. I'll text you my address.'

'Um . . .'

Then Dave leans forward and kisses me, and I swear to you

right now my ovaries actually twist. The kiss, like the first kiss last night, is just soft lip-on-lip pressure for five seconds, but I almost collapse. *God*. The sparks. I'm actually tingling.

'Coming to my place later?'

'Yes,' I say. I'm helpless.

'Don't look so serious, darling,' he says. 'We're going to have some fun.'

# Chapter Twenty Four

Oh God, I adore him.

In the 27 nights since the weekend in Autignac, my entire world
has turned – upside down isn't quite right, it's more like inside-out.
I'm starry-eyed, bow-legged, mushy-headed, chafe-chinned and
swollen-lipped. I'm constantly tingling with adrenaline, post-coital
euphoria and an awful lot of caffeine.

My high starts at 6 am. Dave rolls over, smiles his sexy lazy
smile, and reaches out for me. I fit into him almost perfectly,
one leg draped over his waist, my head on his shoulder, and my
lips against his. We snog lazily for a few seconds until he wakes
up properly, and then . . . well, you know.

Then I hurry home, change and go to work.

My next favourite part of the day, seeing him for the first time
every night. I dash home to shower and dress before hurrying
off to meet him. (Kind of a date pit stop.) I walk up to him, our
eyes meet, he stares at me intensely for a second, and then we
kiss and my brain short-circuits. Sparky McSparkerson.

'Got what you came for?' he always murmurs, and I nod and
pretend to pick up my coat and head for the door. He grabs me
and pulls me back towards him, kissing me again. 'I'm not quite
done with you yet,' he says.

Then we drink mulled wine next to the badly-decorated
Christmas tree in his local pub, grab a very quick dinner, and
go to bed. That's the average school night. On the weekends we

go out to dinner or parties with Sophie and Luke. Robert hasn't been around much, I think he has a few new ladyfriends who are taking up his time and attention.

My discovery that Dave loves friction with his flirting means I spend a lot of time lining up ingenious put-downs. It is, I admit, slightly exhausting. I love verbal thrust and parry as much as the next girl, but straightforward conversation wouldn't go astray now and again. And any real intimacy is so rare, it's practically endangered. Those chats always take place in bed, in the dark. He never reveals much, but when he's giving me all his attention like that, I feel so close to him that it's worth waiting for.

And he's so gorgeous. I mean really, phenomenally, stupidly good-looking. I almost can't believe that someone like him could be attracted to me. I love his total self-assurance, his blasé attitude to everyone and everything and his ridiculous charisma.

I know his confidence borders on arrogance, but I find even that kind of attractive. And he can be a tiny bit selfish sometimes, but I don't mind that either, really. In an ideal world, your boyfri— sorry, the guy you're seeing would offer you coffee in the morning when he makes himself one, right? Maybe give you a towel if you shower at his place on the weekend? I made a sarcastic comment about that last week, and Dave said 'I'm not the cosseting type, angel. You need to tell me what you want. I can't guess your every wish.' Which, I guess, is fair enough.

A couple of times, he's also been a little distant, and it makes me feel sick all day, thinking that he's about to end – uh, whatever this is. But he hasn't. Anyway, I can be distant too. Detached! In control!

Sort of.

The truth is: all of my newfound dating confidence and singledom tactics went out the window the moment we kissed. I'm sure that's normal for the start of any relationsh— I mean, the start of anything.

At least I'm not as nervous around him anymore. I actually feel more nervous when I'm not with him, if that makes sense. When he hasn't got in touch, or when his last text or email was a bit cold or rushed, it's all I can think about. I wait and worry and ugh, it's awful. It's been pretty bad today, in fact.

Dave is drinking in a City pub with his work buddies. He has been doing that a lot recently, unsurprising given it's December, which is a month-long booze-soaked celebration in London. Not me, of course. I'm staying at work late to impress Suzanne. I wonder if I should just go home. But what if he invites me to join? He could be just around the corner . . .

I won't let myself text him first, as per Dave's speech about hating 'text-terrogations' in France. There is an art to being elusive through the medium of text, there truly is. Though it's fucking difficult to practise that art when he's not texting at all. And I've learned that he doesn't like direct questions; if I'd asked 'where are you going tonight?' he simply wouldn't have answered. It's just one of his little quirks.

Mind you, it's always like this. When I think I can't bear to wait any longer, that's when he contacts me. It's like he knows. I just need to be patient and confident and everything will be fine.

I've never had to wait this long, though. I haven't heard anything from him since I left his house this morning.

I stare at my computer screen so long that the words start bending, and I shake my head to force my eyes to focus. I think I'll call Plum.

'Abigay!' she exclaims when she answers the phone. 'How are you, honeytits?'

'Good, fine, good. What are you doing?'

'I'm currently fake-tanning, so you are speaking to me naked.'

'Charming. How's work?'

'Who cares? All I do all day is pretend to be happy and excited about things I hate.'

'Well, that's PR,' I say absently. 'That's why they're paying you the big bucks.'

'I wish,' she snorts. 'I am already in my overdraft. At least having no money will make it easier to diet in January.'

'That's the spirit!' I say. I pick up my mobile phone and gaze at it. Text me, Dave, goddammit.

'What's wrong with you?' she says. 'Something's wrong. Everything alright with Dave?'

'Fantastic!' I say, trying to sound as bright and positive as I can. 'I'll see him later. I've seen him almost every night since France . . . not, um, dinner every night, I just mean, he calls me, and—'

'I get it,' says Plum. 'You're having a lot of sex. But it's natural to feel a bit insecure. Have you had the where-is-this-going discussion yet?'

'Hell, no,' I say, aghast at the idea. 'This is just casual. I'm not insecure.' This is so not true. But I can hardly admit that to myself, let alone to Plum.

'Well, I was totally open with Dan,' says Plum. 'On our fifth date I just said, look, I've been screwed around. I want a real relationship, so if you don't, let's forget about it now. And he loved that and said he did too.' She pauses. 'Sometimes you just have to take a risk.'

'Are you fucking serious?' I exclaim, before I can help myself. That's the absolute opposite of everything Robert's taught me, and the opposite of how I'm trying to act with Dave.

'I like him,' she says simply. 'I really, really like him and I didn't want to fuck around. I used to see getting a boyfriend as the holy grail to escape the sweaty moshpit of singledom – but that's not how it works. You have to wait for the right guy. I met Dan and thought, oh *there* you are. It was different. I can't explain it. . . .'

My instant reaction to this is: *for fuck's sake*. But then I pause and reflect for a second. Did I think 'oh *there* you are'? Not really. Could I say that stuff to Dave? No way.

'Kittenpants? Are you there?' says Plum.

'I've been single for like, five months after seven years of a relationshit. I want to keep this casual.'

'You're lying,' she says. Marvellously direct, these Yorkshire girls. And perceptive.

I pause. Then the words tumble out in a rush. 'I'm scared it's all going to go wrong. I can't be like you. Oh Plummy, I hope it's not a fling, I like him, I do – but pretending to be a bullet-proof bastardette is the only way I know to stay in control, or pretend to stay in control, my stomach is in knots all the time, and—'

'Breathe,' instructs Plum.

But my brain goes racing on. I don't know what I mean to him. Am I his girlfriend? Can a relationship happen without us talking about it? Are there stages? Is there an established time schedule I should know about, like after three months you're properly together? Does it all depend on those three goddamn little words? Why is it so confusing? Why don't I know where I stand? I am insecure! Why am I insecure?

'Are you there?' she says.

'Yes,' I reply, taking a deep, shaky breath. 'If it ends, I'll be fine. I'll get over feeling like I've been plugged into an electrical socket every time I'm within a ten-metre radius of him, and you know, continue with my happy single life. I could do that. I could!'

'Are you sure you're not just addicted to the sex?'

'No,' I say. 'It's not. It's more than that. He's so funny and confident, I love that about him. And when he lets his guard down I just . . .' I trail off.

'Oh, it's the emotional chase, then,' says Plum knowingly. 'Thomasina always says that a self-contained, seemingly unobtainable man who withholds his emotions, or affections, is twice as attractive . . . it's like a game, and every time he reveals something about himself, you feel like you're winning.'

'No,' I say waveringly. Though that sounds scarily accurate. 'What did you think? Do you think he's serious about me?' No answer. 'Do you like him?' Plum and Dan met him last week when we had dinner at Lemonia.

'I'd like to get to know him better,' she says, after a pause. Which means, of course, that she doesn't like him. 'I can't believe you're still at work, by the way.'

'It's fine,' I say, gazing around the half-full, fluorescent-lit office. 'I'm still, you know, over delivering, just like Suzanne told me to. Step. It. Up. Those were her exact words. Step it up, Abigail.'

'What a wanker,' comments Plum.

'Yeah,' I say automatically. I've never thought of Suzanne as a wanker before. A cold slave driver, yes, but I accepted that she was someone who knew how to get the best out of us all.

'How's beautiful Robert the fuckmerchant?' asks Plum. 'I haven't seen him in ages. He must be happy you're seeing one of his best friends.'

'He doesn't seem that impressed, actually. He hasn't been quite himself around me since that weekend in France.'

'Jealous that you're taking his friend away,' says Plum knowingly. 'Such a typical guy thing.'

'They seem to have a complicated friendship . . . highly competitive. They go out of their way to irritate each other.'

'Alphas,' sniffs Plum.

Actually, I assumed the relationship deteriorated when Dave's sister Louisa trampled on Robert's heart, but perhaps Plum's right: they're alpha males who've been pecking around the same field for too long. 'Whatever the reason, Robert and I haven't had much quality flatmate time recently. I miss his grumpiness.'

'I'm sure you'll work it out,' says Plum. 'You get along so well. Why not ask him out for a drink?'

'Nah,' I say. 'Making it a formal drink would be weird. We only

234

ever hung out by accident – because we were both, you know, at home at the same time.'

'You hung out by accident every night and weekend?' says Plum.

'Perhaps our friendship would never last past one of us getting into a relationship. Perhaps we were always going to drift apart,' I say.

'Yeah,' agrees Plum. 'You know, I've slept with all of my male friends. Except Henry.'

'Poor Henry,' I say. 'My mum's dying for me to marry him.'

'Yeah but come on . . . it's *Henry*,' says Plum. 'Anyway, he's in love with Charlotte. Dan and I met them for brunch on Sunday. They're such good fun. Do you think she's smarter than him?'

'I haven't thought about it,' I say, trying to ignore the stab of jealousy I feel: I got the text about brunch, but when I suggested to Dave that we join them, he said 'I already did the friend thing, and anyway, there's only one thing I'm interested in eating this morning, and that's' – well, anyway. He wasn't interested.

'Hmm. Dan's probably smarter than me, but I'm funnier,' she says. 'Abigail! Are you listening?'

'I am!' I say. 'I am so glad things are going so well for you.'

'So am I,' she says. 'All those idiots were turning me into a basketcase. And crazy is so not a good look for me.'

I press 'refresh' on my computer for the eighteenth time since we started talking, and glance at my phone. Nope, nothing.

Plum clears her throat. 'I have to go, my fake tan is dry and my eyebrows aren't going to pluck themselves.'

We hang up, and I go back to staring at my screen again. It's 8.22 pm. Time to go home and wait.

# Chapter Twenty Five

He's never waited this long to call before. What if something's happened?

I take a cab home, rather than the tube, which is an unnecessary expense but I don't want to go underground and lose phone reception. (I know how dismal that sounds, but I'm being honest.)

I take a shower with my phone propped up on the closed toilet seat in case he rings. (He doesn't.) Then I blow-dry my hair and put on my favourite jeans and a casual-but-totally-sexy nude-coloured top and my cosiest socks with the phone constantly in my line of vision so I can pick it up easily if he rings. (He doesn't.) Then I head downstairs for a glass of red wine. With my phone. (As you probably guessed.) In case he rings. (He doesn't.)

I lie down on the couch, wine in hand, legs hanging over the edge, staring into space.

It's past 9.30 pm now. Where could he be? What if he's drunk somewhere, flirting with another girl? What if he's passed out and won't even call me till tomorrow? What if he's changed his mind about whatever it is that is going on between us? What if—

Shut up, Abigail. Calm down. This attitude is so not you. It's (don't say it, don't say it) desperate.

The front door bangs. Robert's in the front hallway, taking off his protective moped gear.

'Hi!' I say.

'Hey,' he replies.

It's been ages since Robert and I last hung out – since before France, now that I think about it – and I suddenly feel elated to see him. I swing my legs off the couch and stand up, smiling brightly.

'Wine?' I say.

'Ah, why not,' he says, sighing, and coming into the room. He's still wearing his suit and looks a bit rumpled and stressed.

'You need a haircut,' I say.

'A shower is more important right now. Very long day. Back in ten.'

He turns and heads straight for his room. I wonder why he's so stressed. He still won't tell me what he does. I've stopped asking.

The living room feels somehow bare and unloved tonight, and not a very nice place to come home to.

So I tidy up, fluffing all the big red cushions and banging the couch into shape, and turn on the fire and the lamps around the room to try to make it feel cosier. Then I open up a packet of pretzels and put it into a bowl for us to have with the wine. There are some tea lights sitting in mismatched tumblers behind the sink, so I put them on the coffee table too. Then I realise they look like an attempt at romance, so I quickly blow the candles out and put them back behind the sink, just as Robert gets back.

His hair is all wet from the shower and he's wearing odd socks with his oldest, most threadbare pair of jeans, and his favourite blue shirt that has too many holes in it. It's done up wrong, but I decide not to tell him that. He looks like himself again. I can't help beaming at him. And not because he's distracting me from Dave not calling. It is just so *good* to see him.

'You cooked!' he says, looking at the pretzels and wine with a grin.

'Never say I don't look after you,' I reply, taking a seat and

237

picking up my glass. He stretches and sits down in his chair with a huffing sound, picking up his glass of wine and holding it up to me. Our eyes meet for the first time since he got home.

'Happy almost-Christmas,' I say.

'Happy almost-Christmas,' he nods, and takes a long sip. 'Ah. That's better.'

There's a pause as we smile at each other. I like his face, I think involuntarily. And not because of the whole handsome thing. I just like it. I probably can't tell him that without sounding like a fool, however, so I take a sip of wine.

'How's Dave?' he says.

'He's good, fine, he's good,' I say quickly. I don't want to linger on the subject in case Robert says something I don't want to hear. 'How's, uh, how's . . .'

'They're fine,' he says crunching a handful of pretzels thought-fully, which is very hard to do. 'They're all fine. How's work?'

I look at him and raise an eyebrow. Work is one thing I don't want to talk about.

'Business as usual, then,' says Robert. 'I thought you were faking work confidence?'

I shrug. 'You can't fake something for that long. Eventually you have to admit the truth, and I hate . . . Christmas decor-ations!' I exclaim. 'That's what's missing.'

'Huh?'

'I was thinking this room felt a bit bare . . . it needs Christmas decorations!'

'Hmm. I've got my sister's old stuff somewhere from before she moved to Dublin . . .'

Robert goes to the hallway cupboard and takes down a very large cardboard box.

'Abby, darling, meet the worst Christmas decorations ever.' Out comes threadbare tinsel; tarnished baubles; knotted Christmas lights; a dilapidated Christmas wreath with some seriously sick-looking red robins attached; eight red candles of varying degrees of use; a CD called *The Best Christmas Album EVER* – and that's just the first layer.

'Your sister seems like she'd be fun,' I say, picking up a staple gun from the box.

'Alice? Oh, she is,' says Robert, picking up a cutlery holder attached to wooden geese swimming in holly.

'What is this?' I say, holding up a stuffed moose with a Santa hat on, with 'Fernie 2002' embroidered on the hat.

'Alice used to staple gun that moose to her front door,' he says. 'Instead of a wreath.'

'May I?' I say, leaping joyfully towards the front door, reindeer and staple gun in hand.

'Ah, the leap of the nimble-footed mountain goat!' he calls after me. 'I'd recognise it anywhere.'

I staple the moose to the door by arms, feet and antlers, and spring joyfully back into the house. 'Shall we get into the Christmas spirit?' I pick up a bottle of Jack Daniel's with a Santa Claus beard attached and waggle it at him.

An hour later, I'm wearing a mistletoe headband. Robert is wearing a Mrs Santa hat with long white plaits. We're singing along to Bing Crosby's 'White Christmas'. I've propped the red robin wreath on the coffee table and put red candles inside, and arranged the baubles in a large glass bowl on the kitchen top. We've also staple gunned fairy lights around the windows (probably a disastrous idea, but at that point we'd already had two glasses of Jack).

'It looks like Christmas with a hangover,' I say proudly.

'I love it,' says Robert, taking a sip of his Jack Daniel's. 'God! I've had a shit week. Thanks for making me do this. You are like human Prozac.'

I grin at him. It feels so easy hanging out with him again. If only relationships could be as easy as friendships. I guess they are, eventually, but first you probably have to go through the trial-by-insecurity phase that I'm in with Dave right now. I want to ask Robert if we can do something together this week, but then I remember that I hope to see Dave every night, so I don't say anything.

Robert starts staple gunning tinsel to the doorway leading out to the stairs.

'That tinsel has alopecia,' I comment.

He gazes at it. 'You're absolutely right,' he says. He tries to rip it down, and shreds hundreds of individual strands of tinsel confetti. 'Bugger!' he shouts. He tries to pick them up off the floor, loses first his balance and then his patience, throwing all the tinsel pieces up in the air and spinning under them. 'Abby, what am I? A snow globe.'

'You're so butch when you're twirling. Like a big galumphing ballet dancer.'

'Well, I trained professionally for years. Till I got in a fight defending a dog from a pack of rabid old ladies.'

I don't mind about Dave not calling, I think suddenly, picking up a half-full bag of chocolate coins from the floor. He'll turn up at some point. And I'm having fun here, anyway.

'I wonder if I'll get a Christmas stocking this year,' I say. 'I think my mother might have outlawed it.'

'I always get one,' Robert says, picking up my legs with one hand and sliding himself onto the couch, then letting my feet plop back down over him. 'My mother tried to stop it a few years ago. She announced that she was tired of spending the whole of December trying to find puzzles and games and toys for three people whose combined ages were almost 100.'

'That is way harsh. What did you say?'

'We pretended to cry,' says Robert. 'Obviously.'

I rest my head on Robert's arm and sigh happily. I feel like I'm home for the first time in weeks, I muse. I can't even remember the last time we sat here together. I remember the first time, after that disastrous date with Paulie. That seems like a very long time ago.

'How old are these?' I say, chewing a chocolate coin.

'At least four years. Possibly five.'

'Mmm, yes, excellent vintage. I particularly like the white specks, they're extra tasty. So . . . Why are you so stressed?'

'Work.'

'Are you ever going to tell me what you do?'

Pause.

'I'm an accountant,' he says.

I start to laugh, then stop. 'Oh, um, really? I thought you were kidding.'

'That's why I never tell anyone,' he says, shaking his head. 'It's an instant conversation stopper.'

'What kind of accounting is it?'

'The heady world of corporate finance,' he says, crunching more pretzels.

'Sexy. Is it your dream job?'

'Erm, yes, I guess so,' he says. 'You know, I ploughed the postgrad, then studied law in the States, then realised I didn't want to be a lawyer . . . I felt like such a fuck up. Nothing fit. But somehow, I ended up in the right place,' he says. 'Everyone does eventually.'

'I hope so,' I say, sighing. 'I can't believe that after all that fuss about not telling me what you do, you're an accountant.'

'I'm private. And I have better things to talk about. Though it's not as boring as everyone thinks.'

'I think you're a control freak,' I say. 'That's why you pump and dump women like you do.'

'"Pump and dump"? Nice. Sex is actually fun for everyone involved, has anyone ever told you that?'

'Ha,' I say, thinking about Dave. There's a pause. 'What are you doing for Christmas, by the way?'

'I'm working, mostly, with a bit of family time. My sister Alice is coming over with her kids. Every Christmas morning should have an overexcited four-year-old, it makes it much more fun for everyone. You?'

241

'I'm in France from Christmas Eve till New Year's Eve.'

'You get along with your parents, don't you?'

'Yes, I love them. But they think we're still aged seven and nine. I swear my mother would be thrilled if I came home with a report card from work at the end of each year.'

'I would have thought you'd love that, too,' he says, and pretends to read from a report card. 'Abigail is a delightfully serious, bright and enthusiastic child, she plays well with others, especially after a few shots . . .'

'Shuddup,' I say, poking him with my toe. 'Anyway, Sophie's leaving early this year to be with Luke . . . I wish I was coming back to London early, then you and I could go drinking and have fun.'

And I could see Dave, if he is even going to be in London. Which I don't know, because he doesn't ever bring up the future, and neither do I. And he doesn't even know that it's my birthday on the 1st of January, because I don't want him to think I'm just telling him so he'll buy me a present. God, the game-playing is getting exhausting.

Thinking all this, I sigh.

'Don't worry about him,' says Robert. 'Dave likes girls who don't chase him.'

'I don't *chase* him,' I say irritably. 'Stop reading my mind. It's casual. We don't ever discuss, you know, feelings.'

'Good. I'm against that kind of filth, myself.'

'Surely you must get fond of your ladyfriends sometimes. You're not a heartless bastard underneath, I know you're not.'

'I get very fond of them. I love their company. I just don't love . . . them.'

'Do they ever fall in love with you?'

He shrugs. That's a yes, then. 'I try to keep that sort of thing, uh, to the bare minimum.'

'Why not just say, I love you, so they feel good, and then hand them a terms and conditions contract saying, limited time only, offer subject to change, etc.'

Robert laughs for a very long time at this. I love making Robert laugh, I think suddenly. He has a loud, unselfconscious guffaw.

'Seriously, don't worry about Dave,' he says later .

'You have to stop mind-reading me,' I say. 'It's getting weird.'

'But it's so easy. You're like a book,' he says. 'A kid's book with very big print. Like *The Very Hungry Caterpillar*.'

'That was my favourite!' I exclaim. 'I used to read it whenever I was upset.'

'Me too,' he says, sipping his drink. 'I hate Jack Daniel's.'

'Me too,' I agree, taking another sip. 'Shall we have another? Oh! I love this song,' I say, as 'Santa Baby' comes on. We both start singing along, with Robert doing a very bad Eartha Kitt impression.

'Is anything happening with Vix, by the way?' I ask, when the song has finished and 'Chestnuts Roasting on an Open Fire' comes on, which neither of us knows the words to. 'Obviously it's difficult because she's in Edinburgh, but are you guys in post-pull contact?'

'I wasn't with Vix in France,' says Robert in surprise. 'I thought you knew that.'

'No,' I say, shocked. 'But – you came downstairs together.'

'We slept in the same bed, me on top of the sheets, and her underneath,' he says. 'There weren't any other beds and we'd been up late, talking about her love life. Nothing else happened.'

I'm stunned. Does it seem odd to you that Robert, the great lothario, would lie in bed with a pretty girl and not make a move? Perhaps he knows it's unwise to plunder the wedding party, as Sophie warned. I'm about to ask him, when my phone rings. Dave! My chest leaps in delight. I reach for my phone and nearly fall off the couch.

'Don't answer too fast,' advises Robert. 'Keep him waiting.'

I shoot him a glare and then hold the ringing phone for a second to compose myself. I look at the screen. Yep, it's Dave.

'Why, hello,' I say casually.

'Why, hello to you,' mimics Dave. 'May I speak to Abigail Wood, please?' He's slurring slightly.

'One second please,' I respond, and then sing some hold music in a very high voice ('Are You Going To Scarborough Fair'), before clearing my throat. 'Hello, this is Abigail speaking.'

'Ah! Abigail. Your secretary was very slow to answer the phone. You should fire her.'

'I shall,' I say. 'I shall beat her thoroughly first, obviously.' My eyes flick up to Robert, who looks like he's checking texts. I wonder if he's listening. 'How may I be of service to you this evening, good sir?'

'It is I who would like to service you, my girl. Very slowly and thoroughly.'

'Everyone's got a dream,' I say.

'Cheeky bitch. Right, my house. Twenty minutes.'

I look out the window. 'It's raining. Can't you come here?'

'Don't go,' says Robert in a low voice. 'Don't let him boss you around.'

'Is that Grandpa Robbie?' says Dave. 'Fine, I'll come there.'

'No, don't,' I say quickly. I suddenly have no desire to see Robert and Dave indulge in their competitive put-downs, or for that matter, to take Dave up to my bedroom when Robert's here. I don't know why, but it would be weird. 'I'll be there in half an hour.'

'Hurry,' says Dave, and hangs up.

The Christmas music has stopped, and I sit back on the sofa next to Robert and smile at him. He grins back, but he's not quite meeting my eyes. The room seems incredibly silent. I take a deep breath.

'Look, I get the picture. You don't like me seeing Dave,' I say, the words tumbling out of my mouth nervously. 'But it's only casual, you know, and I promise not to steal him away from you, and I know you don't get involved in each other's, um, love lives, but I was your friend before I even met Dave, and I still want to be your friend. I also know you guys have a complicated friendship, and I don't want to, um, become a pawn in your stupid macho chess game.' Robert grins at this, which I take as a positive sign. 'So, please, don't be annoyed with me for seeing him. I am having fun. Which is the point, remember?'

Robert nods slowly, drains the last of his Jack Daniel's and Coke, and gets up off the couch. 'Absolutely. Shall I call us a cab to share? Lady Caroline needs me.'

# *Chapter Twenty Six*

The next Sunday evening, when I'm in bed with Dave, something unexpected happens.

'This is nice,' he says, nuzzling me in the darkness.

'Nice?' I say. 'That's the best you can do?'

'This is lovely,' he murmurs, pulling me closer to him. 'You're lovely. I've had the best time this weekend.'

That's because we spent the last two days in and out of bars and bed. And the entire time I had to keep up my slightly tiring sassy-comeback routine. But moments like this, when his barriers are down and it's just us whispering in the darkness, make everything worthwhile.

I sigh happily in the dark and fight the urge to kiss his shoulder.

'I don't think we should give Christmas presents,' I say. I've been wanting to bring this up, mostly because well, I don't think he has any intention of getting me anything, and I don't want him or anyone else to think that disappoints me. I'm totally cool with it. 'To each other, I mean.'

'Is this a trick? This feels like a trick . . .' he says.

'No,' I say, laughing. 'I mean, I know that you've been planning a Christmas extravaganza for me, and everything, but well, I think it'll be easier,' I pause, and add in my faux-sparky-banter way, 'Anyway, more importantly, I don't have anything for you and I simply don't have the time or inclination to battle Christmas crowds.'

'You're so cute,' he says, and we start kissing again. 'You and me,' he says, after a few minutes. 'We should do this. Let's just do it, fuck it, let's do it.'

'Right,' I say, barely breathing in the darkness. What exactly does 'let's just do it' mean, do you think? 'How, uh . . . do you mean?'

'You are a tough little thing, aren't you?' he says. I'm not tough at all, I think, I'm just pretending. 'We make it official,' Dave says, pulling my leg up and around his body. He likes to arrange me like this, pulling and prodding me around him for the perfect cuddle. 'We tell everyone we're together,' he continues, his lips on my throat, kissing and nibbling in between words. 'I've always wanted to be with a girl like you.'

I think I might pass out from elation, but I manage to keep my voice steady. 'I think that can be arranged. I'll have my people call your people . . .'

'She damns me with her faint affection! So elusive. The elusive Miss Wood . . .'

'Sorry,' I say, and pause, staring in the darkness. Can I let my guard down? Can I take a risk? 'I'd love that.' My voice breaks on 'love'. Bugger.

'Good girl,' he says. I wish I could see his face, to see if he looks as happy as I am that we're having this conversation. But I can't. Then he kisses me and as usual, my brain short-circuits.

The next morning, the alarm goes off at 6 am to get us up in time for work. Since it's the week before Christmas, you'd think my office would become a little more festive and relaxed, but no. My entire floor will be at their desks by 7.15 am, latest.

'Do you want a lift home today?' asks Dave, getting out of bed a few minutes later. He's never offered this before, and I've never asked.

'Yes, please,' I say. I can't help but smile from ear-to-ear.

'You do have a sexy little grin, don't you?' he asks, jumping back on the bed and making a grab for me. 'Look at you, with your bird-nest hair. I love it. It makes you even more fuckable.'

'Off! Go and shower and then drive me home or I'll be late for work,' I say, trying to sound cool and tough instead of giddy with elation.

Dave saunters, naked, to his bathroom, and a moment later I hear him singing 'I've Got A Lovely Bunch Of Coconuts'. I snigger to myself. He's so damn adorable.

Except when he takes 30 minutes to dress and do his hair.

By the time I'm home, it's almost 20 to seven and I'm late. I run into the house. Robert is sitting by himself at the kitchen bench, eating porridge and drinking coffee.

'Fuck!' I shout at him, throwing my coat, scarf, hat and gloves on the couch.

'You're late!' he replies.

'Dave's fault!' I yell back down the stairs. I'm feeling tense: we almost bickered in the car. Dave doesn't like other people being irritated with him. Even when he's about to make them seriously late for work. But that's okay. Because he and I are really, officially, seriously-for-serious together.

I shower as quickly as I can, going through my now-regular combing-out-the-bedhair-with-conditioner motion. I dress hurriedly in black trousers and a black turtleneck, frantically blow-dry my hair, tie it up in a very high chignon, and then calm down for a few minutes so that I can apply my make-up properly. (Make-up in a hurry never works out, like eating when running or reading when drunk.)

'It's almost five past seven, what are you still doing here?' I gasp, when I run back into the kitchen. He always leaves by 6.45 am.

'I thought you might need an emergency lift,' he says. 'It's Christmas Eve in four days. No company expects people at work on time.'

'Mine does,' I say. 'A lift would be wonderful, lovely Roberto.'

Robert hands me a coffee and a bowl of porridge and heads up to his room, calling over his shoulder: 'Eat and drink. We'll leave in five.'

Gulping my thanks through coffee, I sit down. The porridge is just how I like it: made with water not milk, plus blueberries and almonds chopped into thirds (not halves! thirds!) sprinkled on top. He returns a few minutes later and hands me a large bag. 'Cold weather kit for the moped. You'll freeze without it.'

'You have spare cold weather kit?' I say in surprise.

He shakes his head. 'I picked it up for you ages ago, but then we haven't been going to work together . . .'

'Thank you!' I exclaim, reaching up to give him a hug. 'That's so thoughtful of you. And practical. How much do I owe you for it?' He leans forward and hugs me awkwardly with one hand, the other still carrying the bag.

'Nothing. It's my treat . . . Try them on.' Robert watches me as I wriggle into the clothes and stifles a grin.

'Am I both warm AND sexy?' I ask. I'm wearing waterproof elasticised black trousers and a matching zip-up coat. 'God! I look like one of those fat cops in *The Fifth Element*.'

'I was thinking more of a giant dung beetle,' says Robert.

I shrug, and waddle noisily towards the front door. 'Let's go.'

I cling like a heavily-padded barnacle to Robert all the way to work, and jump off with a shout of thanks. He nods and speeds away.

Walking through the reception area to the lifts dressed like this is mildly embarrassing, so I just keep my head held high and pretend it's totally normal to look like a giant dung beetle shuffling through the lobby of a large investment bank.

'Looking good, Abigail!' says the security guard, Steve, as I pass him.

'Feeling good, Steve!' I reply, taking out my security pass from my bag to swipe. It's our standard *Trading Places* greeting since we started chatting when I forgot my pass a few months ago. Today he starts laughing at me, clearly tickled by my outfit. I poke my tongue out.

'*Salut*, Abigail,' says a voice as I get into the lift. I knew I'd run into someone. I meet the warm brown-eyed gaze of Andre, the French guy. He hasn't been working in the London office much lately. How typical that I'd see him when I look like this.

'How are you?' he asks.

'Excellent,' I say, flashing a grin at him. 'Please excuse my clothes, I was on a moped . . .'

'Not at all,' he says, making a flicking motion with his hand. 'You always look lovely.'

There is a pause. Thank God no one else is in the lift. I smile without looking at him and keep my eyes fixed on the climbing numbers. He's been sitting near Charlotte and me, and I often catch him looking at me. Third floor . . . fourth floor . . .

'I'm going up to eighth, but . . . will you have lunch with me today?' Andre asks. 'I want to discuss a project with you,' he adds quickly.

'Uh, sure,' I say. 'I'll meet you at 1 pm in the lobby.'

'It's a date!' he says, grinning.

It's not a date, I think to myself. I don't date anymore, because I have Dave. And I really, really do have him.

I grin to myself and fight the urge to do a nimble-footed-mountain-goat leap as I swishswishswish to the ladies' bathrooms, take off all my protective moped gear, and carry it back to my desk.

I take a quick look at my emails and Bloomberg with the front 20% of my brain. The back 80% is thinking about Dave. I am so happy I could burst. I was right!

I knew that if I just stayed in control, and played the cool/detached hand perfectly, that I could win him over. I really am bulletproof.

'Do you have any painkillers?' whispers a voice, and I turn to see Charlotte walking, or rather, stumbling, to her seat. Her hair is in some kind of messy platinum beehive, her skin is blotchy-but-glowing and she's got a guilty grin on her face. 'Henry and I went out for a bottle of wine last night and next thing I knew, it was midnight and we were in some Spanish bar behind Tottenham Court Road dancing to Mental As Anything,' she says.

'You look fantastic!' I exclaim. She does. She looks sex-sozzled and very, very happy.

'Are you drunk? I look like a furball. Have you seen my pash rash?' she grins, giggling helplessly. Her smile is so sweet, even through the stubble rash, and so much nicer than the pale, moochy expression that I knew all those months ago, that I can't help smiling back.

I reach into my second drawer for the morning-after kit I've used regularly since I started seeing Dave. 'Solpadeine, Berocca, toothbrush, deodorant, perfume, face powder, moisturiser, lip balm,' I whisper. 'Knock yourself out. And you should ask Henry to shave.'

'I know! But he's so cute when he's stubbly . . .' she says.

'I should have introduced you two months ago.'

'Yeah, what the fuck took you so long?' she says with a grin, before dashing off towards the bathrooms. I guess she's not rebounding with Henry: no one looks that ecstatically happy with a short-term investment.

The morning goes fast, and it's not until ten to 1 pm that I remember my lunch/date with Andre. Bugger. He's waiting for me in the lobby when I get down there.

'No moped suit?' he enquires, grinning at me. He really is a good-looking man, if you like that olive-skinned chocolate-eyed handsome French thing. But this isn't a date so it doesn't matter what I think of him. I'm sure we'll just grab a coffee and a sandwich from the Italian place, have a quick chat and get back to work.

'Uh, no, no moped suits at lunch' I say. 'So, where are we going?'

'Marco Pierre White,' he says.

Shit.

# Chapter Twenty Seven

I can't wait to tell Robert about this. I'm on an accidental lunch date with Andre.

We're only halfway through our main course at the Marco Pierre White Steak & Alehouse (a restaurant that, from the name, you'd think would have sawdust on the floor, but looks more like a wedding reception, with immaculate all-white decor and mirrors reflecting all the smug diners around us). Already Andre has told me all about his ex-wife, how he misses Paris, his loves (football, Danish design, the Maldives) and hates (the Catholic church, the European Union, Belgians). I definitely have the feeling that this isn't entirely business.

What can I do? I can't ask 'What are your intentions, young man?' I could be wrong, and either way, the ensuing awkwardness would be so awful. So instead, I'm trying to keep my end of the conversation professional-but-charming. It's not easy. He insisted on my trying one of his oysters ('oy-*stares*!') directly from the shell in his hand, and then asked if he might taste my potted shrimps. (I dumped a spoonful straight onto his plate.) Thank God we're both having steak for main course.

He hasn't asked if I'm seeing anyone, and I can't think of a conversation topic that starts 'so my boyfriend Dave and I' without being obvious.

The restaurant is tinkling with the sweet, festive sound of people dying to get plastered. The rest of the diners are 80%

male finance types, all on let's-expense-this-fucker lunches who are laughing loudly and tucking in to the food and particularly the wine with gusto. I feel very out of place.

'This is an exceptional restaurant,' says Andre, sipping his wine thoughtfully and maintaining eye contact with me. 'Elegant. Welcoming. Warm.'

'It is,' I agree. Is it just the accent that makes everything Andre says seem romantic? I've waited for almost an hour for him to bring up the work subject that was ostensibly the reason for today's lunch. But I don't want to be rude. And considering he's French he probably regards food with a practically sexual adoration and doesn't want to sully the meal with work-related talk.

Ah, fuck it. 'So, Andre, what was it you wanted to talk to me about?'

'Hong Kong,' he says. 'Come to Hong Kong with me.'

I am speechless. Is he propositioning me?

'As you know, I'm moving there to start a new regional retail analyst centre. I want you to be vice president of retail research.'

I stare at him for a few seconds. A promotion? In Hong Kong? 'I, um . . . does Suzanne know you are speaking to me about this?'

'No, and I don't want her to,' he says smoothly. He goes on to talk about the team he wants to start, and the role I'd be playing.

I can't think what to say. I have nothing in my brain.

Almost nothing.

Because I hate – *hate* – to admit this, but after six years of working, six years of 7 am starts and late nights and deferred bonuses and anxious presentations and endless hard fucking work, the first person I think of when I'm offered a career-making promotion is Dave.

'What's your, how do you say, stomach tell you?'

'You mean my gut?' I say.

'*Exactement*,' he says.

'That I need time to think about it,' I lie. I hadn't even consulted my gut, I was just picturing myself telling Dave about it, and him asking me – maybe even begging me – not to go, telling me that he needed me and couldn't live without me, that I was the only woman he'd ever – ahem. *God*. Get a grip, Abigail. 'And I'd need to check it all out,' I say, taking out my notebook. Yes. Act positive and rational. You're an analyst. Analyse it. 'If you tell me more, I'll do some research of my own . . .'

'OK. Let's meet again in January and discuss it.' He looks a bit disappointed.

'I'm really honoured, Andre, thrilled, amazing.' Someone hand me an adjective. 'Thank you. It sounds incredible, incredibly interesting, uh, incredible.' Nice one.

Andre goes on to tell me more about the history of the office, and the people currently working there, and their major clients. I make a note of everything, trying to keep my facial expression set to 'interested'.

'I hope it will be motivating for both of us. I have been watching you over the past two months. Suzanne, well, she is . . .' he clears his throat. 'I think you need more authority and freedom to really thrive. I'd like to give you total autonomy.'

'That sounds wonderful,' I say. And it does.

The question I should be asking myself, of course, is the question I never, ever answer: do I even *want* to do this job anymore? I don't know. What do I want? Urgh. Don't think about it . . .

Suddenly my attention is drawn by two familiar figures coming in to the restaurant, and for a second, I think I'm hallucinating. I glance quickly into the mirrors to try to see their faces and gasp.

They walk away from us, right down to the other end of the restaurant, and sit at a table almost entirely obscured from my view. But I get a good look before they sit down. And there's no mistaking who it is.

Dave and Bella.

I feel like I've been kicked in the chest. I can't breathe. What is he doing here with her? Are they friends now? I didn't think they even got on, did you?

'Abigail? Are you alright?' says Andre. He puts his knife and fork down and looks over at me in concern.

'Fine, I'm fine,' I say, putting my hand to my forehead in an attempt to slow down my thoughts. The initial pain has turned into an icy feeling that is washing through my body. They can't see me, but I want to run away – from them, from my thoughts, from work, from everything. I mean, what the hell are they doing here together? They're not friends, they barely spoke to each other in France! What should I do? Confront them? That would be a bit dramatic, wouldn't it? I mean it's just lunch! Then Dave might think I'm overreacting, or being unnaturally jealous. He does hate jealousy, he told me that once, he finds it boring. I don't want to spoil anything just when things are finally good between us . . .

My heart is hammering painfully, oh God, I feel sick.

Let's be positive: they're having lunch, not dinner, right? Lunch is nothing, right? I'm at lunch with Andre! But in that case, why didn't Dave tell me he was meeting Bella today? Then again, he never tells me who he's seeing for lunch. Perhaps he's giving her advice on Ollie. No, that's not likely either. If I walked up to them and said 'fancy seeing you here!', would it be awkward? It totally would. Bella was, frankly, a bit of a bitch in France. And I thought she lived in fucking Bath! God! Brain, slow down! I put both hands to my temples and take a deep breath.

'You are very pale,' says Andre. 'Do you need some air?'

I meet his eyes. 'Yes,' I say. 'I need to get out of here. Do you mind if we leave? I will wait for you outside.'

'No problem,' he says. 'I'll get the bill.'

I run-walk to the door, my head down so that Dave and Bella don't notice me. Not that they're looking around, mind you, from what I can see in nervous, flicky little glances, they're deep in conversation. They look intensely together. Like a couple. An impossibly beautiful, sexy couple.

I think I'm going to throw up.

I get my coat and hurry outside to the street, taking deep breaths as I go.

Breathe, Abigail. Think. What would Robert say about this? Should I call him? No. Of course not. He's all weird about Dave as it is. But if I did, he'd say I was overreacting.

And he'd be right. It's just lunch with an old friend. A family friend! It's nothing. Last night Dave said he wanted to be with me, that he wanted to tell everyone we were together. He said he wanted a girl like me.

Remembering this, my anxiety loosens its stranglehold on my chest just slightly. Enough so I don't think I'm about to keel over.

Calm down. He can have lunch with an old family friend who happens to be a woman. After all, I'm having lunch with Andre, aren't I? And Dave isn't the kind of guy who would cheat, is he?

Actually, he's exactly the kind of guy I'd previously have imagined as a cheater – confident, slick, flirty, with a short attention span . . . but that's a stupid thing to think. What do I know about the kind of man who cheats? Peter – pause to spit – cheated on me! And I was absolutely fucking clueless about it. God, oh God why is this happening. Brain, please stop.

Anyway. She has a boyfriend, Ollie, and yes, they were fighting in France but I don't think they've broken up, have they? So why am I jumping to conclusions?

'Abigail, I am so sorry, perhaps it was the oy-*stare*?' says Andre, coming outside. His face is all worried concern.

'Uh, perhaps it was,' I agree. 'Let's go back to the office.'

The rest of the afternoon is agony. My standard uneasy Daveticipation was nothing compared to this. I can't help it: I'm in hell.

I can't even distract myself: there's nothing happening in the markets. I can't hold a phone conversation. I can't read to the end of a sentence without thinking about what I saw, and I'm obsessively checking my phone. I even take my phone to the toilet with me in case he calls, which is hard, as it's one of those office loos with no cistern so there's nowhere to balance it, so I have to put it in my mouth while I pee. That's probably really unhygienic.

I'm desperate to call Plum or Sophie for reassurance. But their inevitable advice will be to simply ask him what he was doing. I know that's what you're probably thinking too. But I can't. I can't confront him about having lunch with his ex-fling (ex-girlfriend? No, it was just a fling, right? That's what Robert said, wasn't it?). It sounds like I was stalking him, and he'll ask why I didn't come up and say hi right then and there instead of creeping away. If I bring it up now, I'm going to look like a fool.

Oh God. I want to cry.

I head home from work at 6 pm.

I go straight upstairs. Robert's not home. Every step is difficult, and the house feels unusually cold. I have no energy. Angst is so draining.

I lie on my bed in the dark, fully dressed, and stare at the ceiling.

Worst case scenario: it will all end. I'll go back to being single.

That wouldn't be so bad, right? I started this thing with Dave knowing that it could end, that I had to stay in control and not become too smitten, too fast, that I had to be bulletproof . . .

But I'm not. I took a risk. I told him I wanted to be with him last night. I have to see this out.

Anyway, everything else in my world has changed. Everyone else is in love now. Robert is single, but as he said once, he's multiple. Being the only single person in the group would not be fun. I'd be alone every night, with no wingwomen to go out with.

And anyway, I don't want to be single. I want Dave.

I think I must be falling in love with him. This sick, nervous feeling can't be anything else.

My phone rings from deep in the depths of my bag. Moving faster than I ever have before, I sit up and grab the flashing light in the darkness.

It's Dave. 'Hello?' I say, answering too quickly.

'I need you. Naked. My house, 20 minutes.'

'Aren't you going to feed me first?' I say, on auto-witter whilst my mind races. He sounds totally normal. Not like he had an illicit lunch today or has anything to hide.

'I've got something delicious for you to munch on,' he says. 'It's very high in protein. Good for the skin, too.'

I pause. That's normally the kind of absurdly obscene comment that would make me giggle. But I can't. Fear has sucked the giggles out of me.

'Oh, alright, I suppose we should eat before we eat,' he grumbles. 'See you at Odette's in half an hour?'

'Make it an hour,' I say. I need time to prepare, physically and mentally.

'Ah, the elusive Miss Wood. It's a deal,' he says, and hangs up.

I can hardly eat at dinner, or speak, but Dave doesn't seem to notice. He goes on and on about his day, and his latest deal, and tells me I look gorgeous. I'm trying to keep my end of the conversation up, but I feel like a moth pinned to one of those Victorian wall-hangings. Fluttering with panic and unable to move.

'I saw Bella today,' he says, towards the end of our meal, as he pours me another glass of wine. At least I can still drink.

'Really?' I choke out, staring into my glass so I can avoid eye contact. 'How is she?'

'Great, fine,' he says. 'She was in London for a work thing, wanted to catch up. After a free lunch, I expect. She's a bit embarrassed about being such a bitch in France, wanted to apologise. She and Ollie were having problems.'

'Are she and Ollie OK now?' I ask.

'Fine,' says Dave dismissively. He's not interested in other people's relationships, he's told me that before. 'If you'll excuse me, angel, I have to use the – what is it you always say?'

'The euphemism,' I murmur.

'And then I'm taking you home and I want you naked within minutes, if not seconds. Got that? You're looking ridiculously delectable tonight.'

The moment he's gone I nearly collapse with relief. They really were just having lunch! Nothing more! And he told me about it! He wouldn't do that if he had anything to hide! Thank fuck.

I'm overwhelmed with adoration and relief. He is honest. He adores me and wants me. Not Bella.

Dave's iPhone is, as ever, face-up on the table, and it buzzes with a text.

I glance down at it.

You can read texts on iPhones without opening them, and I can't help that I can read upside down from years of sitting across from people in meetings. So I'm really not snooping. The second I read it, I wish I hadn't. The text is from Bella.

*Ha, enjoy. Am home safe. B*

I'm frozen, staring at the text, till it disappears from the screen. It's obviously a response to a text he sent her. Enjoy? Enjoy what? Dinner with me? Why the 'ha'? It sounds sarcastic, doesn't it?

Stop thinking about it, Abigail, goddammit, you crazy fool. You're overreacting again.

A little wispy curl of insecurity winds itself around my chest and settles.

Dave returns and, before sitting down, leans over to kiss me. Our eyes meet as he pulls away and with a little grin, he puts his hand out to tweak my ear. I smile at him and remind myself that he wouldn't be here if he didn't want to be with me. He wants me, not Bella. Me.

# Chapter Twenty Eight

'This has been the slowest Christmas ever,' I say. '*Ever*.'

'I know,' says Plum.

It's December 30th. I've been in France for almost a week. Sophie left on Boxing Day to join Luke at his parents' house in Bath, so it's just me and my parents.

I'm lying on my bed – the bed that Dave and I were deliciously filthy in all those weeks ago – with my legs propped up against the walls. The shutters are half open, revealing a very dark grey sky. Plum's at her parents' house in Yorkshire.

'I am so over my family,' she says. 'If I have to go carolling one more time . . .'

Plum's family Christmases are very traditional. Carolling, church and long freezing walks. The only tradition we have is watching *Annie* on Christmas Day after lunch, with my parents singing along.

'ABIGAIL!' bellows my father from the kitchen downstairs, making me jump. No one bellows like my Dad.

'Oh my God, this is like being six again,' I murmur to Plum. 'Yes?' I call down sweetly.

'There you are. I thought you were lost. Would you care for some soup?'

'It's four o'clock in the afternoon, Daddy,' I call.

'I know. But I thought it might be nice.'

'No, thank you.' I shut my bedroom door. 'That's the eighteenth time one of them has yelled for me today.'

261

'Maybe you're not spending quality time,' says Plum.

'I eat every meal with them, I go to the market with them, we watch movies together, I mean, unless they want to chat to me when I'm weeing.'

'When are you seeing Dave?'

'ABIGAIL!' There's another bellow from the kitchen.

'I'd better go,' I say, sighing. I don't want to answer the Dave question.

'I can't wait to see Dan,' says Plum, ignoring me. 'Did I tell you that he surprised me by wrapping Christmas lights around his willy and singing "Oh Come All Ye Faithful" to me?'

'You did,' I say.

'Are you OK? You don't quite sound yourself,' says Plum.

'Fine, I'm fine, I've just got cabin fever,' I say quickly. The truth is that no matter how much I remind myself that Dave said he wanted to be with me, the insecurity curl won't release its hold around my chest. And it's all because of Bella and that text. It makes it hard to concentrate on anything else . . . I feel very unsettled.

He hasn't called me since I got here. But he does send two or three funny/filthy texts a day, all signed off with an 'x'. Which he didn't used to do. That's good, right? My uneasy longing for reassurance is so severe that when he finally texts, it's like a reprieve from someone hitting me in the face. The relief lasts seconds. Then the chewing, restless worry starts again.

'No problem. You're back tomorrow, right? Are you seeing Dave right away?'

'Uh, no,' I say. Dave hasn't told me when he's back in London, and because I don't want to be needy, I haven't asked. Text-terrogations and all that. 'You?'

'Dan is coming over tonight for dinner to meet my parents and then we're driving back to London together,' she says. 'I've got to go and wrap his presents, actually. Then we're flying to Geneva tomorrow night for the ski trip.'

'Meeting the parents! Good luck,' I say. I cannot imagine Dave meeting my parents. And I don't have a present for him either as all he said about the subject was 'I don't do presents, but I promise to slip you a little Christmas cheer'.

'Alright, darling. Miss you like cock!'

'Miss you too. I'll call you tonight.'

This holiday has been endless. Plum and I have slipped back into talking three times a day, like teenagers. And I haven't thought about my career doubts, and the job offer in Hong Kong, and what I'll do next. I haven't told anyone in my family about it either. They'd just get carried away and that would make it even harder to think clearly.

'ABIGAAAAIL!'

God, it's irritating to be shouted at every 20 seconds. I walk down the stairs, automatically checking my phone and email on the way. Dave hasn't been in touch today, which I think might be why I'm feeling particularly feverish.

'ABI—'

'I'm here,' I say quietly. Dad is standing in the kitchen, saucepan of soup bubbling on the stove, staring at the open fridge with his hands folded thoughtfully over his chest. It's the same stance he uses to watch cricket.

'Oh! Darling. Good. I'm doing the fridge, and I thought you might like to be my little helper.'

When I was five, 'doing the fridge' with Dad was my favourite activity, simply because we almost always found chocolate stashed behind some eggs or something, and we'd share it, giggle furtively and Not Tell Mummy. Now that I'm almost 28 and have my own fridge and chocolates, it's less exciting. But I can't say that as it'll hurt his feelings.

'I'd love to,' I say as enthusiastically as I can.

'So, bub, tell me about your plans for New Year's Eve,' he says a few minutes later, when we're rubber-gloved and ready to go. He starts handing me the milk and juices ('Door first!

Then top to bottom!') and I stack them symmetrically on the bench.

'Um, I'm not sure yet,' I say honestly.

'Your first New Year as a single girl, not to mention your birthday on New Year's Day, you should be out on the town,' says Dad. 'Fun. It's all about having fun.'

God, he sounds like Robert. 'Well, Plum's with her boyfriend, and Henry is at home in the Cotswolds with Charlotte, did I tell you about her? I introduced them and now they're in love. I don't really know what the rest of the uni crowd is up to, I've avoided them a bit since Peter and I broke up,' I'm auto-wittering to hide how distracted I'm feeling. 'I think Sophie and Luke are coming back to London. I guess my flatmate, Robert might be around.'

'Have you been seeing anyone, since, er, you know who?' asks Dad.

Ah, he wants a daddy-daughter heart-to-heart. He always likes doing these over a project. When I was here last summer, just before I broke up with Peter and was mute with anticipatory worry, it took him three similar daddy-daughter projects to get me to talk about it. When I finally did, however, I felt so disloyal to Peter that I could hardly say a thing. I just cried. So then Dad took me to the huge supermarket in Béziers and we looked at the hardware aisle together in silence.

'I have been dating,' I say. 'It's fun. I am very glad I broke up with Peter, put it that way.'

'Good,' he says. 'Anyone in particular?'

'Nope,' I lie. I don't want to talk about Dave. They'll wonder why I haven't mentioned him till now, and why he hasn't called, and why I didn't open a present from him on Christmas Day. I wonder if he's found out it's my birthday on New Year's Day . . . Oh God, I am tired of thinking. 'You know. Taking it casual.'

'There's no hurry. I hope you don't feel pressured to meet someone because of Mrs Mop getting married.'

264

Mrs Mop is Dad's pet name for Sophie. I am Mrs Waterbucket. They've been our nicknames forever, for reasons unknown.

Dad starts handing me the pickles and chutneys from the top shelf of the fridge. Condiments always seemed to me to be an extraordinarily grown-up thing to have in a fridge, don't you think? I used to have loads of chutney-type things when I lived with Peter. Such a different life.

'Earth to Abigail,' says Dad. 'I asked if you'd met anyone particularly nice.'

'Sorry!' I say. 'Mind wandering again.'

'You've always been the same, carrying on entire conversations in your head and exhausting yourself. I think it's the reason you didn't speak till you were three.'

'Till I was three?!'

'Well,' he says, his voice muffled from deep inside the fridge, as he passes me jars of anchovy paste and mussels. I've never seen a fridge so full of non-food food. 'You were always the slowest to do anything, because you thought about it so much first. But then when you actually tried, you were brilliant. Like when you finally started talking, you spoke in full sentences. None of this mama-dada-baba rubbish for you. So I'm sure it's the same with, you know, love.'

'But learning to talk is a bit different from love.'

'Take your time,' he says. 'It sounds ridiculous, but when you find the right person you'll just know. It'll all be very easy.'

'Really?' I say doubtfully.

'Everyone says it, but it's true.' The fridge is empty now. 'Right. Now we wash the shelves.'

Dad is so happy when he's got both sinks full of hot water, splashing soapy bubbles everywhere. He's like a big duck. It drives my mother nuts. On cue, the front door bangs, and my mother walks in. She's been out gossiping with the neighbours, judging by the gleeful look on her face.

'Hands up who wants to watch *Grease* tonight? I just borrowed it from Virginia and Rod up the road!' says Mum excitedly. Sometimes she says things in an eager voice in an attempt to get Sophie and I keyed up about things. I think it worked when we were small.

'Yes please,' I say. 'Sounds great.'

Mum cocks her head to one side and looks up at me. She's a good five inches shorter than either Sophie or I, though she thinks she's very tall. ('I based my whole personality on being tall, I can't change now,' she said once, when Sophie and I confronted her about it.) She also has the ability to pick someone's mood based on the way they're holding their drink.

'Are you alright? You look tired. Are you tired?'

'I'm fine,' I say to the fridge so she can't look at my eyes and see that I'm lying.

'You've been out of sorts ever since you arrived. Have you twosied today?'

'Everything's smashing in that department, thanks, Mum,' I say, giving her the double thumbs up. 'I don't think "twosie" is a verb, though.'

'Thank you, smartypants,' Mum pretends to smack me, but I jump away.

Dad is now standing in front of the fridge, inspecting every corner. 'I think we can probably improve the system, you know, make it more intuitive, streamlined . . .'

'Yep,' I say, trying to give the fridge the attention Dad feels it deserves.

'Vegetables and fruit at the bottom, obviously, and then meat next, and then – and now, this is a bit controversial, but stay with me – the yoghurt and cheeses on the middle shelf, because statistically, I think we reach for them most often.' Dad is beaming with pride. 'Right? And then condiments and mustards and mayo at the top back, jams at the front for brekkers, and voilà. A perfect fridge!'

'Yay!' cheer Mum and I, as applause is clearly required.

When we're done, I kiss him on the cheek and head back upstairs. My mind is an intense whirlpool of half-thoughts and half-worries. I take out my notebook, open it to a new page, and write down what Dad just said.

*When you find the right person you'll just know.*

What a singularly irritating statement.

I start drawing little curls around the sentence.

I wonder if I 'just know' with Dave. I might, you know. I've never felt that crash-bang attraction before. I tremble whenever he is near me, or looking at me, or at the same table as me . . . And when he kisses me, my brain goes into a total arrest.

Is that what it means to 'just know'?

Maybe my insecurity over where he and I are going and my inability to be really, truly open with him is just my inexperience. Or maybe my silly worries about Bella are just distrust left from discovering Peter's infidelity. Or a hangover from all those 'cool! detached!' lectures from stupid old Robert.

From my back pocket, my phone vibrates.

A text! From Dave!

*Hello, my sexy little roast chestnut. I was just looking at photos of you on Facebook. You are scrumptious, has anyone ever told you that? x*

I grin delightedly to myself, and the insecurity curl around my chest disappears. My little Dave-fix. Twenty minutes later, after more redrafts than I can bear to admit to you (because I am a grown woman and should have better things to do with my time than draft the perfect sexy/witty/wry/understated little text) I have a reply to send.

Now, I don't want to pin him down with a text-terrogation, but my natural urge to ask WHERE ARE YOU? WHEN ARE YOU BACK? WHAT ARE YOU DOING? DO YOU MISS ME? WILL YOU SEE ME TOMORROW NIGHT? WHY WILL YOU NEVER MAKE PLANS WITH ME? WHY DID BELLA TEXT YOU? WHY DAMMIT? WHY? is getting harder and harder to ignore. So I've decided to bend the rules and refer – very, very sneakily – to the future.

My reply:

*Stalking is so last year. And yes, I've been told that many times. One more sleep till Abigail is home in London. Hurrah. x*

His immediate reply.

*Hurrah indeed. I've just about had it with my family, too. My sister has gone batshit crazy this year. x*

See what I mean? No details.

I wonder what Louisa has done to get the title of 'batshit crazy'. I think she's the first person I've ever intensely disliked without even seeing her. Anyone who treated Robert that way must be evil. I hope I get to meet her soon.

Another text! From Dave!

*I miss you by the way. See you tomorrow. x*

# Chapter Twenty Nine

It's so good to be home. Our house is still decked out in Robert's sister's Christmas decorations, there's milk in the fridge and crumpets in the breadbin, and it's warm and clean. In short, the place feels loved.

As soon as I got back, I took a shower, dressed in my new Christmas J Brand jeans and a white top, unpacked, put washing on, changed my sheets, rearranged my wardrobe, and played my favourite Roxy Music songs very loudly on the iPod player.

Bored.

I'm trying to manage my Daveticipation. He'll be in touch today. I know he will. He texted 'See you tomorrow'. I have to be patient and not text-terrogate him.

And when I see him – or kiss him – again, perhaps I'll know. Just like my father said.

I wonder what Robert is up to . . . I made him a Christmas card in France. I want our friendship to go back to what it was . . . Whatever he doesn't like about me being with Dave, he's just going to have to learn to live with.

Hmm.

I take out my notebook and look at the sentence again. *When you find the right person you'll just know.* I drew so many little squiggles and arrows around it that anyone analysing that page would think I was crazy and potentially violent.

Very bored. Plum and Henry are spending New Year's Eve

with their respective new partners, Sophie and Luke are driving into London later today . . . DaveDaveDave . . . I wonder what Robert is doing. I'll call him.

'Why, if it isn't the nearly-birthday girl,' says Robert, instead of hello.

'You're not at work, are you? Because it's nearly 5 pm on New Year's Eve and that would be weird. Happy Christmas, by the way.'

'Happy Christmas. And I am at work, yes.'

'Fancy a little New Year's Eve drink?'

'Done. The Only Running Footman in Mayfair?'

'See you there, one hour.'

The Only Running Footman is a loving Christmas hug of an old pub in Mayfair. It's just off Berkeley Square, and during normal weekdays is filled with local suits drinking boisterously. At 6 pm on this dark and frosty New Year's Eve, however, it's surprisingly empty, with just a handful of people in black tie having pre-dinner drinks before heading off to some glamorous Mayfair ball, no doubt. Ever noticed how men always look smug and round in black tie, and women always look sparkly and freezing?

I order two large whiskies and take a seat, my face lighting up as I see a familiar broad-shouldered figure coming in the front door.

'Robert!' I exclaim, jumping up to give him a hug. He looks a bit tired and peaky, probably from working too hard and not eating properly, I muse. And his hair is shorter than I've ever seen it, making him look somehow clean-cut and younger.

'Love the haircut! Can I call you Drill Sergeant?'

'Ah, Abby,' he says, leaning into kiss me on both cheeks, and I give him a hug. He's so big and broad, particularly in all his winter layers and coat. It's like wrapping my arms around a tree.

'Sit down, my boy,' I say. 'You look pale. Have you been eating properly?'

'Yes, Mummy,' he says, taking a sip of his whisky. 'Oh, fuck me, that's good. What is that?'

'Laphroaig,' I say. 'Just one for you, though, princess. You know how you get after a few whiskies.' I raise my eyebrows at him meaningfully.

Robert shouts with laughter. 'Christ! One time! And I drank about a bottle that night, I'll have you know. I'm an exceptional drunk.'

'Of course you are. Now! I made you a Christmas card.'

He opens it. 'You shouldn't have! Ah, really. You shouldn't have . . .' I know I'm a dork, but I made him a little amateur-découpage card with pictures I cut from magazines and discarded Christmas gift tags. There's a moped, porridge, a Bloody Mary, a newspaper, and Don Draper from *Mad Men*, because I think Robert looks like him, and a plum pudding, and a reindeer on which I wrote 'Fernie 2002', and lots of stars.

'It's ugly, but festive, which I think is fitting given what our house looks like right now,' I say.

Robert reads the poem I wrote inside.

'For Robert, so tall and such a grouch, I always see you on the couch, Happy Christmas and New Year, I hope it's filled with lots of cheer'. Wow. That's . . .'

'I know, brilliant,' I say, laughing. 'I was bored.'

'Thank you, Abby. I feel so lucky. Did you make one for Dave, too?' he asks.

'No, just my friends. So tell me about your Christmas. Did Santa find you?'

'Yes, and he brought me pyjamas with airplanes on – my mother doesn't know that I sleep naked—'

'And usually have a girl for added warmth,' I interject.

'—precisely, and my sisters gave me this rather smart coat. What about you, Abigail, my little Christmas fairy?'

'These jeans, and this jumper, and some books, and some of that lemon bath oil from doctor whatever-it-is, and very warm gloves.'

271

'Alice's husband gave her gloves one year and it caused a fight that lasted till February.'

'Schoolboy error. Never give a practical present to someone you sleep with.'

'I'd like to amend that to "or a present that could in anyway insult the recipient, no matter who the recipient is",' says Robert. 'Last year, my mother gave me a book called *Online Dating For Dummies*.' I laugh so hard at this that I choke on my whisky.

'Peter got me a blender once. Practical AND insulting.'

'Louisa once got me a card saying she was taking me to Morocco as my present,' says Robert. 'And then she left me on New Year's Eve so we never went. Which was how she'd always planned it, I guess.'

'That's not funny at all.' I'm shocked.

'I know.' He sighs. No wonder he looks tired, I think. It's the anniversary of his broken heart.

God, I'm dramatic these days.

'Right, well, we're not going to think about her today, the silly bitch. We're going to have another drink and cheer the fuck up.'

By the time we're halfway through the next whisky, the pub is filling up. I have my phone on the table, so I can surreptitiously ensure there's no chance I can miss a call from Dave, but there's been nothing so far. It's 7 pm now. Five hours to go. I just need to be patient. He'll turn up. In the meantime, Robert is doing impressions of his sisters, who always fight like harpies over Christmas.

'I think it's a chemical thing that happens to sisters,' I say.

'Alice is properly grown-up with two children, yet she chased Rosie around the house with a wooden spoon screaming "I know you are wearing my fucking knickers, take them fucking off".'

'I wonder when people actually turn properly grown-up,' I say. 'I don't feel it.'

'I don't think anyone does. Alice says sometimes she sees her kids as really cool housemates with serious dependence issues. So, what do you want to do for your birthday tomorrow?'

'Nothing is planned,' I say, and am about to say 'it depends on Dave' but then I realise how pathetic that sounds, so instead I shrug. 'I always feel like New Year's Eve is the whole world celebrating my birthday a day early, anyway. Maybe we could all go to the pub in the afternoon and just relax. Sophie and Luke and Henry and Charlotte are in London, so . . .'

'Sounds like a plan,' nods Robert. 'And Dave, of course.'

'Of course,' I nod. I glance quickly at my phone. Nope, nothing. I look up and meet Robert's gaze, and before he can mind-read me, I stand up. 'Right! I'm going to the bar.'

There are a couple of girls on a table near the bar, looking at the A-Z map of London.

'Well, that can't be right, that says St James there, but I thought that St James was a park down there,' says one girl.

'That's definitely the Piccadilly Circus region, not St James,' says the other. They're American.

'Hi there . . .' I say. Oh God, why do I always try to talk to strangers after I've had a drink. Oh well. 'Actually, St James is also a very small area just below Piccadilly, as well as a park, and Piccadilly is a long road between Hyde Park Corner and Piccadilly Circus. And that's just a big ugly junction no one goes to if they can help it.'

'Thank you!' they chorus, looking up at me delightedly. They both have perfect teeth, like all Americans. (Damn them.)

'You're so nice!' says the blonde. 'I'm Taylor, this is Bree.'

I order my drinks, and we chat together for a minute. They quickly tell me, in the way of all ambitious new graduates, that they've just finished their degrees in journalism but couldn't find jobs thanks to the economy, so are now travelling around the world and blogging about it.

'We hope to get a book deal at the end, and we'll parlay that into a career in journalism,' says Taylor. 'We have 3,000 followers on Twitter already and it's only been a month. It's called Travel By Proxy.'

They're 21 and they've already got more ambition and career smarts than I do at 28-minus-one-day. When did everyone else figure everything out?

'Can we take a photo of you?' says Bree, brandishing a digital camera. 'Will you be an interview subject?'

'Uh, sure,' I say. Man, I hate photos. 'Do you want to interview a guy too? I feel bad leaving him by himself for too long . . .'

Bree and Taylor turn around, see Robert, and both of their jaws drop. I stifle the urge to laugh. Within seconds, they've picked up their coats, bags and drinks, and are heading over towards him.

'I come bearing gifts!' I beam at him, and make a ta-dah! motion with my hands at Bree and Taylor. They both immediately put on kittenish smiles and Bree pulls down her ponytail, running her fingers through her roots. Robert shoots me a lamb-to-the-slaughter look, before turning to the girls with a smile.

'Hello, Bree. Hello, Taylor.'

'Hello!' says Bree. 'Now! Let me introduce you to Travel By Proxy!' She explains the concept again.

'Abby, darling, you go first,' says Robert.

I nod, sit up straight and try to look thoughtful.

'What's your idea of perfect happiness?'

'Um . . . My friends and a late-night bar.'

'And your boyfriend Robert!' interrupts Taylor.

'Absolutely,' I say automatically. Robert and I look at each other and I fight the urge to laugh.

'What is the quality you most like in a man?'

'Confidence,' I say. 'And charm.' An image of Dave flashes into my head. I wonder where he is, and why he hasn't texted. I—

'What is the quality you most like in a woman?'

'Silliness. And smarts.'

'If you could change one thing about yourself, what would it be?'

'My inability to decide what I want in life,' I say. Robert and I meet eyes again. 'Did you just steal these from the *Vanity Fair* Proust Questionnaire, or what?'

'Not the final one,' says Bree proudly. 'Where do you see yourself in 12 months?'

I'm stumped. I open my mouth to talk and nothing comes out. Robert starts to laugh. 'She doesn't like thinking about the future,' he tells them.

'No, no, I can answer this!' I say. What do I want my life to look like in 12 months? Images flash through my brain: Dave, work, Dave, work . . . nothing is clear. Why am I so indecisive? 'Um,' I say desperately, and cast about for inspiration. 'Well, it'll be New Year's Eve, so I see myself drinking in a pub with Robert.'

'Good answer!' says Taylor. 'OK! Robert. Your girlfriend did so well, let's see how you go!'

'Be gentle,' he says seriously. She giggles and chews her pen. I roll my eyes inwardly.

'OK! OK. What's your idea of perfect happiness?'

'Peanut butter on crumpets,' he says seriously.

'What's a crumpet?' Bree whispers to me.

'It's like a type of bread,' I whisper back.

Taylor clears her throat meaningfully. 'What is the quality you most like in a man?'

'High alcohol tolerance. And loyalty.'

'What is the quality you most like in a woman?'

'Good posture. And loyalty.'

'If you could change one thing about yourself, what would it be?'

'The list is too long . . .' he says, looking at me and smiling.

'Where do you see yourself in 12 months?'

'Apparently I'll be drinking with Abigail.'

'This is great. So great!' says Bree, tapping away.

'Oh my God! Bree! We have to go!' exclaims Taylor, looking at her watch. 'Our New Year's Eve party starts in two hours!'

'You must get tired of girls throwing themselves at you,' I say, after they've left.

'You're the one who dropped them at my feet like a cat with a mouse.'

'I know how hard it is for you to meet women,' I say.

'It used to be. It was only because of those snogging competitions with Dave that I kissed anyone in my teens . . . I was more competitive than I was shy.'

Oh, Dave. Where are you, I think. Why haven't you called.

'He'll turn up,' says Robert. 'I think he's still with his family.'

Our eyes meet again, and I'm about to tell him off for mind-reading, when the girls burst back into the pub. 'We forgot the photo! Some journalists we are!' Bree exclaims. 'OK, smile!'

We both sit up and smile for the photo.

'Come on, you guys! Put your arm around your lady, Robert!'

Robert puts his arm around me. I look towards him, our eyes meet for a second, and I start laughing. This is ridiculous.

'Perfect! So amazing. OK! Call us later! Or we'll email you! Bye!' They run out of the pub again.

'Where was your first kiss, then?' says Robert, after a pause.

'On holiday. A French boy. I was 15 and just happy to get it over and done with. You?'

'I was on holiday too. I was 14. My sister Alice lined Luke, Dave and I up with the other girls and counted three . . . two . . . one . . . LUNGE!'

I'm laughing so hard that I start banging the table with my hand. Ow, that hurts. Must be a bit tipsy.

'Who were the girls?'

'Our sisters, actually,' he says. 'Don't look at me like that! Not our own sisters, obviously. I kissed Louisa who was 19 and, frankly, cradle snatching at the time, Luke kissed Rosie who was 16, and Dave kissed Bella who was 13.'

'That's pretty sick.' Bella and Dave were each other's first kiss? Oh God, don't think about it.

'Yeah, weird, isn't it? Especially considering . . . everything,' he says, then glances at me. I meet his gaze and try to smile.

'Sorry. It was a very long time ago. Do you want a burger?'

'Oo! Yes. Burger. And a beer. And a shot.' I need to erase the image of teenage Dave and Bella kissing.

'Sure you shouldn't slow down?'

'I'm totally fine. When I start doing splits on the dance floor then you'll know I've had enough,' I say. Where is Dave? Argh, the Daveticipation . . . It's nearly 8 pm: he'll be here within four hours. He has to be.

# Chapter Thirty

After we eat, we decide to go to The Punchbowl, another Mayfair pub a few minutes away.

Robert is showing me photos on his phone of his niece Merry, who is four, and Tom, who is two and who has the hugest smile you've ever seen.

'He's the spitting image of myself at that age, by all accounts,' says Robert proudly.

'I always figured you as a grump from birth.' I glance up at him and grin. 'Don't worry, I know you're the Stay Puft marshmallow man underneath. It's a big grouchy facade.'

Robert makes a huffing-laugh sound. 'So is your so-called inability to know what you want in life.'

'Really,' I retort.

'I think you know exactly what you want. You're just too scared to admit it because then you'd actually have to do something about it.'

My face falls. Wow, that was pretty fucking insightful. But I don't want to think about it.

'Too far? Did I go too far?' he says, grinning at me.

'Yes, too far,' I say, frowning up at him. 'That cut me. Deep.'

'Sorry, Abby, darling.' He puts an arm around me and squeezes my shoulder. 'You can say something cutting to me, if you like.'

'OK, I think it's ridiculous that you're still hung up on some absolute bitch who was never good enough for you anyway,' I say, pushing his arm off me. 'I mean, some people are asshats. You have to let it go. You can't control everything in life.'

'Thanks for the advice,' he snaps. 'That's great, from the girl who can't take a risk.'

We stare at each other angrily for a second and then start laughing.

The Punchbowl is the pub owned by Guy Ritchie, and has a more dilapidated air than the cosy-cool The Only Running Footman. The crowd in here seem like they've been here for weeks, sort of glamorous faux-ruffian types who are probably perfectly respectable and work in music or film, plus the inevitable Mayfair tourists and a few New Year black tie types who seem to have forgotten they're meant to be at another party.

Robert heads off to find us a table, and I order two vodka and sodas. Yes. Simple and soothing. It's 9 pm. Dave could turn up at any second, he could be surprising me, he might be texting Robert right now to find out where we are . . . The idea makes me smile.

'You should smile more often,' says a voice to my left. I turn and see a tall guy – mid-30s, slightly scruffy – in a minging leather jacket. 'It makes you much prettier.'

Why do men say things like that? It's not even a compliment, it's saying we're ugly when we're not smiling. I turn back to the bartender and pay for my drinks.

'Guess I'll have to find you at midnight and make you smile,' he continues.

'Guess so,' I agree, carrying the drinks over to the table. As if.

'I came here with Antonia once,' comments Robert. 'It wasn't a good match.'

'I can imagine,' I say, picturing Antonia's all-white Euro ensemble in here. 'Did she wear the white fur gilet? What is that? Albino kittens?'

'No, baby wabbits,' he says, and pauses as we clink glasses. 'God, it probably *is* made from wabbits. Gross.'

'What happened that time you saw her in the airport?' I say, hoping he's feeling more open than usual.

'What? . . . oh. That time. Well, I said "hi Antonia, how are you?". Then she told me what a total bastard I was, how miserable she'd been over me, how if I didn't care I shouldn't have flown out to Milan to see her when she was upset about her dog dying—'

'You did?'

'She was upset!' he says, grinning. 'I didn't think that was *that* romantic.'

'Well, it is. The knight in shining armour act is an obvious aphrodisiac.'

'I did hope I might get some sex,' he admits.

'You're such a gent. So then what happened?'

'And so then I said, I am sorry, it was unfair of me to expect you to be fine with it. And I shouldn't have dumped you by text—' I gasp in horror '—I'm sorry for not answering your phone calls and for refusing to talk about it. I was wrong.'

'God, Robert, I can't believe I ever took dating advice from you. You're such a prick.'

'I apologised to her! And she forgave me. And it wasn't dating advice. It was singledom advice. Huge difference.'

I glare at him. 'Don't change the subject.'

'I said I was sorry. Your lectures made me see the error of my ways . . . or rather, the error of how I deal with the aftermath of my ways.' He smiles angelically.

'A lifetime of bad habits can't be changed overnight. I feel like I should slap you on behalf of the sisterhood.'

'Go for it.'

I raise my hand and slap him firmly across the cheek – not enough to hurt – and he pretends to start crying. I start giggling, I can't help it.

'Such a reprobate, and yet I adore you,' I say, laughing despite myself.

'You do?' he says, brightening.

'But I sure as hell wouldn't want any woman I know going near you with a 10-foot pole.'

Robert's face falls for a second. Then he smirks. 'How did you know my pole is 10 feet? Right. Me to the bar.'

'Another cleansing vodka for me, please.'

Hmm definitely a bit tipsy, applying lip gloss is tough. I'm almost drunk enough to call Dave. I try to weigh up the joy of hearing his voice versus the joy of winning today's phone call powerplay. Perhaps I'll just—

'Are you OK?' I look up. It's Leather Jacket man.

'I'm fine.' I look back at my drink. I want him to go away.

'I saw you slap your boyfriend,' says Leather Jacket.

I start laughing. 'That was a joke! He's not my boyfriend.'

'You shouldn't spend your New Year's Eve with someone like that. Come and sit with us.'

'No, thank you,' I say, smiling as coldly as I can, considering I'm in a really good mood. 'I'm fine, honestly.'

'I think you'd enjoy it. Why don't you give me your number, we can go out sometime. I promise not to give you any reason to slap me.'

He's being too pushy, and he's slurring slightly. I look up at him. 'I'm sorry, I'm seeing someone.'

'Yeah, someone you just slapped.'

'Everything alright here?' says Robert, coming back with our drinks.

'Fine,' I say.

'You watch yourself, man,' says Leather Jacket to Robert, poking him in the chest with an outstretched finger. 'She's too good for you.'

'I know that,' says Robert amiably, sitting down. Leather Jacket throws me a baleful glance as he walks away.

'He's a fucknuckle too. Like most men.'

'Except Dave, presumably,' says Robert.

I check my phone for the fifth time since we got here. Nope, nothing.

'Do you have any New Year resolutions?' says Robert.

'I don't believe in them.'

'They're not imaginary,' he replies. 'For example, I resolve to not be a bastard to women.'

'How noble,' I say. 'I resolve to not have someone be a bastard to me.'

Robert pauses and seems on the verge of saying something. 'Dave—'

My phone buzzes. Dave!

'He just texted me!' I say delightedly, interrupting him. 'He says . . . "With Luke and Sophie now. On the way to London. With you by next year." . . . I wonder why he's with them? And why they left so late?'

'Dave stayed at Luke's last night. They had car trouble today, apparently.'

'Why didn't you tell me?' I say, ignoring the sudden stab of nervy jealousy. Luke's house? Was Bella there, too?

'You didn't ask,' he replies, taking another sip of his drink.

Why couldn't Dave just text me that there was car trouble? Does he not care that I've been waiting all day to hear whether I'd see him tonight? Isn't that kind of inconfuckingsiderate? I sigh. At least he'll still be here by midnight.

''Scuse me,' slurs a voice, and I look up. It's Leather Jacket man. 'I would like you to come and sit with us.' I look up and over at his table, where his two friends are sitting. The table is littered with shot glasses.

'No, thank you,' I say.

'I think you should stay away from this guy.' The words at the end all run into each other. Awayfrmthsguy.

I sit back and look at Robert. He raises his eyebrows. I shake my head to tell him not to get involved.

'Please go away,' I say coldly.

282

Leather Jacket takes a step back and forward in that drunken staggering-on-the-spot way. 'Bitch.'

A split second later, Robert has stood up and grabbed Leather Jacket guy by the lapels. 'Hey. Fucknuckle. She said no. So fuck off.'

Leather Jacket tries to push Robert away, but Robert's taller and stronger than him and won't let go.

I'm not sure what Robert intends to do with him now that he's got hold of him, and Robert doesn't seem sure either. For a second I have the urge to giggle. He said fucknuckle!

Then it all becomes a bit messy. As Robert and Leather Jacket are shoving each other, Leather Jacket's two friends finally notice what's going on and hurry over, one shouting 'Jesus Christ, Damien, not again!' One friend stops next to me, while the other starts hitting Robert in the arm and gets a couple of good swings in before a bartender finally restrains him.

A second bartender grabs Leather Jacket, who wrestles himself away and tries to get Robert in a headlock, resulting in a protracted, imprecise and slightly pathetic scuffly-dance between the three of them for several seconds. I take a second to gaze around the pub, shocked that no one else is trying to stop them, but everyone is silent and entranced. How ridiculous fighting looks. Seriously.

Shaking off the bartender one last time, Leather Jacket punches Robert, rather untidily, in the neck. Robert retorts by punching him, very precisely, in the face. Blood immediately explodes from Leather Jacket's nose.

Two seconds later, Robert faints and crashes to the floor.

Gasping, I hurry over and crouch down next to him, looking up quickly to see Leather Jacket and his mates being dragged outside by the bartenders.

Someone passes me a bottle of water, and I kneel next to Robert's head and try to pull him up. He looks like a black and white photograph of himself. My heart feels like it's stopped beating, all I can think about is Robert.

'Robert, oh please be alright, Robert . . .' I whisper, stroking his forehead. God, he's got lovely hair and such smooth, warm skin.

The rest of the pub is completely silent, looking at Robert passed out cold on the floor and me huddled over him.

Robert blinks a couple of times, and opens his eyes. 'Abby . . .' he says croakily.

He's fine. I sigh with relief. 'I take it you faint at the sight of b—'

'Don't say the b-word,' he whispers, and takes a sip of water.

Someone else brings over a glass of lemonade. Then, like someone turning the music back up, everyone in the pub realises that the drama is over and starts talking amongst themselves again. We are forgotten.

One of the bartenders comes back to chat to us.

'Sorry. We were keeping an eye on those guys all night, we knew they were trouble,' he says. 'Are you OK, mate?'

Robert is now leaning against a table leg, sipping lemonade. Somehow, I've ended up perched next to him stroking his hand and hair, like some kind of tipsy Florence Nightingale.

'I'm fine . . . but I think I need some air. Abigail, will you take me walkies?'

# Chapter Thirty One

'Well, my nerves are still completely shot,' I comment 20 minutes later, when we finally leave The Punchbowl.

'*Your* nerves?' echoes Robert disbelievingly.

He's had two pints of water and a lemonade, and I've had a large whisky (just to calm the nerves). His face has colour again, and we've decided to wait for Luke, Sophie and Dave in a bar in Notting Hill that Plum keeps talking about.

'Fresh air is good,' says Robert, when I suggest a taxi, or that perhaps, for his sake, we ought to go home. (Dave can always join us there, right?) 'I want to walk. It's not that cold.'

I keep my arm around him as we're walking along the top of Hyde Park towards Notting Hill. At first, I was supporting him because he was a little woozy. I felt like he needed looking after. But then it was just comfortable: we walk well together.

'Are you sure you're OK?' I say. 'Do you want me to go and find that guy and beat him up for you?'

'No,' says Robert, laughing. 'Thanks. You're my knight in shining four-inch-heels.'

We stop in two pubs on the way, getting a lemonade for Robert and a whisky for me, then pretend to go for a cigarette and just keep walking with our drinks. We deposit the stolen glasses at the next pub.

'This is one of the naughtiest things I've ever done,' I say, as we wait for our drinks at the second pub.

'Apart from the viola bow,' he says.

'Obviously apart from that,' I nod as the drinks arrive. 'Mmm. Lovely warm whisky.'

'I think you've probably had enough,' he says.

'No,' I say, wrenching my glass away. 'My whisky. Mine.' Robert grins. 'Are you sure you're OK?' I ask again. He doesn't say anything. 'You're embarrassed to have lost control for a split second, aren't you? You are!' I start laughing.

'Ah, you find yourself hilarious, I'm glad someone does,' he says.

By the time we reach the Portobello Star, the whisky has made everything warm and fuzzy. We find a place to stand, smushed against the wall down at the back of the bar with a lot of West London too-cool types and start chatting – or rather, we both listen to my drunken gushing.

'I love hipsters,' I say, as Robert hands me an orangey-whisky cocktail (name? Who can tell!). 'I want to be with a man with a beard before I die. I think it would be warm and cuddly, like kissing a man-shaped teddy bear . . . Oh! That girl is pretty,' I say. 'Look at her, she's just your type. Your two o'clock. I mean my two o'clock, your nine o'clock. I mean . . .' I crack up at myself. 'I can't even tell the time! Ah, you're missing out on beautiful chicks, Roberto . . .'

'You're beautiful,' he says.

I laugh at that, as obviously I must look like a shiny-faced drunkard, and he shakes his head and starts laughing too. I like Robert so much, I think. I feel warm and fuzzy and very happy. He's such a lovely man. I hope he finds true love.

'I hope you find true love,' I say. Oh dear, I *am* pissed.

Robert smiles. How dark green his eyes are, I think. So steady. I feel like I might see double if I keep staring at them. 'I hope I do, too.'

'You're supposed to wish me true love back,' I retort.

'You have Dave,' he reminds me. 'Though I'm surprised you're not pissed that he's so late.'

'Oh yeah. Dave . . .' I say, checking my phone. Nope, nothing, although Robert texted him when we decided to come to this bar. I sigh deeply, my mood suddenly plummeting. 'He'll be here soon . . . He doesn't like to be text-terrogated, and he doesn't like to make plans. So I have to just wait for him. Always, always waiting for him . . . . Which is bullshit, right?' I drink all of my cocktail in one gulp.

Robert nods and then catches himself, and stops.

'And he said he wanted to be my girlfriend and, and, and ever since, ever since . . .' I reach out and, after a couple of attempts, put my empty glass down on the table behind Robert, and try to get the thoughts in my head straight. 'When I hear from him or he's around, I feel alright, more than alright . . . good. I feel good. Plum says I am chasing emotions. But sometimes, not.' Robert is smiling at me, but I've got almost double-vision now. One-and-a-half vision at least. 'Oh, Robert. I am tired of this powerplay, I am not the player, I am not playing the powerplay. You know?'

'Are you in love with him?' asks Robert. I only just hear him saying it, the bar is so loud.

'I don't know,' I sigh. 'I don't, um, don't know,' I look up at Robert and start laughing. 'I don't know seems to be my catch—' I hiccup – 'my catchphrase.'

'That's a terrible catchphrase,' he says, with a grin.

'My dad says, the right person, I'll just know. Most annoying thing in the world.' I can't tell Robert about how my brain short-circuits whenever Dave touches me, and that it's that reaction, above anything else, that makes me feel he might be the right man for me. I can't even remember what that feels like, or even what he looks like. I can't remember anything right now.

'You're not making sense,' says Robert.

I look up at him and grin happily. What were we just talking about? I forget.

Suddenly the DJ stops the music, and the crowd starts counting.

'Ten! Nine! Eight . . .' Robert and I join in, in that excited and totally unselfconscious way that you do when you've been drinking for hours.

'ONE! HAPPY NEW YEAR!' screams the crowd.

I grin at Robert and stand on tiptoe to reach up and give him a smacking Happy-New-Year cheek kiss, when someone elbows me violently in the back and I'm shoved forward, my mouth landing forcefully on his.

'Whoops', I think, and go to say it, but I can't, because all of a sudden his arms are around me and his lips are on mine and we're kissing, properly kissing, and his lips are so warm and my heart starts beating wildly and I don't want to stop and everything around me goes whoooooooooosh . . . Seconds, minutes – I don't know – later, we break apart.

The instant that Robert's lips are off mine, I put my hands on his chest and push him away from me, trying to catch my breath. Or my thoughts. Whichever comes first. (Neither do. The slackers.)

My heart is hammering so loudly in my chest that it almost hurts.

'Happy birthday,' he says. He looks as surprised as I am.

'I . . . I—' I'm horrified. I keep meeting his eyes and then looking away. I didn't push him off me fast enough, we shouldn't have kissed, I didn't stop it, Dave, his friend, my boyfriend, oh God . . .

'I'm sorry,' he says immediately, reading my face.

'No, I'm sorry,' I say. I feel completely sober all of a sudden. 'I'm going . . . I'm going . . . to the bathroom.'

I pick up my bag and turn to push my way through the crowd.

A glance in the mirror is every drinking girl's nightmare: my make-up is AWOL on my red face, my eyes are glittering weirdly, and my eyeliner is very badly smudged.

'Fuck,' I say. My mind is racing. Fuck, I just kissed Robert, my best friend, my boyfriend's best friend, fuck, Dave, my boyfriend, is he my boyfriend? He must be, he said he was, fuck, I just kissed Robert, I liked it, did I like it?

288

At least I'm sober.

'Fuck,' I say aloud again.

A girl comes out from the toilet cubicle behind me. She's very pretty, and wearing a tiny green dress with her hair in a funky beehive. Why do I look so drab, I think irritably. My jeans and plain top looked so classic and fresh when I put them on, now I look like a nun. A J Brand-wearing drunk nun who just cheated on her boyfriend and jumped on her best friend. Fuck. I look in the mirror again, and notice that the girl washing her hands next to me is crying silently.

'Are you alright?' I say automatically.

'Fine, fine,' she says, and wipes away a tear. 'My boyfriend and I broke up on Boxing Day,' she adds, her voice choked with tears.

'Shit, I'm so sorry,' I say. 'That's so awful. Are you having an awful night?'

She shrugs, heaving an enormous make-up bag onto the sink. 'I knew I'd cry at midnight, so I brought my entire make-up bag,' she says, laughing through a small sob.

'I've got eye drops,' I say helpfully. 'And . . . mints, and powder, and perfume, and Benefit High Beam, and, let me see . . .' I open my make-up bag and put it next to hers on the sink. 'Just help yourself. At least you don't look like you came straight from a triathlon, like I do.'

'I've got foundation,' she says, grinning at me. 'And a Q-tip that you can use to fix your eyes.'

Ah, the power of make-up to bring girls together. I don't want to think about Robert, or what just happened, or what's about to happen. So instead, as we pass Bobbi Brown Shimmer Brick and MAC Smoulder back and forth, I counsel my new friend Millie on her break-up, which she said she could see coming all through Christmas, especially when he gave her a book with the '3 for 2' Waterstone's sticker left on.

'Who got the other two books?' I say.

'That's what I want to know!' she says and we cackle with laughter.

'Well, frankly, I think you are much better off without him,' I say, handing her MAC Nuance blush.

'I know,' she agrees, handing me some Benefit Hoopla bronzer. I never wear bronzer. Hey ho. In for a penny.

'And,' I say a moment later to my new, tanned reflection. 'I think that you're going to meet someone tonight. Someone,' I pause to add some more to my nose and chin 'to make you forget all about him.'

'You know what I want?' she says. 'I want a fling. It was an intense five months with that dickhead. I want something casual. With lots of sex.'

I pause, and look at her. 'Then I have just the man for you.'

We traipse back down the stairs together. Yes, I will introduce Millie to Robert, and that will make him happy, then I will go home and to hell with it, I'll call Dave and tell him he's missed me, I mean, that I've missed him, and that he needs to come over and have sex with me and that will fix everything. Yes. Good plan.

Then I look over to where Robert is waiting for me and see my sister and Luke and . . .

Dave turns and, grinning, grabs me and lunges into a huge kiss. Immediately, the electrical reaction is back, like someone flipping a switch in my body. I'm tingling all over, but I'm also horrifically conscious of Robert watching us. Robert, who I just kissed. Oh God, did that really happen? It doesn't seem real . . .

'Happy New Year, angel,' murmurs Dave, standing me back up and looking into my eyes. Holy blue eyes. Can he read my guilt? I blink and look away. 'And apparently happy birthday. Right, now that's done, I'm getting drinks.'

I am quickly enveloped in a happy birthday hug from Sophie and Luke, who are ranting about their nightmare drive from Bath with pit stops for wine and how Sophie and Dave are annoying drunks and Luke is an 'annoying sober'.

I haven't dared to look at Robert yet. Instead, I pull forward Millie and introduce her.

I notice Dave appraising Millie's body with a practised eye. I wish I looked hotter tonight. I want him more than ever. I don't even care why he's late anymore. (But oh God, please let it not be because of Bella.) It's so good to see him that the relief has overtaken everything else . . .

I want Millie to talk to Robert, but when I finally look over at him, he's expressionless, staring into space. Luckily, Millie takes the initiative, and puts her hand on his arm, smiling up at him.

'Robert, Abigail tells me that you protected her virtue earlier . . .'

'Uh, yeah,' he says, without looking at me. 'I did.'

'What? Story!' says Sophie.

Robert and I manage to tell the entire Punchbowl punch-up story, together, without our eyes meeting even once. We both leave out the fainting bit automatically. I don't want to drop Robert in it, and he doesn't seem to want to talk about it either.

God, I feel self-conscious. If they'd walked in 15 minutes earlier . . . No, don't think about it.

'Well, that all sounds very chivalrous,' says Dave, who returned with drinks halfway through the story. 'Well done, Robbie. What a brave boy you are.'

'He was, actually,' I say, suddenly irritated by Dave's usual jealous ribbing. 'It was amazing.'

'It sounds wonderful,' says Millie, smiling up at Robert. He looks down at her with a little grin on his face. Good, he's back to normal. Great.

'Birthday lunch tomorrow?' Sophie says to me.

'Yes please,' I say. 'But no singing. No cake. None of that shit. Henry and Charlotte will be back too.'

'Half of our mates are at a ball tonight,' says Luke. 'So they might come along tomorrow.'

'What ball?' I say.

'A charity ball. Organised by Louisa's husband,' says Luke in

291

a low voice. 'Dave refused to go, said it was a waste of his money. He caused a massive fight.'

'It *is* a waste,' says Dave, placing a lazy hand on the back of my neck and stroking it. I fight the urge to purr, then glance at Robert, and for a moment our eyes meet. I look away quickly. 'I'm not giving my hard-earned money to the impoverished hamster association.'

'It's the RSPCA,' says Sophie. 'You know that.'

'I like to choose the animals I help,' he replies. 'Dogs, yes. Cats, no. Horses, yes. Parrots, no. And I've always thought the RSPCA was a front for a vice ring of some kind.'

'You just don't like her husband,' says Luke.

'Well, he's a wanker,' says Dave. 'And a ponce. That's why I try to undermine him at every given opportunity.' He pauses. 'It's actually a beautiful thing.'

He glances at Robert, who has turned to talk to Millie and hasn't heard a thing. In a flash I realise that despite the competitive put-downs, Dave and Robert really are best friends. They may operate an official policy of 'don't get involved', and he couldn't stop the way his sister behaved with Robert, but he's clearly been a complete prick to her and her husband ever since.

Seeing this twisted display of friendship and loyalty makes me suddenly adore Dave even more.

'You secretly love Robert, don't you,' I whisper.

'I do,' he nods back, and winks at me. 'But don't tell him.'

I flashback to Robert and the kiss(es) again, and am knocked out by guilt.

Good, loyal, and frankly, adorable Dave. Bad, disloyal, horrible Robert and me.

Luckily, Luke is telling stories that cover my self-reproaching silence. Luke's mother got drunk on Christmas Day and announced she wasn't slaving over the fucking turkey this year, she wanted to 'eat white fucking chocolates in front of Miracle On fucking 34th Street like everyone fucking else'. Luke's Dad has never knowingly touched an oven, so Luke and Bella had to make Christmas lunch, and as a result they didn't eat till 10 pm and the turkey was cold in the middle.

Apparently Bella and Ollie were fighting the whole time, again.

'It's actually getting kind of boring,' says Luke. 'I asked her to dump him, just to give the rest of us a break, but it seems that's out of the question.'

I steal a glance at Dave, but he doesn't look interested. He looks over at me and grins. 'Let's get out of here,' he whispers into my ear, pulling me towards him. 'I'm not quite done with you yet.'

I'm torn. I've been craving this, the moment I could binge on class-A Dave, for over a week, but now I kind of want to party with my sister. Then again . . . I glance over and see Robert whispering something into Millie's ear. She giggles and swivels her eyes up at him flirtatiously.

'Let's go,' I nod. 'We're staying at my house, though.'

'With pleasure. *Au revoir*,' everyone, I'm taking Abigail home to ravish her.'

My eyes dart back to Robert as I kiss Sophie and Luke goodbye. He's not looking at me. I say a quick goodbye to Millie, who seems to have cheered up considerably.

'See ya,' I say in the general direction of Robert.

'See ya,' he echoes.

We leave the bar and Dave takes my hand. 'It's very good to see you,' he says. 'Now let's get you out of those wet things.'

As we get in a cab, I cast one last look back at the outside of the Portobello Star, surrounded by the usual intrepid, freezing smokers.

What just happened? It doesn't matter. Don't think about it.

# *Chapter Thirty Two*

You want to know how I've dealt with it? I've totally ignored it. Or tried to, anyway.

The kiss was nothing, we'd drunk enough booze to kill a dog, or at least I had, and, you know, shit happens. We'd just been through the whole fight-faint trauma, and it was the anniversary of his Louisa thing, and I was knocked into him, it really was a total accident. I don't even remember it that well.

I admit I feel horribly guilty. But it happened, and there's nothing I can do about it now. It was a drunken mistake.

So there's no point in thinking about it, right?

It helps that I haven't really seen Robert in the fortnight since New Year's. He's out a lot, and so am I, of course. When I do see him, we both act perfectly polite and friendly. It's not normal between us, it's even less normal than it was at the end of last year . . . but it's fine. It will be fine.

And guess what. My Dave insecurities are over! More or less. I've put them down to general dating inexperience. I hadn't started a relationship in seven *years*. I didn't know how to feel like part of a couple. And seeing him with Bella at lunch that day, as innocent as it obviously was, well, it just played into my silly insecurities. So it's no wonder I obsess slightly, I mean, obsessed. Past tense. Right? Right.

I've even got used to his inability to 'cosset'. And I've tried to be demanding a couple of times over the past few weeks, just to see what happens. Not much, usually.

'Coffee,' I said when we woke up this morning.

'I'd love one, my little bowling ball,' he whispered, snuggling into me.

'Why am I a – oh,' I said, blushing in the darkness. 'No, I want you to get me a coffee.'

'Tell you what, how about you get us coffee today, and I'll time you, and then tomorrow I'll get it, and we'll see who's faster?' he said, nibbling at my ear. I shivered in delight. And so he got his way, as he always does.

Not that much else has changed. I still wait for him to contact me, and making a statement with a rising inflexion, so it sounds like a question, is the only way that I can get him to talk about his plans.

For example, this morning, as he was getting dressed and I was savouring the last few minutes in bed before I had to get up and hurry home through the cold, I said 'I expect you have a day of excitement and thrills ahead of you,' with my voice rising inquisitively on 'you'.

'I'm having dinner with Mother tonight,' he said.

'Fun,' I replied, thinking how much I wish he'd ask me along, but that it's just not his style. Sigh.

Then he leaned over and grinned at me. 'Why don't you come along?'

'I'd love to!' I gasped, before restraining myself. Cool, Abigail. Detached. 'I mean, sure. Where are we going? What time? What should I wear?'

'Questions, questions,' said Dave in mock-irritation. (I think it was mock.) 'I don't know yet. I'll let you know later. Now get up. You're not making me late again.'

It's 4 pm now, you'd think 'later' would mean 'before the end of the work day', wouldn't you? There's no point in calling him. I did it the other week to confirm what time he wanted to meet for dinner, and he snapped 'as soon as I know, I'll tell you. Don't nag me' and hung up. He said sorry about it later – he's abrupt when he's busy; it's not personal – but you see, it's not even worth trying. It'll just upset both of us.

I press 'refresh' on my emails again. Nothing. Maybe he's changed his mind, or maybe his mother has said she doesn't want to meet me.

Cripes, and I was just boasting about how almost-not-insecure I am these days . . .

January has been quiet at work, but the big report I was working on during most of November and December has done well. We got our bonuses in early January, and mine was better than it has been in years. I'm saving it for a rainy day, maybe if Dave and I were ever to . . . anyway.

Today Andre, who I haven't seen since before Christmas, is back in London and has suggested we meet downstairs at 4 pm and head out for '*un* café and a chat'. I guess it's to talk about that Hong Kong job. It's probably blown over entirely, so it's a good thing I haven't seriously thought about it . . . I glance over the cubicle divider at Charlotte, who's typing with a little smile on her face.

'Say hi to Henry for me,' I say.

'What? I'm not – I'm actually working on a – I'm not –' she pauses and giggles. 'OK, I am.'

I wish Dave and I sent emails all day. But he says it distracts him. Sometimes he sends naughty texts.

Charlotte's work phone rings, and she answers it with a cara-melly, 'Charlotte Barry . . .' I'm transfixed for a second. She never used to talk like that. Is that why she's getting so many phone calls recently?

'I can see why you'd think that, Ed, but actually, we believe that it's going to far exceed expectations next quarter,' she says, swivelling her chair round to look up at me. I mime drinking a coffee and she shakes her head and winks. God, she's sassy these

296

days. 'Well, that's exactly right,' she says, swivelling back. She's taken the brains she always had and added confidence. And now she's unstoppable.

I sigh, and walk to the lifts. I still don't know what I'm doing here. I'm in a holding pattern. I feel kind of depressed and lacking in energy. It could be SAD, you know, I haven't seen sunlight in days.

Maybe it's just this office and Suzanne that need to change. Maybe moving to Hong Kong is the answer.

For a brief moment I picture myself living in Hong Kong with Dave, both of us working hard and sharing a fabulous, busy, joy-filled life . . . it seems a bit of a stretch, doesn't it? But I can't imagine a future without him, either.

'Andre!' I say, walking up to him in the lobby. He turns around. He's tanned from skiing for the past two weeks, probably in Courcheval or Chamonix somewhere.

'Abigail,' he says, leaning over to kiss me hello on both cheeks. I wasn't expecting this, and start slightly, before recovering.

'*On y va?*' he says, and continues to speak in French. 'I know you speak French, Abigail. I've seen your CV.'

'I'm shy,' I reply, in French.

'Ha. Cheer up. I have some news that will make you show me that lovely smile.'

He should really stop flirting. We work in finance goddammit.

I plaster a businesslike smile on my face as we walk towards the Italian coffee shop. The two men behind the counter act as though they haven't seen me in an age, though it's been since exactly 8.04 am this morning, when I did the latte run for Charlotte and I.

'Firstly, how are you? How was your Christmas?'

'Great,' I say, lying just a bit. What am I meant to say – 'quite dull, mostly marked by a deeply uneasy yearning with just a little bit of insecurity, and climaxing in a guilt-inducing near-scandal when I jumped my best friend'?

'You have been travelling a lot?' he asks. 'Is Suzanne making life hard?'

'No,' I say. Why is he asking that? Is that code for 'you look like a miserable shit'? I'm fine. I'm totally fine!

'I have the official job offer for you. I wanted to get you out of the office because, well, what's that saying? The walls have eyes.'

'Ears,' I say, stalling. 'The walls have ears.'

'Right. Guaranteed bonus first year, and we'll double your base salary. We'll cover relocation costs, help you find an apartment . . .'

Without even thinking about it, I start talking specifics with Andre. Years of training, I guess: I want all the details. I'm not saying yes, but I can't help but nod and smile a lot. It's a ridiculously good offer, and I suddenly realise that I really would be pretty stupid to turn it down. It's more money than I've ever made. I'd get away from Suzanne, lead my own team, and get to run research analysis my way. Whatever 'my way' is.

All I have to do is move to Hong Kong.

'So, I think the next step is for you to visit the Hong Kong office, meet the team,' he says, watching me carefully.

'OK,' I agree. It seems easier than saying no. Or yes. Whichever I decide.

Andre starts telling me all about the team he's setting up, their projects and the logistics for my visit. Suzanne can't find out about the job offer, not that she'd be devastated to lose me, but just because cross-team poaching is messy and frowned upon. That doesn't make it any less common, of course.

We decide I'll fly out in mid-February – in a month – for a four-day visit, timed to coincide with a Luxury In Asia trade show that I can use as my excuse for Suzanne. Andre will already be there and can show me around.

I've never been to Hong Kong, and part of me is excited. The other part of me is distracted. As per fucking usual.

Four days (five nights!) without Dave would suck. I wonder what he'd think about the job offer?

Goddammit. I am a grown woman, I should make career decisions based on what I want. I should be genuinely thrilled and flattered too. What's wrong with me?

I get back to my desk and stare at my computer all afternoon. At 5.50 pm my phone buzzes and, I swear, I nearly purr with happiness. It's Dave. We're meeting his mother at the Orrery in Marylebone at 8 pm, which doesn't give me a lot of time.

Shouting 'bye' to Charlotte, I pick up my bag and coat and dash for the lifts, then take a taxi home. Thank God that Robert's not home yet, I muse, the awkward small talk is really getting annoying. I can spend an intense hour getting ready.

Dinner with the mother of my boyfriend. Wowsers, this is a big deal. Now that I know I'm definitely going, I can embrace the emotion that I've been stepping around all day. I'm nervous as hell. But this will be great! This will bring us closer together.

I don't know what the story is with Dave's father, by the way. I don't know if he passed away or left Dave's mother, and I don't want to ask. Dave never discusses him, and I've never remembered to ask Luke or Sophie. I wonder if I could call Robert to ask – ah, no. I can't. Not anymore.

I shower and blow-dry my hair in the feverish way I always do when I'm hurrying to meet Dave. Now comes the hard bit.

Dressing for his mother.

Hair down or back? Ponytails are too girlish, but hair down could be seen as sexy, and I shouldn't wear black, it's a bit funereal. Mustn't look too serious. Or too sexy or too demure or too fashionable. Not jeans, she might hate jeans, and God, not a short skirt, she'll think I'm slutty. Blazers are too boxy, cardigans too casual, my Christmas cashmere jumper needs hand washing and I'm never home long enough to do it, a pretty blouse would be ideal but it's freezing outside, and I can't just wear a long-sleeved shirt . . . Oh God, I could cry. I feel like

I'm hyperventilating. I wish I was better at clothes. Fuck it, I'm calling Plum.

'What up, A-Dawg?' she says cheerfully.

'Don't talk street to me. I'm meeting Dave's mother tonight. Sartorial nightmare.'

'Your high-waist dark grey trousers, pair them with the silky top from Cos and a black cardigan over the top, plus your black LK Bennett heels. Very mother-in-law friendly.' Plum is talking with the seriousness of someone giving CPR instructions in an emergency situation. Can you believe she knows my wardrobe this well?

'Not my mother-in-law, but yes, perfect,' I say, my despair immediately lifting. God, I love Plum.

'Almost mother-in-law, whatever. Wear your pearl studs, and no perfume, what she doesn't notice she can't dislike. And make sure you wear a sensible scarf, hat and gloves, it is January and she'll think you're far more practical than you are.'

'Yes, ma'am,' I say obediently, trying to think where my old gloves are. I lost my new Christmas ones on New Year's Eve and haven't replaced them. (Urgh. New Year's Eve.) 'Thank you, you are brilliant.' And so calm, I think to myself. That's the Dan effect. I wonder what effect Dave has had on me.

'My pleasure,' she says. 'Remember, she has to fucking love you, because her son does.'

No he doesn't, is my instant thought, as I hang up.

I look at myself in the mirror for a few seconds.

Does Dave love me?

I *hope* he does. Or will. Or might . . . But I can't even think of Dave and love in the same sentence.

I certainly don't want to say it, or even think it, until he does. I feel giddy when I'm with him and long for him when I'm not. And that's enough. For now, anyway.

# Chapter Thirty Three

It's about halfway through dinner that things hit a real low-point.

'Dave, I can't *believe* you never even *mentioned* Gail to me!' says Dave's mother. She raises a glass of wine to her lips. 'I really *don't* know *what* I'll do with you, darling.'

I think about correcting her to say 'Abigail', but since I've done that six times in the past hour, there's really no point. So instead, I smile and wait for Dave to reply.

'It's ABI-gail, Dottie,' he says. He calls his mother by her first name. 'And well, I don't discuss my personal life with you.'

'You wouldn't have a life *at all* if it wasn't for me! Me and my *wonderful womb*,' she says. She turns to me and winks. 'Am I right?'

'Dottie . . .' says Dave warningly.

'He hates the word "womb",' she says to me confidingly, yet loudly. 'Womb, David! *Vagina*!'

Dave's mother is, shall we say, surprising. I'd expected a sophisticated older lady. Very slim, with tennis-playing arms, a blonde bob and a calm, brittle exterior. In other words, a peroxide Anna Wintour.

I got the blonde bob bit right, but the rest very, very wrong.

Dottie is a Rubenesque, heavily made-up woman, poured and tweaked into a very tight dress. Since her fourth glass of wine, her conversation has pinballed all over the place. We've heard about the contractor renovating her house ('That dreadful man! His eyes! On my pins!'), the difficulties of dating for the over 50s ('I never thought I'd say it, but bald men really do try harder') and the love woes of her *bichon-frise*, Mr Mitzy ('Retarded detumescence, the vet called it. I said I don't care, make it go away!'). She's also on first name terms with all the waiters.

'This restaurant does *not know* how to make a decent risotto,' she says, pushing her plate away and taking out a packet of Silk Cut. She speaks in *very clear italics* for dramatic emphasis and, I think, to escape any enunciation problems caused by excess wine. 'Raymond! Take it away! I'm going outside. For *a fag*. Abigail?'

'Uh – I don't –' Actually, I'm in the kind of stressed mildly-drunk mood where a cigarette would be great, but I'm on auto-lie, programmed to not smoke in front of the mythical-disapproving-mother-in-law. Plus, the idea of being alone with her is scary.

'Yes, you fucking do,' says Dave irritably. 'Take her outside, please.'

Once outside, in the freezing January air, Dottie breaks into a gusty rendition of 'It's Harry I'm Plannin' To Marry'. I smile awkwardly. What the devil do I do now? Join in?

'Well, *cheeky* David to surprise me with you like this,' she then says to me through a haze of smoke. 'I had no idea he was even *seeing* anyone! He's *such* a bachelor. Don't you think he's *extraordinarily* handsome? I tell you, if I was 15 years younger . . .'

Creepy. I know boys' mothers always adore their little princes, but Peter's mother never acted like this. And surely she means 30 years younger?

'Yes, he's lovely,' I say eventually.

'I said to him recently: you'll end up *old* and *alone* like me if you're not careful!' she exclaims joyfully. 'But it's different for men!'

I nod. She's scaring me.

'I've been seeing this *fabulous* gent who lives in Marbella most

302

of the time. *Wonderful* lifestyle out there. Wants me to move in with him,' she says, dragging quickly and repetitively on her cigarette so it burns down to halfway in seconds. 'Ever since David's father—' she pauses, and suddenly her eyes are filled with tears. I put my hand on her arm instinctively.

'Oh – God, Dottie, I'm so—'

'*Sorry*? Why would you be sorry, it wasn't *your* fault, was it?' she snaps. 'Let's go!'

I stub out my cigarette in the little bin left for smokers, and then pick up Dottie's cigarette butt from the ground and put it in there, too, and follow her inside.

'I took the liberty of ordering coffees,' says Dave pointedly.

'I'd *love* a little nibble on something sweet,' says Dottie, taking another slug of wine. She looks completely normal now, no sign of the recent near-hysteria. (Me? I'm shell-shocked.)

'I'll get you a Wagon Wheel on the way to your hotel,' snaps Dave.

'I'm *so sad* Louisa couldn't join us,' says Dottie petulantly. So am I, I think. I'm dying to meet the bitch that broke Robert's heart. I asked Dave a few times, till he said 'what's with the Louisa obsession?' so I stopped.

'I'm not,' says Dave. 'I've had enough Louisa to last me till next Christmas.'

'*You* picked those fights, David.'

Dave ignores his mother, and thankfully, the coffees arrive. I'm so nervous that I've been totally silent most of dinner, unable to think of anything to say and, when I do, unable to say it out loud. But I can't just sit here mute, either.

'Coffee! I love coffee!' I blurt out, apropos nothing.

Oh, Abigail. Why don't you just read the fucking menu aloud?

When dinner is finally over, we drop Dottie off at her hotel, and continue in the taxi back to Dave's house. We haven't spoken to each other since we left the restaurant. I clear my throat, but he doesn't even turn away from the window.

There's a gulf between us. There always is.

I don't know what's going through his head, just that he's in a bad mood. Or maybe he's tired. I can't tell the difference. Perhaps he's regretting asking me along tonight, I think glumly. Probably thinking how much he wishes he wasn't with me. Oh God, this isn't right. Something is wrong, something is missing . . .

And then Dave turns to me.

'Abigail, angel, I'm so sorry,' he says. 'I thought she'd be better than that.'

'She was lovely,' I say untruthfully. What does he mean, 'better'? Less drunk? Less prone to singing/crying fits and professions of motherly lust? 'She got a little upset outside. About your Dad.'

He sighs, and then leans over and takes my hand. It's the first non-sexual physical affection I've ever had from Dave. 'Thanks for coming with me,' he says, holding my hand up to his lips and kissing it. 'I needed you.'

'Do you want to talk about it?' I say. I think I already know the answer, but I'm so thrilled to have him be even a tiny bit open with me that I can't help myself.

'No. Now come here.'

He pulls me over to his side of the taxi and kisses me. For the first time ever, it's tender, and I actually feel close to him. I don't know why his mother was crying, or why tonight was as difficult for him as it clearly was, but I don't care. All I need is Dave to be near me, and to want me as much as I want him. Everything must be OK if he's being like this, right? That uneasy feeling I had that something is wrong . . . it's nothing. It must be nothing.

'You're delightful,' he murmurs, in between kisses. 'It's always good to see you, always.'

My heart leaps with joy. Everything *is* fine! I knew it was.

By the time we get home (I mean, to his place), he's cheered up considerably. Dave doesn't enjoy introspection; his moods are unnaturally buoyant. It's infectious to be around: when he's happy, I'm happy.

I now feel open enough to tell him about what I'm doing this weekend, rather than sneaking them in around his plans as I discover them on the fly, the way I usually do.

'A tasting at Luke's wedding venue?' he responds at one point. 'They should do a marriage tasting . . . you could get the cold shoulder, a long-term huff, a touch of a temper tantrum, and endless arguments about whose turn it is to spend Christmas with whose family.'

'Cynic,' I say. I'm lying in his bed, as he puts away washing and hangs up his laundered shirts.

'Well, I'm not sure what I'm doing. JimmyJames wants to go to some party in Islington.'

'That sounds fun,' I say, as coolly as I can. (He's discussing plans! In advance!)

'Shall we do it? OK, I'll tell him we're in,' he stands in front of his open sock drawer and sighs. 'I am thirty fucking years old. I should be able to find a matching pair of socks.'

Encouraged by this new perfect-boyfriend side of Dave, and anxious not to lose his attention, I lean back and sigh deeply. 'I'm having a work crisis, Dave,' I say. It's time to tell him about the job offer in Hong Kong.

'Really, angel? Do tell . . .' he says, peering into the sock drawer. 'I've never even fucking owned a pink sock. Where did you come from?' He holds the pink sock up to the ceiling. 'I shall call you Bethany. Bethany, the mysterious pink sock.'

I giggle. Dave picks up a stray white sock, folds them together and starts singing 'Bethany and Ivory'.

'Um, well, I don't love my job. And I don't know if it's my team, or the job, or the industry . . .'

'No one loves their job,' he says, walking into his bathroom and coming back with a toothbrush in his mouth. 'That's a fact.'

'Don't you think I should care about what I do between 7 am and 7 pm every day?'

'You don't have any other interests, do you?' says Dave,

around his toothbrushing. 'It's not like you love photography, or interior design, or flower arranging . . . so what the fuck else would you do?'

'Um . . .' I can't think what to say. He's absolutely right.

'You're not going to magically discover some perfect career that'll make you dribblingly happy for the rest of your life. Just accept that you're like everybody else, angel.'

I feel hurt by this, but I can't think why. He's not being mean exactly. Just truthful.

'I was offered a—'

Dave holds a hand up to interrupt me, goes back to his bathroom, spits out the toothpaste, rinses and pads back into the room. 'Enough job talk! It just reminds me of my own career dissatisfaction. My bonus had better be the size of Birmingham this year or I'm going to crack skulls. Those people don't appreciate me.'

'I don't think anyone's bonus is going to be good this year,' I say. Dave's bonuses, past, present and future, are one of his favourite subjects, I've noticed.

'Well then, let's not talk about it again, hmm?' Dave looks over at me and smiles lasciviously. 'Are you naked, young lady?'

I nod my head coyly. In this conversation, at least, I know just what to do.

'Shocking,' he says. 'I'll need to see that for myself.'

# Chapter Thirty Four

I still haven't brought up the whole Hong Kong thing. And it's been almost a month.

I keep telling myself I'll do it tonight, and then . . . I never do. If I tell Dave about the trip I'm supposedly taking (this week!, oh God) to go to the Luxury In Asia conference in Hong Kong, then I'd have to tell him about the job offer, and I'll be forcing a conversation titled Where Is This Relationship Going. I don't feel quite, um, confident enough to do that yet. So the flights are booked, the hotel is booked . . . but in my head, I'm not even sure if I'm going. There hasn't been a good time to tell Dave, anyway. He's been more distracted than usual lately. I think his work is making him very stressed – he often works so late that we don't even see each other for days. But one thing hasn't changed: whenever I'm about to see him, my stomach churns with nerves.

I'll bring it up with Dave tonight, I will. I will. And I'll email Andre to confirm it. He and I have been emailing a lot – work stuff, but a bit of banter, too. Maybe working with him would be different from here, maybe I'd like it. Oh God. I have to make a decision soon.

I look around at the frenzied boredom that characterises 4 pm on a Monday in my office, press 'refresh' on my email, and sigh.

I mentioned the job offer to Sophie and Plum over our Sunday night supper at Sophie's house last night. Their shocked reaction quickly convinced me that mentioning the trip wouldn't be a good idea.

'You're moving . . . to Hong fucking Kong?' said Plum in disbelief.

'No, no, I don't know, maybe,' I said, stumbling over my words. 'I don't think . . . I don't know. I was offered a job, that's all.'

'I thought that you weren't sure about your job.'

'That it doesn't make you happy.'

'I wasn't,' I said, adding more grated cheese to my baked beans and buttering another slice of toast. Sophie doesn't make a huge effort for these Sunday suppers, but they're very comforting. I always think that toast smells like a hug. 'I'm not, I mean . . . I don't know. Yet. But it's good, right?'

'It's fantastic! I mean, congratulations! As long as it's what you want,' said Sophie.

'What does Dave think?' asked Plum.

'Nothing, I haven't told him,' I replied, frowning to myself. 'No need . . . to . . . for that.'

Sophie and Plum exchanged a glance. Wait a fucking minute, I thought, I'm not the one who has a glanced exchanged about her. If anything, I am the one exchanging said glances, dash it. But I didn't feel up to confronting them.

'Not yet,' I continued hurriedly, biting into my toast. 'What's the point? Since, as you say I'm still, uh, working things out. It's my decision. Enough about me, anyway. Let's talk about something else.'

'How's dishy old Roberto, my favourite fuckmerchant?' said Plum.

'Something apart from him,' I said. They both looked at me. 'Robert and I . . . well, we've grown apart.'

It's undeniable. We don't email or text the way we used to. I rarely see him, and when I hear him and walk downstairs to say hi, the front door bangs and I can hear his footsteps hurrying away. He's avoiding me.

I can't exactly talk to him about it. What would I say? 'Oh, Robert, by the way. Kissing you was a huge mistake and I regret it. I can't bear the thought that I cheated on Dave with you. I know you regret it, I also know you disapprove of me and Dave for some mysterious stupid macho reason, but come on, let's be buddies?'

No. That's not what grown-ups do. Grown-ups just pretend everything is fine and get on with life. Even though I miss him. And I wish everything could just go back to the way it was.

Sophie and Plum looked at me sympathetically, and I suddenly felt like crying. Instead I tried to act philosophical.

'Perhaps you can't have a best male friend and a boyfriend.'

'What about Henry?' said Sophie.

'Doesn't count. We've known him way too long.'

'You can't get rid of long-term friends without something viciously spiteful happening, like someone deleting you on Facebook,' added Plum.

'Why isn't Henry here, anyway?'

'He's cooking dinner for Charlotte.'

'He'll make a fabulous wife one day.'

Then Plum dropped a bombshell.

'I've quit my job. I'm starting a graduate diploma in Fashion Media Styling at the London College of Fashion.'

Sophie and I immediately started whooping our excitement and congratulations.

'When did you decide this?' I asked. Plum looked absurdly happy.

'Remember that day you asked me if I loved my job? That started it . . . I've always wanted to work in fashion. I was just too fucking scared to admit it because then I'd have to actually do something about it.'

I felt a lump in my throat. Why do I want to cry, I wondered – jealousy? No. Worry about my own lack of career focus? No, not that either.

309

Then I realised that it was because that's what Robert said to me on New Year's Eve. Back when we were still best friends and everything was so warm and easy. He said that I was too scared . . .

The friendship is over. I need to just accept that.

With steadfast effort, I blinked back the tears and grinned at Plum, and luckily she and Sophie had moved on to talking about Sophie and Luke's pre-wedding trip to Chicago this week.

Now, sighing deeply, I look around the office again. It's a real London February day: the sun has called in sick. It's bitingly cold outside yet the office air-conditioning is still on 'high'. The fluorescent lighting, the grey carpets, the airlessness . . . Oh God.

I fight the urge to bang my head against my keyboard. Instead, I press 'refresh' again. Email from Dave!

*Can you meet for a quick drink tonight? Need to talk.*

My stomach feels like someone's kicked it. 'Need to talk'? Does that sound bad to you? No flirtiness, no 'x' at the end? I reply:

*Of course. Everything alright? x*

He replies almost immediately, and I'm seized by a fearful sick feeling.

*Meet me at The Magpie at 6 pm.*

Something is wrong. He was fine when I saw him yesterday. It was Sunday morning, so we slept in, I made us coffee, then later on I went home to change and met the girls for dinner. He spent last night with his sister Louisa, so I didn't see him . . . Perhaps they had a fight, and his digital coldness has nothing to do with me. The insecurity curl around my chest flickers, but doesn't go away. 6 pm? I can't wait that long! This is Daveticipation on steroids.

I gaze at my computer screen, watching the clock in the bottom right corner move. 4.41 pm.

My phone rings. It's my boss.

'Suzanne,' I say quickly, trying to sound as confident and busy as I can.

'Abigail, come in here please,' she says.

310

'Of course,' I say brightly. I walk over, fighting the urge to run. Why does she scare me so much? I miss my old boss. He just left me alone.

'The last six weeks have been abominable,' she barks, without any kind of prelude, the moment I step into her office. 'The only reason we're still breathing is because of Charlotte. Your sales calls have dropped to an all-time low. You haven't done anything proactive—'

'I finished the Brazil project,' I interject feebly.

'And did fuck-all with it,' she snaps. 'I thought we had an understanding, and at the end of last year, I saw a real change in you. Now it's like you *want* to be fired. You haven't taken your eye off the ball, you've put the fucking ball down and walked away from it entirely.'

'I know,' I say quickly. 'I'm sorry, I'll . . . I'll fix it, I'll step it up. I've had personal—'

'I don't care,' she says. 'Fix it. Go to the conference in Hong Kong. When you're back next week, I want to see a difference.'

I haven't had personal problems, I think to myself as I walk out of her office. I've just been preoccupied.

Maybe I do want to be fired.

I head straight to the bathrooms, lock myself in a cubicle, and sit on the closed seat. I want to cry, but I can't find the tears. All I have is a huge, thudding sense of foreboding. Dave . . . work . . . Dave . . . work.

I lean forward on the seat, looking down at my shoes and try to line them up perfectly against the tiles. It's impossible; the tiles are made of unevenly overlapping linoleum. It bothers me every time I pee.

Just a few months ago, I felt like everything was perfect! I remember thinking that I was invincible. *Bulletproof.*

Where did that *go*?

I count to 100, wash my hands and walk back to my desk. Charlotte's away skiing with Henry, so it's even quieter than

311

usual. It's now 5.21 pm, and the sky is almost dark. I go to work in the dark, I come home from work in the dark. Oh God, I hate winter. I hate this office. I hate everything.

I'll tell Dave about Hong Kong tonight. Dave, tonight . . . ugh . . . The minutes creep by until finally, finally, it's time to go.

When I get to the pub, Dave is leaning on a stool against the wall, texting someone. He glances up and immediately assumes a blank look that's clearly intended to give nothing away. Oh God. My nervousness has never felt like this. I think my hands are shaking. I'm too scared to check.

I walk up, smiling twitchily, but he doesn't smile like he usually does, just leans over, very quickly kisses me hello on the lips and takes my coat off.

'Can I get you a drink?'

'Yes, please,' I say. The insecurity curl around my chest has become a boa constrictor. I try to smile and play the cocky card. 'Red, I think, if you're amenable.'

Dave smiles tightly, through pursed lips. 'I'll get you a glass, not a bottle. I can't stay long.' He heads to the bar.

He's totally about to dump me.

Breathe, Abigail. Breathe.

I sit down and gaze around, hyperventilating through the knotty fear-pain. I feel flushed, though I don't know if that's from emotion or because it's so hot in here.

'Here you go,' he says, coming back with a small glass of red.

'Thanks,' I say, taking a huge gulp.

'Abigail,' he starts, then looks at me and smiles as though seeing me for the first time. 'You have a red wine smile, angel.'

He called me angel, I think, the knotty-pain easing for a second. Maybe he's not about to dump me.

He takes a sip of his beer and pauses for a second, looking at me. 'I'm going away. For work.'

312

'Oh, great!' I say in relief. He's not dumping me! 'I mean, oh, well, that's a bummer. Where are you going? When?'

I see annoyance flicker across his face. Shit, he's in one of those moods where he hates questions. Or talking.

'Asia, mostly,' he says abruptly. 'Singapore first, then from Friday afternoon I'll be in Hong Kong for the weekend . . . Then Beijing, then Shanghai, then Tokyo.'

'I – I—,' I say faintly. I want to tell him I'm going to be in Hong Kong too, and make him say that it's hilarious that we'll be there at the same time, but I don't know how. I'm too scared it will annoy him more. (And yes, I know how pathetic that sounds.)

'Hong Kong will be,' he agrees, taking out his phone and glancing at it. 'It's my favourite city after London.'

There's a pause. I try to think of something to say. 'Well, I just got a text from Sophie, she and Luke are heading to Chicago for a pre-wedding break, he got a trip with his work, so she's joined him out there—' Stop gabbling Abigail, you tool.

He finishes the rest of his beer in one gulp. 'Right. I have to go. I'm taking the early flight tomorrow, so have to sort some things out. I'll be in touch, OK?'

'Cool,' I say. What I want to say is: I'll miss you, will you miss me, is everything alright, why do I still feel sick, I'll be in Hong Kong too, please don't leave . . .

He grins briefly, puts his coat on and checks his phone again. 'Take care.' Then he kisses me very quickly again and walks out of the pub without looking back.

I pick up my bag shakily. There's a text from Suzanne.

*Where are you? Come to my office immediately. Urgent project.*

313

# Chapter Thirty Five

Just over 48 hours later, I'm on a plane to Hong Kong.

This is my plan: I'll land at 5 pm Thursday afternoon, Hong Kong time. I've got a meeting with Andre on Friday morning, and then I'll call Dave and say 'Guess where I am?' And then we'll be in Hong Kong together for the weekend! I'll pop over to the Luxury In Asia conference at some point so Suzanne doesn't suspect anything, but mostly I plan to be in bed with Dave.

And everything will be fine.

Why am I doing this? For the job? To escape Suzanne for a week? So Dave will want to move to Hong Kong with me – after all, he did say he loved it? Or so he'll decide that he can't live without me in London and beg me to stay? Or am I actually only flying because he's here and I have a horrible sinking feeling something is wrong? I don't know. But I can't stop myself.

Anyway, looking at this another way makes me feel kind of empowered. As Plum said, sometimes you just have to take a risk. No one can accuse me of being too passive now.

I am shattered, by the way. That 'urgent project' that Suzanne needed me for was a non-stop nightmare. I got four hours' sleep on Monday and Tuesday night, worked all the way through till 8 pm Wednesday night, then went straight to the airport. I haven't even had time to call Sophie or Plum all week. I've survived entirely on chocolate, stale sandwiches and coffee. In the back of my head I've been constantly running over the conversation with Dave in the pub. What did it mean? Why was he so odd? So now here I am, strapped uncomfortably into my economy seat, hurtling towards Hong Kong.

I tried to eat, couldn't, tried to read one of the trashy novels I bought at the airport, couldn't. I tried watching old romantic movies but cried so much during *When Harry Met Sally* that the guy next to me offered me his hanky. So embarrassing.

All I want to do is sleep. When I try, questions – worries – flash through my head.

Why won't the knot of panic and fear in my stomach go away? Why do I feel like I'm chasing him? Why do I feel sick, all the time?

God! I need to calm down. Caaaalm. Too much caffeine not so good for Abigail.

I'm overthinking it. He was probably just stressed on Monday night. That's all. He hasn't texted since he left London, but he did reply 'thanks . . . I'll try' when I texted him 'have a good flight'. He must be really busy.

And this Hong Kong job has been on the cards for ages, the fact that he's here this weekend is just serendipitous. It's not like I'm, you know, following him. Not really.

I take out *Vogue*, but am unable to read to the end of a sentence. So I start watching *High Society*. God I love this film. I detest most musicals as much as the next girl, but this one is special. Bing Crosby, Frank Sinatra, Grace Kelly, beautiful mansions and clothes and songs and everyone gets tipsy and behaves inappropriately . . . I mean, what's not to love?

It strikes me for the first time, however, that the plot is pretty spurious. She's marrying a pompous bore called George, but flirting outrageously with Frank's Mike and is secretly still in love with her ex-husband, Bing's Dex the whole time. Why wouldn't she admit that she's in love with Dex? Don't you think she'd figure it out before the very end? Why is she making life so deliberately difficult for herself?

My mind wanders exhaustingly like this for the entire flight. I'm physically exhausted, but too keyed up to sleep. So I drink coffee to keep me going, and pace up and down the aisles. I can't eat anything. The knot in my stomach doesn't leave much room.

Eventually we start our descent. All I can see out the window is light grey clouds and dark grey hills and a grey tarmac. This is like a dream.

The company has corporate rates at the Mandarin Oriental, so waiting for me on the other side of baggage claim is a driver in a red-and-black uniform holding up a sign with ABIGAIL WOOD written on it. He escorts me to a waiting Mercedes Benz, with bottles of water and wet towels in the back.

I take my phone out of my bag. It's out of battery. Shit. No charger, either. Never mind. I know Dave's number off by heart if I have to call him . . . He's not landing till tomorrow, so I wasn't going to call him till then, but God, I don't know if I can wait that long.

The drive from Chep Lap Kok airport to Hong Kong Island is surreal. February is winter here, too, but it's humid and only slightly chilly: completely different to London. The sun sets – or rather, as I can't see any sun, it gets darker and darker – as we drive over enormous bridges linking islands covered in low grey mountains, and past huge estates with 50-storey apartment blocks lined up next to each other.

Then Hong Kong city finally appears in an explosion of light. It reminds me of *Blade Runner*: futuristic and strange and beautiful. Hundreds of skyscrapers of all sizes and angles are lit up in front of a grey mountain. It's like a different planet, I keep thinking. Another world.

I'm so tired.

We drive through a long tunnel that I assume must be underneath the Harbour, and emerge on Hong Kong Island, on a motorway that snakes above the ground. First, we pass apartment buildings, but they're quickly replaced by office blocks with shiny, reflective windows, reaching up farther than I can see. It's beautiful, I think absently. So beautiful. I wonder where Dave is. I blink, and it takes a long time to open my eyes again.

After a few more minutes, we turn into a driveway. Another red-and-black uniformed man opens the car door, and I walk into the marble lobby of the Mandarin Oriental.

As I wait to check in, I gaze around. Everyone else in this lobby looks rested and well-dressed. I look like a piece of used chewing gum in comparison. I can feel how dry my skin is from the flight and the lack of sleep. I really need a shower and my teeth feel fuzzy – oh, my turn to check in.

'Do you have a Nokia charger?' I say, after they hand me my roomcard.

'Certainly, Miss Wood,' says the concierge. 'We'll find one and send it right up.'

God bless company expense accounts, I muse, as the bellboy shows me my hotel room. It really is the most beautiful room I've ever seen. It reeks of expensive masculinity, with a huge walk-in shower, separate bath and a mirrored vanity area with sink. The thought pops into my head: Robert would love this room. Oh God, Robert. I haven't seen him in days.

I tip the bellboy and collapse straight onto the bed.

I need sleep, I need it like oxygen, but my body is buzzing with caffeine and worry.

Opening my laptop, I quickly check my emails, just in case Dave has been in touch . . . Nothing. I can't be bothered to open any other emails. You know, I still have an acidy ache in my stomach, no matter how much I try to deep breathe it away.

The concierge calls. They're having trouble finding an old Nokia charger. God, why didn't I bring one?

Then, finally, eking out the pleasure of waiting to do it, because once it's done I can't do it again, I pick up the hotel phone and dial Dave's number. He's still in Singapore, but I can't wait till tomorrow. I need to know everything is OK, then I can sleep.

Please pick up, please pick up . . . God, my heart is thumping.

Straight to voicemail.

I leave the following message: 'Hi! It's me . . . Just, uh, calling . . . send me an email when you can. My phone's out of battery, but I have something, uh, exciting to tell you . . . bye.'

Yep, a pretty shit message.

I hang up, the insecurity curl tightening around my chest. Deep breath, Abigail. Take a shower, go to sleep, and when you wake up, everything will be fine. Dave will turn up, he always does.

After asking the concierge to hold all calls (it's only midday in London and Suzanne will probably try to track me down), 'unless you find the phone charger,' I say as clearly as I can, I get into bed and close my eyes.

# Chapter Thirty Six

What follows is a 12-hour nightmare.

My brain won't stop racing, I'm hot and cold by turn, tossing and turning, in and out of shallow sleep. I don't know if it's tiredness or the insecurity curl just making its presence even more keenly felt, but my stomach is a bubbling, churning mass of nerves. My brain darts between work and Dave, work and Dave, neither thought giving me any rest or relief, just worry, worry, worry . . .

I beg the universe to let me sleep, then, since the universe isn't answering, I call reception about the phone charger.

At 7 am, unable to stop myself, I dial his number again. Straight to voicemail. I don't leave a message, and instead dial room service to get a bucket of coffee. I need to be on form for my 9 am office-tour-and-brunch meeting with Andre, and my eyes feel so tiny and heavy I can hardly see.

The coffee doesn't help. I'm a total zombie.

'Are you hungry?' asks Andre, when we're finally sitting down to eat in the hotel coffee shop.

'Starving,' I lie.

I'm too exhausted to be hungry. I look down at the pancakes set in front of me, and suddenly can't remember the last time I ate. We're having brunch in the hotel coffee shop, and all I can think about is bed. This is hell. I am in hell.

'So! Tell me what you think,' says Andre.

He means about the office. We just saw it: the 67th floor of a building on Queens Road. It's raining today. I think the greyness of the Hong Kong day is made darker by the skyscrapers, too. There's no sunshine here.

'Great! Beautiful office. Really. Beautiful.'

I'm not lying: the office is stunning, as offices go. Expensive, and slick . . . and just the same as London.

That was my first thought. The shades of grey, the rows of desks, the fluorescent lighting, everyone in suits, all busy and stressed . . . It felt horribly familiar. Apart from getting away from Suzanne, what's the point in moving, when the office and the job fills me with the same tired ennui as London does? When I think about it, I want to lie down, close my eyes and wail.

I'm just overtired, I remind myself, trying to chew a bite of pancake, as I watch Andre's mouth moving, talking endlessly about his plans for me and the team. And I need to see Dave. As soon as I do, everything will be fine.

I feel like I have no saliva in my mouth.

I take a sip of orange juice to force the pancake down, and almost gag. I meet Andre's eyes, which are so brown and warm. I feel odd and removed from everything. Whenever I blink, my eyes burn.

Somehow, I get through brunch and promise to meet Andre at 3 pm to go to the Luxury In Asia conference. I'll check my emails, and fuck it, I'll try to call Dave again. I can hardly keep my eyes open. It's 3 am London time and I haven't slept in . . . I don't know how long.

I walk slowly into the hotel lobby, and stop at the concierge to ask if they've had any luck finding an old Nokia phone charger. Why, oh why didn't I get a BlackBerry or an iPhone like everyone else?

As I'm standing at the desk waiting, I hear a ping, and automatically glance behind me. It's the lifts. And that's when I see them. For a moment I think I'm hallucinating, because this can't be real. This can't possibly be real.

It's Dave and Bella.

They step into the lobby and he turns, looks at her and murmurs something, and she grins blissfully and reaches up to put her arms around him. They start kissing, right there, just 20 metres away from me.

I draw in a sharp breath, a bursting shocked feeling in my chest. This can't be happening, no, no . . . They're still kissing, they're still kissing!

Any second they're going to see me, they're going to turn around and see me, but I can't move. Dave's hands are in her hair, her arms are around his back. It's like something out of a fucking movie. They look so happy, so completely together, oh God, I can't bear this. I am going to scream.

'Miss Wood? Ma'am, we have your phone charger—'

I ignore the concierge, my eyes still glued to Dave and Bella, wave after wave of freezing cold horror washing through my body. I clutch the desk behind me for support. I feel sick, I think I'm going to vomit. They're kissing so passionately that I feel like I'm intruding by watching. But he's my boyfriend, he was, he is . . .

Dave pulls away and gazes into her eyes for a few seconds, and murmurs something. I've never seen him look that tender, that happy. He's never, *ever* smiled at me like that. Bella smiles back and murmurs something, her eyes never leaving his. Then Dave leans over to press the lift button, and as a ping sounds again, walks her backwards, still kissing her, back into the lift. She's giggling into his lips as they go.

The lift door closes.

I turn back to the concierge, my breath coming out in jagged gasps. My face is hot and tingly. My eyes are losing focus. Where did the sound go?

The next thing I feel is the floor hitting my face.

# Chapter Thirty Seven

I fainted. Obviously. Which caused a nice amount of drama.

The hotel staff were wonderful. They carried me to a private office, gave me tea, mopped up the bloody cut on my cheekbone, put ice on the swelling on my eye socket and asked me a hundred times if I wanted a doctor. When I finally convinced them I was fine, and just needed sleep, they helped me to my hotel room.

As soon as I was alone, I collapsed in a hysterical heap.

I didn't know what to do with myself. I didn't want to call any of my friends or my parents or my sister. I suddenly realised that flying to Hong Kong without telling them looked not just rash, but actually crazy.

So I sobbed on the floor of my hotel room.

Question after question zipped through my head, each worse than the last. Should I have known when I saw them having lunch alone? Am I incapable of having a faithful boyfriend? What the fuck is wrong with me? I cried and cried and cried.

Then I started to wonder if they were still in the hotel, and my imagination went wild. Were they having sex right now, just a few floors away . . .? Were they talking about me or – oh God, laughing at me! Would Dave feel bad if he knew that I was here? Would he beg me to forgive him? I tried to plan horrible things to say to him if I could. And I cried some more.

Then my tears stung the cut on my cheekbone. And I cried some more.

Like an emotional masochist, I searched for sad thoughts that would upset me more. I thought about how everyone has found love except me. Even Peter, horrible Peter who also cheated on me, is in love with someone else. I am the only single person I know, apart from Robert, and my friendship with him is over. I miss Robert, I thought pitifully. And I cried some more.

I thought about all my dates. About all the sweet, kind men who'd asked me out, and I'd heartlessly ignored, ensconced in my little arrogant bubble that I'd thought was so funny and cool. I am a horrible person and I don't deserve to be happy, I thought. Karma really is a bitch. And I cried some more.

I thought about flying home to London. I thought about walking back into the office, knowing that I was Suzanne's bitch for the rest of my life. And then I just didn't think I could physically get off the floor of my hotel room. I didn't want to be here, but I didn't want to be there either. I didn't want to be anywhere.

I was hysterical with sadness and self-pity. Whenever I almost felt better, I'd remember Bella and Dave in the lobby, looking like the happiest people in the world, and I'd find fresh tears again.

And then, after about seven hours of non-stop crying, there was a knock at the hotel door. And well, you know what happened then . . .

It was the wrong man on the other side.

It was Robert. He looked like shit: almost grey with tiredness, his suit all crumpled, no tie, hair even more unkempt than usual. He charged in, shouting at me. I screamed at him, collapsed on the bed and cried myself to sleep as he stroked my hair. All I kept thinking was, thank God, thank God he found me.

When I wake up, it's the next morning.

The sun has finally appeared, shining brightly through the windows, and Robert is sitting at the desk, working on his laptop. My hysterical, horrified feeling has lifted, but just slightly.

'How did you . . . why are you here?' I croak. 'How did you find me?'

Robert turns and grins at me. He looks tired. 'Good morning to you, too. On Wednesday, I knew Dave was away, but I hadn't heard you in the house. Dave wasn't answering, so I rang Sophie, who rang Plum, who rang Henry. Charlotte said you might be in Hong Kong at some conference. Then I rang Dave again. Bella answered by mistake.'

'They're here together, Robert,' I say, little tears running down my face.

'Yes, they are . . .' he says, more gently. 'And when I realised that you were in Hong Kong, and so were Dave and Bella, and you wouldn't answer your phone or emails . . . well, I figured something like this must have happened. It's pretty fucking hard to go accidentally missing in this day and age, Abigail, well done.'

'Sorry . . .' I murmur, feeling the cut on my right cheekbone gingerly. All the flesh around my right eye is throbbing.

'And your parents were hysterical by that point, so I decided to come out and find you myself,' he said.

'Oh God. My poor parents. I really . . . I really fucked up. Should I call them?'

'I already have. I didn't sleep much last night. Jetlag.'

'You're so good to me,' I say. 'Thank you.'

'I'd alerted everyone that you were missing. It was my fault that everyone was panicked. I felt responsible.'

'I should have told someone . . .'

'It's fine. I called everyone the minute you fell asleep, everyone knows you're here.'

'I'm sorry I called you a stalker.'

He smiles. 'That's alright. I know you didn't mean it.'

I shuffle to the bathroom and start crying, yet again, when I see my face. My eye is bruised and swollen, and the cut on my face is a bloody scar.

'My outsides match my insides,' I say, through my tears, as I get back into bed. 'I fainted, Robert, when I saw them I fainted . . .'

'I know, the room service guy told me when he brought dinner last night,' he says gently. 'Don't worry. I'm sure you're a fast healer . . .'

'At least I fainted properly. Unlike some people, who just collapse.' I smile at him, a tiny grin that almost hurts my face. How long has it been since I smiled? My smile muscles must have atrophied.

'Are you actually being competitive about fainting?' he says, laughing.

'I think I'm coming down with something,' I say. My throat burns when I swallow. 'Everything in my body hurts.' When I close my eyes they ache, and I feel exhausted despite just having slept for hours. I wonder if this is what heartbreak feels like. Thinking this, yet more tears run out of my eyes.

'Cry all you want,' he replies, and his matter-of-fact tone makes me stop. 'I'm ordering breakfast. And you're eating everything.'

Over toast and scrambled eggs, I tell Robert a little about how I'd been feeling about Dave, and how the other night I knew something wasn't quite right.

'Do you think he was cheating on me the whole time?' I ask Robert in a tiny voice.

'Maybe,' he says. 'I had my suspicions in Autignac that weekend. I think Ollie did too. That's why he left.'

I think back to the funny atmosphere over the weekend in France. Dave ended it by going to bed with me, though. That must have driven Bella crazy. Perhaps that's why he did it, I think, and feel a clawing pain in my chest.

Robert sighs. 'I blame myself. I should have said something about it. But I didn't want to cause trouble if there was no reason . . .' He rubs his eyes with his hands. 'I'm so sorry. He's my oldest friend, but . . . I thought it was best not to get involved.'

'I think you're pretty involved now,' I comment. 'What did you say, by the way, when Bella answered Dave's phone?'

'I said, "you fucking idiots", and hung up.' He grins.

I smile back, my insides twisting at the thought of Bella with Dave, Bella answering his phone, Bella in Hong Kong with him, Bella in bed with him . . .

'But why cheat on me with her? Why not just go out with her again?'

Robert shakes his head. 'That's a long story.'

'Tell me,' I say.

'Well . . . Dave and Bella went out, as you know, about six years ago. It had been coming on for years, they've always gravitated towards each other at our yearly family holidays . . .'

I grimace, remembering the first kiss story.

'But then Dave would bring a girlfriend one year, and she'd bring a boyfriend the year after, and it set up a sort of mutual antagonism. They were constantly snapping at each other.'

'Dave loves that sort of thing.'

'Right. So they finally got together one summer. It started in June, and went on for a year. It was very intense. We'd never seen either of them so happy.'

I wince slightly at this.

'Sorry, Abby, darling, are you sure you want to hear this? Right, now you can have pancakes because you ate all your eggs like a good girl.'

'Finish the story,' I croak, pouring maple syrup over my pancakes. I'm really not hungry but I know that eating will make Robert happy. Right now, I'd do anything to make him happy, I'm so grateful to him for rescuing me.

'Well, the following summer, Dave and his mum Dottie were walking on the beach and discovered his dad, Angus. Kissing — more than kissing, I think — Luke and Bella's mum.'

I'm too stunned to speak.

'Luke doesn't know, neither does Bella. They never will, neither will their father. Their mother swore that it was nothing and begged them not to tell her family. But unfortunately it was the fifth time Dottie had discovered something similar . . . And she'd been best friends with Luke's mum for years, too. So then Dave's parents split up. Dave's dad is now remarried and living in Monaco.'

'Dave never talks about him,' I murmur.

'Dave has completely cut him out of his life. And he couldn't bear keeping it all a secret from Bella. So he broke up with her.'

'And I thought you and Louisa were the only big family holiday scandal,' I comment.

Robert grins wryly. 'It was the same year.'

'How do you know all this? He told you?' I can't imagine Dave confiding in anyone.

'No,' says Robert. 'I ran into him straight after he'd left the beach and knew something was wrong . . . I calmed him down. We never talk about it now. He said he never wanted to tell Bella about it, or remind his mother of it. The only way to do that was to break up with Bella.'

I sigh, and close my burning eyes.

The pancakes and eggs and toast are churning unhappily in my stomach. What a mess. What a horrible, horrible mess.

'Why did you suspect something in France?'

'When we were in the courtyard, Ollie and I walked in to the kitchen to get wine, or something, and saw Dave and Bella talking. He was holding her hand. It looked somehow . . . intense. They sprang apart when they saw us, and Bella and Ollie went to bed soon after that.'

'I still don't see why . . . why he had to pretend to want to be with me.'

'I think he does . . . or did. I think he wanted it to work with you, it would have made life easier, particularly with the wedding coming up, where he knew Bella would be . . . But he's still in love with her.'

'Why did he bring her to Hong Kong?' I say, in a little mewing voice. 'Why did he lie to me?'

'I don't know,' says Robert softly.

'I think I'm going to be sick,' I say.

'Don't be so dramatic,' says Robert, rolling his eyes.

'No, I mean, I really think I'm going to be sick.'

Robert just gets me to the bathroom before I start throwing up.

# Chapter Thirty Eight

I can hear Robert talking on the phone. He sounds angry.

'You must have a doctor on call. She's been completely out of it for 24 hours, it could be serious. Fine.'

He hangs up. I try hard to open my eyes and can just make out Robert standing next to the bed. 'Thank you,' I try to say, but I have no voice, so it comes out in a husky whisper. I'm boiling hot and my bones are aching, I feel like I'm sinking through the mattress.

'I feel sick,' I whisper. Slightly redundantly.

'I've got some cold and flu medicine for you, Abby, darling. I rang my mum, I think you just have the flu . . . Try to keep it down.'

I lift my head off the pillow and drink the orange liquid that he offers me.

'Good girl.'

'Don't push your luck,' I whisper.

Robert grins. 'Well, at least you're talking. It's been a day since you made any sense.'

'So it's Sunday?'

'Brilliant deduction. Listen, do you want to have a bath so I can get housekeeping to change the sheets? Between the vomit and the sweat, the bed is pretty minging.'

I blink slowly and nod. Oh, nodding hurts. Won't do that again.

329

I fall into a mini-sleep while he runs me a bath and then shuffle to the bathroom. As I pass the toilet, my legs buckle, and I get my head over the bowl just in time to throw up the cold and flu liquid. It tastes so nasty, and I feel so sorry for myself, that I start crying. Again.

'Oh, Robert. I feel like I'm dying.'

'Self-pity alone isn't fatal, Abby, darling,' he says, picking me up and helping me into the bathroom. 'Do you need me to help you bathe?'

I narrow my eyes at him. 'No. I'm good, thanks.'

He grins and shuts the door behind him. I have a long bath, then wash my hair, dry myself and dress in the clean t-shirt and shorts that he's left for me. The whole process is absolutely exhausting. I wrap my hair in a towel turban, and clamber back on the magically-clean-and-new bed. My body aches so much. I want to roll over but I don't have the energy.

'You need to dry your hair,' says Robert.

'I don't care,' I say, and am asleep in seconds.

My dreams are exhausting. I'm always running, trying to find someone, but I don't know who. Now and again I throw up, but I'm not sure if it's in my dream or reality. Then I dream about trying to find my parents, but when I do, my dad is shaking his head in disappointment. I'm sorry, I keep saying in my dream, I'm so sorry.

I'm very hot, and someone makes me drink lots of water, and at some point I hear two voices in the room, but I can't catch what they're saying.

The next time I'm properly awake, it's Monday night.

'I'm starving,' I murmur.

Minutes – or hours, I don't know – later Robert is next to me, spoon-feeding me chicken soup. I'm too out of it to even be embarrassed or make a sarcastic comment. Then I fall back to sleep. This time, my dreams are easier, and the stress and panic is gone.

When I wake up again, it's early evening. The sky outside has a soft peachy glow.

I feel almost normal.

I blink a couple of times. How light my eyelids are today! I stretch, noticing the long-sleep stiffness in my arms and legs has replaced the heavy ache of the last few days. Then I roll my head up and look around the room. Robert's at the desk, on his laptop.

'Hey you,' I say. My voice is back, but croaky, so I clear my throat and say it again. 'Hey! You.'

Robert turns around. '"Hey you?" Is that all you can say?'

'I'm much better.'

'I can see that.'

I sit up in bed, and the sudden movement makes my head spin. 'Whoa. Low blood sugar level. What day is it?'

'Tuesday. I'll order you some food,' says Robert, grinning.

It's so lovely to see him smile that I beam back. Then I replay what he just said. I've been sick for *four days*? 'Robert, have you been here the whole time?' He nods. 'Thank you. I don't know what would have happened without you.'

He picks up the room service menu. 'It would have been . . . difficult.'

'Did I have swine flu? Bird flu?' I ask cheerfully, hopping over to the mini-bar. It's so good to feel like myself again. 'If I don't eat something now, I'll pass out.' I tear open a Toblerone and start munching.

'Two ham and cheese toasted sandwiches, two vegetable soups, and lots of warm bread rolls please,' says Robert into the phone. 'And two large apple juices.'

'I'd like a burger and chips and a beer, actually,' I say, through a mouth full of chocolate.

'No. And by the way, it wasn't swine or bird flu. Just plain ol' gastric flu combined with total exhaustion and mild hysteria.'

331

'Well, that sucks,' I say in dismay. 'I was sure it was more serious than that.'

'Sorry. Did you know you giggle in your sleep, by the way?'

'Really? How adorable of me.'

'Ah, it's good to have you back to your annoying self again.'

I lie back on the bed and look around the room. My suitcase has been unpacked, and is standing in the hall next to a carry-on case and suit carrier.

'Where have you been sleeping, Robert?'

'Next to you on the bed, some of the time,' he says, typing at his laptop again. 'But you thrashed around and talked a lot. So I slept on the floor a bit, too,' he pauses and looks over at me. 'I'll get my own room now that you're feeling better. I didn't want you to wake up and be sick and alone.'

'You're so lovely,' I say, without thinking. He looks so exhausted. I bet he's barely slept at all.

Robert shakes his head and frowns, turning back to his laptop. 'Anyone would have done the same.'

I can't quite wrap my head around the fact that we're in Hong Kong and that Robert flew all the way here to find/rescue/nurse me.

I think back to my flight, which has taken on a strange fuzzy haze, and my nightmarish hours in the hotel, and then – gingerly, like someone testing a sprained ankle to see if it still hurts – to seeing Dave and Bella kissing in the hotel lobby. Did that really happen?

Strangely, that memory doesn't hurt as much as it did before. It feels like a scene in a movie seen long ago.

So – to test the potential pain – I think about Dave lying to me. And about the fact that he could have been cheating on me the whole time with Bella. The girl he always loved. I feel a dull ache, but the searing, clutching, shocked pain is gone. The urge to cry is gone.

'I don't feel that upset about Dave anymore,' I say in astonishment. 'Not like I was.'

'Good. He's not worth it.'

'Perhaps the hysteria was shock and tiredness. Or perhaps the last four days was a concentrated mourning period,' I say thoughtfully, chewing a piece of Toblerone. I think about the flight, the first night in Hong Kong, the sleepless, obsessed feeling when I didn't know where he was. What was I thinking? 'God, what a nightmare. Perhaps I went temporarily crazy.'

'Perhaps,' echoes Robert distractedly.

'I've missed my flight to London!' I gasp. 'It was last night! I should call work, I need to get back—'

'No way. I've told your office you're very sick, there's no rush.'

'Should I call Andre? I was here to talk about a job, I—'

'For once in your life, stop being so conscientious. I delayed your flight by a week, but you can change it whenever you want. Just relax.'

I lie back on the pillow, processing all of this. 'You're like my guardian angel.'

'That guy Andre sent you those flowers. Someone else called Rich sent you those other flowers. You're quite popular in the Far East, aren't you?'

I can hardly even remember the meeting with Andre. How would Rich know I'm here? . . . Oh, Henry.

'Maybe I should call Rich,' I muse aloud. 'He's Henry's brother, you know, we dated a couple of times. Though he might want to go out, or something. I'm definitely not ready for anything . . . like that. Probably best to ignore it.'

I shuffle to the bathroom and take a look at myself. My hair is so greasy it's changed colour, and I'm very pale and visibly thinner, especially around my face. The cut on my cheekbone has almost completely healed, and my black eye is now just mildly greeny-yellow. My first black eye, I think mournfully, and I couldn't even really enjoy it.

I lift up my top a few inches and see that my stomach is concave, and my hipbones are protruding more than normal. Why is it that I can't help but be slightly thrilled at this? I mean it's wrong, surely.

I shower, dress in very old jeans and a white top (there's no Pretty With A Punch today; I'm not feeling pretty and I'm too weak to punch), and stretch out on the bed. Robert is still working. I can see out the window to the twinkling lights across Hong Kong Harbour. I wonder where Dave is, and if he's with Bella. I want to ask Robert, but at the same time, I'm not ready for the answer.

How could I have gone from confident bastardette to insecure man-chaser in the space of just a few months? Dave was the cool one, the detached one. I was . . . it's like it wasn't even me.

Perhaps we all have a desperate little bunnyboiler inside us, just waiting to hoppityhop out. I remember Plum acting *un peu* psycho around previous boyfriends, and even Sophie. I always thought, that could never happen to me. What is it about some men that make us crazy? I didn't feel loved, I wasn't ecstatically happy . . . I just wanted him. And I wanted him to want me.

And for what? For a spark when he kissed me?

Then again, it was a pretty fucking good spark.

I sigh deeply.

'You alright?' says Robert, sitting next to me on the bed. He reaches out and strokes my head again, and I look up at him and think for the tenth time today how glad I am that he's here. And not because he rescued me from a misery meltdown and nursed me back to health. But just because there's no one else I'd rather see.

I smile at him, and he smiles back. For the first time since I woke up, I feel calm. What's done is done.

'I'm fine,' I say. And I mean it.

Room service arrives, and we set ourselves up on the little sofa-coffee-table area and start eating.

'I don't think food has ever tasted this good,' I say, tearing into my ham and cheese sandwich.

'Take it easy, Abby, darling,' he replies. 'Chew. Please don't relapse. I've never seen someone throw up green bile before.'

Raising an eyebrow sternly whilst chewing with enthusiasm is almost impossible. Try it.

'You scared the shit out me when I arrived. All that screaming and crying. I thought you'd lost it.'

'I had. But then I found it again.'

'He's not worth it,' says Robert.

'I know. I can't, um, explain why I acted the way I did.'

'You can't control who you fall in love with.'

'Well, you should be able to . . . anyway, it wasn't love, it couldn't be. It was more like I was addicted to him,' I say slowly. 'I wasn't happy. But I couldn't . . . control myself.'

Robert nods. 'I know exactly what you mean.'

'Are they still in the hotel?' I say quietly.

'I told them to change hotels.'

We finish our meals in silence, but again, I'm struck by how calm I feel. Like I'm exhaling a breath that I've been holding in for months.

After dinner, I call my parents and Sophie and assure them that I'm not on the verge of death. And then, because I'm shattered again, I put on clean pyjamas and curl up on the bed. Robert has been working the whole time. It is only midday in London, I guess.

'Does your office mind you being out here?' I say.

'I had to come here sometime in Q1 anyway. I've got a full day of meetings tomorrow.'

'You're an incredibly good friend, Robert. I can never repay you for this.'

He makes a dismissive snorty-huff sound, but he's grinning.

Especially considering we've barely spoken in weeks, I want to add, but don't. I don't want to spoil it. This feels almost like our old friendship. I grab the remote and shift position slightly, lying down on my stomach.

'Come and watch Hong Kong TV with me. Ooh! Hong Kong MTV. Awesome.'

'Alright,' says Robert, standing up and coming over to the bed. 'But you'll have to stop hogging the Toblerone.'

# Chapter Thirty Nine

'I'm good as new, Roberto,' I say when I wake up the next morning.

'Good,' he says. He's at the desk, working. Again.

I stretch my arms and legs and yawn noisily. How very nice it is not to want to throw up.

'I will never take being well for granted again.'

'I'll get my own hotel room today, then.'

'Shame. Camping out here last night made me feel like we were escaping reality.' The reality of Dave and Bel – ah, don't think about it.

'Alas, my reality has followed me. I have to go to a meeting. Sure you're feeling OK?'

For a second, I consider calling Andre or checking my emails. Or calling Henry's brother Rich, so he can take me out for a flirty lunch. But I feel like being alone. How unlike me. 'I think I'll go for a walk today.'

Robert hands me a bowl of porridge and a spoon. 'It took me a long time to convince them to put chopped almonds on top. I'll be back by 8 pm tonight. Take it easy, alright?'

I beam at him as he leaves, holding my toasty warm porridge bowl against my chest, feeling like a small child. Then I start watching children's cartoons in Cantonese. Foreign language TV is a great way to keep the brain empty, but occupied. This one is about a pig, and from the looks of things, he can't stop farting. It seems hilarious. Then I order a large pot of coffee.

There's a knock on the door a few minutes later, and marvelling at the speed of room service, I skip over to the door to open it.

But it's not room service. It's Dave.

'Abigail.'

My heart is racing in shock. 'What do you want?' I say, without thinking.

'May I come in?' he says tentatively. I've never seen him look so nervous.

I think for a second. 'No.'

'I just wanted to say . . . I'm sorry.' He can't meet my eyes. 'I didn't mean to hurt you. I really didn't . . . This thing with Bella goes back years.'

'I know.' He doesn't look as gorgeous as I always thought he was. In fact, he looks sort of . . . small. And pale.

'Robbie told me how ill you've been. I feel fucking awful, Abigail, I'm so sorry.'

'You spoke to Robert?'

'He didn't tell you? He came down and gave me hell a couple of days ago. Bells, too.'

At the mention of her name, I automatically flinch. *Bells?*

'It's not her fault, Abigail,' he says quickly. 'It was all me. I made her miserable . . . for years. And, um, I really *wanted* it to work with you, I just . . . I did like you.'

'Well, good for you,' I snap, and try to close the door. I don't need to hear about how he tried to force himself to be with me. In fact, I don't want to see him ever again.

'Please, let me finish. The thing with Bella, I never stopped . . .' he pauses, and sighs. 'We broke up years ago. We tried to be friends but it wasn't possible. It never is, not really.' He's lost in thought for a second. 'Then after Christmas she sent me a letter . . . anyway, I didn't know what to do, it was torture, I was involved with you, but also with her—'

'Am I supposed to feel sorry for you?' I say acidly.

338

'I can't erase what we did. I was trying to get out of it without hurting anyone. Then I had to come here for work and I was talking to Bella, and it was a crazy last-minute decision . . . She feels awful, she has been so upset about hurting you . . .'

'Poor little Bells. Well, I have to go now, Dave.'

He finally meets my eye. He looks like he might cry.

I shut the door, turn around, and slide to the floor, and gaze into space for a few minutes, thinking.

Suddenly, all I feel – all I really, honestly feel – is pity for them both. Poor Dave, for being in love with someone else and knowing it would hurt his mother if he continued to see her. Poor Bella, for having her heart broken all those years ago, and never knowing why. No wonder she became a bitter cow. They loved each other and couldn't be together.

What a mess.

I don't even want to cry about it now. I feel sort of . . . dry. I have no tears left for him.

A few minutes later I get up to let the real room service in, and after showering and dressing, I decide to go for a walk around the hotel. It's gorgeous: calm, understated and luxurious.

Eventually, I find myself on a walkway over a busy, traffic-filled road that links the Mandarin Oriental to Prince's Building. I look out the walkway window, and see that almost every building is connected to its neighbour by at least one or two walkways. How funny.

I get a latte from a cafe in Prince's Building, wander through antique and print shops, and find myself on another walkway heading to Alexander House.

There's nothing I have to do. And nowhere I have to be. With no destination, no map, and no agenda, I'm free to just wander. It's something that I never do in real life. Even on shopping/coffee/whatever days with the girls, I have a list of errands to run, shoes to look for, dates to think about, texts to send. Busybusybusy.

But not today.

The French have the perfect word for it: '*flâneur*'. It means to stroll around aimlessly but enjoyably, observing life and your surroundings. Baudelaire defined a *flâneur* as 'a person who walks the city in order to experience it'.

As Plum would say, I'm flâneuring like a motherfucker.

Up some escalators and I'm in another walkway over a much wider road with trams zinging back and forth underneath, over to a building called Landmark.

Landmark is enormous: three floors of fun wrapped around a central courtyard where, for no particular reason that I can discern, a small orchestra is playing tunes from Hollywood musicals. I start singing along to 'What A Swell Party This Is', and walk around, looking into windows and sipping my coffee. Marc Jacobs, Dior, Chanel, all packed full of people . . . This city is luxury-crazy, I muse.

Eventually, after various escalators and detours, I walk out into the street. There are red cabs bottlenecked at traffic lights, and serious, New York-style crowds of people. I walk up, cross the road at the lights, and meander along Queen's Road. I pass street hawkers selling pashminas, and wander up and down alleyways packed with stalls selling cheap watches and silky dressing gowns. I walk into a make-up shop called Sasa, and spend £80 on Lancôme skincare that would cost hundreds at home. I walk in and out of Chinese herbal stores, electrical shops, fashion shops and shoe stores. Some of the brands are international, like The Body Shop and H&M, and some must be Hong Kong born-and-bred, such as the delightfully-monikered Wanko.

I decide to get deliberately lost, and turn up a steep hill. The crowd thins slightly, and I cross over two roads till I reach what's clearly a nightlife area that's apparently called Lan Kwai Fong. Every shop front is a bar. I walk into a Happy Days-themed sort of place called Al's Diner. It's empty, with bored waitresses gossiping in the corner, and a jukebox video screen playing Bruce Springsteen.

After ordering a burger, fries and a Heineken, I take a seat at the window and gaze at the people walking past. Lots of business people, a few tourists. Everyone is walking faster than Londoners do: in a hurry to get somewhere. A Porsche speeds down the hill, narrowly missing an old man in pyjama-style trousers and a white vest, wheeling an ancient bike with a huge basket attached. He shouts after it. I don't need to speak Cantonese to guess what he is saying.

I wonder if this is what Dave loves about Hong Kong, I think involuntarily.

Don't think about Dave, I quickly tell myself.

What kind of person must I be to have lost my way so badly, so quickly? I thought I was so clever, so sorted with my glib approach to dating and singledom . . . what a terrible mistake. I knew nothing. I still know nothing.

Thinking this makes me sigh.

I realise, with a jolt, that I essentially ignored all of Robert's surviving singledom tips throughout my entire time dating Dave. My bulletproof dating stance crumbled like an airplane cookie in the face of a handsome, uber-confident man with a sharp line in banter.

I sip my beer. Everyone on the street is seriously rugged up, I notice. The average Hong Kong woman is wearing tights, boots, a hat, gloves, a scarf and an overcoat and it can't be less than 15 or 16 degrees today, i.e. practically swimming weather to the average Londoner.

A man and a woman step up onto the elevated area outside Al's Diner. As they walk in, I meet eyes with the woman and I smile without thinking about it, just as my burger and fries arrive. Mmm. Fries.

'OK, so let's say we start in May,' says a voice. I turn slightly, and see the man and woman now sitting just a few feet away from me. Darn. There goes my quiet time. 'We'll have it wrapped by July and can then start shooting in New York, Zurich and London after the summer.' He's Irish.

'May is pushing it,' replies the woman. She's Canadian, I think.

'This is what we have to work with,' he says. 'I don't want to be in southern focking China during July and August.'

'I'm still not convinced Guangzhou is the right place for the shoot,' she says. (I know I'm eavesdropping, but I can't help it.) 'And that conference was a waste of time. We need to show growth in Asia so that we can highlight the ridiculous money, the total conspiracy that all these luxury brands are—'

'Well, you're the one packaging it to be lowest common denominator,' interrupts the guy.

'Was *An Inconvenient Truth* lowest common denominator?' she snaps. 'Was *Sicko*? No. It's accessible but not stupid. There is a difference. If you can't tell it, you're stupid too.'

'I've missed working with you,' he says, laughing.

They pause as the waitress brings out their food. I'm fascinated by their discussion and dying to join in. Being starved for conversation is probably another after-effect of being in bed for five days.

'This is a recon trip, OK?' she adds, after a moment. 'That's the point. So we cross Guangzhou off the list and keep going.'

'We won't be allowed to film in the industrial cities around Shanghai and Beijing,' he says. 'The pollution is bad press for the Chinese government. They're only going to allow us in if we present China in a positive light and show them the dailies.'

'Well, I'm not a fucking propaganda merchant,' she replies.

There's a moment of tension. Then he starts laughing and she joins in.

I clear my throat. I'm dying to say something, but perhaps I'll look crazy, or like an eavesdropper. Hey ho.

'Excuse me,' I say, turning to them. They both turn to face

me politely. Shit. What am I doing? Fuck it, I've started now . . . 'I didn't mean to eavesdrop, but, um, I was . . .'

The Canadian woman grins. She's only a little bit older than me, I think. Early 30s, with long brown curly hair that needs a cut. Slightly hippie-ish. The Irish guy is older; tall with slightly thinning hair, wearing a zip-up parka.

'But if you're looking for a Chinese city that's not too polluted and that's growing really fast despite the recession, have you thought about Beihai?'

'We have,' says the man quickly. He's not interested in talking to me. 'We crossed it off the list. Filming isn't allowed.'

'Oh,' I say, abashed, and slightly surprised. Beihai is one of the fastest-growing cities in the world, and the beaches are supposed to be beautiful, I would have thought they'd be thrilled to get publicity.

'You're thinking of Baotou,' says the Canadian woman to the man.

'Am I?' he says. For a second, I think he's going to be rude again, but then his face creases up with laughter. 'Sorry. I can't keep track of the focking names.'

'Ignore him,' she says to me. 'He's just a know-it-all.'

'China has 100 cities with more than one million people. It's a lot to keep up with.'

'What else do you know about Beihai?'

I pause, and think for a second. 'You're filming a documentary on the recession, right?'

The woman looks surprised, and grins. 'More or less.'

'Well, Beihai was also part of the Silk Road two thousand years ago, so there's that angle. These days it's the fastest growing city in the world. It's also a major tourist destination for mainland China and they're trying to make it an international one, too. And it's cleaner and prettier than some other areas.'

I pause, and flush. I didn't mean to start making a speech, but she's got such a nice open face. I instinctively warm to her.

343

I thought the guy was ignoring me and typing into his BlackBerry, but then I notice that he's actually making notes.

'B-E-I-H-A-I,' I say helpfully.

He glances up and grins. 'Thanks.'

'I'm Katherine, by the way. I'm the producer.'

'Abigail,' I say. We shake hands.

'Ronan,' says the Irish guy, offering his hand to shake. 'Executive producer.'

Katherine looks at him and barely conceals a snort of laughter. She looks back at me and grins. 'How do you know so much about China?'

'Uh, I'm a research analyst for an investment bank in London,' I say. 'I specialise in luxury and Asia.'

Their eyes light up.

'Tell us *everything* you know,' says Katherine.

344

# Chapter Forty

'Your skin is very dry,' comments the beauty therapist.

'I've been sick,' I say apologetically.

'Bad condition. Pores enlarged. Wrinkles too deep.'

I'm only fucking 28, I want to say. But instead I smile hopefully. 'Can you fix me?'

After the manicure-pedicure fiasco (apparently my toe-claws were unacceptable), the waxing humiliation (I think I know the Thai for 'forests of Borneo' now) and the body scrub meltdown (it hurt! I kept making little shrieking noises), I am becoming accustomed to short Chinese women making tsk-tsk-tsk sounds when they look at me.

But I'm so relaxed that I don't mind what anyone says.

In fact, I've had one of the best days in recent memory: first, the calming flâneuring and people-watching, then a life-changing hour talking to Katherine and Ronan (I'll tell you all about that later), then I went shopping on my one-beer-buzz on the way back to the hotel and fell asleep for an hour. I woke feeling better than I have in weeks, did my first nimble-footed-mountain-goat leap in months and at 4 pm headed to the hotel spa, where I am now. I've nearly finished my two-hour pampering session. All that's left is my hot stone massage.

Robert left a message on the hotel phone telling me he'd be back at 8 pm. I hope he wants to go out for dinner. I do. I feel so rejuvenated by the day's events. I smile thinking about them.

'No smiling!' snaps the woman.

'Sorry!' I exclaim, and start to giggle, and after a disapproving pause, she joins in.

After my facial, I get a hot stone massage. I drop off to sleep at one point, then wake myself up snoring and drooling lightly. God, the poor masseur. She finishes with a scalp massage that makes me feel awake and energised again, and I shuffle back to my hotel room in my robe and slippers feeling better than I have in a week. (It's probably not the kind of garb the Mandarin Oriental really approves of for its public areas, but to hell with it.)

Back in the room, I wash my hair, blow-dry it with the pleasingly powerful hotel hairdryer, and dress in a short, sleeveless white dress that I bought today, plus my favourite green high heels. I take a long time to apply my make-up, just for the sheer pleasure of being able to look like something other than a scab for the first time in days. Smokey grey eye shadow and lots of mascara, some careful blush, bronzer and illuminator to fake better health . . . I also bought a little gold clutch today, so I put my lip gloss and credit cards in that.

I look at myself in the mirror with satisfaction. I feel like me again.

I stride over to the mini-bar – these being stride-enforcing heels – and open it up. Wild Turkey! How Thelma and Louise of me.

I mix it with a Coca-Cola, then lie back on the bed and start watching a Cantonese soap opera. You can actually tell what's going on with these soap operas by the body language. An older lady with drawn-on eyebrows – a sort of Chinese Joan Collins – is trying to split up a younger couple. The guy is either her lover or her son, it's hard to tell. I have a flashback to Dottie for a second. How devastating to find your best friend and your husband together. No wonder Dave wanted to do anything to protect her. I just wish that 'anything' hadn't included 'fucking with me'.

I hear a scratching at the door and the card-lock buzzes.

'Honey, I'm home!' calls Robert, walking in to the room. He's wearing a dark grey suit and looking, I suddenly think, absurdly fucking good. It's so nice to have him here.

'Sharp suit,' I comment from my vantage point on the bed.

'This old thing?'

'Can we go out to dinner, please? I want to see Hong Kong at night from somewhere other than this room.'

Robert frowns at me. 'Sure you're up to it?'

'I feel great. And I had a nap this afternoon! I'm good as new.'

# Chapter Forty One

The Peak Tram is an old-fashioned trolley car that travels almost horizontally up and down the biggest hill on Hong Kong Island. It's a clear night and the view is incredible: hundreds of buildings and thousands of twinkling lights stretching all along Hong Kong Island, and across the Harbour in Kowloon. One skyscraper looks like an enormous nose-trimmer, another like a Toblerone bar. The 80-plus storey buildings continue as we climb the hill. I can see into apartments, I can even see people watching TV and eating dinner with their families. It's surreally cheering.

The sky still isn't properly dark, though it's 8.30 pm; it's that same sort of purplish-grey that I noticed from the hotel room every night. I realise now that it's the lights from the city reflecting off the clouds. It probably never gets really dark.

It only takes about 10 minutes to reach the top. Towards the end, when it's really steep, my stomach flips, reminding me of the feeling I had when Dave first kissed me. Perhaps that spark was just fear, I think to myself, and grin slightly.

'Enjoying yourself?' says Robert.

'Yes,' I say. And it's true. I am. I feel calm and happy.

We're eating at a place called Pearl on the Peak, and the main reason we're here, I see immediately, is the floor-to-ceiling windows with views over the whole of Hong Kong and Kowloon. It's incredible, like looking onto another universe. Robert has reserved the front window table. We sit down and start looking through the menu.

'This is the kind of menu I call Fun With Food,' I comment. 'Shavings and oils and *veloutés*, oh my.'

'I know. Have you been to L'Atelier du Joel Robuchon? We should go, it completely freaks your tongue out, in a good way. Oh, and St John Bread And Wine. Nose to tail eating . . . Seriously amazing meals. As long as you don't think too much about the fact that you're eating, like, a deep fried pig's head.'

'I could handle that. My dad used to make us eat raw fish eyes when we were little.'

Robert looks horrified. 'What!'

'I know. He thought it was funny. He'd bet us that if he ate it, we had to. Then he'd eat it. So . . .'

'So? So nothing! So you say, no thank you, Daddy, I have to go and practise my viola now!'

I laugh so hard at this that nearby diners look around.

We order, and when the waiter has poured our wine, I hold up my glass.

'Thank you again for finding me and looking after me. You're the best friend a girl could have. Even better than a dog.'

'Abby, stop saying thank you. I'm here for work, anyway. It's no big deal.'

'You need to learn how to accept a compliment.'

We smile at each other for a second. I've got used to Robert's unwavering eye contact. In fact, tonight I'm finding it very hard to look away. It's kind of soothing.

'So, I have some news,' I say. I've been waiting to share this, but needed a drink in my hand to really do it justice. It's that kind of news. 'I met some people today who are making a documentary on the luxury industry and the recession. One of those bigger budget, movie-style documentaries, you know, like Michael Moore's films? And we talked for an hour and—' I beam at him, and the words tumble out in a rush – 'They want to meet when we're back in London and I think they're going to offer me a job because they said "we need you on this project, you're perfect for this, let us talk to our backers and we'll come back to you".'

'Holy shit!' says Robert. 'Are you serious?'

'Yep. They said I'd told them more in an hour than their team of researchers back in London had in two months. Then they asked if I'd ever considered leaving banking and I said every single fucking day of my life.'

'That's so perfect!' He leans over and clinks his glass against mine. 'Here's to you, you little research geek!'

'To me!'

'You must have really impressed them.'

'Well, I'm quite an impressive person,' I say. Robert arches an eyebrow and I grin cheerily at him. 'I know the luxury industry inside and out. I'm a natural choice for the subject. But also . . . I love research. I love discovering things . . . No matter what the subject, I think maybe it could be something I'd be good at . . . um, I don't mean to sound arrogant about it.'

'You don't. It's refreshing to see you so enthusiastic about your career.' I make a face. 'Career isn't a dirty word, sweetpea. And I think you'd be brilliant at it too. Surely it'll be a salary drop though?'

'I don't care. I've got some savings, not quite enough for a deposit on a house if I had to—' I pause. Shit, I'm talking about putting a deposit on a house? How unlike me. 'Money isn't that . . . it's just not everything to me. I'll still earn a decent salary . . .' I pause, slightly embarrassed to have talked about myself so much. 'So, how was your day?'

'Good. I'm looking into a deal that my company wants to get involved in. But I don't think it's quite right.' He frowns and shakes his head. 'Ah, it's boring.'

'Tell me, damn you,' I say.

'Well. We think a Chinese company is going to buy us out.

350

We don't want them to. So I've been talking to another company instead. It's all very cloak and dagger.' He pauses. 'As cloak and dagger as my job gets, anyway.'

'God, you're right. That *is* boring.'

'Really? OK then, tell me more about resea—' Robert closes his eyes and pretends to snore.

'I hope my stomach is up to this,' I say, as our first courses arrive: plates of mixed crostini heaped with exotic rich toppings like wild boar.

'Are you feeling OK?'

I grin at him, chewing happily. 'Food is good.'

'God, you're deep. *Food is good.*' I snort with laughter, and he grins at me. 'The first time I came to Hong Kong, Louisa joined me and I brought her to eat here. She hated the menu and made us get a taxi back to the hotel so she could get a burger and chips.' He shakes his head. 'What a pain in the arse.'

I almost choke on my bread roll. 'You think she's a pain in the arse now?'

'I always did,' says Robert in surprise. 'The problem with Louisa – and Dave, really – is that they're absurdly likeable, even when they're being absolute bastards. That sort of charisma, well, it's addictive to be around.'

I nod. I bet I don't have that kind of charisma.

'The good news is that you can become immune to it,' he says, leaning in to me conspiratorially.

'But you're not immune to it,' I comment, smearing more butter on the roll. This is the best butter I've ever eaten. 'You're still in love with her.'

'I most certainly am not.'

'But you got drunk when you saw her at that party back in September . . . you go quiet whenever her name is mentioned, and, um—'

I'm desperately trying to think of reasons that I'm so sure he's not over Louisa. I just am, that's why.

'I got drunk that night because she tried to come on to me when her husband was talking to someone else, and it was the only way I could get her to stay away,' he says. My jaw drops in shock. 'I go quiet whenever her name is mentioned because my mother always told me if you can't say anything nice, don't say anything at all.'

'But you're commitment-phobic . . . and a slut!' I exclaim.

Robert shouts with laughter. 'You say the nicest things. Maybe I just haven't met the right girl yet . . . but I like sex.'

'Poor Robert. Looking for Miss Right.'

We eat in silence for a few seconds. I'm trying not to show how stunned I am.

'Can I ask you something?'

I look up in consternation. 'What?'

'New Year's Eve,' he says in a low voice.

'Oh.' I don't know what to say. I was hoping he wouldn't bring that up. 'That.'

'I'm glad . . . that we're fine about it now,' he says, watching me carefully. 'We were pretty hammered.'

'We were indeed,' I nod. For the first time in weeks I let myself remember our kiss, the feeling of his arms wrapped tight around me in the corner of the hot, noisy Portobello Star, and feel my face go red.

But I don't know what else to say, and thankfully, the waiter comes to top up our wine.

'Tell me about Cyrano de Bergerac, then,' he says, changing the subject. 'You told me I was like him.'

'Not exactly,' I say, laughing. 'It's a French play, I studied it . . . It's about a man with a huge nose who was sure this beautiful woman, Roxane, could never love him because of it, so he helped the handsome but stupid Christian de Neuvillette woo her, by telling him what to say. Like you helped me woo those guys at speed dating.'

'We "wooed" them?'

352

I grin and raise my hands to the ceiling. 'Woo-woo.'

'Wait. Are you saying I have a huge nose?'

Robert turns to show me his profile and I pretend to study it. Actually, his nose is perfect. Very strong but perfectly proportioned to his face. But I'm not going to tell him that.

'It's passable,' I say.

'I've been meaning to rent that Cyrano film. Or at least *Roxanne*, the Steve Martin version.'

'That film is brilliant! I love Steve Martin.'

'Have you seen – ah, what's it called, hang on—'

'*The Man With Two Brains*? *The Three Amigos*? *Dirty Rotten Scoundrels*? I've seen them all.'

It's halfway through our second course that it hits me that I'm laughing more with Robert than I ever did with Dave. We've been telling stories about our first day at school (I was the only child in my class who could already read, write and do additions and subtractions as I'd forced my dad to teach me; Robert cried the whole time for his mummy and had to sit on his teacher's lap all day – 'I still get emotional when I smell Chanel No. 19.'). Then we talked about books, and travel, and a thousand other things that somehow, we never covered in all those lazy weekends and easy evenings we spent together.

It's so effortless to be with him, compared to the pressure of pre-rehearsed quick-pat statements I had with Dave. The thought crosses my mind: this is the best date I've ever been on.

And I drop my fork.

'Everything alright? Do you feel ill?' says Robert.

Pause. I glance up at him and smile self-consciously, feeling my face tingling. I bet I'm blushing. 'Totally fine.'

I'm arguing furiously with myself: this isn't a date, this isn't a date . . . Oh God, I hope he can't mind read me . . .

'So, tell me more about your day. Do you like Hong Kong?'

'I love it,' I say, happy to be distracted from my brain. 'I flâneured around, you know. Walked without a destination.

Explored without a purpose. It's the first time I've had a day with no to-do list in . . . I don't know how long. It was kind of a revelation, actually. Stimulating and yet . . .' I search for the right word. 'Peaceful.' I pause. 'That probably makes no sense.'

'I know exactly what you mean,' says Robert. 'I was stranded in Rome because of a BA strike once. I had two full days and absolutely nothing to do. I walked around noticing things I'd never noticed on previous trips, ate four-course meals all alone . . .' he pauses. 'I've been to Rome a couple of times before and since, but that's the trip I really remember.'

'We run around too much. In London, I mean. It's too hectic. We never do . . . nothing.'

'That's the way life is though. No matter where you live. But perhaps we should turn our phones off and – what was the word? – *flâneur* more often than we do.'

'I wonder if it's possible to *flâneur* with someone else. Or if true solitude is the only way to be that reflective.'

'I think it depends who you're with. Remember that day you and I walked to Regent's Park?'

I nod.

'I saw things that day that I've never noticed before or since. How the trees were planted to give the park space and balance. How there are always clusters of people and pockets of beautiful empty park. And I clearly remember one little boy who fell over and was crying hysterically, isn't that weird?' he pauses. 'I wonder where he is now.'

'Probably reading *The Very Hungry Caterpillar*.'

He glances at me and grins. 'Hopefully.'

'I loved that day too. It was very relaxing.'

'It was,' he agrees, and glances up at the same second that I remember his little temper tantrum that day. 'Until I flipped out, obviously.'

'Ah, yes, lashy,' I say, grinning. Robert looks deep into my eyes and grins and for a second, the expression on his face changes into something more intense . . . I look away quickly. Shit.

When we finish dinner, Robert asks for the bill, and despite my protestations, won't let me pay. Just like a date, I find myself thinking. Oh God, this is just like a date.

We get a taxi down the Peak – cue: lots of highly winding roads that cause us both to skittle back and forth across the back seat into each other, though I'm trying my hardest to hang on to the door so I don't land on top of him – and end up back at the Mandarin Oriental.

'Let's have a quiet drink here,' he says. 'If you saw Lan Kwai Fong at night, you'd never want to go to bed.'

The sophisticated, understated M Bar is on the top floor of the hotel. There is a sprinkling of people at tables around the bar, polished types who have that international-rich-interesting persona down pat. We sit at a low table in the far corner with views over the Harbour.

'Hong Kong is so beautiful,' I say, turning to Robert. 'No one ever says how beautiful it is.'

'I know,' he smiles at me. Our eyes lock, and I feel myself flushing again. I look away and pick up the drinks menu.

'I'll have an Old Fashioned,' I say quickly.

'Whisky, very healing for the stomach,' he comments.

We sit in silence for a few more minutes, gazing at the view. The silence isn't awkward, however, it's just so peaceful. Our drinks arrive. Robert raises his glass.

'To you. And to your brilliant new career.'

We clink glasses. I have found a brilliant new career, I think happily to myself. I know it's right for me. I am sure I can do it. I even think that maybe I'll be good at it. I can finally leave banking, finally stop pretending to be someone I'm not. Even if the job doesn't work out, if the producer Katherine didn't mean what she said, I am still going to pursue this as a career.

'Remember that time at New Year's, when you said you

thought I knew what I wanted in life, but I was too scared to admit it?' I say.

'Yes,' he says.

'You were right. I need to quit my job, to get a life that I actually . . .' I pause, thinking. 'That I actually want and will enjoy. I'm a shit research analyst . . . But I was too petrified to admit it. It's hard for me to, um, make decisions.'

'You were just waiting for the right time and opportunity,' he says, smiling easily at me. 'Now it's here.'

'It is,' I agree, taking a thoughtful sip of my drink and gazing out the window for a few seconds. 'I feel like I'm at a turning point in my life,' I say, turning to him. 'I finally know what I want.'

'I do too.'

For a second we lock eyes, and all of a sudden, my heart starts hammering. I have the presence of mind to turn to gaze out the window again. Though the view isn't as magnetic anymore.

'Another drink?' he says. I nod frantically, unable to speak. He waves the waitress over to order.

What's going on? Something is clicking inside me, like someone turning a key in a lock. Don't think about it, I tell myself. Just look out the window and think about talking with Katherine and Ronan today. Think about my new life, my new job . . .

The bar is almost empty now. I turn back to Robert. Our eyes meet yet again and I find myself unable to look away. I feel tingly and warm . . . He smiles at me, a tiny smile that's almost more in his eyes than on his face, and I grin back automatically.

Then, slowly and calmly, Robert reaches across the little table and takes both my hands in his. I look down at our hands and back up at him.

'Abby, darling . . .' he murmurs, leaning forward.

I snatch my hands away as the waitress approaches with our drinks. For a second reality reasserts itself. I'm in a hotel bar with Robert. My best friend. What am I doing? Why am I feeling like this? When the waitress leaves, I don't look back at Robert, and instead focus on my drink.

'You look beautiful tonight, by the way,' he says, interrupting my self-terrogation. 'I don't think I told you.'

'Uh, oh, um, no,' I stammer, and take a long, very slow sip of my drink, staring pointedly at the glass. After fifteen seconds my lips start to freeze on the ice, and I am forced to look back at him.

'Are you tired?' asks Robert.

I turn to look at him and nod as my heart starts hammering again. Where did this come from? I feel like I've been possessed.

'Shall we head back downstairs? I've got the room next to yours, by the way. I just need to call reception and get them to bring up the key.'

I clear my throat. 'Right then, let's go to my room and call them.' Act normal, Abigail.

We walk, side-by-side but not touching, out of the bar in silence, then stand in the lift in silence, then walk – yep, in silence – down the corridor to my room.

When we get to the room, Robert walks straight over to the TV and starts playing with the remote control.

'I'm DJ,' he calls. 'You're bartender.'

'Smashing. I'm just going to use the, uh, euphemism.'

I walk into the bathroom unsteadily. I can still feel the whisky burning in my throat.

I pause in front of the bathroom mirror and look at myself. I look less shiny and flushed than I'd have expected. I lick my finger and run it under my eyes to fix an eye liner smear. Why am I trying to fix my make-up? I'd better eat some toothpaste. Why would I eat toothpaste? Who is going to be smelling my breath? Don't answer that. Answer this: What the fuck am I doing? Six days ago I was hysterical over Dave. No, don't answer that either. And don't think about Dave.

I lean over the sink, rest my forehead against the mirror, close my eyes and take a deep breath. My heart is racing thunkety-thunk, and my fingers are quivering. But not with nerves. With excitement.

And this is not like the nervous excitement I felt around, well, you know who. It's different. It's more like an unbearably delicious, certain, sweet anticipation . . . like I know what's going to happen.

Do I know what's going to happen?

Without pausing to – consciously, at least – answer my own questions, I walk out of the bathroom.

Robert is sitting on the bed watching a Cantonese pop video. He glances up as I approach and then grins back at the TV.

'Check out Faye Wong! I think I might be in love with her.'

I reach out to Robert's arm, pull him up to stand in front of me, and for a second we lock eyes. Then I lean forward and kiss him.

My first thought, after the shock of fuck-I'm-fucking-kissing-fucking-Robert, is, oh my God, yes, yes, yes, this is what kissing is *meant* to be. He's so warm and strong and such a perfect kisser, I feel like my whole body is melting, like I'm thawing out for the first time in days, months, years . . . For a second I sway, my knees tingling, but then his arms wrap around me so tightly that I wouldn't move even if my legs gave way completely.

*Yes, yes, yes, yes, yes, yes, yes, yes. . . .*

This isn't what I expected. This isn't what I remember from New Year's Eve. All I recall from that is the whooooosh feeling. Then again, this is a sort of whooooosh feeling too. But I'm far more sober, so I can concentrate instead on his hands on my neck and face and hair and oh God, the delicious smoothness of his lips, the warmth, the melting warmth . . .

*Yes, yes, yes . . .*

We kiss like this, slowly and deliberately ('necking', I believe is the term) for the length of four Cantonese pop songs. Then

358

Robert takes one hand away from the back of my neck and, without breaking the kiss, reaches for the remote control and turns the TV off. I giggle at the smoothness of his action, and he pulls away and grins.

'Nice move, Romeo.'

'I practised it when you were vomiting.'

I look up at him. You're so gorgeous, I think. I know you inside and out, and I adore you. His eyes don't leave mine, and I'm not nervous, or fluttery, or helpless, or any of the emotions that I would have felt if he was – you know. That was sparky and scary, this is warm and sure . . . Thinking this, I reach up and start kissing him again.

After a few more minutes of kissing, I start (full disclaimer) pushing things faster than he is. With both hands, I shove him down flat on the bed, half-sitting, half-lying on his chest and start unbuttoning his shirt.

But Robert stops me. (Irritatingly.) He grabs my wrists and pulls me down over him, and then rolls over so he's lying on top of me. Pinning my arms to my sides, he kisses my neck and I shiver in delight, and crane my neck to kiss along the line of his jaw, nibbling that soft little patch of skin just under his earlobe till his breath comes out in a gasp.

'I want you,' I murmur without thinking, and well, it's a pretty goddamn sexy thing to say. (Try it.) Robert certainly thinks so. He looks intently at me, then rolls back so I'm on top of him again. My arms are now properly free, and I start unbuttoning his shirt again. (I'm quite determined like that.)

'You sure about this?' he says, as he sits up so I can pull it off. When I finally tear my eyes away from his body (holy pectorals, Batman) I notice that his face is more serious than I've ever seen it before. 'Totally sure?'

'You know I'm sure,' I reply, and grin at him. 'Your chest is surprisingly hairy.'

'I hope I can't say the same thing about you.'

I start to laugh, and it's like this that we continue, teasing and undressing each other. And then we're naked and well, we stop giggling, and well, it all becomes rather deliciously intense.

Now, you know how I feel about discussing the gory details. I don't see you having sex, and I'm sure you don't want to see me either – but I have to tell you one thing. It has never. EVER. Been like this. It's a bit of everything by turn, and absolutely perfect altogether: slow, fast, quiet, loud, rough, tender, smooth and just absolutely fucking incredible. The second time is faster, more passionate, more urgent, more grabby. And the third time is achingly sweet and slow and sleepy.

(Sorry, am I boasting?)

'Abby, my darling,' he murmurs much, much later, as we lie draped over each other in the darkness, the light from Hong Kong's never-dark sky coming into the room. 'Cripes, that was . . .' he pauses as I pinch his arm for making fun of my words. 'Smashing.'

'That was rather nice,' I agree softly. I am so sleepy.

'We have to talk about this,' he whispers, a few seconds later.

'Later.' A tiny alarm bell is ringing somewhere in my head. I ignore it. 'Later.'

He wraps his arms around me and I fall asleep.

# Chapter Forty Two

So here I am.

Naked. In Hong Kong. Where I came to chase/surprise my boyfriend. And where I ended up having ecstatic sex with my best friend Robert. Three times.

My eyes open wide and I look around. God knows what time it is, but the room is dark. At some point last night – between sex *deuxiéme* and *troisiéme*, I think – Robert closed the curtains. I have a clear memory of his rather delightful nakedness silhouetted at the window, and then he turned and smiled at me, and I ordered him back to bed.

I've just realised that this is the biggest bed in the world, by the way. We're marooned together in the middle, with miles of space reaching out to the edge. I'm lying on my side, and Robert's arm is tucked over me. I can tell by the way he's breathing that he's sleeping. I try to wriggle away, and his arm tightens around me in his sleep, pulling me towards him. He's so warm and strong, and breathing slowly and deeply. He's like a fucking bear in hibernation.

My eyes adjust to the light and I crane my head to see the bedside clock. It's 6.34 am. Oh God. I need to think.

Come on, Abigail. Use your brain.

You're lying in bed next to a guy who has slept his way through most of London and the Home Counties, with pit stops to Europe and the States for variety. The biggest lothario you've ever met.

A man who has made 'playing the field' an Olympic sport. Sure: he has never been anything but a good and loyal friend to you. But he is a lothario nonetheless.

So be honest with yourself. The way you couldn't be about Dave. See this situation for what it really is.

This was a bad idea.

This was just sex.

We got carried away.

Maybe it was the only way to end a week as intense and crazy as this one. I mean, he flew all the way to Hong Kong to find me. Maybe it's the Florence Nightingale effect: I fell in lust with my nurse. Or maybe it's good old-fashioned knight-in-shining armour appeal.

And remember, Robert's a rescuer by nature. He rescued me on every bad date I ever had. He punched that guy on New Year's Eve. He even flew to be by the side of Antonia when her dog died. It's not meaningful. He likes helping people. It's just who he is. He's got a saviour complex.

And dinner last night felt . . . I don't know, different, special, it really did. But we're in Hong Kong and it was my first time out since recovering from the twin perils of gastric flu and Dave. And yesterday was such an amazing, genuinely life-changing day, what with discovering the documentary job . . . All these things combined to make it feel special. But it was just sex. It's only ever just sex for Robert, remember? As he said, he hasn't met the right girl, but he likes sex. And when you think about it like that, the way he acts doesn't sound *that* wrong.

And I don't want to indulge in the emotional chase again, either. Another self-contained, gorgeous, confident, funny, seemingly unobtainable man? No wonder I'm drawn to him. I'm like a little sniffer dog for bastards. And Robert would be a bastard to me in the end. I'm certain of it.

What was it that sequin girl said at that party? She said he makes you feel special. Like he's going to look after you. Well, no shit, Sherlock.

What else was it she said? I can remember it perfectly . . . 'He always says how he's not looking for a relationship but he's so kind and sweet and hot and seems like perfect boyfriend material. But it's all a front, it's a game to him, he's just a big fucking slut.'

If it's a game, then he's the only one who ever wins. Which means the other person always loses. And I don't want to lose again. I might be a big fucking slut too, but I'm not stupid.

I'm not like every other girl he's been with, the ones who expect more. I know I can't change him. Sophie said he was unobtainable, that he was a womaniser. And that girl at the party said Robert has sex three times and then says it's better if they keep it casual.

Well, we had sex three times.

So that means he'll do his disappearing act when he wakes up.

Maybe I'll just beat him to it.

What would happen if I stayed? I briefly try to imagine it. Let's say that he doesn't dump me when he wakes up. Then what? We go back to London, still living together, and what – friends? Lovers? Dating? It would be awkward, he'd be tense and distant, and I'd be nervy and worried, and our easy friendship would be truly over, he would just dump me in the end. After everything that's happened, I can't do that. I need to protect myself.

For the first time in my life, I'm going to be decisive.

And I'm going to leave him before he can leave me.

I slither down the bed slowly, out from under his arm. Robert's breathing doesn't change. I tiptoe into the bathroom as silently as I can, turn the shower on and stand under it motionless, my face upturned, letting the water beat down on my face.

I know I am right.

Everything with Dave combusted because I ignored everything I knew about surviving singledom. I wasn't in control, I wasn't detached, and I certainly wasn't fucking bulletproof. I recite Robert's original surviving singledom tips, whispering them to myself under the shower.

**Be cool**
**Be detached**
**Act brutal**
**Stay in control**
**Bulletproof**
**Always leave them before they leave you.**

I'm going to leave without waking him, fly home to London, and by the time he gets back, we'll be over this blip. Our friendship has survived blips before, after all. It was just a one-night-stand.

How's that for detached?

I finish showering quickly, apologising to my poor hair for yet another traumatic yanking-the-comb-through-conditioner experience, and smear some moisturiser on my red stubble-rashed cheeks. Then I dress quickly, and throw all my clothes and toiletries into my suitcase. Robert doesn't stir.

Should I leave him a note to say I'm totally fine about what happened last night? That everything is cool between us?

I rip a page out of my notebook, grab a pen from the desk, and think for a second.

*Fun night. Thanks for everything. Heading home to London. See you later.*

That about sums it up, right?

I stop, just as I'm leaving the room, to watch him sleeping. His hair is flopped out over the pillow and his jaw is even more stubbled than usual. He looks like a superhero playing truant: strong and warm and God, so tempting.

For a second, I pause, and take a step back towards him. Maybe I could just get back into bed. Kiss him awake and . . .

But then I remember that if I don't do this now, then he definitely will. I'd rather leave than be the one left behind.

I hurry down to the hotel lobby, pay my bill – making a mental note to not resign before these expenses are approved by work, haha – and request a transfer to the airport. I'll sort my flight out once I'm there. I take out my now-charged phone, still containing tens of texts messages I need to return, and once in the car, start replying one by one. Every text that I send is the same.

*I'm fine . . . gastric flu is a mean little bitch. Home tonight. See you this weekend? X ps Dave and I broke up.*

I can't wait to get home, I tell myself. I'll do washing, I'll call the girls, I'll sort my career out . . . I'd better make a to-do list.

Flipping to a new page in my notebook, I start writing a list. I want to Google Katherine and Ronan, and their company, Intuition Films. I think I have dry-cleaning to pick up, too, and I need to order some more contact lenses. It's Dad's birthday in two weeks, so I must buy a present. Ah, the satisfactory diversion of a list.

Fuck me, I feel strong all of a sudden. No, I feel . . . bulletproof.

I get to the airport, march straight up to the British Airways desk and ask to change my flight. Fortunately for me, there's one in an hour, so if I hurry through security, I can just make it.

By the time I'm on the plane, I'm exhausted again. I don't know how much sleep I got last night, but it can't have been more than a few hours. I wonder if Robert's still sleeping. He'll be relieved when he realises I'm gone, so he doesn't have to deal with it. He really will.

I start making notes on ideas for the documentary. I need

to find out more about it, but off the top of my head I can think of a dozen specific stories that illustrate the idea of the luxury myth. I close my eyes as the wheels lift off the tarmac, and by the time the seatbelt sign has been turned off, I'm asleep. I don't wake up till we land in London.

# Chapter Forty Three

'And you haven't spoken to him since then,' says Plum.

'Nope,' I say.

'Is he back?' says Sophie.

'Yep,' I say.

'Are you avoiding him?' asks Charlotte.

'Nope,' I say.

'Won't it be totally weird to still live with him?' asks Plum.

'Absolutely not,' I say. I look at each of their concerned faces in turn, and then over at Henry, who is bashing his face against a French-fry-stuffed double cheeseburger. He stops, mid-chew, and looks over at me guiltily.

It's Thursday, and we've met up at The Bountiful Cow in Holborn for a catch-up dinner. It's the first time I've properly seen everyone since I got back from Hong Kong last week. Thank God, every non-work moment has been all about Sophie's wedding. (Discussing seating arrangements is, it turns out, highly calming.)

'Look, guys, it's not a big deal,' I say, picking up my half-eaten burger and handing it to Henry, who layers it carefully into his existing burger. 'He got home from Hong Kong a few days ago. I'll run into him in the house at some point.' Sophie makes a worried face. She's convinced I'm hurting his feelings, but I know I'm not. 'Soph, Hong Kong meant nothing to him either, I guaran-fucking-tee it. I was the nearest thing in a 32-B. That's all.'

'If you say so,' says Sophie cautiously, exchanging another look with Plum and Charlotte.

'What?' I snap. This exchanging-looks thing is so exasperating when, you know, I'm not involved.

'Why did you leave?' they say in unison. Plum adds 'the fuck' between 'why' and 'did'.

'It was a one night stand!' I reply. 'That's what you do. One person leaves. And I'd rather leave than be the one left.'

'But . . . he flew all the way to Hong Kong for you,' says Charlotte.

The girls start talking all at once. 'He looked after you when you were sick.' 'He's so gorgeous.' 'You get along so well. You'd be a great couple.' 'Poor Robert! Imagine how he felt, waking up alone!' 'He could be your motherfucking soulmate!'

'And he's a total dude,' interjects Henry, burger finished and paying attention at last.

I close my eyes and sigh. They just don't understand. All of them are born-again incurable romantics, who lucked into happy relationships, despite having no singledom survival skills to speak of.

And they don't know Robert like I do.

'He was thrilled to wake up all alone in Hong Kong so he didn't have to deal with me. I made his life a hell of a lot easier,' I say. 'And Plum? There is no such thing as soulmates – sorry, "motherfucking soulmates".'

There's a pause. I know they're exchanging another look, but I keep my eyes on my fries.

'Is it alright if Dan joins us?' says Plum eventually.

'Luke's coming too,' says Sophie. 'He'll be here in 20 minutes.'

'So when does the new job start, anyway?' says Plum.

'Monday. And I'm resigning tomorrow,' I say, taking a sip of wine. My appetite has dropped off a cliff since I was sick in Hong Kong, but my thirst remains undiminished. 'Suzanne's back from wherever the fuck she's been. That'll be . . . interesting.'

'You'll be fine,' says Charlotte supportively. 'Suzanne has to give you immediate gardening leave. Imagine the information you have access to. It could be devastating for the company.'

I nod mutely. Naturally, I've spent the past few days making a copy of every file that could possibly come in handy. But I won't even say that out loud.

I smile to myself, thinking about my new job. Ever since Katherine formally offered me a job at Intuition Films, her production company in Soho – at, surprisingly, a salary not too far below my current one – I've felt energised and positive about my career. I could never imagine even saying that before.

It's only a six-month contract. Katherine said, 'Let's take it to the end of this project, and then see how we are.' But I know I can parlay the contract into a real career. They want me straight-away. And I can't wait to get started.

Last time I saw Suzanne was just before I went to Hong Kong, when she gave me the full banshee treatment. And now I get to tell her – professionally and politely, of course – to 'step it up' her arse. I can't wait to tell Robe— ah, never mind.

Dan and Luke arrive, and we get caught in ordering another round of drinks.

'How are you, sweetheart?' asks Luke quietly, when everyone is distracted by Henry loudly forcing Charlotte to order a dessert so he can really eat two.

'Fine, I'm fine,' I say quickly, smiling at him. I only saw him briefly during wedding planning sessions on the weekend; he said placement brings him out in hives.

'Dave called me last night, told me the full story about Bella and him getting back together over Christmas,' Luke says quietly. Not the full story, I think to myself. You'll never know that. I haven't told anyone what Robert told me about the family holiday scandal, and I don't intend to.

'I can't . . . I don't know what to say,' Luke looks at me guiltily. 'She's my sister but I didn't see that coming. What a

369

fucking mess. As for the Robert thing – Sophie told me, I hope that's OK—'

'It's fine,' I interrupt him firmly. 'I promise. I'm completely fine.'

'How can you always be fine so motherfucking quickly?' hisses Plum, who's clearly been eavesdropping. 'And by the way, have you thought about the fact that you'll see Dave—' She pauses, and pretends to spit over her shoulder – 'and Bella at the wedding in like, three weeks?'

'Of course I have,' I say, aware of Luke and now, oh great, Sophie and Plum staring at me worriedly. I'm determined not to let my romantic nightmares (read: massive fuck-ups) affect their wedding day. Think about it: because of me, half the wedding party isn't speaking to the other half. Talk about a shit bridesmaid. Dan, Henry and Charlotte are now all staring at me too. God, sometimes I wish we all weren't quite so close. 'It's not a big deal. We're all grown-ups. There won't be a scene. I'm not upset anymore.'

'Well, I fucking am,' comments Plum. 'I never liked the guy. Dave never bothered to talk to me on nights out – I wasn't a friend or a potential shag, so I was a non-entity. I hate that.'

I flinch. I wish I'd noticed that. 'Well, I don't think seeing them will upset me, anyway. Dave was a mistake, that's all.'

Plum interrupts. 'But the fucknuckle cheated on you and lied to you.'

'Thanks for the recap,' I say. 'But honestly, it's just, uh, it's over and done with. I'm fine. I lost my head, not my . . .' I pause, embarrassed, but I can't not finish the sentence now. 'Not my heart.'

'That makes sense,' nods Sophie, and quickly changes the subject.

This probably doesn't make sense, but when I do think about the three months I was with Dave, I feel like that whole period – the crazy nerve-wracking insecurity, the desperate dash to

370

Hong Kong, the devastating lobby revelation – all happened to someone else. Someone who wasn't me. Not the real me.

When I think about it, though, this happens all the time. Everyone I know has dated a bastard, and why? What makes women so smitten with men like that? Men who never call; who always keep us waiting; who don't introduce us to their friends; who refuse to stay at our house; who are bored by any topic not involving them; who never do much to make us feel secure or special or loved; men who, in summary, aren't *mean*, exactly, but aren't exactly *nice*, either? I can't think of one truly kind thing Dave ever did for me (not counting in bed) except make me laugh. And laughing is – while crucial – not enough. Not by itself. He's a real – what's that term I heard someone use recently? Cockmonkey. That's what Dave is. A cockmonkey.

And moreover, he's a sad cockmonkey. Because he's been in love with someone else for years, and felt unable to be with her. No wonder he was cold and hard inside: he had to be.

Anyway, I have better things to think about.

Who would have thought it could be so satisfying to figure out what you want in life, and try to make it happen? You know, I always used to imagine that happiness was all about accomplishing your goals – that you could only be satisfied after ticking off every little thing on a long list of things to do. But now I'm not so sure. I think that going after your dreams is even better. Because when I wasn't striving to achieve anything, I wasn't excited to wake up every day. But I am now.

'I'm not playing a drinking game!' I hear Plum shouting from the other end of the table. 'My entire life is a drinking game, Dan. And the rules just keep getting more and more complicated.'

'It's not a drinking game,' he replies, and starts singing. 'Plum Enchanted Evening . . . ha! I win.'

'Ummm . . . Dan! I feel like a woman,' she says.

'What are they talking about?' I ask Luke. We're all staring up at them, and Plum is laughing hysterically and smacking the table with her hand.

'I think it's a game involving inserting someone's name into a song title,' he says.

'I read about a game like that in a book once,' I say.

'Sophieeelin' good,' sings Luke. 'Duh-duh. . . . duh-duh . . .'

'Luke, luke, luke, luke of earl . . .' she replies. They high five.

'Oh, baby do you know what that's worth? Oo, Henry is a place on earth,' sings Charlotte, her voice trailing off hopelessly towards the end.

'That was rubbish,' says Henry. 'Charlotta shakin' going on!' he starts playing the drums on the table.

'That's not her name!' shouts Plum.

'Suck it, Plum!' replies Henry.

Everyone starts arguing all at once. Nothing rhymes with my name, I think sadly. And no one is even trying.

'Abigail away, 'gail away, 'gail away,' sings Plum. I look up and she meets my eye with a smile. Trust Plum to be the one to realise how much it sucks when you're single and everyone pairs up to play a game. Then I realise what song it is.

'Are you telling me that the only song that my name fits in is by fucking Enya?'

Charlotte turns to me. 'There's a guy at the bar looking at you,' she says.

'Not interested,' I say immediately. 'I'm not playing that game anymore.' And I'm not. I don't even look up to see what he's like.

'You fucking what?' says Plum, in shock.

'I'm going to enjoy being single,' I say.

'You are?' says Charlotte, trying not to look surprised. I ignore the subtle stress on 'you'. Now the entire table is listening to me. Again.

'Yep,' I say breezily. 'I tried so hard to avoid Lonely Single Girl Syndrome before,' (out of the corner of my eye I see Dan mouth

372

'what?' at Plum) 'but I think it's now time to embrace it. Singledom is safe.' I stand up, handing Sophie money for the bill for later. 'I'm off. Early start for Abigail tomorrow.'

'Are you sure?' says Sophie, standing up to hug me goodbye. 'Is this because the boys are here? I can tell them to leave if you want girl time,' she whispers.

'No, no, of course not,' I say quickly. 'Honestly. Tomorrow's a big day. I'm resigning, remember?'

# Chapter Forty Four

The next morning isn't worth talking about until 10.42 am, when I'm sitting with Helen from HR and my boss Suzanne, who repeats the following two words several times, with increasing aggression and incredulity each time.

'Documentary research.'

'Yep,' I beam. 'On the recession and luxury markets.'

'I'm afraid we'll have to ask you to leave the building immediately,' smiles Helen. She's warm and chatty, with a soul of steel.

'No problem,' I say, smiling warmly back.

'Get your stuff. Security will be with you in 10 minutes,' snaps Suzanne.

Man, she is so pissed off. I feel like clapping my hands.

'Great! Thank you so much. Cheers. Thanks!' I say brightly. I stand up and fight the urge to execute a nimble-footed-mountain-goat-leap out of the room.

I walk back to my desk as fast as I can without running, jump behind Charlotte and shout 'BOO!' She jumps and starts to giggle nervously. People don't shout 'boo' in this office. Ever. I quickly whisper what happened in the meeting, just as the security guard arrives. It's Steve from the front desk.

'Hi, Steve,' I say, beaming at him.

'Ready to go?'

'Will you carry me out of here like Richard Gere and Debra Winger in *An Officer and a Gentleman*? Maybe I can wear your hat?'

Steve laughs so loudly at this that the entire floor looks over. Grinning, I pick up my bag. There's nothing else I need. I took the few personal things I had home last week.

'I'll call you later,' says Charlotte tearfully, hugging me.

'I'll miss seeing you every day. But you're dating Henry now so you won't get rid of me. It was all part of my evil plan to make you a best friend.'

Charlotte grins, and as her work phone rings, reaches over to answer it. She's way better at this job than I ever was. And she actually likes it.

As Steve walks me out of the building, I cannot stop smiling. I feel so happy.

'See ya, Steve!' I say, hugging him goodbye. He looks slightly surprised, but grins and hugs me back.

'Bye bye, Abigail. You take care.'

He leaves me to take a deep breath of lovely clean, cold air. It's sunny and blue-skied. The perfect day to be post-employed.

I'm no longer a research analyst. I'm not working for an investment bank. I don't start work before 7 am every day, or make announcements to testosterone-fuelled trading boys.

What an utterly brilliant feeling.

Smiling to myself, I take out my iPod and start listening to Phoenix, till I remember Robert introduced me to them, and then put on my 60s mix. No memories there.

Smile firmly plastered back on my face, I walk towards Fleet Street, and then up to Covent Garden. The piazza in Covent Garden is so beautiful and yet it's somewhere Londoners practically never go, I muse. I walk up, my heels catching on the cobblestones, looking at the buskers and the tourists.

I'm not sure what to do with a free day. I haven't had one since . . . ah. Hong Kong. Since I flâneured.

And automatically, my mind goes back to Robert. I'm trying not to think about him, as you've probably picked up. There's just no point. What's done is done. And every time I wonder if maybe, just maybe I shouldn't have run out and left him in the hotel room, I tell myself to shut the hell up.

He hasn't exactly been knocking down my door, begging to talk about it either, you know.

I wander in and out of shops and try to engage myself in people watching, but it doesn't take. I'm not peaceful inside. I should be – I've quit my job, I'm starting a career that I'm excited about, I'm finally free of my stupid self-imposed dating pressure and the ensuing disease that was Daveticipation . . . yet something's not right.

Then I get a text. It's from Robert.

*Heard the job news from Luke. Well done. You deserve it. JimmyJames is sleeping on the couch for a few weeks. Hope that's OK. R*

I'm stung by the formality of signing off with 'R'. As though I wouldn't know who he is, wouldn't have his number saved anymore. I bite my lip, and draft a reply.

*Thanks . . . No problem about JimmyJames . . . happy to have him around!*

I deliberate for a second. Is that an appropriate response? What else can I say? Are you OK about Hong Kong? Are you upset with me? Is our friendship over? Can we ever go back to how things were? Should I be more friendly, say how excited I am about the job? No, I shouldn't. He clearly doesn't want to be friendly. I'll even take out the thoughtful ellipses. I edit my text:

*Thanks. No problem re JJ. A.*

Send.

I walk all the way home, head up to my room and work on my documentary research for a few hours, texting Sophie and Plum in an attempt to arrange something to do tonight. But no one's free. I could go to a party that one of the university lot is throwing, or I could force myself on any of the couples if I really wanted to, but I don't. So I keep working.

At about 8 pm, I hear noises downstairs. Robert and JimmyJames!

Inviting them to share a takeaway would be a good way to start mending our friendship, surely? I apply some lip balm and walk downstairs. Be cheerful, I tell myself. Be relaxed.

Robert and JimmyJames are lying on the couches watching a football match.

'Hi guys,' I say, smiling as brightly as I can, leaning against the doorframe.

'Hi,' Neither looks up from the TV.

'How are you, JimmyJames?'

'Alright, Abigail, my darling?' says JimmyJames, turning his head to wink at me. 'Thanks for letting me crash. I promise you'll hardly know I'm here.'

'No problem! Would you like Thai for dinner? I'm about to order . . .'

'Nah, we've got pizza on the way,' says Robert, without even turning his head. He picks up the remote control and turns the volume up.

'OK,' I say as cheerfully as I can. There's a cold feeling in my chest. I've lost my appetite all of a sudden. I get a yoghurt from the fridge, and eat it standing up at the kitchen bench. The ads come on, and Robert comments on the Cadbury's ad, but I can't quite catch what he's saying. JimmyJames laughs and agrees. It's like I'm not here. I can just see the back of Robert's hair and his long legs stretched out on the coffee table. I remember what it feels like to have my hands . . .

Stop it.

I put the empty tub in the rubbish bin, and walk upstairs. Neither of them says a word to me.

Fine. If he wants to be cold, I can be cold too.

# Chapter Forty Five

Monday morning, and the first day of my new job – no, my new *life*.

The winning I'm-not-from-an-investment-bank-I'm-a-totally-cool-media-person-like-you outfit: my favourite J Brand jeans, layered long-sleeved white T-shirts, a big loopy scarf and a sharp navy jacket. Hair in a very high messy bun. I tie the laces of my new leather Converses with a sigh of happiness (goodbye achey work heels!), and survey the results in the mirror. I don't need Pretty With A Punch anymore. I wear what I want, and I just feel like me.

Robert's already left of course. JimmyJames has bombed the living room with shoes, clothes, coins, scrunched up bits of paper . . . At least it'll be annoying Robert too, I think grimly.

I've stayed out of their way since the takeaway incident last week. It hasn't been hard, thanks to all Sophie's wedding admin. I never thought I'd hate something as innocuous as a wedding programme, but once you've folded 120 of the little fuckers and laced ribbon through the corner, you're ready to punch a vicar. The wedding is in three weeks. Just three weeks till we're all at the same bridal party table. Dave. Bella. Robert. And me.

The office is in an old building on Dean Street, and at exactly 9.58 am, after two calming coffees and a deeply enjoyable Soho-people-watch, I walk in. I'm not nervous, bizarrely. I feel calm and excited, but not nervous. Now that I think about it, I haven't been nervous about anything since Hong Kong. I've literally been cured of nerves, my long-time nemesis . . . Perhaps it was the shock of seeing Dave and Bella. Or the shock of waking up next to Robert.

Thinking this, I walk into the building laughing out loud, and a security guard watching TV at a desk gives me a funny look.

I prepare my first 'enthusiastic new employee' face. What I'm not prepared for is Katherine, who runs down the stairs two at a time, and leans in to give me a double cheek-kiss hello and a warm hug.

'Wonderful to see you!' she exclaims. 'How are you?'

'Fantastic!' I say. 'How are you?'

'Frantic. I'm so glad you're here. Right. Let's go.'

Intuition Films is on the top floor, and I note with another thrill that there's no irritating security tag needed to get in to the office. Huge windows line one side of the room, real windows that can actually open over the Mary Poppins rooftops of Soho. The office is a warm, creative mess, with eight people stationed at computers, several couches stacked here and there, film posters all over the walls, and Roxy Music – ah! Roxy Music! – playing softly. I can see a tiny galley kitchen where a young guy in skinny jeans and a hoodie is buttering some toast.

'This is your desk,' says Katherine, depositing me next to a large desk in the far corner, next to the window. A new-looking laptop is sitting there waiting for me. 'Most days we start at 10ish, and finish at 6 pm or so. Everything should be set up. If you need anything, call me or ask Robyn, the office manager,' she turns and points back to a blonde woman at the other end of the office. I nod. 'We've got a Luxury Project production meeting at 11 am. I'll come and get you.'

I can't describe how interesting my day is without sounding like, frankly, a total geek, but it's incredible how my interest in the luxury market and finance is fired up, simply by looking at it from another angle. We need to make the main finance stories of the past decade both interesting and digestible, and I have loads of ideas. At first, I'm a bit timid, but by 1 pm, when we wind up the production meeting, I'm talking quite volubly and happily to Katherine and Jeremy, the junior researcher and toast-butterer. We have a rough outline of how we're going to progress the research, and the production assistants have a list of immediate to-dos.

'By the way,' says Jeremy to Katherine, as we're leaving the office. 'Ronan rang earlier. Asked me to fast track that research on the France project. Is that OK?'

'Yes, we've had some interest from HBO,' replies Katherine. 'We need to get everything together for a meeting in LA next month.'

'What's the France project?' I ask.

'It's our first non-documentary feature . . . we've got an amazing script, it's a four-part historical drama on Blanche of Castile. She was the wife of—'

'King Louis the eighth,' I say. 'Um, I wrote my university thesis on her. I have a degree in medieval French.'

Katherine stares at me for a second and starts laughing hysterically. 'Of course you do. Christ! I'm so glad we met you.'

Jeremy grins. 'So am I. I've been completely fucking lost.'

I smile happily. I don't think I've ever had a work day like this in my life.

The next few days fly past, a blur of meetings and research and ideas that all cement my feeling that this really is the career I was meant for. I tend to stay at work later than everyone else, never leaving before about 8 pm. I can't help it: I feel so lucky to have this job. I don't want to let them down.

I fill up my evenings catching up with the girls, and even arrange to meet up with a few old friends from the university crowd. Anything not to be at home.

Apparently Peter has moved in with the girl he went travelling with – yep, the one he had an affair with. The news doesn't affect me at all. It's like hearing gossip about someone who I've never even met, isn't that odd?

On Thursday, I have a few after work drinks with my new colleagues but feel too shy when they all suggest going for dinner. I will, one day. But not yet. Instead, I head home. I'm positive the boys will be out tonight, so I'll have the place to myself.

Having JimmyJames here has made the no-man's-land territory of my friendship with Robert easier to bear, I reflect, as I walk into the bombsite slash living room. In other ways, it has made it much harder. I wonder if we would have talked about things by now if we'd found ourselves alone.

Then again, there's nothing to really discuss, is there? No.

I think I have to move out. I mean, I know I do. I've been putting off thinking about it (how unusual for me). But this cold awkwardness can't go on . . . or rather, it will probably go on forever. So I should just get out, right?

I put some washing on and head upstairs to take a long, hot bath. I try to read *ELLE*, but I can't concentrate, so I just lie back, watching the steam evaporate off the top of the water. Eventually I shave my legs, since I may as well, and apply a facemask. After about half an hour, the water starts to cool, and my periodic refills aren't hot anymore either. I dry myself, dress in my warmest pyjamas, and do something I've been looking forward to since, well, forever.

I throw out my old work uniform – I mean, clothes.

All those awful old Pink shirts I kept for emergencies, when nothing else was clean. The black trousers that I really hate, but kept because I couldn't be arsed to buy a new pair I'd hate just as much. The brown trousers that were good for bloaty days. That cardigan that I always took with me in summer, because the air conditioning was so brutal. The black top that I never, ever liked, but that came in handy for when I just didn't have anything else.

I take particular pleasure in throwing out a pair of mid-winter boots that I only wore because they straddled the tenuous ground between stylish, warm, and work-appropriate.

Now I can wear what suits me. Do what I want. Stop faking it.

Once all my clothes are safely in rubbish bags, ready to give to the charity shop; and my leftover clothes are hanging happily in the wardrobe, I light a candle, lie back on the bed and pick up my book.

And then, out of the corner of my eye, I see a big cardboard box in the corner: my personal things from work. Including the waterproof wet-weather moped gear that Robert bought me, that I only wore that one time. That was so kind of him, wasn't it? So very typically quietly thoughtful and generous, the way he always is – was – to me.

I wonder where Robert is right now.

He's probably out with JimmyJames. And he's getting on with his life. I'm here, getting on with my life. We're just not friends any more, simple as that.

It shocks me how much this thought hurts, like seeing a bruise on your shin the morning after a party and giving it a good poke to see just how bad it is.

Robert isn't my friend anymore.

The thought is so painful that I gasp.

In an effort to distract myself, I open my laptop and check my emails. There's just one email: from an account called . . . Travel By Proxy.

I smile in delight and open it and there, in my inbox, is a friendly little email from Bree with a link to their blog entry for New Year's Eve.

It's titled: **Robert and Abigail**, and is followed by a photo of Robert and me from New Year's Eve. We're sitting at that cosy table in The Only Running Footman, his arm is around me, he's grinning at me and I'm laughing into the camera. I've never seen a photo of us together before. We look stupidly happy.

I start reading their intro.

*We met Robert and Abigail at a quaint little pub in Mayfair. London-dwellers, City-workers, these two were the most relaxed and friendly of everyone we met in the UK's capital. They could hardly talk without looking at each other, smiling at each other, and even touching each other. True love. All together now: awww . . .*

Corny. And they completely misinterpreted the relationship between us, too.

Fucking hell, I miss him.

I do, I really miss him. I stare at the ceiling for a few minutes, thinking about the past six months. About all our nights out together, and cosy breakfasts in the warm kitchen when it was still dark outside, and silly texts and emails. All the lazy Sundays reading the papers together and having peanut butter on crumpets, and impromptu drinking sessions in The Engineer, and the Christmas decorations night, and New Year's Eve, and Hong Kong . . .

I'd love to tell him all about my new job. He'd get a kick out of it, I know he would.

Tears well up in my eyes. I feel indescribably sad. There's a lump in my throat the size of a goddamn golf ball and I feel . . . what is this feeling?

I know what it is.

I feel homesick.

I lie back on my pillow, gazing at the ceiling. This isn't the same feeling I had about Dave at all. I don't feel that sharp nauseating shock, or that hope-crushing rejection. That was different.

This is pure, unadulterated sadness.

The friendship between Robert and me is over.

After staring at the ceiling for a few more minutes, I pick up my phone and call Sophie.

'Ahoyhoy,' she says, instead of hello.

'I miss him, I miss Robert, and we'll never be friends again,' I say, and just saying the words aloud makes me so sad that I almost start crying. I control myself, however, and take a deep shaky breath. 'Sophie? Are you there? I said I miss Robert.'

There's a pause. I hear some scuffled sounds, and then the sound of a door closing.

'Right I'm alone now. Continue.'

'I just . . . I miss him, I don't know how else to say it. I've never felt like this. I'm . . . homesick for him.'

'Homesick?'

'I feel an ache in my throat and my tummy. Just like that feeling at school. I've never felt like this about anything else. I miss him.'

'You miss him . . .' says Sophie slowly. 'Maybe you should tell him?'

'I can't do that,' I say, aghast. 'It would be weird. I just have to accept it and move on.' Silence. 'I was kind of hoping you'd agree with me on that one. Maybe give me some tips on how to do it.'

Sophie takes a deep breath. 'Don't you think that maybe – maybe – it's odd to be more upset about Robert than you are about Dave?'

'No. Anyway, I was more upset about Dave before he dumped me . . . I have a new theory that I worried about it so much beforehand that when it happened, it hardly hurt at all.'

'Huh,' says Sophie. We talked about Dave quite a lot when I got home, obviously, but she still doesn't believe me when I say I'm fine. 'That explains why you didn't seem quite yourself at Christmas.'

'What?'

'You were a bit, uh, tense . . . Mum and Dad kept cornering me to ask what was wrong with you.'

'I was temporarily insane, that's all. Dave was a drug.'

'Well, he's an asshole drug,' says Sophie, adding loyally: 'And if he knew how amazing and wonderful you are, he would never have . . .'

'Honestly, Soph, you don't have to say that,' I interrupt. Funny how even thinking about Dave seems like a waste of time. 'Anyway, maybe he and Bella belong together.' I still haven't told Sophie about Dave's dad and Luke's mum, of course. It would just put her in an awkward position, to know something like that about her future mother-in-law, something not even her fiancé knows. And besides, it's really not my secret to tell.

'I'm playing nice for the wedding because you can't de-bridesmaid your treacherous bitch of a sister-in-law without causing a huge family ruckus. But the minute it's over, I intend to unleash hell on her.' This is such an uncharacteristic thing for Sophie to say that I almost want to laugh, but the lump in my throat is aching too much.

'Huh,' I say instead. If I start to laugh, I think I'll cry at the same time.

'So . . . Robert? What are you going to do?'

'Mmm,' I say, trying to control the tears welling up in my eyes. 'Well . . . what do you think I should do?' I say eventually.

Sophie pauses for quite a long time. 'Darling, if you can't see how you really feel about Robert, then I don't – I don't know what to say.'

'What do you mean, can't *see* how I *really* feel?'

There's another pause.

'Luke and I, um, we kind of thought that you guys would, I don't know . . .'

'What?'

'Get together.'

'No!'

'But you get along so well, there was all that sexual tension—'

'What? There was not! When was there sexual tension?'

Silence. Fucking hell, *why* is Sophie so good at holding her tongue?

'We get along – sorry, we *got* along, past tense – so well because there was no sex involved. Robert is a playboy, remember? We were only ever friends. I loved his company . . .' I pause, thinking.

'Can you honestly tell me you don't think he's handsome? Just a teeny bit?'

I don't say anything. I'm staring at the Travel By Proxy photo of us. He's absurdly good-looking. 'It doesn't matter. Robert never saw me like that. He doesn't find me attractive.'

'You don't know that. Perhaps he didn't make a move earlier because you were his flatmate, or because you are my sister. Don't shit on your doorstep, and all that. And then you were seeing Dave, anyway.'

'Um,' I say. I'm thinking. Robert paid me lots of compliments. Mostly under the influence of alcohol, admittedly. And in Hong Kong, when we were in bed, he said some very—

'He's been different, since he met you, you know,' says Sophie, interrupting my reverie.

'He has?'

'He spent more time with you than he ever did with the boys, or with any of his ladyfriends, or whatever it is you used to call them. He used to spend a lot of time alone . . . he was a grouch.'

'He did? He was?' I don't think he's a grouch at all. I did, but only till I got to know him. Now I think he's lovely. In every possible way.

'Yes,' she says impatiently. 'You're so blind, Abigail.'

'I am?'

Sophie starts laughing at my parrot-questions. I don't say anything, but start chewing my bottom lip, lost in thought.

'I need to think.'

'Yes, you do. Love you.'

'Love you.'

I don't want to think about Robert and whatever it is that Sophie's suggesting. Because if he ever liked me like that . . . *if* he ever, ever did, and I never let myself even think about it because I assumed he wasn't interested, and then *if* after we finally succumbed to the chemistry and affection between us and slept together, I discarded him like yesterday's crumpets then . . . well, then that's one almighty fuck-up.

I can't bear the thought of being in bed tonight with just my

386

brain for company. So I take an antihistamine, one of the drowsy ones, and am asleep in minutes.

I wake up at 3 am to the sound of shouting.

And giggling.

Then I hear Robert's voice, and JimmyJames' voice. And then more giggling. Not just giggling. *Girlish* giggling.

'Fucking hell,' I say aloud.

Then someone puts music on. I can hear JimmyJames shouting along to the lyrics.

That's it. It's the middle of the night. I'm not putting up with this. I have a new job, goddammit. I need sleep.

I get out of bed, still in my pyjamas, and start padding furiously down the stairs. I'm almost at the bottom when I hear Robert's voice.

'Turn that shit down,' orders Robert. I can tell by his voice that he's been drinking. It's too loud, and he thinks he's whispering. 'My flatmate is sleeping.'

'Your flatmate, hmm, is that what you call her these days?' says JimmyJames, hiccupping. The music is instantly turned off.

'That's what she is,' says Robert shortly.

'Do you have any lemon for my vodka?' says a girl's voice.

'Picky little thing, aren't you?' says JimmyJames.

'I'll have some lemon, too!' says another girl's voice. 'Robbie, I love your place!'

Then I hear JimmyJames and the first girl in the kitchen, giggling and flirting as they get a lemon out and cut it. But it's not them that I'm concerned about. It's Robert and the second girl. I can't see them, but I can hear them clearly. They can't be more than eight feet away.

'I think I've broken my toe,' says the girl. 'Robbie, would you come and look at it?'

'Uh, of course,' he says. I hear the couch squeak. They must be sitting on the couch nearest the hallway. 'What nice toes you have . . .'

387

'You should see my arse,' she says, and laughs hysterically at her own joke.

In the dark, I make a how-disgusting face. What a tart. Robert wouldn't go for that, would he? Suddenly there's complete silence. JimmyJames must be kissing the first girl. Nothing else would shut him up for this long. Is Robert kissing the second girl? I hold my breath, willing one of them to talk.

'It's not broken,' says Robert. I sigh with relief. He was just looking at her toes. 'You'll live to wear heels again.'

'Oh thank you, Doctor Robbie,' she says. 'So . . . want to give me a tour of the house? I think we should give those two a little privacy . . .'

'Uh, sure,' says Robert. Another couch-squeak indicates he's standing up, and I immediately lurch up and start creeping backwards up the stairs. I don't want him to know that I'm here, don't want him to know I'm listening, and don't want him to see me in pyjamas when he's with this girl with the incredible toes/arse. I get to Robert's landing just as they come around the corner to the bottom of the stairs, and speed up the second set of stairs to my room as fast as I can. (Thank God for all that nimble-footed-mountain-goat practice.)

'Ooh, three storeys, it's huge!' says the girl.

'Uh, it's just a funny-shaped little place, really, cut out of a big old house, you probably didn't see the front entrance,' says Robert. 'My flatmate is asleep upstairs, so please be quiet . . .'

'Oh, she won't hear anything,' she scoffs. 'So what's in here, then?'

I'm at the very top of the stairs, in the darkness, holding my breath as I look down on them. I can't see their faces, just the bottom two-thirds of their bodies. Robert is wearing jeans and his khaki shirt. And the girl's wearing a purple dress, black patterned tights and knee-high boots. She looks like a fucking go-go dancer, I think viciously. She's quite tall and slim. Taller than me, I'd guess. The thought makes me narrow my eyes in dislike.

'Well, that's the bathroom, obviously,' he says. 'And that's, uh, my bedroom.'

'Will you show me?' says the girl.

I roll my eyes to myself. Christ, Robert's not going to fall for that, is he?

I peer down again, and fight the urge to gasp aloud: the girl is suddenly right in front of Robert, pressing herself against him . . . they must be kissing. Are they kissing? They are! I can hear a squelching sound.

'Mmm, very nice,' she says. I fucking hate this chick. I don't even hate Bella but I really hate this go-go girl. 'Come on then, show me your room.'

There's a pause. Please say no, Robert, I think. Make up an excuse.

'Perhaps we shouldn't,' he says. 'It's a terrible mess . . .'

'We can keep the lights off,' she giggles.

Then the door to his bedroom shuts, and I'm left standing in the dark, panting in horror.

How could he do that? How could that have just happened?

I turn around and head back into my room. I'm having trouble breathing properly, but I think that's probably from holding my breath for much of the last five minutes. My heart is beating so loudly that my ears hurt. I get back into my cold bed and lie there, staring at the ceiling, feeling the ache in my stomach get bigger and bigger. I press my fingers against my ears and try not to imagine what might be going on just one floor below me.

Just one thought keeps running through my brain.

This is wrong. This is all wrong.

# Chapter Forty Six

There's no point in thinking about it, you know. I can't be angry with him for bringing home someone else. I left him in bed in Hong Kong. I walked out on whatever had just started between us. And even if I hadn't, who's to say that he wouldn't have done the same to me? Just because I've realised whatever it is that I've realised about how I feel – or might feel – about him does not mean that he realises the same about how he feels – or might feel – about me.

If that makes sense.

So there's just no point in thinking about it.

Thank God for work. It's the only thing that gets me out of bed, the only thing that keeps me sane and smiling. When I've filled up my brain with facts and figures and stories and people and events and ideas, then there's no room for any thoughts of Robert. Even when I'm not in the office, even when I'm with Sophie, or the girls, or Henry and Charlotte, I just witter away and try to focus on what I did today, what I'll do tomorrow. Work.

Until the moment I get into bed. Then I close my eyes and am instantly transported back to Hong Kong. Back to the hotel room. Back to the moment after dinner when I walked out of the bathroom, grabbed his arm and – well, you know the rest. I replay it over and over again in my head, and then fall asleep and dream about him. It's been three weeks since that 3 am shock realisation on the stairs. Three weeks since I finally became conscious that I – well, never mind. Let's just say that the home-sick feeling was just the start of it.

And this isn't Lonely Single Girl Syndrome, or desperation, or anything else that I used to worry about when I was freshly single, either. This is just a sad, empty yearning that won't go away. And there's nothing I can do about it.

When Plum established that I wouldn't even say Robert's name out loud, she figured out what had happened, and after five hours of trying to convince me to tell Robert how I felt, suggested I date other men, just to see if it could help me 'move on'. But I can't even imagine dating anyone now. The thing I loved most about the dates I went on before was talking about them with Robert afterwards.

Every time I've seen Robert, I've been unable to even look at him. Fortunately, JimmyJames is still staying with us, so they seem to be on a permanent booze-bender, and only come home to sleep. And anyway, Robert doesn't look at me either. It's like he hates me.

Thinking about it makes me feel like lying on the floor.

Even when I've just woken up in a suite at the Charlotte Street Hotel, as I have today.

It's Sophie and Luke's wedding day, and we're all staying here as it's just a few streets from the tiny Marylebone church where they are getting married. Sophie asked me to share her bedroom, and I agreed on the proviso that she doesn't try to cuddle me. (From family holiday experience, I know that she's like a little koala and I'll wake up on the far corner with her hanging on to my back.)

I've been awake, thinking about work and trying not to think about Robert, for God knows how long. Sophie is still sleeping soundly, facing the other way, her breathing deep and even. When we were little, I was prone to nightmares – roosters, sausages, elves. You name it, I had nightmares about it. My parents – understandably – would get a bit grumpy after the sixth night

391

in a row of me climbing in with them. So I would go and get into bed with Sophie, who was all warm and peachy and never stirred. She's just the same now as she was then: kind and calm and generous. Tears prick my eyes as I think about it. Now she's getting married, and hopefully going to have little warm peachy babies of her own. I hope she has two girls. Sisters are special.

I can't imagine that the whole marriage-and-motherhood thing will be happening for me anytime soon.

Sophie answers the wake-up call from reception, and rolls over to face me. We meet eyes for a second and grin.

'Happy wedding day!' I shout. The tears threaten to spill, but I blink wildly at the ceiling and they recede.

Sophie sits up in bed and squeals.

I head into the bathroom, clean my teeth and splash some cold water on my face. Last night's dream was eerily real. I dreamed that I stayed in the bed in Hong Kong, and Robert woke up and kissed me, and everything was different . . . I point at myself in the mirror. Just. Stop. It. Today is about Sophie, not you.

I bound back out and jump on the bed, shouting 'mawwiage!' I'm ready to go into a whole Princess Bride act, but—

'You talked about Robert in your sleep last night,' she interrupts.

'I dreamed that we were burgled. I was probably saying "robbers, robbers,"' I reply quickly.

'No, you said "I'm so sorry, Robert. I'm so sorry."'

'Ha,' I say.

Sophie looks at me and shakes her head. Thankfully, I'm saved by a knock at the door, and I race to answer it. It's Vix, who looks, as usual, hung over.

'Hotel bar. JimmyJames. Robert,' is all she says, walking straight over to the bed and getting in next to Sophie.

We had a rehearsal dinner last night with the entire bridal party, did I mention that? Even Bella and Dave.

What does it say about my state of mind that I barely even noticed those two?

The entire bridal party, plus our parents, sat at a long table at Elena's L'Etoile. Robert was right down the other end, laughing with JimmyJames and Vix all night. We didn't speak, though he did say 'hi, Abigail,' when he first arrived. I said 'hi, Robert,' back. (Ah, quite the conversationalists.) Fortunately, dinner started late, so at 11 pm when Sophie announced that the bride needed beauty sleep, I left with her. Bella tried to catch my eye twice – she was on the other side of the table and three down – but I ignored her. Dave was on the same side of the table as me, and very subdued. I barely noticed him. Once, his presence would have electrified me.

'Was last night difficult?' whispers Vix to me.

'No, not at all,' I assure her.

Sophie overhears. 'Was it alright with Dave' – she pauses, and we all pretend to spit over our shoulder, and then look back to her as though nothing had happened – 'and Bella?'

'It's cool. They mean nothing to me.'

I can't mention this in front of Sophie as we've all agreed to not rock the bridal boat: Vix cornered Dave before dinner last night and said, 'Listen to me, you little fuckwipe. Tomorrow is about Luke and Sophie. Not you, and not Bella, and not Abigail. So behave, and be nice, and tell Bella to wipe that pout off her ugly mug, or I'll stab her in the eye with my fag.' Ah, Scottish girls. So direct.

'Well, I've left Bella out of all the fun maid stuff, anyway,' says Sophie. She's started calling us maids, rather than bridesmaids. 'I told her we're getting dressed separately and I'll send her the hair stylist later.' Vix and I start to laugh: Sophie's never been so vengeful in her life. Thanks to marriage, or maturity, or good ol' filial loyalty, she's finally able to get angry. 'She can suck it. No one fucks with my sister.'

'Yeah,' echoes Vix. 'I'm not even gonna talk to her. And I'm going to be an absolute bitch to Dave whenever I see him, forever. So there.'

'You say the sweetest things. Beauty bomb!' I say, emptying the bag on the bed. Out rolls Frederic Fekkai and Kérastase deep conditioner, REN face masks, Clarins Beauty Flash Balm – which Vix falls upon with little cries of joy – and a Philosophy Microdermabrasion kit. The girls immediately start noisily deciding which they'll need, and I smile to myself. I knew they'd like this stuff.

'I fucking wish you'd let us fake tan,' says Vix petulantly, after she's combed through the deep conditioner and is spackled with a face mask.

'My wedding, my rules,' says Sophie calmly. 'Trust me. In 20 years, we'll all be laughing at fake tan photos the way we now laugh at perm photos.'

Room service arrives with French toast and extra strong, extra-milky coffee, Sophie's pre-chosen wedding day breakfast.

'We're having champagne, too, but not till later,' she adds cheerfully.

'I made some playlists for this bit,' I say, slotting my iPod into the speakers next to the TV. 'Going To The Chapel' comes on.

Vix is increasingly hyper, dancing around while Sophie exhibits a strange bridal calm. I join in as best I can.

Another knock at the door indicates that the manicurist from Return to Glory is here. Then the hair and make-up people arrive, just as our mother comes in, enquiring how everyone slept, and fixes me with a stare from across the room. She was giving me the gimlet eye all last night too. To escape her, I run to the bathroom.

'When did this wedding become a movie shoot?' I hear Sophie saying in surprise. 'There are more helpers than there are bridesmaids.'

'I just wanted to make sure we weren't rushed,' says my mother. I wash the mask out of my hair, shampoo, shave my legs and do all the requisite grooming rituals that a good maid should, and then, I stand for a long time under the boiling hot water of the shower. It reminds me of that hotel shower. When I lay on the floor for an hour and cried over Dave.

God, what a waste of tears.

I dry myself, fasten my hair in a towel turban, wrap a robe around my body and come out of the bathroom. Vix has gone to shower in her room.

'What on earth is up with you, missy?' asks my mother, who is sitting with the manicurist. I sit down on the opposite side of the room, and the hairstylist starts combing out my wet hair, a hairdryer tucked under her arm.

'I can't hear you,' I mouth to Mum, pointing at the hairdryer.

'It's not even on!' she exclaims.

At that moment, the stylist switches on the hairdryer. I beam at my mother and shrug, and she rolls her eyes and starts talking to Sophie. I meet eyes with the stylist in the mirror and she winks at me.

Continuing like this, I'm saved from talking about Robert or what on earth is up with me for hours. There's always someone around, or something to do, and soon it's time to get dressed, and then we open a bottle of champagne. And then, finally, we're all ready.

'Good luck today, darling,' I say, leaning over to give Sophie a hug. 'I love you.'

'I love you too,' she says, wrapping her arms around me tightly. 'I want you to be happy. I really do.'

'I will be. I mean . . . I am.'

She pulls back and looks me in the eye. I look away first.

'Let's go.'

# *Chapter Forty Seven*

Walking down the aisle as a bridesmaid is terrifying. I cannot imagine how nerve-wracking it must be for the bride. Practically everyone I know, all our family members, everyone that has seen Sophie and I grow up, is in the church. And they've all turned around to stare.

Bella goes first. Then Vix. Then me. And then Sophie, on my Dad's arm.

As I walk up the aisle of the packed little church, I try hard to keep my eyes on the black and white floor tiles and Vix's steadily advancing feet, so that I can match her pace. When I get halfway up the aisle, a collective gasp tells me that Sophie has just entered the church, and – thank God – no one is looking at me anymore. That's when I raise my eyes and find myself looking straight at the groomsmen.

There's Luke, with a huge smile on his face.

Dave, staring straight ahead, his face blank.

JimmyJames, clearly deeply hungover.

And then Robert. Looking right at me.

Our eyes meet, and for several seconds, I get tunnel vision. All I can see is his face, his eyes staring at mine. Everything in my vision apart from him goes fuzzy. I'm trying so intently to read his expression that for a split-second, I stumble over the hem of my dress and break the stare. When I right myself and look back, he's not looking at me anymore.

Hardly breathing, I take my place next to Vix as calmly as I can, and turn to watch my sister coming down the aisle.

She's wearing a long off-white silk dress, in a sort of bias-cut, with her dark hair long and wavy. (Her something old is our mother's earrings, her something new is the dress, her something borrowed is again the earrings, and her something blue is a pair of sky blue heels. In case you were wondering.) I'm wondering why people always cry at weddings, because really it's just a weird pagan ritual, when I turn to look at Luke's face. His entire face is creased up in a smile so wide it looks like it must hurt and just as she reaches him, his eyes fill with tears. And then I start crying, too.

Sophie laughs, and leans up to kiss him and whisper something in his ear, and he nods and uses one hand to quickly flick away the tears. They both turn to the front of the church.

I look next to me and see that Vix is also crying. We meet eyes and immediately start to giggle. Vix makes a small exploding sound.

Bella flinches, as though she thinks we might be laughing at her, but doesn't turn. We've successfully avoided her all morning, she didn't even come with us to the church. The bridesmaid dress Bella chose doesn't suit her, I note with satisfaction (okay, I don't hate her, but I'm allowed to be happy when she looks bad, right?). Like ours, it's soft pale grey, but she's wearing a knee-length halter neck style that makes her look both slutty and wide. Vix is wearing a below-the-knee strapless style that suits her, with some serious upholstery keeping her puppies under wraps. My dress is very plain: just below the knee and sort of draped, with a low back. As we're turning to face the front of the church, I look out to the congregation and glance at Plum, who makes a gesture to my dress, and gives me the thumbs up, mouthing 'fucking fab!' Sartorial approval. I almost laugh again, and just control myself.

The rest of the ceremony passes by in a blur. I can't see Robert, despite straining to out of the corner of my eye. Then the vicar pronounces them husband and wife, and everyone starts cheering and whooping, led by JimmyJames and Vix.

We follow Luke and Sophie back down the aisle, but my chance to see Robert is stolen as two of my younger cousins come up to give me a hug. This is followed, when I get outside, by crowds of our family and friends who want to kiss and hug us all. The so-called reception line for said kissing and hugging is a total shambles, because JimmyJames wants to talk to Vix and Luke won't stop kissing Sophie. I can't see Robert in the crowds of people, and when the main person I don't want to see – Dave – comes towards me and looks like he might start to speak, I grab my great-aunt, give her an enormous hug and pull her over to speak to Dad. Crafty old me.

It's the bridal party's job to ensure that all 128 guests make it to the reception. As we start shepherding people out of the churchyard, it's already a mess, with people stopping to chat and ambling out onto the road.

'Help,' I say beseechingly to JimmyJames and Vix, who are standing near me bickering flirtatiously.

'Yeah, James,' says Vix. 'I thought you were a take-charge kind of guy.'

'Right, screw this,' says JimmyJames. He puts his fingers in his mouth and lets out a huge whistle. 'Everyone! Hold hands! We are going to do this in an organised fashion!'

If you haven't seen 128 people in cocktail attire holding hands and snaking through Marylebone, well, you haven't lived. Since the hand-holding order came when everyone was still mingling and talking, we're all placed quite randomly, and there are relatives holding hands with friends holding hands with parents etc. It makes everyone giggle and breaks the ice. It's a gorgeously sunny day and unusually warm for March, which always makes Londoners a bit giddy.

I'm holding hands with Vix and my Uncle Jim. I can't see Robert.

The reception is in a tiny mews off Great Titchfield Street: a huge, all-white photography studio with huge floor-to-ceiling glass doors along one side, opening out onto a hidden garden, where there are two large outside bars set up. This is also where, for a few deeply stressful minutes, the bridal party has to take group photos. I can't bring myself to look at Robert, or Dave or Bella for that matter, but Vix keeps up a running patter that makes Sophie and I laugh constantly.

Thankfully, waiters with large tumblers of champagne on ice are waiting for us as soon as photos are over. I stride away from the bridal party as quickly as I can and start chatting to the guests.

'Champagne with ice cubes! Very unconventional,' I hear one of Luke's Dutch aunts say sniffily. 'Like the shoes, I suppose.'

'Try it, you might like it,' smiles Sophie as she passes. She'd warned me that some of Luke's relatives wouldn't approve of the reception venue. But since she caved on the church ceremony – religion not being her cup of hot cha – she wouldn't budge on anything else.

The aunt takes a sip, makes a face, and then takes a much longer sip, turning away. I meet eyes with Sophie and wink. All her planning and worrying is going to pay off.

Suddenly, Vix grabs my hand and hisses 'Follow me!' She marches me inside, past the long banquet-style dinner tables, through the kitchen and out into a little side alley where the bins are. She's clearly downed a few glasses of champagne already, and her dress is *un peu* wonky.

'I think your boob is plotting an escape,' I say. 'Why are we here?'

'We're having a secret fag away from the crowds,' she says, yanking up her dress. 'And by the way, I slept with JimmyJames last night. I wanted to wait till after the ceremony to tell you.'

'What!' I gasp. 'OK, now I need a cigarette.' I light one, take a drag and cough profusely. I haven't smoked in months.

'How could you go for a fucking cigarette without me?' says Plum, jumping through the doorway, followed by Sophie.

'Why is it the only maid I can see is the one that I don't even like?' asks Sophie. 'Bad maids! Bad.'

'Vix is the baddest maid of them all,' I say.

'I slept with JimmyJames last night,' she says again.

Everyone screams. I scream again, too, just for the fun of it.

'Hello, ladies,' says a male voice. We all turn around: it's Dan. 'Ah . . . I can see this is a willy-free VIP area. Can I get you a drink?'

'You can get us a bottle,' says Plum, leaning over to kiss him. 'All good?'

'JimmyJames and I are taking bets on which one of you lot falls over on the dance floor first,' he says.

'That's so romantic,' says Plum. 'But don't worry, sugarnuts. I'm a sure thing.'

Dan leaves, and we all turn back to Vix, who has a satisfied little grin on her face.

'Tell me motherfucking everything,' say Plum, as Dan returns with the bottle of champagne and four glasses and then dashes off. 'Love you, baby!' shouts Plum after him.

'Well, he's been calling and texting and emailing a lot since that weekend in France,' says Vix, downing her first glass of champagne and pouring another. 'And he makes me laugh so much . . . he's interesting and smart. And he's an amazing kisser. I mean, what else is there in life?'

'Amen, sister,' says Plum, clinking glasses with her.

'I thought you were with Robert in France?' says Sophie.

'Don't be silly, Robert's in love with Abigail,' Vix says, and then claps her hand over her mouth. There's a pause that seems to last forever, and then everyone looks at me.

'No, he's not,' I say. 'He's not,' I say again, and then look up to meet all of their eyes. 'Is he?'

Vix shakes her head. 'I promised him I wouldn't say anything.'

400

'Robert did *not* tell you that he was in love with me,' I say forcefully.

'Not in those exact words,' she says. 'But we talked until 3 am in France. He talked about you a lot. He's always looking at you. I asked him directly, and he didn't answer . . . but it's so obvious to everyone, except you.'

I stare into space for a moment, chewing my lip, and then shrug. 'Well, it doesn't matter. We don't speak anymore. We're not even friends. If he ever felt that way . . . it's gone now. I heard him bringing some random girl home the other night. He's an incorrigible ladykiller. He will never change.'

'JimmyJames told me that,' says Vix. 'But he also told me that Robert didn't do anything, and that the girl stormed out of the house after being in his room for about ten minutes, interrupting JimmyJames' little snog in the kitchen,' she adds proudly. 'Now that he's my boyfriend, he'll have to stop that behaviour, obviously.'

'He's your boyfriend?' exclaim Sophie, Plum and I in unison.

'Everyone's asking if the bride has done a runner,' Luke pokes his head around the doorway. 'You're hiding next to the bins?'

'Sorry, darling,' says Sophie. 'Come on, girls. This conversation will have to wait.'

# *Chapter Forty Eight*

Inevitably, when I sit down after an hour of mingling like a good little bridesmaid, the first person I see is Robert. He's sitting in a little bubble of his own, and looks nearly grey with nerves. I can't say anything to calm him, either; he's on the opposite side of the long bridal table from me, and we're both at the very end.

We couldn't get further away from each other if we tried.

Oh God, I feel bad for him. The best man's speech. He's been dreading it for months, and I didn't even help him. I was too busy obsessing about Dave, and thinking about my own problems. I suck.

I wonder if I should – no. I can't go and talk to him. It wouldn't make any difference. I fucked it up. I just have to get through today, go home, and get over it.

I sigh, and look around the room. The wedding is a success so far. You'd never know half the bridal party isn't talking to the other half. I've barely even seen Dave and Bella. The champagne has been flowing like, well, like champagne should. I'm meant to be next to JimmyJames, but he hasn't sat down yet. Diagonally across from me is my father, who will be next to Vix and Sophie if they ever stop butterflying.

'Alright, Daddy-o?' I ask across the table.

'I am, indeed,' he says, taking out his notes for a once-over. Despite the fact that he too, has a speech to make, he radiates his usual calm. 'All good here.'

I think back to our conversation in France. *When you find the right man you'll just know.*

I think that maybe I found the right man, but let it slip away. I loved being with Robert more than anyone else in the world. In fact, I remind myself again, the happiest I've ever been was when he was my best friend, my drinking partner, the person I confided in and laughed with, and read papers with, and ate dinner and breakfast next to . . .

And then when we finally got together; finally knocked down all the stupid barriers separating us, I left a note thanking him for the 'fun night' and got on a plane to the other side of the world.

What if he'd done the same to me? I would have been devastated. It was the worst thing I could have done. Then again, I remember wryly, he programmed it into me with all that 'always leave them before they leave you' stuff. He taught me to be a bastard. So no wonder I behaved like one.

'Ha,' I say aloud.

'Enjoying the day, darling?' says Dad across the table. 'I want to hear more about your glamorous new job, by the way. Hollywood, watch out, eh?'

'It's a documentary, Dad. It's not that sexy,' I say, grinning.

'By the way, I don't think much of that Dave fellow,' he whispers.

'Dad! Shush!' I say. My dad is good at many things, but whispering isn't one of them. We're always trying to drown him out in restaurants when he makes a comment on what someone else is wearing/eating/saying.

He shrugs nonchalantly. 'I was talking to him about you and Sophie and he left me, mid-sentence. Very bad manners. I think he might be a bit of a prat.'

I grin. 'I think he might be a bit of a prat, too.'

He nods. 'Thought so . . . ah, Robert!' he says, calling up the table. 'How are you feeling?'

Robert looks over, glancing quickly at me, and then smiles greenly at Dad. 'A bit ill, to be honest, Mr Wood.'

'Call me Ross,' says Dad. 'You'll be fine. Just speak from your heart. And when in doubt, raise a toast.'

Robert grins, and nods. 'Thanks for the advice, Ross. If you could raise a lot of toasts in your speech so the crowd is nice and drunk for me, that'd be great.'

My dad laughs at this. 'No problem. Now, did you happen to catch the results of the Six Nations today?'

What the – since when are Dad and Robert besties? I think back to last night. They were sitting opposite each other at the rehearsal dinner. Clearly they got along.

After a few minutes, Vix takes her seat, and my dad turns to talk to her. I've been pretending to look around the room and smile at people. But the minute he's not talking to my dad anymore, I look back at Robert. Our eyes meet and, just like in the church, everything else around him goes out of focus. Instant tunnel vision. Oh God. I don't know if I can bear this.

'Good luck,' I say, but my voice comes out in an almost whisper. I don't even know if he can hear me.

He smiles, but it doesn't reach his eyes. A heavy, sinking feeling overwhelms me. If he ever did think of me as anything more than a friend, he certainly doesn't now. I'm not even a friend. I totally and completely fucked it up.

Everyone starts cheering and clapping again, as Sophie and Luke walk through the reception and take their seats. Luke is high-fiving people on the way and Sophie is laughing at him. They're the most relaxed newlyweds I've ever seen.

When they reach our table, Sophie sits down, and Luke, still standing, clears his throat.

'My wife and I . . .' he begins, predictably, and everyone cheers. JimmyJames and Vix are whooping. '—would like to thank you all for coming. I'll be giving my speech a little later, but for the

404

moment, let me raise a quick toast to all of you. May your champagne bubbles rise up to meet you.'

I take a slug of champagne and immediately have a coughing fit as it bubbles up my nose. Note to self: champagne is not for slugging.

My Dad now stands up to give his speech. 'As father of the bride, it's my pleasure to make the first speech. For those of you who don't know me, my name is Ross – that's "Ross, Sir" to you, Luke . . .' I look at Robert again, and lose track of what my father is saying. Robert really looks like he might pass out. I wish he'd said he didn't want to do the speech, really, someone shouldn't feel so sick on what's meant to be a joyous day, don't you think? JimmyJames could have done it, or fuckhead, I mean Dave.

'. . . so on behalf of my wife and I, and all the guests today, I'd like to wish you health and happiness for the rest of your lives together.'

'To health and happiness,' echoes the crowd. I mouth the words absently. Robert's gone even paler.

'Nice one, Ross,' says Vix, winking at my Dad as he sits down.

'Try to control yourself around me, Victoria,' he says drily, though I know he's secretly thrilled.

The waiters are serving the first course now. JimmyJames and Vix are flirting noisily with each other across the table, thank God. I can sit here in silence.

I take a bite of scallop and look up at Robert again. He's seated next to Luke's mum on one side (who, I've noted with interest, looks like hand-churned Dutch butter wouldn't melt in her mouth). She is talking to Dave on the opposite side of the table. I can't see his face, but I imagine he's pretending to be equally charmed. I wonder if she knows she is the reason Dave broke up with her daughter, and the reason his mother is an unhappy lush. She must know she helped to break Dottie's marriage up. She must, surely.

What a mess. My family is so boring in comparison.

'Hello, high table,' says Plum, trooping up with Dan in tow. She crouches next to me. 'What's up, pussycats? Anything from the evil duo?'

'Shurrup,' I hiss, and turn to JimmyJames before my dad can overhear and start asking questions.

'So, Abigail,' says JimmyJames. 'Vix tells me you've changed your career.'

'Uh, yes,' I say turning to him. 'I did. I mean, I am. Trying to.' I can't seem to get thoughts straight in my head. 'Plum is, too.'

'Indeed I am,' Plum says, smiling beatifically at us. 'I was working in a job that wasn't emotionally or intellectually satisfying. So now I work in fashion.'

Vix cracks up, and then stops. 'Shit, sorry. I thought you were making a joke.'

Plum and Dan, who are already pretty tipsy, start telling a story about one of the Dutch relatives who tried to start a drinking game during the first course, and was told off by the vicar. I'm now facing the wrong way to see Robert. Maybe he should just pretend to faint or something to get out of the speech. I've never worried this much about someone in my life.

'I think you should move to London and live with me,' I hear JimmyJames shouting – he's obviously aiming it at Vix but it's in my ear.

'Alright,' she says, looking over at him.

'Really?' he exclaims.

'Yeah, OK,' she says, a grin spreading across her face.

'Wooo!' screams JimmyJames joyously. He turns up the table to face Robert. 'Rob! I'm moving out of the house of the rising singles and into cohabiting bliss.'

Everyone at the table turns, and I feel Robert, Bella and Dave staring in our direction, and my skin crackles with heat. Fucking hell, when did I start blushing again?

'I can't see your mother approving of you two living in sin,' says my dad to Vix.

'It's holy flatrimony,' hiccups Vix, looking at JimmyJames adoringly. 'Till the lease do us part.'

As Plum and Dan return to their seats, the waiters start clearing plates, and I steal yet another look at Robert. He now seems to be in a kind of trance. I'm not even sure that he's breathing.

Then, when all the tables are clear, Luke turns to Robert and whispers in his ear. Robert nods, and stands up. Oh God, it's time.

Immediately, the crowd shushes itself, and everyone turns to listen. He stares straight ahead, and for several petrifying seconds, I think he's not going to say anything at all.

Then he clears his throat and starts talking.

'When Luke asked me to be best man, I almost cried. Partly, yes, because of the honour, and all that stuff,' he says. The crowd, already well-lubricated, titters. 'But mostly, because I realised I'd have to stand up in front of a large group of astonishingly good-looking, well-dressed people and talk about,' he pauses, and puts every bit of dramatic emphasis into his next word: '*Love.*'

The crowd all laughs again. What was he so worried about, I wonder. He's great.

'Now, you may not know this, but there's only one thing that will petrify a 31-year-old single man more than public speaking. And that's love.' I smile up at him. All the colour has rushed back into his face. 'So, I'm going to start this gently, for everyone out there who's as scared of love as I've always been . . . I've known Luke a long time, and I can confidently state that since the moment he met Sophie, he's been happier than I've ever known him. He laughs longer. He talks louder. He smiles more. In short, he's the man that I think he was always meant to be . . . but it took the appearance of Sophie, of beautiful, calm, loving Sophie, to make him that way.'

Everyone cheers at this point, and I glance up at Sophie and Luke with tears in my eyes. It's true. They were meant to be together.

'Now, as I am still – very – single and alone, I've had a lot of time to reflect on the art of finding love. My mother always told me that you have to slay a lot of dragons to get to the princess –' there's a whoop from the audience – 'and I think that's true, but the dragon that you really have to slay is your own fear of – now bear with me, this is going to sound soppy – your own fear of taking a risk for love.' He pauses for a second. Everyone is listening intently now. 'Luke's risk was walking into that pub when he first saw Sophie. Most of you already know this story: he was walking past The Walmer Castle in Notting Hill, saw her through the window, knew she was the one for him, and then sat alone at the bar for two hours, drinking alone, until he had the courage to talk to her.'

'Is that why it's called Dutch courage?' shouts someone from the audience, to general groans.

'I was going to make that joke, but I dismissed it as too lame,' deadpans Robert quickly, and everyone laughs some more. 'For Luke and Sophie, it was, more or less, love at first sight. Now, this is a story that has always scared me.' Robert waits for the laughter to subside, and continues. 'Because: what if he didn't walk in to the pub? What if he never found the courage to go and talk to her? Some of us think the way they met sounds easy, but it would have been much easier for Luke to walk away. It's always easier to walk away.'

I look down at the table for a second. I found it easier to walk away.

'It's braver to stay. It takes courage to stay.' Robert clears his throat, and pauses for a second. 'I am sure I speak for all the single people here when I say that I don't want to ever lack that courage. I don't want to lose my best friend and my true love, just because I wanted to stay in control and not take a risk. Even if they walked away, even if they ran to the other side of the world, even if I thought that I didn't have a chance in hell, I still want to know that I did everything I could to make it happen.'

I blink, and replay the past sentence in my head. What?

Robert clears his throat. 'So, ladies and gentlemen, if I may, I'd like to encourage you to turn to the one you love – or, if you are between loves right now, then the nearest person of the opposite sex, provided of course that their significant other doesn't mind – and tell them that you love them. No caveats, no limited time only, no terms and conditions: be true to yourself, take a risk, and tell them you love them. To love!'

There's a roar of 'I love you!' and 'To love!' from all over the room, as everyone stands up and raises their glasses, cheering and clapping as they go. I can hear Henry whooping particularly loudly. Talk about a crowd-pleaser.

And me? I can hardly breathe. All I can do is stare at Robert.

He is leaning forward, resting both his hands on the table, with his eyes shut. Look at me, I think as forcefully as I can, please look at me.

Robert takes a deep breath, opens his eyes and a beat later, looks over at me.

For a long moment we look at each other, and for the third time today, everything around Robert's face goes out of focus. All I can see is him.

That speech really was for me, I realise. It was all for me.

'I love you,' I say.

He can't hear me, because of the noise all around us. But he can read my lips.

'I love you,' he says back, and his face cracks in the hugest smile.

I smile too, and suddenly feel like there's a light beaming out from the centre of my body, through every inch of my skin.

That's the spark I've been looking for. The spark is the feeling that you were born to be this happy. And that's how I feel right now.

# *Chapter Forty Nine*

'I love the way you do thumbs up, like the Fonz,' he says.

'I love the way you take up every inch of space, wherever you are, like a big shaggy dog.'

'I love the way you take everything and nothing seriously.'

'I love the way you take me seriously.'

'I love that your brain is always working on three things at once.'

'I love the way you're so serious on the outside and so silly underneath.'

'I love that about you, too.'

'I love the way you squeal like a girl.'

'I love the way you arrange the cutlery in the dishwasher according to type.'

'Well, forks and spoons always fight . . . I love your face.'

'Ah, damn you, I was just getting to your face . . .' he says, and leans forward and we start kissing again.

Not that we've really stopped kissing. At every full stop, sentence clause, and sometimes just between syllables, we've kissed. After Robert's speech, and the seemingly never-ending main course (during which we found it nigh impossible to break eye contact), and Sophie and Luke's first dance, Robert could legitimately stand up and ask me to dance.

Eleven songs later, we're still dancing together, hardly moving, our arms slung around each other. I'm not sure who else is dancing. All I can see is Robert.

'I'm so sorry that I left you in Hong Kong,' I say, for the hundredth time.

'That's OK, darling. If I were you, I would probably have done the same,' he says.

'Sophie once described you as London's premier playboy,' I say. 'Sure you're ready to trade that title in?'

'So utterly, utterly ready. You know, I think I've loved you since you told me the ending of that *Simpsons* episode.'

I laugh. 'Why?'

'It's just not what I would have expected from a girl like you.'

'I guess that's what girls like me are good for. The unexpected.'

'You are. You definitely are.'

We start kissing again.

'My face hurts from smiling,' I say.

'I'll kiss it better later.'

'I love you.'

'I love you.'

Yep, it's pretty nauseating. I'll excuse you from hearing any more of the love talk.

At some point over the next few hours – it's all a bit hazy for me; I'm drunk on kisses – Sophie and Luke cut the cake, and the wedding band leaves, and the Pixies cover band arrives. This is quite a departure in musical tone, and after watching Vix, JimmyJames, Charlotte, Henry, Plum and Dan charging around playing air guitar and leg guitar, Robert and I decide to head outside to the garden bar.

'Do you want a shot?' says Robert. 'Liquid confidence?'

'Get thee away from me, Satan,' I say.

'Hi there,' a voice interrupts us. It's a very well-turned-out blonde woman in her mid-30s, wearing an expensive-looking long, mint dress and a slightly déclassé faux-mink stole. 'Beautiful speech, Robert. Can I have a word? In private?' She looks at me pointedly.

'No,' he says abruptly. 'You can't.'

He takes my hand and as we walk off, I finally twig.

'That was Louisa!' I exclaim.

'Yes,' he says, grinning. 'The silly bitch. Constantly trying to get a piece of me.'

'I want to meet her,' I say petulantly.

'No, darling, you really don't,' he says, kissing my hand.

I can't help it. I turn around and meet Louisa's heavily-kohled eyes. She's staring at me furiously from the doorway. I give her the biggest smile I can muster, and then turn to Robert, grab him by the tie and pull him down for a huge kiss.

'Lovely,' he murmurs, 20 seconds later. 'But don't think I don't know whose benefit that was for.'

'Just marking my territory,' I say amiably.

'Robert, excellent speech,' calls my mother, gesturing with a martini glass like she's Dorothy Parker. She's on the other side of the bar with all my aunts, who are gazing at Robert like he's something to eat. Which he is. But only for me.

'Let's run away,' I say to him.

'Anything you want,' he replies.

Then a bartender comes up and hands me a note.

*I'm sorry. I can't explain it or make up for it. But I am sorry. Bella.*

I crumple it up and throw it in a nearby ashtray.

'Bella or Dave?' guesses Robert.

'Bella,' I say. I shrug. 'It really doesn't matter. I don't care about them.'

'Neither do I,' he says, smiling into my eyes. He hasn't let go of my hand since we started dancing. It feels very natural. In fact, it feels – what's the word? Right. 'I only care about you. And I care, a little bit, about getting us both another drink. One second . . .'

Robert turns to a nearby waiter, and I grin to myself and gaze around the outside area happily, and then catch my dad's eye. He looks pointedly at Robert and then at me, and winks.

I wink back. He was right, I think. He was right and Robert and I were completely and utterly wrong. When you find the right person you'll just know.

'We've broken every single one of your rules,' I say to Robert, as we turn to face each other again and he hands me a glass of champagne.

'Rules?' he says, leaning over to give me a thoughtful little nibble-kiss.

'The surviving singledom rules. Your entire speech was about how the only way to find love is to not be cool, or detached, or brutal, or bulletproof. How being in control and walking away is cowardly, how you must be brave and take a risk.'

'As long as it's the right person—'

'But still, it's the opposite of the rules,' I insist.

'They weren't *rules*, darling,' he says. 'They were just . . . silly. I was trying to help you feel better about being single because the whole thing seemed to stress the hell out of you. In an absolutely adorable way, of course.'

'It did,' I admit. 'Though as you'll remember, I was brilliant at singledom for a while. Then I crashed and burned.'

'Good thing you won't be single again, then,' he says, leaning forward to kiss me.

'Darn,' I say. 'I really think I would have nailed it this time.'

# The Rules of Surviving Singledom

~~Be cool~~ Be silly
~~Be detached~~ Be direct
~~Act brutal~~ Be kind
~~Stay in control~~ Let yourself do whatever you want
~~Bulletproof~~ Have an open heart
~~Always leave them before they leave you~~ Be true to yourself
and everything will work out.

I'd like to think that I'm adorable when I'm writing. That I sit here, chewing my lip endearingly, as I search for the perfect phrase or word. In reality I'm a panda-eyed harridan, sighing and swearing and bashing the keyboard furiously, with the occasional joyous laughing fit at my own hilarity, and far more frequent hair-pulling tantrums when I decide the whole thing is awful and I suck. So the biggest thanks has to go to Paul, for putting up with me during the writing of *A Girl Like You*, and even marrying me just after I finished it. I love you. You are the best. I am sorry about the sex bits. I promise I was thinking about you the whole time.

Thanks to my agent, Laura Longrigg, for being so perceptive, encouraging and brilliant about writing and reading and oh, everything. Thanks to my delightful editor Sammia Rafique, for falling in love with *A Girl Like You* straightaway and for her endless positivity. Thanks to Jill Grinberg for her encouragement, support and our long, lovely conversations. Thanks to everyone who read *The Dating Detox* and emailed me to say hi. Thanks to the people who emailed a Bastard name suggestion and story to Name That Bastard (not to mention thanks for going through all those dreadful breakups just to help me name the dude). Thanks to all my friends called Dave for not minding that their name is, apparently, the biggest bastard name of all. (Hey, internet polls don't lie.) Thanks to my non-Dave friends and family for being encouraging and cool and funny.

415

Since we're here, thanks also to Nora Ephron, Helen Fielding, Elizabeth Gilbert and Jilly Cooper, for being deliciously smart, funny, insightful and more-ish writers who inspire me to try to be as deliciously smart, funny, insightful and more-ish as them. And thanks to you, for reading this far. You must be bored by now, surely. In fact, to paraphrase Ferris Bueller: you're still here? It's over! Go home . . . Or, go to the next page and read a bit from my first novel, *The Dating Detox*.

# PART ONE

# Changing How You Think

# THE DATING DETOX: A Sneak Peek.

At 5.30 pm exactly, I leave work as quickly and quietly as I can to head down to meet Bloomie in a bar about ten minutes' walk from South Kensington tube station. I'd like to get a black cab, but can't quite justify it. (I spend an inordinate amount of time justifying the expense of black cabs to myself. My two go-to excuses are that it's late so the tube could be dangerous. Or that I'm wearing very high heels.)

On the number 14 bus on the way down the Fulham Road, I try to talk myself into being in a good mood. Despite the universe throwing every happy loved-up person in London in my path tonight (how can they all find love and not me? How can the drab little beige thing in front of me be calling her boyfriend to say she'll put dinner on for when he gets home? Why, damn it, why am I unable to achieve that?), it's not actually that hard. I'm cheery by nature, I love after-work drinks, I love Bloomie and I love the place where we're meeting. It's a restaurant called Sophie's Steakhouse, but we only ever go to the bar part. It's not quite a pick-up joint, but not all couples; not too rowdy, but not too quite; not too cool and not too boring. In short, it's the perfect place for the freshly single.

I push past the heavy curtain inside the front door, and see the usual young, rather good-looking West London crowd. There are some gorgeous men in here, as ever, though I know they're probably a bit rah-and-Rugger-Robbie for me. A few floppy-haired

Chelsea types in red corduroy trousers (where do they sell those things and how can we make them stop?), a couple of older business-type guys waiting alone in suits for wives or girlfriends, and I can sense, but not see, a group of five guys having an early dinner in the restaurant part, as they turn around to look at me as I come in. I know it's only because, well, I'm female, but still. It's gratifying. Especially today.

Bloomie is, as usual, about half an hour late, so I kill time reading the fun bits of the paper someone else has left behind (you know, the celebrity bits, and the movie and book reviews). As soon as she arrives we start as we always do: with a double cheek kiss and a double vodka.

Things move swiftly from there. I don't want to get hammered tonight as it's only Wednesday and payday isn't for another ten days, but quite soon we start going outside for cigarettes (neither of us smoke, except in situations of extreme stress, like last night, or drinking, or, um, gossiping on a Saturday, or sometimes on the phone), which is a sure-fire sign we're here for the long haul.

Before I know it, I'm slapping the table with one hand to emphasise my point (which point? Who can say? Any point! Pick a point, please), and making dramatic absolute statements that start with 'I will NEVER' and 'There is no WAY'.

From drink one to two we talk about Posh Mark, from drink two to three we talk about Eugene (the extremely lovely guy she's been dating for a few months. She calls him The Dork because who the sweet hell is called Eugene?), with a quick side-wind into talking about Bloomie's recently-redundant-and-leaving-soon-to-travel-the-world flatmate Sara, from three to four we talk about the state of the economy. (Just kidding! We talk about Posh Mark and Eugene again. Obviouslah.) Then drink five hits. And the thoughts that have been percolating in my brain all day tumble out.

'Bloomie. Bloomster. Listen to me. I can't do it again. I can't do it again.'

'What? Drink?' Bloomie is writing The Dork a text, with one eye closed to help her focus.

'No – I mean, yes, I'll have another drink . . . um, yes, a double, please. I can't . . . I can't date anymore, I can't do it, I'm useless at it and I can't do it.' I'm hitting the table so hard to emphasise every point that my hand starts tingling.

'Get a grip, princess.'

'Seven years of this shit, Blooms. Six failed relationships. I don't want to do it anymore. I just want it all to go away.'

'It's seven years of bad luck, that's all. Wait!' Bloomie throws up her hands melodramatically. 'Did you break a mirror when you were 21?'

'I mean it . . . I can't do it again. The whole dating thing is fucked. You see someone for ten minutes in a bar and they chat you up and ask you out, and boom! You're dating, but how can you possibly know if they're really right for you?'

'Well, you hope for the best,' shrugs Bloomie, with all the confidence of someone in a happy relationship.

'No. I can't bear it . . . The nausea, the hope, the waiting for him to call, the nausea, and on the rare occasions that everything is really good and he likes me and I like him, the nausea of waiting for him to dump me. As he will, because he always does, no matter who the fuck he is. I've done it too many times, and I look back on them all and feel so angry at myself for dating them in the first place . . . And have I mentioned the nausea?'

Bloomie looks at me and frowns.

'Is this really about Rick? Because I swear to God, that guy was . . .'

'No,' I interrupt quickly. 'Of course it is not. I am over him. I really think, I mean I know, I know I am over him.'

'OK . . .' she says doubtfully. 'Why don't you just concentrate on work for a few months and not worry about it? That's what I did after Facebook guy and it was the best thing I could have done. And after Bumface. And The Hairy Back.' These are her

421

ex-boyfriends. She pauses. 'I always concentrate on work, actually.' She starts to laugh. 'Imagine if I hadn't had such a shit lovelife! I'd never have had any promotions.'

I look at her and sigh. I've never had a promotion.

'I am a failure at my job, Bloomie. Today was . . .' I close my eyes. I can't bear to think about work. I've told Bloomie about my inability to deal with Andy before, and she suggested ways to handle it, but I'm just not able to tackle things like she does. (I believe the technical term is 'head on'.) 'It's nothing, it's not worth even discussing. I should just quit my job. I'm so bad at it. I'm a failure! At everything!' Oh, there goes the drama queen again. Sashaying away.

'Hey. Come on. You're great at your job,' she says loyally, reaching a tipsy hand out for my shoulder. 'Though I wish you'd be as ballsy with them as you are with us.'

I raise a doubtful eyebrow at her. 'Being ballsy with my best friends isn't exactly hard. It's the rest of the world that's difficult.'

'I had a bad day too,' says Bloomie supportively. 'You know, this is the first time I've left work before 8 pm in a month. I hate it.'

She so doesn't hate working late, but I'll leave that. 'Really? Are you OK? What's happening?' I take a sip of my drink. I'm hungry, but the drinks here are expensive, and dinner will have to wait till I get home.

'Don't you read the papers, darling?' she says, laughing. I notice, for the first time, the bags beneath her eyes, and that her nails are uncharacteristically bitten. 'It's more that nothing good is happening . . . I just need to keep my head down and not lose my job.'

'Oh, um . . . yes,' I say, stirring my drink. When it comes to the world of finance, I'm clueless. Have the banks started collapsing again? I always picture them tumbling down piece by piece. 'I'm sure you won't lose your job, Blooms.'

'Yeah, yeah, it'll be fine,' Bloomie says, making a batting-away motion with her hand. 'And The Dork is an excellent distraction. That's what you need. You need a Dork to distract you.'

'No,' I say, and sigh deeply. 'I can't make the right choices no matter what I do . . . It will never work out for me. Never. And I don't want to try anymore.'

'I know you,' says Bloomie, laughing. 'You say that now, but tomorrow you'll see some hot dude in a bar and think, yes, please.'

'Exactly! I even walked in here tonight checking the guys out and wondering which of them might ask me out. I really do think like that, and I've been single for less than 24 hours. What the hell is wrong with me? I'm in a vicious circle where my life revolves around dating, but dating is bad for my life. It's called an addiction!'

'No, it's not. It's called being a single in your twenties.'

'Well, I'm over it,' I say. 'I'm sick and tired and fed up with the whole fucking thing. As God is my witness, I am not dating anymore.'

'You're not religious, Scarlett O'Hara,' says Bloomie, poking her ice with her straw. 'You're not even christened.'

'OK then, as Bloomie is my witness . . .' I pause for a second, and slam both my hands down on the table so hard that the bartenders look over in alarm. 'Yes! Yes! I will officially cease and desist from dating and everything to do with it from this moment forth. No more dating, no more dumpings. Officially. For real.'

'No men?'

'No men.'

'No sex?'

'No sex.'

'No flirting?'

I pause for a second. 'No obvious flirting. But I can still talk to guys . . .'

'You need to draw up a no-dating contract, then.'

'Do it,' I say, taking out a cigarette and perching it in my mouth expectantly.

'We'll call it the Love Holiday!' says Bloomie happily, looking through her bag for a pen.

'Love Holiday? That sounds like a Cliff Richard movie. No, it's a . . . it's a Sabbatical. A Dating Sabbatical.'

'What if you meet the man o' your dreams?'

I roll my eyes. 'Come on. What are the odds of that?'

Bloomie cackles with laughter. 'When will you know it's over?'

'Six months. That's the average Sabbatical, right?'

'Dude, seriously. That's a long time to ignore real life, even for you.'

'That's the point . . . OK, three months.'

'Right, I need some paper. I'll ask the bartender. And shall we have another drink?'

As Bloomie heads towards the bar, I gaze in delight at all the men I won't be dating. I feel deeply relieved to have the whole issue taken away. I can't believe I never thought of this before! I am brilliant! High-fives to me!

The next morning I wake up with a predictably dry and foul-tasting mouth.

I open one eye, noting thoughtfully the crusty-eyelash sensation that means I demaquillaged imperfectly, and discover a piece of paper on my right breast. Naturally, dear reader, you're one step ahead of me – I'd expect nothing less – and you know already that this piece of paper will be the list that I remember reading (with one eye shut, due to mild vodka-induced double-vision) as I went to sleep last night.

THE DATING SABBATICAL RULES
1. No accepting dates.
2. No asking men out on dates.
3. Obvious flirting is not allowed.

4. Avoid talking about the Sabbatical.
5. Talking about the Sabbatical is permitted in response to being asked out on a date. Until then it would just intrigue them and be another form of flirting and in fact be taken as a challenge.
6. No accidental dating, ie, pretending you didn't arrange to meet them just for a movie or something when you blatantly did.
7. No new man friends. It is just as confusing. And it would open up opportunities for non-date-dates, ie, new-friend-dates, which are just the same as dates, when you get down to it.
8. Kissing is forbidden. Except under extreme circumstances, ie, male model slash comic genius is about to ship off to sea to save the world and as you say goodbye he starts to cry and says he never knew true love's kiss.
9. Actually, if you meet a male model slash comic genius who is about to save the world, you can sleep with him. Otherwise keep your ladygarden free of visitors as it will complicate matters. None. At all.
10. No bastardos.

I signed it and Bloomie signed it. Our signatures have, unsurprisingly, slightly more flair than usual. In fact, I've added an 'Esq' to mine. Hmm.

What the hell is a ladygarden?